Praise for *To Elena*

Though God is always at work, there are times when his mighty hand is more readily discerned. Elena Bondar and her family lived in such times. Read her story, and watch how she faces one challenge after another by praying and trusting in God's goodness and how, each time, he provides. The reader cannot help but lift words of praise to God for his faithfulness to these people.

—Patricia Devine, missionary serving in Bible translating

To Elena

THE TRUE STORY OF ELENA BONDAR

To Elena

P. GIFFORD LONGLEY,
VERA BONDAR ABBOTT

To Elena

Edited by Kalyn McAlister

Independently published in the United States of America

ISBN: 9-781549-949524
1. Biography & Autobiography / Religious
2. Biography & Autobiography / Historical
16.11.24

Dedication

To my mother,
Elena Ivanovna (Nosova) Bondar,
whose faith left no room for fear

—Vera Bondar Abbott

Whoever does not carry their cross and follow me cannot be my disciple. Suppose one of you wants to build a tower. Won't you first sit down and estimate the cost to see if you have enough money to complete it?

—Luke 14:27–28

Acknowledgments

I give my sincere thanks to everyone involved in this project, especially the following:

To God almighty, Creator of the universe, the beginning and the end, Savior of the world, King of kings and Lord of lords, everlasting Father, Prince of peace. Without you, there would be no book.

To Alexei Karpenko, the one who shared his faith without fear. No prison could hold you; no sentence of exile could stop you from spreading the gospel. Only eternity will reveal how many souls you pointed toward Christ through your sufferings. Thank you for giving up your life to save others.

To Elena, my mother, who taught me courage and faith in God. I would not be here if you were not willing to give up your life in obedience to God. While you suffered carrying me, underneath were the everlasting arms of God. You called me Vera: "Faith." Indeed, I was born because of your faith.

To Arkadiy, my father, who taught me perseverance and the preeminence of honesty and faithfulness no matter what the cost. You taught me to put God first.

To Pana, my aunt, whose suffering and persecution are the reason we left Irkutsk and the impetus to our miraculous escape into Germany. Your sponsorship enabled our entire family to come to the United States of America where we found freedom.

To Luba, my older sister, without whom this book would be incomplete. You filled in many facts that I would not know because I was too young to remember. You are the archive of our family history. I bothered you day and night for information and took you away from all that you had to do in your own busy life. You did it all willingly and with love. Your name is Lubow: "love." You have always lived up to your name. I always look up to you. You taught me so much.

To Nadia, my younger sister, who completed the desire of Papa's heart, the third daughter he always wanted. Your name is Nadiezda: "Hope." Truly, you were the ray of hope during the trying time when you were born. Thank you for keeping this project in your prayers.

To Dr. George Boltniew, a dear friend who also survived WWII and lived among us in the refugee DP (displaced persons) camps. Thank you for your input of the "Abduction" of Georgiy, our Opa. You remember it well! I pray that God will continue to use you as you serve him among the Slavic people and protect you as you continue to travel extensively into Poland, Ukraine, Belorussia, and Russia, bringing hope to the lost and oppressed people. We will remain friends forever.

To Eldon, my husband and best friend. Thank you for your patience during this past year. You stepped in to do my errands, cooked dinner, and helped with research and scanning those old photos and many, many other things while I sat at the computer for hours translating Mama's Russian documents into English. Thank you for standing behind me and continuing to encourage me. I appreciate you so much. It has been a joy to share my life with you. I will always love you.

To all you who encouraged me to write this story—you know who you are. You prompted me to start seeking God's will regarding this project, and God answered in his time.

To you who have endorsed *To Elena*, taking time out of your busy schedules to read the draft and share your encouragement. It means so much to me. I am forever grateful.

To P. Gifford Longley, you are a gifted writer chosen by God in answer to my prayers to put this true story of *To Elena* into print. Thank you for taking time away from your own projects to complete mine. It was a joy working with you. You have taught me so much. God bless you always!

—Vera Bondar Abbott

Foreword

The idea of writing this book has its roots way back in 1969, the year Eldon and I were married. We lived then in Berkeley Heights, New Jersey, and attended a church, Long Hill Chapel, which was located in nearby Chatham. There were many young married couples in that congregation, each longing for fellowship and Bible study. To meet this need, a group was formed called "Homebuilders." Seventy-five couples started attending the events, so many that we divided ourselves into a series of small groups. This gave everyone a better chance to get to know each other. The small groups then rotated once a year so that, over time, we got to know everybody. In this way, we developed some great and lasting friendships—many relationships that continue even to this day.

As we assembled in our groups and studied the Bible together, we learned where we were from, where we grew up, and the circumstances of how we had become Christians: how each of us came to faith.

As others told their stories in these small meetings, I shared that I was born in Siberia. Since that was so different to these mostly American-born folks, questions always followed. I told them some of my family history and how we escaped the Soviet Union during World War II. Word of my story got around, and I was soon asked to share it (my testimony) at a Homebuilders banquet.

You must first understand my thoughts on hearing this. *I am not a speaker. I am petrified to stand in front of a crowd.* I was not sure I wanted to do this. But I was continually asked if I would.

I started to pray to see if I should.

I realized right away that if I were to speak, that I needed information from my mother; far more than the bits and pieces that I knew just from listening to her stories as I grew up. So I asked Mom to write down everything she could remember.

Mom was still busy at that time, busy raising the last six of her nine children. So getting her to write for me became a long and drawn-out process. Then as I began to receive her notes and stories, I needed to translate them from Russian into English. At last, I was getting the material I would need to put together my testimony.

There was a lot to tell. My task was to sort through all this and find the bits that best synthesized her life and pertained to mine.

Since I was not a writer or speaker, I needed to spend a lot of time in prayer. I asked God to guide my thoughts and give me the words to say. The purpose of my talk, after all, was to give God the honor and praise that he deserves, for he is the one who has done so much in Mom's life and in mine.

In 1975, I finally agreed to tell my story. I had finished all the translating and understood the facts in the right order. The Homebuilders group set the date for the banquet. The planning of the event began.

"Who will take care of the food for the banquet?"

"Let's ask Vera to prepare a Russian meal."

I was young, energetic, and able, so I agreed.

I thought it would be nice to have something different for the meal. I decided on borsch and blintzes, thin crepes filled with cottage cheese, sour cream and applesauce. I was told that seventy-five couples had signed up for this banquet. There would be 150 mouths to feed.

I made the borsch the day before the banquet using large lobster pots. The blintzes, with the help of volunteers, were done ahead of time as well; but the filling couldn't be done until the day of the banquet. So I spent that day in the church kitchen, while a good friend watched my two small children.

A set-up crew did a great job decorating the hall. The tables looked beautiful. The background music, a CD from the Russian Balalaika Orchestra, was just the right touch.

When time came for me to speak, I literally stepped out of the kitchen and walked straight up to the podium. Being so busy with the cooking, I'd had no time to worry about being in front of that large group of people.

As I started to speak, I felt the Holy Spirit was with me. Once I'd begun, I was so engrossed in the telling of the story that I was not at all nervous. I felt as I finished, that every listener had been touched.

Then dinner was served.

We brought out the massive order of food (four lobster pots of borsch and some six hundred blintzes). Delicious smells filled the room. The borsch and the blintzes were loved by everyone. Every last bit disappeared.

The banquet ended, and a line of guests came by to give me a hug and tell me how much my story had touched their hearts. Several said, "This should be written in a book." That thought had never entered my mind. I pursued it no further.

In May 1979, Eldon and I moved to Hingham, Massachusetts. We started attending church there at South Shore Baptist. The pastor came to our house for a visit. Eldon told him that I was Russian and had an interesting testimony. The pastor asked if I would be willing to share my story during an evening service. I said I needed to take time to pray about it and to prepare.

Soon after, I agreed and gave my second talk. This time, I did not have to prepare a banquet. But again, afterward, many told me, "You should write a book."

Word spread to others that I had a compelling testimony. I started to get calls to speak at different churches and various women's banquets. Each time I spoke, I heard the same thing, "This should be recorded in a book."

I started to ask the Lord, "Are you the one telling me to write a book?" But my fears persisted. "Lord, I have no talent for this. I am not a writer. I am not a speaker. Yet, Lord, if it is your will, I am willing." I added a caveat, "But you will have to find someone to help me."

I knew that before I could ever write this deeply personal account, I needed permission from my parents, permission to share their story with the world. Second, I needed more material. Both of my parents gave their blessings, and then Mom followed by giving me a pile of poetry she'd written during my growing up years in refugee camps. She included also bits and pieces of stories she'd written over the years since.

But I had no time then, no time to look at Mom's words. I was too busy raising our three children. For many years, her papers sat in a drawer.

I thought about the project from time to time. I prayed that the Lord would show me how to go about this effort. "Who can I ask to help me?" I imagined writing to some well-known Christian writers. I could send them a tape and ask them to listen. Would they consider helping me to write the book? I wondered, *How much will it cost? Can I afford it?*

But nothing ever came of it.

Years passed.

Throughout our marriage and wherever we lived, Eldon and I have always committed our homes to the Lord by making them available to host people. In our minds, we did this for the glory of God, the One who blessed us in so many ways. We used our home to share his blessings with others.

We opened it to missionaries, refugees, and others with a need.

In 2014, we received an email from our own South Shore Baptist Church missionaries, Matt and Grace Dorn. They'd just sold their home in order to move out west to start a new work. It would be several months before their new assignment commenced, so they needed a temporary place to stay. Eldon and I prayed about it and then offered them a room in our home.

As we lived together, we had many conversations around the dinner table. One evening, Matt Dorn mentioned that fellow church member, Peter Longley, had written two books on the history of his family. I soon borrowed copies. I finished reading both books in one week. I was captivated.

I immediately thought I should ask Pete if he would be willing to help me in the writing of my book. I thought, *He is right in my own church, and we can get together and discuss this whole huge project.* I imagined no better opportunity.

To my delight, Peter did not hesitate to take on the project. Thus I was assured that God had steered me to him. I was overjoyed! With tears in my eyes, I prayed, "Lord, can this be?"

As Pete and I began this project together, I thought about the many steps that had led me here. My three children were now grown and on their own. I had the time to spend in translating all of Mom's manuscripts. And Pete would do the writing.

I have been praying about this project for thirty years.

This is God's perfect timing.

—Vera Bondar Abbott

Notice to the Reader

In the spring of 2015, I was approached by Vera Abbott, who had an idea of writing her own book. She described that idea. We later met, mapped out a plan, and came to an understanding of how we would work together and how to proceed.

This book is Elena's story. It is told in the style of historical fiction: to live inside the characters as they experienced life, to see the events unfold "in the moment" in the same way they must have seen them. This necessarily involves taking and turning the retrospective and first-person narration of Elena's original texts into simple past tense, while imagining (inventing) necessary bits of story that do not appear in her manuscripts. Historical and geographical context had to be added for the reader to make sense of the storyline.

Elena's manuscripts by themselves are stunning in their detail—what she thought and, in many cases, even what she said and what others said to her. It is remarkable how many of these conversations she recorded; she was a skilled and prolific writer. But more than quantity, quality, and detail of information, Elena also spoke from the depths of her heart. She spoke what she was thinking at the time, her emotions, her desires, her hopes. This human side of her, I did not need to invent.

I have truly enjoyed being involved in the writing of this book, feeling the tug that this is a story that has to be told, that those old manuscripts should not be forgotten. Having completed this work, I have now seen the life of a woman who endured incredible hardships without being crushed by them and to do so on the strength of her faith. I also have fallen in love with her message. It is a message of indelible hope and courage proven over and over again in her life to be based on the only thing that matters: the only hope, the only faith, the only love—the love of Jesus.

When you have read her story, I hope you will agree.

—P. Gifford Longley

Introduction

On October 25, 1917, Vladimir Lenin, the leader of the Bolsheviks, led his leftist revolutionaries in a revolt against the Russian Provisional Government. That event culminated decades of political and social unrest and launched a civil war between those that supported the old monarchy and the new locally elected councils of workers and peasants: the soviets. Russia would never be the same.

The social causes of the Russian Revolution stemmed from centuries of oppression of the lower classes by the tsarist regime. The vast population, most of them poor farming peasants who did not own any land, felt that land should belong to those who worked it. With oppression as a backdrop, the arrival of industrialization created large urban centers where there was opportunity to work for wages that would better feed the family, to acquire new skills, and to achieve at last a sense of personal dignity. But when workers got to the factory to begin their new careers, what they found was shocking. They fell victim to unimaginable working conditions with eleven-to-twelve-hour workdays, six days a week, and harsh, dangerous settings. The rising number of workers at the factories made for severe housing shortages. In 1904, the average apartment in the Russian capital of St. Petersburg housed sixteen people, eight per room. Apartments generally had no running water, and the resulting piles of human waste in the streets soon posed a major health risk. This mix of appalling living and working conditions, amidst a semblance of rising self-respect, created an environment ripe for strikes and protests. This new proletariat would rather strike than work, as they had so little to lose.

The clash between workers and government came to a climax on January 22, 1905, when protests outside the Tsar's residence grew violent and the Imperial Guard fired into the unarmed demonstrators. The result of this "Bloody Sunday" was more than one thousand casualties: those wounded, shot to death, or trampled in the ensuing panic. A crippling general strike ensued.

Tsar Nicholas, a deeply religious and conservative man, had been ruling the people of Russia under what he saw was a divine right: that his authority had been granted him by God. His idealized vision of his monarchy had blinded him to the actual state of the country and made him unwilling to accept progressive reform that was bubbling up from the unwashed and ungodly masses.

But the events of Bloody Sunday did have a sympathetic impact on Nicholas. He responded in his October Manifesto, which established a democratically elected parliament: the first State Duma. But a year later, he enacted new laws that limited civil rights and undermined the power of the Duma. He would later dismiss this body when it proved uncooperative. In doing this, he planted the seeds of frustrated unrest. Revolutionary ideas and violent outbursts targeting the monarchy would now become the norm.

Since the Age of Enlightenment, Russian intellectuals had promoted societal ideals such as the dignity of the individual and the right of having a voice in government. Russian liberals and populists put forth their ideas in speeches and pamphlets, many founded on the writings of Karl Marx and Friedrich Engels, nineteenth century German philosophers, economists, sociologists, and revolutionary socialists. The theories of Marx and Engels, commonly referred to as Marxism, held that human societies progress through the process known as "class struggle" (the conflict between the ownership class and the dispossessed laboring class). They argued in *The Communist Manifesto* that class antagonisms under capitalism would result in the conquest of political power by the working class and the eventual establishment of a classless society: a communist utopia. The Russian liberals and anarchists that became familiar with Marxism were soon seeking opportunity to carry out organized revolution to topple capitalism and to bring about a communist utopian society, seeing this as the only solution to battle the iron fist of a dithering leader that paid no attention to their real needs.

The outbreak of World War I (the Great War) in August 1914 initially quieted the constant social and political protests in Russia, as the people united with the Allies against a common external enemy: Germany and the Central Powers. In a visible political stroke, the Russian capital was renamed Petrograd to sound less German.

Patriotic unity did not last long.

As the war dragged on and casualties mounted, protests increased against the government, protests for peace, and cries for food. War had disrupted agriculture, but was truly only partly to blame for the food shortages. The main cause of shortage was hyperinflation, the devaluation of the ruble through the government's practice of printing money to finance the war effort. By 1917, the price of food was four times what it had been at the start of the war. Labor strikes and food protests arose in greater fervor. And while Russian armies suffered one defeat after another at the hands of the Germans, cries rose to a fever pitch that Tsar Nicholas II was unfit to rule.

On February 22, 1917, a series of strikes broke out in Petrograd. A rally known as "International Women's Day" was held the next day. Fifty thousand women marched to demand bread. Within days, virtually every industry in the city had been shut down. Workers filled the streets from every vocation: industrial, commercial, service, white-collar, teachers and students. Riots ensued.

To restore order, the Tsar sent what was left of his war-torn army out into the streets. But the soldiers were afraid to confront the protesters, many of whom were women. Instead, they began to mutiny, joining in the rebellion. The crowds then tore down symbols of the Tsarist regime as the masses flew out of control. All sense of government authority collapsed. It had not helped that Nicholas had dismissed the ineffective Duma that morning.

Remnants of the Duma quickly organized the Provisional Committee to restore law and order, while members of the socialist movements established the Petrograd Soviet to represent the workers and soldiers. By March 2, amidst the chaos, seeing no hope that his rule could continue; Nicholas abdicated his throne. He and other members of his family were placed under house arrest in the imperial residence at Alexander Palace. A spirit of elation and excitement spread over Petrograd.

Under the rule of the new Provisional Government, Russian political exiles were allowed to swarm back into their homeland. Among them were Vladimir Lenin and many of his Marxist-Leninist cohorts. Lenin had been protesting against the Tsarist regime since the 1890s, when he translated *The Communist Manifesto* into Russian and became a political activist. His ideas about the use of violence to remove the government had placed him at the head of the Bolshevik ("Majority") Party in their quest for control of the new Russia. His voice became the rallying point.

In July, a group of Bolsheviks stormed Alexander Palace. They escorted every member of the royal family to the basement where they were shot. Then in October, the Bolsheviks seized control of Petrograd, threw out the

Provisional Government, and established the new Russian Soviet Federative Socialist Republic.

At the beginning of 1918, the Bolsheviks relocated their capital to Moscow. From there they appointed themselves as leaders of various government ministries and seized control of the countryside, establishing the secret police (Cheka, later NKVD) to quash dissent. To end Russia's participation in the first world war, the Bolshevik leaders signed a peace treaty with Germany in March.

After the removal of the Provisional Government in October 1917, civil war erupted. Three factions competed for rule: the Bolsheviks ("Reds"), the antisocialist factions ("Whites"), and the non-socialist factions. War continued for four years as the Bolsheviks expanded their power and systematically eliminated opposing voices. In 1922, the Revolution concluded with the establishment of the Union of Soviet Socialist Republics (USSR).

While the most visible events of the multiyear period known collectively as the "Russian Revolution" took place in Petrograd and Moscow, the political and social changes, including the rules of land ownership, swept across the entire empire. These reached even to the businessmen, peasants, and poor farmers who lived in Siberia, distant people whose existence and lives had been largely removed, even oblivious to clashes of the political elites. But no one within the vast borders of the USSR could now escape the Revolution, its ideas or its power. If you did not like the new ways, you were suddenly an enemy of the state.

Enemies were to be eliminated.

Prologue

"Wake up, Panchak!" Krasnov yelled. He shoved the guard's chair back. It teetered on its hind legs.

Panchak lurched awake; he flung his arms and legs out to keep from falling backward. The chair stabilized, and then the front legs slammed back down onto the stones. Panchak dug his fingernails into the armrests and glared up at Krasnov. He remembered afresh why he hated his job so much. He snapped, "You try and stay awake all night down in this *rat hole!*"

Krasnov clenched his jaw. He detested insubordination and fat people, and Panchak was a slob. But Panchak was his most feared guard. So what was he supposed to do, fire him?

The guard rubbed his eyes with his big hairy mitts, stared at the floor, then shook himself. At last, he looked up and strained in the dim light to make out the whites of Krasnov's eyes.

Krasnov eased himself and refocused on why he had come. He placed the paper down on the desk. "We're sending out 'twenty-two-twenty-seven' this morning."

The guard picked up the sheet and tilted it toward the lamp. He read the name a second time, then nodded as he pushed himself to his feet. He picked up a lamp. A smile lifted the corner of his wide mouth. He looked at Krasnov. "*Khah-rah-shoh.*"

The two men scuffed along the uneven cobbles that led down the dank hall to the cells. When they arrived at the designated prisoner's cell, Panchak handed the lamp to

27

Krasnov, reached over his gut, and fumbled with the keys. They braced themselves as he undid the latch and pulled the door open. Krasnov held his nose.

A wave of stench poured out into the hall.

Krasnov raised the lamp up high into the door opening. The tiny black cell was shaped like a chimney, not much wider than a man. There stood the prisoner, propped into the corner: pallid, sleeping restlessly.

The guard hesitated at first to touch him. But gathering his resolve, he grabbed the cleanest parts of his coat with his fists and pulled him rudely out onto the floor. The prisoner fell forward, hard onto his head. He rolled to his side, moaning.

Panchak looked up at Krasnov and grinned. Then he started kicking the prisoner. He flailed his arms and legs wildly like a marionette, throwing his massive weight into each kick.

Krasnov interjected, "If he passes out, you're going to have to carry him."

Panchak stopped, now breathing heavily and sweating amidst the fecal stench. He wiped his brow with his sleeve, bent forward, and yelled, "Get up, you pig!"

The prisoner rolled silently to his knees. It took some time and effort, but he was able to push himself up onto his feet. He staggered, then gained his balance.

Krasnov addressed the prisoner, "I tell you, as a member of Cheka, that we're sending you to Siberia, where all you enemies of the state *deserve* to go."

The prisoner kept silent.

"Did I see you smile?" blurted Panchak. He swung his arm around and plowed the prisoner in the jaw. The force of his fist made a crunching sound as it connected.

The prisoner hurled to the side and bent toward the floor, holding his face with his long skinny fingers. He choked, then vomited out several teeth. Catching his breath, he composed himself as best he could and raised back up to face the men. Blood drizzled from his lips down onto his unshaven chin.

Krasnov ordered Panchak, "Go, clean him up or he'll make everyone else on the train puke."

The guard grabbed the prisoner by the mop of his hair and dragged him toward the exit. The prisoner lurched along, barely able to keep to his feet, weak from starvation and torture. At the end of the old hall, they stepped outside onto the prison grounds. The sun was nearing the horizon, and the sky was beginning to glow. There was an outside shower there with a catch basin for a drain.

The prisoner was ordered to strip, which he did without any sense of modesty. He had lost all dignity many months before. He laid his filthy clothes to the side.

"Throw them in the bin." Panchak pointed to the trash barrel. "We will have new clothes for you."

"We have no other clothes." Krasnov interrupted. "He will have to wash those rags and put them back on."

Panchak nodded.

The prisoner showered without soap. The water was numbingly cold. But at least it was still summer and the air was yet warm. After he washed himself, he rinsed out each of his garments and put them back on. His jacket, though, this he did not wash.

Panchak complained.

The prisoner appealed through his blood-soaked lips, speaking softly, "It will keep me warm as I dry out." He shivered as he stroked his hip pockets, feeling the contents. He held the fabric close.

Panchak reared to strike the prisoner again, but Krasnov grabbed the guard's shoulder, and nodded his consent to the prisoner's request.

They needed now to bind the prisoner. Panchak walked over to the wall. There were iron cuffs there, hanging from hooks. He grabbed a pair and paused to study the wall to his right. The once-white stucco was spattered in dried blood, riddled with bullet holes. He stared at the ground, crimson from the executions the day prior—thirty-two enemies. The blood lay thick like syrup, swarmed by flies; the smell was repulsive. He was going to have to get the new guard to clean that up. That was not *his* job. He smirked as he walked back to the convict.

The guard bent and clamped the leggings onto the prisoner's emaciated ankles. Dissatisfied with their loose fit, he grunted and shoved himself back to his feet, now standing close before the captive. He puffed his foul breath into the detainee's face. "*O-kei*. Let's go now."

The two men grabbed the prisoner's arms and swung him around toward the gate. Two more guards with rifles greeted them at the massive iron doors: the only opening to the compound. Krasnov showed them the papers. The gates were opened onto the street.

The prisoner stepped through the opening and glanced up at the eastern horizon, seeing the rising sun. He squinted his eyes shut. The sight was simply too bright for him, having spent so many days in the blackness of his castle cell. As they walked down the road, he turned his head away from the light, glancing back at the pale ramparts, plastered walls capped with red tiles, topped by spirals of barbed wire—walls that had secured his home for the last year.

Down the hill and little more than a kilometer away, the men arrived at the train station. The scene was alive with activity. There were factory workers disembarking for their day's labor and many members of the Russian military, wearing their drab green uniforms.

Krasnov led them through the crowds and beyond the station, out into the train yard. The people they passed stared at the spectacle of the prisoner led along in irons. Many turned away, repulsed by his pathetic appearance. Others purposefully fixed their gaze on him, sneering, scoffing, and dispensing a punishment of derision.

The three approached a train sitting in the siding, making ready to depart to the east. The engine puffed out great billows of steam and soot that ascended high into the air. Behind it trailed a long line of gray boxcars, extending around the bend and out of sight.

Several hundred meters down the tracks, they came to a temporary shelter. A sign hung from the canvas marquee emblazoned with bright red letters: "NKVD." Several officials stood in its shade, proudly wearing their tan uniforms, armed with black pistols on their belts. Their caps identified their order: blue visors with red bands marked on the front with a red star surrounded by a hammer and sickle, the mark of the Soviet secret police.

Krasnov approached an official seated behind a table. He planted both feet and straightened to attention, reached up, and snapped a salute. "I have a prisoner here, exiled to Siberia." He pulled out the paperwork.

The official returned the salute and took the document. He studied it a moment and set it to the side. Laid before him was a large notebook. He lifted the cover open, laid it flat, and patiently flipped through the pages toward the back, coming finally to the one he wanted. He ran his finger down below the last entry and barked, "Prisoner number?"

"Twenty-two-twenty-seven," said Krasnov.

The official dipped his pen into the ink and began to write. He paused and looked up, for the first time addressing the prisoner, "And your name?"

The prisoner nervously stroked the hip pockets of his jacket. He cleared his throat, nodded, and addressed the official in a gentle voice, "My name is Alexei Karpenko."

Part One

1

"You all are *good* people, and…and I love you all." Such were Elena's last words as she slumped to her knees, closed her eyes, and collapsed onto the stage. The spotlight remained on her a few seconds, and then the theater went dark.

A single set of hands clapped with enthusiasm.

The lights came back up, revealing the director, who stood alone at the front of the empty theater. "Wonderful! Marvelous, my dear!" He pulled his hands to his heart and tilted his head with a sigh.

Elena sprang to her feet and ran to the front of the stage. "So can I be Larissa? Please?"

"My dear, sweet Elena, you *are* Larissa." Director Mikhailovich extended his arms up toward her. Elena ran down the steps and flung her arms around him. "Now there is still so much more work we have to do to get you ready."

Elena leaned her petite form back and gazed up into his face.

"And when we are done, my dear, then I shall take you back with me to Leningrad, and we shall show them all; we shall show them the best *Ostrovsky* they have ever seen! For you, my sweet little Elena, *you* are a star."

Andrei stepped out from the shadows of the wing and onto the stage. He cleared his throat deliberately to remind them they were not alone.

Elena ignored the young man as long as she dared, holding onto the director, closing her eyes and feeling the glow, hoping that feeling would not end. At last she let go and turned toward the stage.

Andrei stepped forward stiffly. He tugged and smoothed the pockets of his uniform. He removed his hat, bent forward, and stared into Elena's eyes. "Yes. That was quite nice. Umm, I mean you had me entirely convinced." He would not permit himself to make eye contact with the director.

Elena strutted up and onto the stage, straightened as tall as she could, and threw her brown hair and shoulders back. She tilted her hips with each stride, confidently capturing his gaze, holding him prisoner with her smile. She came up close. "Well, I am glad you liked it."

Andrei snapped out of his trance. He leaned back and nervously felt his bright red collar, took a firm hold of his hat, and returned it to the top of his head. Like a soldier coming to attention, he spun toward Mikhailovich and gave him a stern look.

The director fumbled with his script. He looked down at the podium and fidgeted with the pages, putting them in order, though there was no need. Agonized, he turned away, facing the empty seats. He tensed and waited, hoping the Young Komsomol leader would just leave without incident.

"Come, Elena." Andrei's voice cracked. "Can I...can I take you to dinner?"

Elena peered up at him and paused. Though she had all the appearance of a young woman, she was only fifteen. She well understood what her mother would think of a girl her age having a close relationship with a man of twenty-six. She deflected. "How nice of you to offer. But you know better. You must first speak to my father to get his permission."

Andrei could not conduct such a private conversation onstage. He took Elena by the arm and walked her toward the wing. "Yes, I know all about that." He looked around backstage. Seeing no one, he continued in a soft voice. "You know..." He glanced down at her dress and collected his words. He was enticed by Elena's clothes, clothes that made her stand out from all the other girls in the village, clothes she had designed and made herself. This dress was deep red, with beautiful embroidery on the front. "I appreciate how you make so many decisions on your own. I...I mean how you are not held prisoner to the old ways."

Elena aimed to be esteemed and behaved in many ways to earn it: her choice of dress, her mannerisms, and her flirting. But she was too wise to fail to recognize what was happening right then. She knew he was hopelessly infatuated with her, that he would say almost anything to get her alone. But she would have none of it. "I am having dinner with my family this evening." She was curt. "The same as always."

Andrei realized too late that he had moved too fast. He tried to swallow the apple-sized lump in his throat. He turned back toward the stage and changed the subject. "In our meeting last night, we were talking about new members, and..."

"I really need to get going now." Elena walked away toward the stage door and stepped out onto the street.

Andrei followed after her, jogging to catch up. He continued, "You know we have a list."

"A list of new members? How nice."

"No, not new members. I mean...I mean we have a list of troublemakers."

Elena stopped in her tracks.

He explained, "Troublemakers....you know...'enemies of the state.'"

She leaned toward him and whispered, "Enemies?"

Andrei stiffened. "Yes. Anyone that would hate our government, that would resist the modern ways of the Party, that would work to destroy the good we bring for all the people." He had longed to be this close to her. He studied her face as she listened, examining her soft skin and her moist, red lips, staring into her brown eyes. She was hanging on his words now, and he was desperate to maintain his control. "We have many comrades, many eyes to see, and many ears to hear. And when we *know*, we will not hesitate to *act*."

Elena was disarmed by his sudden confidence. He was normally so nervous when he was around. But this rashness, this boldness was all new, so different. She felt a chill and backed away. "What do you mean, you will *act?*"

"We will do what we always have done." Andrei looked around again, up and down the street. It was a small town: a few shops, the Universal School, the theater, several homes. It was early evening; the light was fading. There were but a few pedestrians coming and going, concluding their business—but none near to them, no one that could realistically hear what he was about to say. "We execute those that cannot be reformed. But before that, because we want to give everyone the benefit of the doubt, we send the enemies here to Siberia, where we can keep an eye on them."

Elena's mind flashed. It dawned on her why Andrei had been inside the theater. She had heard the things that had been said, rumors, about Director Mikhailovich. He had been exiled there from Leningrad, sent to Bunbuy for speaking out on his political views *and* because he had been wealthy. Now it must be true. She recognized why Andrei had been at the theater so many times. It was to keep an eye on the director. And she had thought Andrei had been there just to get close to her. What a fool she had been! She swallowed hard. "You say, 'we'?"

"We?" Andrei straightened tall and tugged on his uniform. "The Komsomols, of course." He wet his lips. "I want you to come to our meetings to hear what we do. There are a number in your theater group that have joined—people your age. We would love to have you."

Elena turned away. She stared at the house across the street. "When do you meet?"

"*Sreedah*, at seven o'clock in the evening."

"Hmmm." Elena's mind drifted. "I think I am busy that night." She turned back to him, tilted her curvy form, and placed her hand on her hip as she met his eyes.

His voice rose in pitch. "W-well, maybe you can come another time?"

"Hmmm." She refused to say yes or no; just blinked at him, confidently back in control. "I do have to go now."

Andrei removed his hat and tilted forward in a bow. "Then I shall see you again tomorrow."

Elena turned toward the dingy house directly across from the theater. "We'll see," she said as she walked away.

As she approached the house, the front door swung open. Out stepped Anna, her younger sister, who ran down the steps to greet her. "We have a guest with us for dinner."

Elena paused. "A guest?"

Anna's words flew out with enthusiasm. "Oh, he is a very nice man. He is new in town. I met him this afternoon, and *of course*, I invited him home for a good meal. He...he doesn't have a job, you see. So he *has* to eat something. Right?"

Elena studied her sister's face, aglow with kindness, her eyes alive with what seemed like a million thoughts, so busy, so evident of how smart she was. Anna had been able to go to school. She was four years younger, yet she had taught Elena math, how to count, how to read. Without this little bundle of energy, Elena would not have learned a thing. "Right," she replied.

Anna jumped back up the steps and pulled the door open and held it there for her sister. The smell of fresh baked bread greeted Elena as they stepped inside into the main room. This was the largest room in the modest three-room structure. It had a small sitting area, the kitchen, and a long table where they ate their meals, always together as a family.

Everyone was in their places at the table, waiting for Elena: Mother, Stepfather, Elena's two stepbrothers and stepsister, and the guest seated nearest the door; his back was to her.

Elena had barely a moment to size him up, noting right away the tattered shoulders of his jacket and the bits of gray sprinkled in his filthy matte of hair.

Anna tugged on Elena's sleeve. "Here is our guest."

The man pushed his chair back, rose to his feet. He was quite tall. He turned to Elena and studied her face. He leaned forward and held out his hand. "You must be Elena?"

Elena was unexpectedly arrested by his presence, fixated by his disheveled appearance. She hesitated, remembered the importance of hospitality, and then laid her palm in his. "Yes."

"I am most pleased to meet you." He gave her hand a gentle squeeze as his eyes made contact with hers; eyes filled with kindness. His smile broadened as he continued, "And my name is Alexei Karpenko."

2

Elena stared at Karpenko. He was a mess. He probably had lice, and she had just held his hand. She cringed. She glanced at Anna wondering what she had been thinking when she invited this beggar into their home—a bum, apparently a criminal, ineligible to work, an "enemy of the state." She turned toward Mother.

Akulina had been studying her daughter's reaction on greeting the stranger. And she was appalled by what she had seen, knowing exactly what Elena was thinking. Her displeasure screamed from her eyes. *Elena! Stop judging! Please, just be gracious.*

But no words needed to be exchanged.

Elena's face went blank. She stepped to the front of her chair opposite the guest and sat right down, looking anywhere *but* at Karpenko. Everyone else did the same.

Elena's stepbrother, Semion, sat directly across the table, next to Karpenko. He was two years older than Elena and took devilish joy in being her primary source of irritation. He lifted his hand beside his face to shield his mouth from his guest's view, then silently lipped something at her.

She paid him no attention.

Akulina examined the table. The food was on the plates: slices of beef, potatoes, and beans. "Semion. Would you kindly start the bread around?" She picked up her fork. "And let us all eat while it is hot."

The family's many hungry hands sprang into action, grasping the knives and forks, clinking the china.

Karpenko spoke, "Excuse me. Would you mind if I prayed before we ate?"

The clinking stopped.

Elena turned toward Mother at the head end.

Mother glanced at her husband, Sidor, down the table to her left and then faced her guest. She laid her implements down. "Why, umm, yes, Gospodin Karpenko. Yes. You certainly can...uh, of course."

Karpenko clasped his hands together, closed his eyes, and tilted his head downward.

But no one else did. Instead, they stared at him as he opened his mouth to speak.

"Dear Lord, I thank you so much for this kind family here. These are such wonderful people, good people. And I am so grateful that they have opened their home to me, a total stranger. I am indeed thankful for their hospitality and for this food, which smells now so wonderful and has been prepared with such care and love. *Thank you*, Lord, for providing all of it, for all this kind nourishment. And thank you, Lord, for bringing me here to this great home. Please, Lord, *bless* them all. I pray this in Jesus's name. Amen."

Elena had watched Semion the whole time during the prayer. He made faces, lifted his eyebrows, puffed out his cheeks, and wagged his tongue. He had heard none of Karpenko's words. Yet as soon as Karpenko spoke the "Amen," the young man's mouth shut tight, concealing his disrespect.

Mother broke the silence. "Thank you. That was very nice." She looked individually all around at her family and wrested back her control of them. She could not permit them to be rude.

Stepfather waited no longer. He glared at Semion. "I'll take some of that bread, young man."

Semion had seen that look in his father's eyes before. He swallowed hard and promptly picked up the basket. He handed it across the table. Sidor tore off a piece of the warm loaf and handed the basket to Elena.

Elena looked up at him. She, too, understood his resolve. No words were necessary. If there was *anything* to be said about the stranger, it would be said later, and in private. She handed the basket across to Karpenko to keep it going around the table.

The mealtime that followed was the quietest Elena could ever remember.

After the meal, Anna and Larissa (Elena's stepsister) began to clear the table, taking the dishes into the kitchen. Elena picked up her plate and stretched across the table to take Karpenko's. But before she could, he picked it up and offered, "I would like to help." He stood and gathered the utensils, then followed the women into the kitchen.

Mother was taking the plates and stacking them onto the washboard.

Karpenko addressed her. "Gospozha Briuchanova, may I do the dishes?"

Mother turned to gently correct him. "*Akulina*...you may call me Akulina." She leaned toward him and smiled. "Thank you for offering, but the girls can do that." She turned to Elena. "Go and fetch the water, my dear."

Elena stepped forward to retrieve the metal bucket beside the sink. But before she could, Karpenko took hold of it. "Please. I would like to help. I-I always helped my wife, doing the dishes. It is the least I can do to thank you for the meal." He raised his eyebrows toward Akulina and waited.

Mother hesitated and then gestured. "The pump is out here, on the side to the right." She grinned. "It will give you a good workout."

As soon as Karpenko left, Elena stepped up close beside Mother. "So may I go now? Please? I will do the dishes tomorrow." Her mind was racing with energy, already forgetting about the guest, moving onto the next thing.

"Practice?" Mother asked.

"Of course." She took a deep breath. "Oh, and I got the lead part in *Without a Dowry*...Ostrovsky's play. I am going to be Larissa." She turned and looked at her stepsister, who had the same name. "Not *you*, of course." Elena was beaming.

Mother turned toward Sidor, who was leaned back in his chair, bathed in the warm glow of the lamp. He had closed his eyes, tilted his head back, exhausted from the hard day's work in the fields, his mind ready to drift off into another world. Yet he had heard the entire exchange. He was a man of few words and very proud of Elena's talent, particularly pleased by the free tickets the whole family got to the theater because of her involvement there. He opened his eyes and looked at his wife. He said nothing, just turned to Elena and nodded his consent.

Elena pumped her fists with joy.

She ran to her room, stopped to look in the mirror, combed her hair, straightened her collar, pursed and wetted her lips, pinched her cheeks for color, straightened her back, puffed out her chest, and then ran back into the main room. She was out the door in seconds, shouting, "See you all later!" as she left.

3

The actors and stagehands assembled on the stage to hear the final words of the director and then were dismissed. Several left, but a group of four young women remained on the stage, talking. Elena stood among them, fully engaged in their banter.

A young man had watched the practice from the darkened theater. As the others filtered out, he jumped up on the stage. He walked up to the women, his eyes fixed on Elena.

"Mitia!" Elena exclaimed.

The other girls turned to face him and swooned. He was very tall, a handsome, yet familiar sight.

Elena's eyes narrowed. "Why are you here?"

"I, uh..." Mitia fidgeted. He stuffed his hands in his pockets, uncomfortably aware that he had become the center of the whole group's attention. He lowered his eyes and took a deep breath. "M-my mother died. I, uh, I came home to help the family."

The girls crowded him, soothing. "Oh...Oh, so sorry." Mitia Pavlovich had been a part of their theater group for years, but was older than them. He had gone on to get a formal education at the university in Kansk. He was a terrific dancer and was well liked by everyone. One of the girls stretched up and gave him a hug.

Mitia patted her on the back, blushed, straightened, and pulled back. He took a step away, quick to refocus on Elena.

"I-I would like to speak with you. Uh, unless...unless you have to go."

The other three girls didn't hesitate.

"I have to get going."

"Me too."

"Yes, it is late."

They grinned at each other as they walked away, leaving Mitia and Elena together.

Mitia looked all around. Others lingered; they were not fully alone. He whispered, "Let's see if we can find a better place to talk."

He guided her through the stage door and outside into the evening air. There was a garden beside the theater. He took her to an empty bench there, illumined by the glow of the backstage window. Together they sat.

Mitia fumbled with his words. "H-how long have I known you?"

"Why, since we moved to Bunbuy. I was twelve then. So I suppose it has been three years."

"Yes. That is right. And I was nineteen. So it *has* been three years."

"Um hmm." Elena nodded. She strained in the shadows to see his face, trying to make out his eyes, to see what he was thinking.

Mitia clasped his hands together. "Well then, I think it is time."

"Time? Time for what?"

"It is time to make it official."

"Official?"

"Yes, that you will be my girlfriend."

Elena had suspected his words, feared the subject. They had spent so many evenings together during the summer. Several times, Mitia had asked her to be his girlfriend. Each time, she had told him no, that she was too young to be anyone's girlfriend. And then he went off to school, and she had finally been able to relax, to put his tireless requests out of her mind. Now here he was again, coming on so serious. She wondered how she could end this discussion, how to get out of there without hurting his feelings. She took a deep breath and looked straight at him. "You know I am too young to make this decision. I am only fifteen."

"Yes. Yes. But I am young too." Mitia summoned his resolve. "Our parents...mine, yours...they want us to marry, and I want to marry you, to *someday* marry you. And while I am away from you at school, all I can do is think of you, and how others want to see you. And I...I don't want to lose you, because I want you to know that I love you."

Elena stood. She well understood the plans of *others*: the many times she had heard Mother and Stepfather talk about how good it would be for her to marry Mitia. But that had only ever been someday, at some undefined future time, *after* she had the chance to finish growing up, to get her education, and experience more of life—and maybe even after meeting someone she really loved. She had to slow him. "I have no intentions of thinking of marriage at such a young age. I cannot commit myself to such a thing."

Mitia rose to his feet directly in front of her. He was more than six feet tall, while she was less than five. He towered over her.

Elena looked up at him and grinned. "Now think about it. How can I be your wife? You are so tall, and I am so short."

He put his hand on her shoulder. "You are not shorter than my mother; and I am not any taller than my dad. So that will not make any difference in our marriage." Mitia studied her face.

She turned from him. "Even if I do decide...*someday* decide to marry you, I...I cannot give you my answer while I am so young."

"Why?"

"I am too young to make such a serious decision, and I...I do not want to feel tied down." Elena took several steps away. "I am very independent and want the freedom to see others before making that decision. After all, you are away all winter, and I am here alone. When others want to go out with me, I want the freedom to do so and not feel guilty...guilty because I gave you my word."

Mitia inched closer. "I will not be jealous if you see others. I want you to have that freedom." He leaned forward. "No one will know that you have committed yourself to me. This would be between you and me alone. It will be later, after I finish my education. Then you will be old enough to get married. We will wait for each other."

Elena had run out of words. She folded her arms.

Mitia raised his hand to his forehead. His shoulders sagged. He pleaded, "You should feel sorry for me. I have just lost my mother and now am an orphan. She...she *wanted* me to marry you. And now your answer to me will be a healing balm, *as I mourn her.*"

Elena suddenly did feel sorry for him. Her mind flashed. She remembered the many times Mother and Stepfather said they loved Mitia, and Pana (her sister) said the same. She weighed his many good qualities; qualities that would make him a good husband for any woman. He was comfortable to be around, smart, and not bad to look at, and he never drank and did not smoke. Elena pondered her culture with so many arranged marriages. She looked up. "All right. I will agree to marry you."

Mitia took her hand. "I am the *luckiest* man in the world."

At that moment, the light from inside the theater went out, leaving them in the dark. Mitia took her by the hand and walked her across the street to her front door. There they said goodbye.

Elena came into the darkened house, burdened with a heavy heart. She went straight to bed, but could not fall asleep. Instead of being happy, she felt sad. Her mind raced. *What have I done? What if I meet someone else that I fall in love with? What will I do then? I gave him my word, and he knows that I am trustworthy. How will I then tell him I love someone else?*

Then the worst thought came. *Do I really love Mitia?* Elena could not convince herself that she did. Wrestling, she considered Mitia's good qualities. *He is surely a wonderful person. He is smart. He always takes care of me. All this good I see in him. But someday I will have to kiss him.* At last, she concluded. *I do not love Mitia...not as I should.* She regretted she had made a hasty decision and was overwhelmed with guilt. She could not sleep all night.

In the early morning, while it was yet dark, she heard the sound of Mother in the next room, preparing their breakfast. She dragged herself out of bed and into the kitchen.

Mother turned and looked at her. "What is wrong, *milochka?*"

Elena shoved her hair back and out of her eyes. "I have made a *terrible* mistake. Mitia asked me last night...he asked me to marry him...not right away, of course...but I told him 'yes'...and now I am committed to him forever...and I do not love him...and I do not have the freedom to engage with someone that I *do* love." Elena began to cry.

Mother set her work down and stepped across the small room. She gathered Elena in her arms and held her tight, soothing her. "*Moya dorogaya dochinka.*"

"And now my whole life is *ruined!*"

Mother let her cry.

"And I want to be able to see other boys, but then I will feel guilty because I have given him my word. And I want to be able to find someone that I love."

"Yes. Yes." Mother moved them toward the table. They sat down.

Elena's face was red. She wiped her eyes.

"You know, my dear, Mitia is quite a good young man for you to find. He is one of the best. You should not feel guilty about giving him an answer. You will love him for his character and because of his love for you. Do not be afraid. You are really too young to understand real love. That will come as you mature. Love is not the only thing to look for.

"A person also needs to look at all the qualities of the person that she plans to marry. It is his qualities...his qualities that you will live with." She reached across and laid her hand on Elena's. "You should be happy that such a wonderful person wants you for a wife. Remember that he is everything we could wish for, for our daughter. You should be very proud of that, and not fill your mind with fear."

Elena had quit her sobbing. She studied the calm of Mother's face. This was a woman that had been through so much in her life. Her first husband, Elena's father, the two of them had married for love. And then after the Revolution, he had run away, run away to Mongolia, hoping to hide the family gold from the hooligans. And when he returned, he contracted typhus and died. Soon after, the Communists took away nearly everything. And Mother and Auntie were forced to split up the family. Fearing she would lose the rest of what she had and be sent to prison, Mother decided at last to marry Sidor, widower of her sister. Then she could return to her childhood home with a different name, safe from the confiscations. If there was anyone who understood

love, family, and commitment, it was Mother. Elena p
her other hand on top of Mother's and squeezed it.

Sidor stepped into the kitchen. He saw them seated
the table.

Mother read his eyes. "We are just having women talk."

Sidor turned, headed back into the other room.

Elena pushed her chair back from the table. "No. Don't
go, Papa. We are done. I am going to help Mama with the
eggs. Would you like the usual?"

Sidor grunted. He sidled over to the table and sat down.

Sounds came from the other room, indicating the others
were up and getting dressed. The long workday was getting
underway. The farm chores were calling everyone. There was
no more time to waste.

And as the routine of day came over Elena, her many
hard chores, she became resolved about her life. Marriage to
Mitia seemed a certainty. He would soon go away to school.
She would be free to see others. He would not be jealous.
And Elena would someday be his wife.

4

Elena rowed with the current, guiding her little boat downriver. There had not been much rain since August, so the flow was steady and easy, the water peaceful. As the sun came up, the larches glowed brilliant yellow against the backdrop of green spruces that lined the banks. The late autumn air was chilly and fresh, the morning spectacular.

Elena steered her rowboat around the last bend. Ahead, the cows stood on the banks taking their morning drink. They lifted their heads and watched her, mesmerized by her familiar approach.

Elena was the first to arrive; the others from the six families followed soon after. They came, young and old, carrying their milk jugs. Some also arrived by boat, others walked, taking the road that twisted and turned beside the bends of the river. They kept their cattle and other livestock there, several miles from the village, where the fields were abundant with good grass for feeding. The task of milking was routinely done in groups, because afterward all that milk had to be brought back in large buckets. It was a heavy job that needed many hands.

At midday, after the milking was complete, the workers gathered wood and lit bonfires to cook their lunch. They brought out eggs and butter and made *kasha*. The eggs were also served cooked: scrambled, hard-boiled, and sunny side up, all to everyone's liking.

After their meal, it was time to go home. Some carried the milk along the road, while others took theirs in their boats. They sang songs as they went along, those on the roads and in boats followed together in the singing. They sang a familiar refrain with a deliberate rhythm.

Kalinka, kalinka, kalinka moya!
V sadu yagoda malinka, malinka moya!
Akh, pod sosnoyu, pod zelenoyu,

Spat' polozhite vy menya
Ay-lyuli, lyuli, ay-lyuli, lyuli,
Spat' polozhite vy menya

Little red berry, red berry, red berry of mine!
In the garden is a berry, little raspberry, raspberry of mine!
Ah, under the pine, the green one,

Lay me down to sleep,
Oh, swing, sway, Oh, swing, sway,
Lay me down to sleep.

The villagers enjoyed being together, united by their work, unified like family. The older folks rushed to get home as they had other chores yet to do. But the youngsters were in no hurry. They savored and stretched out their time together, and their parents allowed them to lag behind.

Elena pulled her rowboat up to the dock. It had been a hard row upriver, straining against the current. She unloaded the milk containers and then made several trips to deliver them to the store. Afterward, she took her family's portion home.

Back at the family farm, she found her stepfather at the barn, hard at work. He had the wagon there filled with grasses: oats, buckwheat, and rye. She helped him unload it, tie the grain into bundles, and carry it in for storage. It was heavy work, but Elena was used to this and loved being around Father. He was happy as he worked and sang songs. He often told her, "If you are happy, you will always have good health."

After her chores were complete, Elena finally returned to the house. As she entered, she found her mother in the kitchen, just beginning to prepare their dinner. Karpenko was there seated at the table, making brooms for the winter.

Elena studied him and playfully chided, "I see you are doing my job again."

His face brightened. "I am glad to help, to do all I can."

Karpenko had by now become a fixture in their home, doing odd jobs, installing electric lights, using his skills as a former electrician. And he was there every evening since that first night. But he looked so different now. He was cleaned up, his hair cut and groomed, his face shaved. Mother had repaired his tattered jacket and made him a new shirt and pants. Her good meals had fed life back into his eyes.

He gave her a friendly greeting.

"Lena, would you like to make the dough?" Mother asked.

"Gladly." Elena always enjoyed helping her mother. She was more than a confidant; in many ways, Mother was her best friend.

Elena mixed the ingredients and worked them together in a bowl. She poured a big lump of dough out onto the table beside Karpenko, then rolled the dough back and forth in firm and even strokes, beating out a rhythm. As she rolled, she sang slowly and deliberately, "*Ka-lin-ka, ka-lin-ka, ka-lin-ka mo-ya!*"

As she sang, Karpenko picked up Sidor's violin. He pressed it up under his chin, seized the bow, and joined her in the tune, following in perfect time and pitch.

She peeked up at him, winked, and quickened the pace. "*Kalinka, kalinka, kalinka moya!*"

Karpenko kept up with her lead. When she got very fast, he switched to staccato, picking at the strings. He joined her with the singing.

They finished the verse together. "*Spat' po-lo-zhit-e vy men-YA!*"

Karpenko strummed the last string and slammed his hand over the bridge to silence the instrument. He flipped his chin up in emphatic flair.

Elena stared at him with a broad grin. They both broke into laughter as Mother applauded.

Elena sighed. "You play so well! And you have such a lovely voice." She picked up a towel and wiped the flour from her fingers. "Do you know any other songs?"

"Yes. I will play for you." He pulled out a chair and sat.

Elena sat next to him, engaged in the moment. Karpenko tucked the violin under his chin. He adjusted the instrument to the right angle, placed his left fingers on the neck, and raised the bow high. He closed his eyes and pressed the bow onto the strings with confidence. His body swayed as he perfectly played the tune, a sweet hypnotic chorus. After he played the tune through once, he began to sing, "*Pust' Iisus Moyim Serdtzem vladeyet.*"

Elena closed her eyes and basked in the beauty of the song. When he finished, she gazed at him and sighed. "That was so lovely. I felt lost in the tune. But...but I did not understand the words."

Karpenko set the violin down. He reached into his hip pocket and pulled out a small tract. He handed it to her. "If you read this, perhaps you will understand. And if not, then we can talk about it."

Elena was suddenly suspicious. Karpenko was, after all, an exile, an enemy, an enemy for some reason unknown to her. She wondered if he could be trusted. She studied him as if seeing him for the first time; for she had never engaged in his after-dinner discussions. Every evening she had run straight out to practice while the rest of the family talked. All she could confirm about his character was what she could see with her own eyes, that he was always pleasant, and always considerate of others. Setting her suspicion aside, burdened to be polite, she took the tract from him with a quiet, "Thank you."

Karpenko nodded, then looked back down at the violin. "I used to play for my children all the time. That was their favorite song."

Elena detected a sudden sadness in him. And as she looked into his eyes she had the sense she was understanding him. But she immediately felt like she was entering a world where she did not belong. It was an awkward feeling. She decided she should not open a discourse. She said nothing more.

After dinner and after she returned from the theater, Elena sat down by herself at the table in the quiet of the kitchen. She pulled out the tract, curious to read it, but not in the least driven by interest in the content. Rather, she was always looking for opportunity to practice her reading, fighting back at not having been able to go to school.

Elena labored with the text, sounding out the words. She made it most of the way through. The text was all about Jesus, justification, faith, and grace—it was an explanation of theology. The little she understood was of no interest. At last, she grew weary. It had been another long day and she could no longer keep her eyes open. She closed the tract, put it away, and went to bed.

The next day, after dinner, she handed it back to Karpenko.

He asked, "Would you like to talk about it? Do you have questions?"

She took a breath and carefully chose her words. He was obviously proselytizing, and she needed to end it. "Thank you for sharing that."

Karpenko recognized her disinterest.

"I really have to get going to rehearsal now." She took a step toward the door.

Karpenko got up and opened the door for her. He studied her eyes as he quoted her a scripture she would have seen in the tract. "You will know the truth, and the truth shall set you free. So if the son sets you free, you shall be free indeed."

Elena hesitated a second, then thought it better to say nothing. She was anxious to get to the theater.

She turned and stepped outside, her mind singularly focused on how she would say her lines.

5

Elena arrived at the theater before everyone else, as usual. She preferred to get there early to avoid the crowd, to be able to take her time to read the notices on the bulletin, since she read so slowly. There were no newspapers in the village, nothing delivered to homes, nothing to buy. So everyone came to the theater to read the bulletin to find out what was happening.

She started at the top with the national news, the big headline: "Trotsky Arrested:" his traitorous plot against Stalin; "Riots in Vienna:" strikes by the socialists; "Nazis Acquitted:" for political murder in Germany. By comparison, the local news seemed to be so mundane. There were the results of the "Harvest" and the story on the "First Snowfall." There was an entire section on "Goods for Sale:" canned jellies, new boots, and custom seamstress services.

Finally, she came to the section "At the Theater." Her interest at last was piqued. She read about the coming production. "Friday & Saturday Showings" of "Pushkin's *Eugene Onegin*, starring Elena Nosova in the leading role of Tatiana." She pored over the article from beginning to end, twice.

Just below this article, another caught her eye.

INTERESTED IN GODS—A Baptist exile Alexei Karpenko has come into our village preaching and teaching others to join his capitalistic religion, poisoning them with his ways. He is staying a great deal of time at the home of one of our star performers, Elena Nosova.

She has become his close friend, and he has caused her to convert, to adopt his uneducated ways. Soon she may become a nun.

Elena stopped reading, faint with shock, incredulous. *Did someone really write this? Am I dreaming?*

She looked around, saw no one, took a deep breath, and read it a second time. She read it all the way through in total disbelief. The only thing *not* a lie was the fact that a guest had indeed been visiting her home. The rest was fantasy. *I pay no attention to Karpenko or his teachings. I...I do not believe in God!*

Elena formed her hands into fists and glared at the notice. *The whole town will soon be reading this...this bunch of lies! How humiliating!*

Elena stood there several minutes wondering what she should do. But it was hopeless. She couldn't pull the notice down. That would be a crime against the government. And even if she did pull it down, the bulletin only exposed at last what people had been whispering amongst themselves, what they had been plotting, what they really thought of her. There was nothing now to do but leave, leave the theater. *Whoever wrote this will have to pay for what they have done!* Her decision became final. *I am not going to show up for practice. I am through with this play. I am done with this theater!*

She left.

No one saw her leave.

Coming back into the house, she found her mother alone in the kitchen. Mother looked at her, puzzled. "Why are you back so soon?"

"I don't want to talk about it." Elena stifled her anger as best she could. "I, uh, I have to work on my sweater." She removed her hat and coat, picked up the basket with her knitting, and sat down at the table, avoiding eye contact.

Mother stood a moment, holding her dish towel. Then thinking it better to let her daughter cool down, she went back to work, drying the dishes. She assumed there would be a better time to talk about it...later.

Thirty minutes passed.

There was a knock on the door. Mother glanced at Elena, closer to the door than she was. She hesitated. Elena made no move. Mother stopped what she was doing, walked over, and opened the door to peek outside.

One of the members of the theater club stood on their stoop.

"Gospozha Briuchanova, good evening."

"Vasily. How are you?"

"Is Elena home?"

"Yes."

"May I speak to her?"

Mother opened the door and moved out of the way.

Vasily stepped inside and saw Elena sitting at the table, knitting. "What is the matter, Comrade Nosova?"

Elena purposely ignored him.

"We thought you got sick or something, and I see that you are just knitting, while all of us are waiting for you at practice."

Elena set her knitting down and glared. "You might as well stop waiting because you will never see me in that theater again!"

Vasily's eyes widened.

"I am done with the theater." Elena picked up her knitting and went back to work on it.

Vasily lingered a moment, fidgeting. At last, he put his hat on and left. Mother closed the door behind him. She turned and studied Elena, who kept her eyes trained on her knitting. Again, Mother decided that now was not the time to talk; so she went off to her room.

Late in the evening, there was a second knock on the door. This time, Elena answered. She pulled the door open a crack and looked out. The production manager, Victor Belyakov, stood alone on the stoop. Before he had a chance to speak, Elena addressed him sternly, "I already told Vasily that you will *never* see me in that theater again!" She gripped the door, ready to slam it in his face.

Victor removed his hat and pleaded, "This was not something that you should take so seriously. We were just playing a joke on you. You should not pay so much attention to it."

Elena took little solace from the apology. She held her breath and clenched her jaw as the veins in her neck popped out. At last, she sighed, calmed herself, and spoke deliberately. "I meant what I said. I am *not* coming back." She shut the door.

The evening became late. Elena was thinking she should go to bed. But then there was a knock on the door once more, a gentle tapping.

Immediately, Elena got up to answer it, hoping her family might not be disturbed. She peeked outside through the window and recognized the man standing at the bottom of the steps wearing a uniform. It was Andrei, the secretary of the Young Komsomols. She grabbed her coat, threw it on, and stepped outside into the frozen moonlight.

Andrei looked up at her on the steps. "They need you for this performance." His words spilled out in clouds of steam. His lips shivered. "What are you thinking, Comrade Nosova? You cannot do this."

"But I am doing it."

"But think what you are doing. You are causing them to cancel the performance."

"You and your comrades were not thinking what you were doing when you posted the article about me on the bulletin for the whole village to see...and I am just doing to you what you have done to me."

Andrei looked at her with big eyes. "Well, why are you getting friendly with this Baptist? If you weren't, this article would not be posted."

"You all are *liars*."

Andrei folded his arms as he stared at her. He breathed in and out several times, his breath condensing in the moonlight.

Elena stepped up close to him. She narrowed her eyes and fixed them up at his. She was resolute. "No matter what you say, no matter what you do, I *will* not go."

Andrei put his hands in his pockets. He bit his lip, turned from her, and walked away.

6

The entire family was assembled for breakfast when the knock came sternly on the door. Elena jolted. She looked around the table. Everyone had stopped eating.

Mother got up. She set her napkin on her chair, strode to the window, pulled back the curtain and peered out. She raised her hand to her mouth. "Oh my!"

Elena and the others crowded around her at the window. A group of Soviet police stood in the street in full uniform. Andrei was at their front. Behind him stood a man surrounded by the police. It was Karpenko.

Mother opened the door and stepped out onto the stoop. She stared at Andrei.

Andrei addressed her, forcefully, "We are sending this man to the Far East. He is here to say goodbye."

Elena squeezed outside and stood beside her mother, shivering without her coat. She shifted left to right, straining to see past Andrei, hoping to get a look at Karpenko's face. Andrei continued his prepared speech, loud enough for curious neighbors to hear. He pointed at Karpenko. "This man has turned the star of the club into a religious nut. He is an enemy of the state."

Elena was chilled by the words. She looked at Karpenko. She knew he had done nothing wrong. *He is suffering because of me...because of the lies told about me.*

Karpenko clanked forward in his ankle chains. He focused on Elena. She stepped down, frustrated at the senseless spectacle. She drew close to him; the exile looked like he had been beaten, his eyes black, his lips swollen. She appealed to him, "Gospodin Karpenko, you are educated, a man of good character. Why do you prefer to suffer and leave your wife and children...b-because of your preaching and belief in God?" She studied his eyes, recognizing at last his crime, why he had been exiled. "If you just keep quiet, *if you had kept quiet,* then you would have been left alone, and you would be with your family."

Karpenko spoke softly and with confidence, "If I keep quiet, the hills and rocks would cry out about his greatness."

Elena was puzzled.

Karpenko reached into his hip pocket and pulled out a small book. He extended his hand forward. "This is for you."

Elena trembled in the cold. She glanced at Andrei, looked again at the book, then took it.

The Young Komsomol leader seized Karpenko by the arm and pulled him with force. The police gathered around him. They led him away down the street.

Mother rushed inside. In a moment, she burst back out the door, down the steps, and chased after them, yelling, "Wait!"

Andrei looked back at her and glared. They stopped.

Akulina ignored the leader. She forced herself between the police and stepped to the front of Karpenko. "I have a daughter in Vydrino. Her name is Pana." She slipped a piece of paper into his pocket. "She can help you."

Karpenko nodded in appreciation, then turned his head downward, studying his chains.

Andrei shoved her aside and scowled. "Let's go."

They took control of Karpenko and led him away.

* * *

Back in the house, the family returned to the table in silence, shaken by what they had just seen. Food suddenly seemed of no interest.

Father grabbed his hat and coat. "I need some air." He put them on and stepped outside. The boys and Anna followed, leaving their half-eaten plates.

Mother began to clear the table.

Elena joined her in the work, washing the dishes. After a few minutes, she worked up the courage to speak. "I don't understand. He should have kept his religion to himself. He was such a nice man…a gentleman."

"That's the Communists." Mother bent and scraped the perfectly-good, uneaten food into the trash. "There is just no freedom for men to think for themselves." She seethed. "The *Communists!* They destroyed our lives, took everything we owned, and killed a lot of our family. They caused starvation in the whole country…the sicknesses that killed your own father and grandfather." She turned from her work and looked at Elena. "If there was no Revolution, you could have been educated. But they caused this pain, the disasters in the whole country. This is not life. This is persecution!"

Elena studied Mother, encouraged by the strength in her voice, her certainty, her courage. Mother had seen so much and survived. She had perspective. She was to be admired.

"Mama, tell me again about Papa."

Mother raised her brow. "Ivan?"

Elena nodded. She longed to remember the better days, before the Revolution, when she was a little girl in Kondratyevo. She grew up there in a large home with a big family, including Father's brother, Don, his wife and children, and Father's elderly parents. They had been a tight knit family of twelve.

Mother brightened. "Oh, he was such a *handsome* man. He was short and brown-headed just like you. But he never said very much. He didn't need to.

"We would sit around the table. Your uncle Don played his accordion, and we all sang. But your papa, he never sang. He sat back and watched. When Uncle Don joked and made all you kids laugh, then Grandpa Nosov took his big wooden spoon and rapped Uncle Don on the head. The whole room exploded in laughter. But it only took your papa one word to stop it. Immediately it was quiet; even Uncle Don.

"That was your papa: his quiet strength."

"And Uncle Don? Whatever happened to him?"

Mother's face went blank. She picked up a plate, rinsed it, and handed it to Elena to dry. "No one knows for sure. He was all alone at the house when the government goons, the villains seized the place. When Auntie and I returned home, they wouldn't let us live there anymore, and Uncle Don was gone. We asked and asked the NKVD, but they never told us a thing." Mother picked up a handful of knives and forks. "At least we know what happened to your uncle Vlas. They took him to the river and forced him down through a hole in the ice." She dropped the flatware in the dishpan with a splash. "It was a terrible thing. It was *evil*."

Elena shuddered. The two said nothing more as they finished their work.

They returned to the table to sit. There lay Karpenko's book.

Elena picked it up and looked at Mother. "What should I do with this?"

Mother stared at it a moment as peace filled her eyes. "Put it in our hope chest as a memory from Gospodin Karpenko."

Elena thought about it. The hope chest was where the family kept mementos, the valuable things. She agreed. It seemed a nice thing to do.

7

BUNBUY, IRKUTSK OBLAST, SIBERIA
DECEMBER 4, 1927
LATER SUNDAY MORNING

After Father returned from his walk, he and Elena left to go fishing, the usual Sunday routine. They gathered their rods and tackle and began the two-kilometer walk to the river.

Father could no longer contain himself. "Now the family cannot go to the theater free of charge!" Tickets cost fifty kopeck each—three rubles for the entire family. They were in the habit of going twice in a month, what would have been the cost of one month's rent. He launched into Elena. "And you will be responsible if we wind up in jail too. You are making a laughing stock of all of us." He put his head down and quickened his pace.

Elena was blindsided. She stopped, shook herself, then jogged to catch up. "How is it that they could lie like that and it is okay, and I stand up for myself and it is *not* okay?"

He took a deep breath, slowed his pace. He held his hand out, palm down. "I just want things back to *normal.*"

"Normal?" Elena fumed. "*Normal* is coming to an end. You should sell the house and all the farm equipment and the animals and...and move to the city."

Father scoffed. "You *are* becoming crazy."

"I am not crazy. The Komsomols are taking away the farms, seizing them for the government. They call it 'collectivization.' You should sell now; get something before you have nothing." She caught her breath and then dove even deeper. "Some of the money you get will get me some

71

education. You will lose everything *anyway*. Why not sell now?"

"Where did you hear all this? They cannot enforce collectivization." He looked her up and down. "You are just a kid. How do you know all this?"

Elena knew her stepfather had never been persecuted, not in the way she and Mother had. He had no idea what that was like. *What can I tell him? What will wake him up?* Her mind flashed. She thought about her friend Dimitri, the son of a wealthy merchant. The Komsomols had taken his family's store this past summer, and he had escaped to the Far East. He escaped because Elena had found out from Andrei that it was going to happen, and she had secretly warned Dimitri beforehand. *Should I tell that to Father?* She hesitated. *I cannot tell on Andrei. He told me in strict confidence. The Komsomols will think Andrei cannot be trusted, and he will be persecuted. And he has been nice to me.* She backed down and changed her tact. "Well, I just think it can happen."

Father shook his head. "And why do you need an education anyway?"

"I would like to go to college."

"We have no money for that. And why do you want to leave us? You already know how to read and write."

"I should at least go to trade school...to the School of Sewing and Design."

"You sew beautifully now. You do not need more education than that. You crochet and embroider and knit. And when you get married and have children, you will not need more education. You will be too busy taking care of them."

They'd had this discussion many times before; always ending in the same infuriating way. Elena bit her tongue. They stayed quiet the rest of the way to the river.

When they arrived, they studied the scene. The river was white with ice, frozen solid. Elena's shoulders drooped. She loved to fish with Father, to spend hours every Sunday out on the river with him. But today they could not fish. She'd half feared it. The temperatures had been frigid the last five days. She shrugged and looked at Father. "I guess that is it. Here is winter."

They turned and walked back home; keeping silent the whole way.

Elena went to her room. Her stepbrothers and sister were out, off doing something. She had the room to herself, and she was in no mood to speak to anyone. She flopped on her bed and stared up at the ceiling. Memories of her childhood flooded her mind.

She was six years old when the Revolution came to Siberia. Someone had informed Mother that children were being taken from wealthy families, taken for reeducation into the communist doctrine. Her family was indeed wealthy. Her father and two brothers were merchants selling fabric and other goods. They had the large store in Kondratyevo, a farm, and a big house.

Then the horrors of life began.

Immediately, Father escaped to Mongolia, while Mother broke up the rest of the family. She sent her children to live in the homes of people that she trusted, scattering them to other villages. Elena was separated from her cousin, Klava, her best friend.

Even at six, Elena was old enough to be a helper at her new home. She worked very hard. She took care of horses and worked in the fields, did the laundry, and washed the dishes. In the winter months, she knitted, crocheted, and did spinning-wheel work. Her guardians paid Mother for Elena's labors, sending the payment, payment in flour.

Mother was able to make bread with it and survived that year. So in a sense, Elena had worked to keep Mother alive.

During this time, between age six and twelve, Elena cried a lot, constantly lonesome for her family. And it was in this time that Father returned home, only to die soon after from typhus. Grandfather also died from typhus, and Grandmother became paralyzed by it. She did not survive for long.

Elena understood she lived in evil days, and it was not her parent's fault that she had to be put away to live as a slave to strangers. So she became obedient to those with whom she lived and did everything they told her to do. Obedience of her parents had dominated her life. But now she felt a change coming. She wondered, *Can I continue to obey them? Can I return to the theater?*

Elena felt alone. She remembered the recent times, better times, her popularity. She had become the "star" of the theater. Everyone loved her. She embraced all the practice, all the dance rehearsals, all the time spent memorizing her lines—none of these efforts were exchanged for getting out of housework. She loved being an entertainer. *But who have I been entertaining?*

The NKVD.

The Komsomols.

Elena was suddenly sickened. *I have been their puppet...part of creating "normalness"...giving the people of the village something to do, some distraction while their farms are systematically stolen, while those that are educated and wealthy are hauled off to jail...or worse.*

She resolved to never go back. This would be the first time to disobey her parents, a violation of her very nature. And that really hurt.

So the theater was done. *Now what?*

Elena sat up and stared out the window. She hated the thought of staying in Bunbuy, living in a small village, and being a farmer. She desired to leave, to get ahead somehow. But she needed a higher education. She could not even work in an office without an education.

But Papa will not pay for me to go to school.

Yet she could be married to an educated person. They could live well together. They could get out of the village. But she wanted to be on an equal level with her husband.

Mitia?

Elena saw it coming, unavoidably. She would marry Mitia, a man she did not love.

As she stared out the window, it began to snow. The Siberian winter was closing in. How could she escape her life? She felt sorry for herself.

I am done with the theater.

I am disobeying my parents.

I will never get an education.

I will marry Mitia.

I will, oh…oh…There is no escape!

Yet before she gave in completely, a thought flashed into her mind. She felt a sudden and insatiable sense of curiosity.

Elena got up and stepped purposefully out of her room. She came into the living area, drawn toward the corner.

There was the hope chest.

She lifted the lid and looked in at the many items: the family silver, photographs, a painted rock she got from Nana. Amidst these mementos lay Karpenko's book. She grabbed it and looked out the window. No one was around. She returned to her room and closed the door.

Elena sat on the edge of her bed, holding the book in her hands. She felt the warmth of the brown leather cover, the edges all worn and bent, the binding cracked.

Karpenko must have carried this for years.

The front surface of the book was bumpy, embossed with many ordered dots and lines that surrounded the four edges and made an ornate border, decorated, intertwined with grapevines and leaves. In the center of the cover was the shape of a cross.

Curious, she thought.

Elena opened the book. Inside the cover, she found that Karpenko had written something to her: two simple words: "To Elena."

8

Elena turned to the next page of Karpenko's book, the title page. It read, "The New Testament of our Lord Jesus Christ with Psalms in the Russian Translation." She felt a chill, like she was holding something forbidden. She got up and went to the next room to confirm no one was at home. She returned to her bed, turned the page over, and continued to read.

It was the gospel of Matthew. She read the genealogy and understood nothing. She turned the page. Here she came upon the birth of Christ and started to understand what she was reading. This was something she had never heard about, and she was always interested in learning something new. She was engaged. She read for several hours and then returned the book to the hope chest. No one saw her.

Elena continued this pattern of reading in secret for several weeks. All the while, the chill dread of being discovered never left her. She only read when no one was in the house. And the more she read, the more she wanted to know. Who was this Jesus?

She read about people coming to Jesus to be healed of every kind of sickness, so large crowds followed him. They listened to him speak, "Blessed are the gentle...blessed are the merciful...the pure in heart...the peacemakers." He taught how to behave toward others: to not be angry, to make friends; and when slapped in the face, one should "turn to them the other cheek." He said that when someone was sued for their shirt, that they should also give their jacket. Jesus instructed, "You should not hate those that hate you," rather "love your enemies and pray for those that persecute you." And, "Do not judge others so that you will not be judged." And, "Treat people the same way you want them to treat you." These words of Jesus were to her a revolution. People did not normally act like that.

She read about the religious leaders, the Pharisees. They were the wealthy ruling class, the people who studied the scriptures. They knew the scriptures and all the traditions better than anyone else. They began to follow Jesus around, curious to hear what he had to say. The Pharisees soon questioned Jesus's authority to say, "Your sins are forgiven." This, in their minds, made Jesus equal with God, which to them was a horrible sin. They watched as Jesus broke their customs and healed people on the Sabbath, the day on which no one should work. Healing to them was "work." They rejected Jesus's good works and rejected his words. They seethed inside as Jesus openly ridiculed the Pharisee's own double standard, their hypocrisy, for they invented rules they could not violate in order to legally avoid helping widows and those in need. Jesus called them a "brood of vipers," like "whitewashed tombs, which look beautiful on the outside, but on the inside are full of dead men's bones and all sorts of impurity."

The Pharisees sought to silence Jesus. They paid an informer to reveal where Jesus could be found at night, when there were no crowds—none of those who adored Jesus could be there to stop them or see what they were doing. They seized Jesus and put him on trial. They brought in false witnesses to lie about Jesus. They convicted him. They hung him on a cross. And there he was executed, but not before he said kind words of those killing him. "Father, forgive them, for they know not what they do."

Elena felt sorry for Jesus. She hated what was done to him. But she had seen it before.

Karpenko.

What did he do wrong? All he ever did was speak his mind. He was good and kind. And they lied about him...the Communists! They just wanted to shut him up. And if he would not keep quiet, he would be shot. He, too, would be executed.

She knew then this little book, this forbidden book, was the truth. She was drawn to the words, words that commanded her how to live and to love others. She wanted to do the correct thing, to do good. As she studied the book, she judged her own life, her qualities. *I do not lie, cheat, or swear. I want to be fair to everyone, to the best of my ability.* This same integrity and honesty she saw in Jesus. With time, she fell in love with Jesus; he became the ideal to follow.

*   *   *

Elena at last decided that she had to get out of the house to break the boredom of the winter. She went to the theater.

It was morning, before the time of the practices. There was a room in the back of the stage where Director Mikhailovich lived. She entered the stage door and worked her way forward, through the labyrinth of sets in the back of the wings. Before she got to his room, she found him standing out on the stage, facing the empty seats.

"You are here," she said as she entered.

"Elena!" He turned and welcomed her with open arms. "What brings you here?" He directed her to the center of the stage where there were some chairs. They sat down. "You are not coming back, are you?"

Elena shook her head. "No. No. No." She pulled her arms out of her jacket and draped it on the back of her chair.

"I just need to get out of the house. This winter is endless." She finally got comfortable and looked at him with admiration. "I need someone to talk to."

Mikhailovich leaned forward. "It is good you came today. I am leaving tomorrow."

"*What!* Really?"

He breathed a happy sigh. "My three years are up. I am going home to Leningrad."

Elena was stunned.

"Yes. It is true." He leaned back, cupping the back of his head with both hands.

"W-what will you do?" Elena knew he could never work again, not as an engineer. He would forever be labeled an exile.

"The theater, of course. I can get a job there…directing." He reached across and put his hand on hers. "You should come with me."

Elena raised her brow in disbelief. She pointed at herself.

"I'll make you a *star*."

"Oh no. Not me. I am done with the theater."

He waved his hand. "Hmmm, listen, I had nothing to do with that—"

Elena cut him off. "I know. I know. I trust you. If I didn't, I would not be here. You are a man of integrity."

He smiled and nodded. "We had a very hard time after you left. It was not easy to find your replacement; and then they were never quite as good as you, my dear."

Elena blushed.

"The NKVD and Komsomols were very surprised you had become interested in Karpenko's ideologies."

"I wasn't!" She caught herself, realizing the irony of how things had changed since then. She wasn't interested before, not while Karpenko was here. But she was now. She wondered, *Can I tell him what I think now? What will he think of me?* She swallowed and pressed forward, wondering if he was a man like Karpenko. "You are an exile. Exactly what did…"

"What did I *do?*"

"Uh-huh."

"Nothing. I did nothing except get a good education, work hard, and eventually become wealthy." He scowled. "They took everything. *Everything!* I suppose I could just have handed it all over and said nothing, just like my partner. Inga, my wife, she said I should just keep quiet. She warned me I would get arrested; I should stop saying what I thought. But no. I went on and on."

"What did you say?"

"Oh, I called the Communists liars, said that they were stealing what they did not earn, that the masses did not understand, were blissfully ignorant with their new freedom in the Revolution; but that they would eventually find out they had no freedom at all. Then they would rise up and throw them all out."

"Freedom?"

"Yes. Freedom to think for yourself."

"Freedom of religion?"

Mikhailovich looked at her. He hesitated. "Well, yes. I suppose. But that is not what I really mean."

Elena took a chance. "You know, I have been reading a Bible."

He studied her face as a stern look came over his. He turned away and looked out into the dark and empty seats of the auditorium. "Well, you certainly should keep *that* to yourself. *Me?* I never had time or energy to think about God. Besides, this whole world is so messed up, so filled with corruption. I don't know how a god could ever let that happen." He turned back to her. "That is not the main point.

The main point in this Russia is that anyone who is educated, anyone who has money, anyone who tries to think for themselves, *that* person is a threat. And threats have to be eliminated."

Elena felt suddenly insecure. She had wanted to share her thoughts with the director to tell him about the excitement she had found, this new discovery, this Jesus. But she could see that would go nowhere. Mikhailovich was an educated man. He had no time for superstitions, no time for religion. And yet he was a man she looked up to. He was smart and cultured. She thought again about the theater, her many good days there, how popular she had been, how everyone had admired her. *What happened to that old Elena?...the Elena that had never heard of Jesus?*

Mikhailovich had been studying her face, the torture in her eyes. He could see she was burdened with something unspeakable. Yet in this culture, such was to be expected. It was best to say nothing. He did not pry.

At last, she spoke. "Do you think you could really make me a star?"

"If I ever see you again, my dear, sweet Elena, it will be in Leningrad. And in Leningrad, you will be a star; if I have anything to say about it."

Elena felt the conversation had nowhere left to go. She got up and said a few more words of kindness to the man who had so long been her mentor and encourager, put her coat on, and then departed to go back home.

The next morning, the family was assembled for breakfast when there was a gentle knock on the door.

Mother got up and answered it. She turned to Elena. "It is Victor Belyakov, for you."

Elena got up and stuck her head out the door. "I told you. I am not coming back."

Victor's face was lined with worry. "I know…I know. But that is not why I am here."

Elena tapped her foot, waiting.

"It is Director Mikhailovich." He hesitated, then stared down at the snowy ground. His face turned just as white.

"Yes. What about the director?"

Victor gulped and looked up. "He…he has been shot…*executed*."

9

Elena continued to read Karpenko's book in private. She pressed on through the other three gospels: Mark, Luke, and John. Each gospel told the story of Jesus over again, but each from a different perspective, the viewpoint of another eyewitness to his life.

She found on those pages an unexpected aspect of Jesus: his authority. He had power over sickness, for he healed people. He had authority over demons, as he cast them out. He had authority over nature, for he calmed the stormy sea. He had power over death, even his own, for he rose again from the dead and appeared afterward to many of his followers. Surely, he showed power in all the things he did, power and kindness.

But she was most taken by the power in his words, the wisdom of his words, for he never backed down or apologized for anything he said. He boldly called himself equal with God—that is what got him killed. No, he was more than just a good man. He was the Son of God. And he called others to follow him. She pondered. *Should I follow him too?*

Then she saw the conflict coming, conflict from believing those words.

I cannot live the way a Christian should live. There is no one here who believes like me, believes in life after death. I will forever be alone in my faith. I will be persecuted. And when the persecutions start, I will deny my faith anyway. What is the use in trying?

I should just live like everyone else; forget this Jesus. What is the point in worrying about eternity or worrying about God? Whatever happens to everyone else will also happen to me. Right?

I...I am thinking about this too much. I need to move on. When spring comes and then the summer, I will go to the park. I will see the people dancing. I will forget all about this.

For days this battle raged in Elena's heart. She had no one to confide in. No one knew she had been reading the Bible. There were never religious discussions in her home. And even if she dared to tell her parents, they would not understand her struggle. And neither would anyone else. She was truly alone.

Yet despite the looming trouble, Elena could not stop herself from feeling drawn to follow Jesus.

How can I forget him? I feel connected to him somehow. How can I leave him? Maybe I could find a church, find other believers, a place where I can worship.

But in her society, her godless culture, she knew this would be hard. There would always be fear, fear to follow Jesus.

But I know different now. He holds the truth. I must follow Jesus.

Can I?

* * *

The last of the snows melted and spring finally came. The trees and flowers had begun to bloom, while Elena remained alone in her house, held captive to her solitude, a prisoner to her struggle.

On the first bright morning, the sun streamed in through the windows and fell on her as she was seated in the kitchen. She awoke to the warmth, stirred at long last from her stupor. Moved to change, hoping for fresh air, she got up and opened all the windows in the house. A breeze swept through the rooms. It brought with it the sound of music.

She looked out across the street at the park beside the theater. A band was playing. People were dancing. Many of the villagers were out on the street walking, enjoying the first fine day. They stopped to watch the band, caught up in the beauty of the moment. They had forgotten the doldrums of the Siberian winter. They had forgotten the monotony of their existence, if only for this short happy time.

Elena felt detached from them.

They do not believe in God.

But as for me, if I live to be seventy or eighty, even if I have to suffer, it will be worth it, as long as I have Christ. He is offering me so much more than a life of temporary happiness here and now. He says, "I am the resurrection and the life. He who believes in me will live, even if he dies." He is offering me eternal life!

Without him, I have nothing. Whatever happens here is temporary, joy or troubles will soon be forgotten. I cannot bargain with Jesus, "I will follow you only if no one persecutes me and my life is happy."

He says, "Come to me, all you who are weary and heavy laden, and I will give you rest. Take my yoke upon you and learn from me, for I am gentle and humble in heart, and you will find rest for your souls. For my yoke is easy and my burden is light."

He also warns, "He who is not with me is against me, and he who does not gather with me scatters."

Elena resolved. *I will follow him. I will follow him no matter what happens. There is no turning back.*

Elena had never prayed before, yet she felt the urge to do so now, to affirm her decision, to make a commitment. She went into her bedroom and got on her knees. She looked out through the open window. She could see the park and all the people dancing to the music.

She closed her eyes and prayed, "Dear God, you know my heart. You know the struggle I face. But I am committing myself to you. I know you will be with me, that you will carry me through whatever my future holds. I need you every hour of my life. I am not perfect...oh, how I know that! I need you to rescue me. I want eternal life, to be with you when I die. But even more, I need you now, today. I need you with me forever. Thank you, Jesus. Praise your name!"

Elena lifted her head and gazed out the window. As she watched the dancers, tears flooded her face. But they were not tears of sadness. They were tears of incredible joy.

She knew she was different from them now. She knew she had been transformed.

And she was sure right then she would never be alone.

10

When Elena's parents came home from the park, they found her standing in the kitchen, beaming. Father was in an obvious mood, focused on the daily tasks to be done, so he wanted in no way to get sidetracked by what he presumed to be a lengthy discussion. He glanced at her, blinked, and immediately went outside to get to work.

Mother's curiosity was insatiable, seeing such a change in her daughter's demeanor. "What happened to you?" she asked.

Elena clasped her hands to her chest "I have asked Jesus into my heart, and now I am so happy!"

Mother's face turned ashen. She looked Elena up and down. "What have you done? Have you lost your mind?"

"Oh no, Mama, I only believe in God now. That is the difference."

They sat down together at the table. Elena explained to Mother her journey of the past three months and the certainty she had found in her new faith.

"Well, my dear," said Mother, "you are *really* strange."

Elena nodded, an acknowledgement of just how strange she *had* become, but not shrinking back or intending to hide it. She was energized by her discovery of the truth. Undaunted by Mother's response, Elena pulled out Karpenko's Bible and began to read aloud some of what she considered to be the most convincing passages.

Elena put the book down and looked seriously at Mother. "Do you believe in God?"

Mother looked away uncomfortably. She spoke quietly, almost a whisper, "Yes."

"Do you believe in eternal life?"

Mother turned back awkwardly. She stared at Elena and nodded. Then, overcome with insecurity, Mother got up and left the room. As she walked away, she muttered, but Elena heard it, "What has become of my daughter?"

Elena went to help Father with the chores. They were tilling the earth and planting seed. Most of the time, they were focused on their labor or too far apart to speak. But when they took a break to get a drink from the well, it was then that Elena could no longer contain her thoughts. She poured out her discoveries on him. He let her speak her mind, avoiding engagement and not changing the subject, showing a respectful silence entirely consistent with his quiet persona.

Elena finally confronted him. "Papa, do you believe in God?"

Father stared at her. His eyes narrowed. He finally spoke. "No." It was an answer that had no anger, no emotion. He raised his cup to his mouth, finished his drink, wiped his lips off on his sleeve, turned, and walked back to his plow.

Elena's parents grew concerned about her new belief and strange behavior. They became fearful of what could happen to her, having witnessed what had become of Karpenko. So out of their concern, they forbade her to keep reading his book.

But Elena would not be stopped.

She needed to find a place to go, away from their eyes, where she might continue her study. Since the time when she was a child, she had been afraid of cemeteries, afraid out of superstition, all those dead people lying under the earth. But Elena, in her newfound faith, had no more fear of death.

She knew the cemetery was a beautiful place. It was like a park full of flowers. It was also a quiet place, a place where she could be alone. She went there to read her Bible and to pray. No one bothered her there, at least for a while.

Semion, her stepbrother, had been spying on Elena. He knew what she had been doing. While Elena was out in the fields working, he took her Bible from the hope chest and hid it. Later that day, he came into the bedroom and found her lying on her bed, crying.

He stood over her. "I never heard of anyone crying over a book."

Elena looked up, her eyes blazed at him.

"What is wrong with you, Elena?"

"Please give it back. Please!"

"I can't."

"What do you mean you can't?"

"I burned it."

"What!" Elena jumped to her feet.

"Listen. You are smart, but now you've become stupid. You have lost your mind because of that book." He turned away. "I did what was best for you. That is why I hid...I mean, I burned it."

Elena grabbed his arm. "You didn't burn it, did you?"

Semion kept looking away. "I did. I burned it."

"Your fear of this book is why you have such hatred in your heart. You are afraid of the truth. Your hatred is not good. It will destroy you."

He turned back, glaring. "You are the one being destroyed by the book."

Elena grew shrill. "You need to have a conscience, stop torturing me, and return my Bible. Remember that life is in the hands of God! And if God punishes you..." She caught herself, realizing her emotions had taken her where she did not want to go. She lowered her voice and calmly continued,

"Think about this, Semion. Please give me the freedom to just believe what I want." She let go of his arm.

He stared at her a second, turned and walked out of the room.

Semion kept the Bible hidden from Elena for three months. During that time, Elena asked him for it many times. Yet he was surprised that she seemed no longer angry with him.

Finally, he softened and approached her kindly. "So how are you doing?"

"Huh?"

"Oh, I mean, you know, that joke I played on you...hiding your Bible."

"Joke?"

"Yeah. Joke. I mean..." Semion cleared his throat and stuffed both hands in his pockets. "Okay. I will make a deal with you. You sew me a new shirt, and I will give you back your Bible."

Elena grinned. "I will be glad to sew you a shirt and *more*, if you want."

Semion hurried out of the room. In a few minutes, he returned with the Bible. He handed it to her.

Elena took it in her hands, pressed it to her heart, and jumped up and down. She threw her arms around him and said a silent prayer, *Thank you, God. Thank you for hearing my prayers. And thank you for giving me patience.*

Since then Elena carried her Bible wherever she went. She continued to read it in the cemetery every Sunday and on any day off. There were woods and a wide field past the cemetery, and she found there a better place to spend time by herself. There was a huge tree that had stood out in the middle of the field. It now lay on its side, uprooted in a recent storm. Curious to see it, she wandered out through the tall green grasses and wild peonies to get a closer look.

Half the roots were sticking up in the air, next to a big hole that was lined with soft grass and moss. She climbed down into the hole and spent several hours alone there, reading and praying; confident that no one could see her. She was grateful for this place of solitude and peace, and returned there regularly.

When Elena was not working or alone in her secret place, she spent time with her friends and anyone else who would listen as she shared with them about her newfound faith. She expected that some sort of persecution would eventually find her, as many of her contacts were engaged in the Young Komsomols. Yet the Communists left her alone. No one reported her to the government. She was encouraged by this; sure that God was lending her protection.

But there were others that abandoned her friendship because of her new belief. One was her dear friend, Olga, a daughter of the village orthodox priest. This priest forbade Olga to associate with Elena any longer. And there were others that stopped calling on her or turned away whenever they saw her coming.

Despite losing friends, she continued to find comfort in the field with the huge hole, comfort from her best friend, Jesus.

One day, while she was in this hole, she heard a voice. "Oh my goodness. How did you fall into this hole?"

She looked up and saw three adults staring in at her.

They climbed down into the hole to help her get out. "Are you hurt?"

"No. I am fine. I am just sitting here."

A strange expression came over their faces.

"Look. She has a Bible."

"She is reading out here in a hole."

"She must be crazy."

"She is afraid she will go to prison."

One of the men grabbed her by the wrist and dragged her up to the surface.

"She is already in prison, out here in this hole."

"She is just a girl, and she is giving up her freedom for silly superstitions."

When they all got back to the surface, they dusted themselves off. Elena said nothing, embarrassed that she had been found, but more bothered by her lack of freedom.

One of the men took her by the shoulder and pointed her toward the town. "Let us go now," he said.

They walked her back to her house and said nothing along the way.

And they did not report her.

11

When Mitia Pavlovich returned home from the university for the summer, he was anxious to reunite with Elena. He came to her house to call on her. Elena stepped outside and descended the steps to greet him. Mitia reached his arms out toward her excitedly. She embraced him politely, then backed away.

Mitia stood tall, smiling with anticipation, overjoyed to see her again. He studied her wavy hair, shimmering in the sun, the color of roasted chestnuts, perfectly combed. She seemed to him more beautiful than he remembered. He asked her nervously, "Would you like to go to the theater?"

Elena responded coolly, "Maybe we could go to the park."

Mitia felt the change in her. Still, he persisted. "Okay." He held out his arm. She took it and they walked together across the street. Music was playing and there was an open area where people were dancing.

"Would you like to dance?" he asked.

Elena shook her head. "We can sit and watch them a while."

They found a grassy spot in the shade of a tree and sat down together.

Mitia lowered himself, staring at her. They had always danced when they were together. She was a terrific dancer, and they were quite a sight when they were moving together. He worked up the courage finally to ask, "How come you do not want to dance?"

"I am through with dancing."

His brow raised. "Through with dancing?"

Elena leaned on him, held his arm, and gave it a gentle squeeze. "I am not through with *you*. And I will dance again, someday. Just not here. I am through with dancing in Bunbuy."

She went on to tell Mitia the whole sad story of the joke that had been played on her, the big lie about her becoming a follower of Karpenko, and her newfound disgust at the thought of entertaining anyone from the theater group or the Young Komsomols, the Communists. She continued, "But it is really ironic."

Mitia had been watching the dancers. He turned and refocused his attention on her.

"I wasn't following Karpenko's teachings then." She took a breath. "But I am now."

Mitia leaned toward her, puzzled.

"I believe in Jesus. He is the Lord of my life. He has brought me new purpose; and my sins are forgiven."

Mitia's mouth dropped open. He had never heard anyone talk like that. It made no sense, like she was speaking a foreign language. He hesitated, then shook his head. He turned back toward the dancers. "Well, it makes no difference to me. I still intend to marry you."

Elena drew closer. She explained to him the circumstances of her isolation over the winter, the details of her many findings in scripture that led to her decision. Yet he seemed unmoved by her passion. He was disinterested, disengaged.

Finally, she confronted him, "Do you believe in God?"

He kept his eyes ahead. "I never much thought about that."

"But there is so much out there, *so much* in God's creation that tells us about him. He has a plan for all our lives, if we will just pay attention and listen. And he will transform us by his grace."

He finally turned to her. "I can see that you are different. I...I felt it since I first saw you again."

He lowered his gaze to the ground. "You *have* been studying this a long time. And I can see that it takes a lot of time to come to your understanding." He wet his lips. "But I do not wish to deceive you. Right now...here, today...right now I cannot commit to try and understand it all, this Christianity. I can't."

Elena held his arm tight and said a silent prayer.

He placed his hand on hers and whispered in her ear, "But I do feel something. I will tell you. I have always thought there is a God."

Elena was comforted by his honesty and hopeful for another day to talk about it. They enjoyed the music and quietly watched the dancers together for a while. Afterward, he walked her home.

Mitia continued to call on Elena. They talked of their plans for the coming year. He had just one more year in Kansk before he graduated.

Elena lamented, "I would like to go to school."

"Why don't you?" he asked.

She studied his eyes. She appreciated his kindness, how he was thinking of her.

"You should go, do it. You could go to trade school."

Elena's eyes brightened. "Sewing school?"

"Yes."

* * *

Since Elena's secret hiding place was exposed, she looked to find another.

On a Sunday afternoon, she ventured far beyond the woods and field, down a long and seldom-used road to the other side of the wetlands. She saw a fence there that she climbed over. There were rose hip bushes growing in abundance. In their midst, a massive tree stood straight and tall. She worked her way around the prickly bushes to the far side of the tree.

The ground was soft there, covered with needles. She sat in the shade and looked all around at the nature, shielded from the view of the road by the broad trunk of the tree. Birds were singing, and butterflies flitted among the brilliant red rose hips. She felt secure in God's presence there, disregarding any danger from the wild animals said to frequent the area. She opened her Bible, read it, and prayed for several hours, grateful for the solitude.

* * *

As summer wore on, Elena was working with Father in the fields, cutting the grain. She was at his side when she worked up her courage to speak with him on a tired old subject. "I want to go to school this fall."

Father swung his sickle hard through the grain. He kept his eyes focused downward at his work. But he had definitely heard her.

"You need to sell everything, get some money now before the Communists take it all away. We should move from here, while we have a choice. It will be safer in the cities."

Father took several swift hacks at the stalks. "If everyone goes to the city, where will people get food? Who will feed them? The farmers feed everyone."

Elena went back to her main point. "I want to go to trade school. I want to learn to sew better so that I can get a job."

Father set his tool down, knelt, and grabbed up a bundle of grain. He turned to face her, holding the sheave upright. He looked up at her as she pulled twine out from the pocket of her apron and tied the stalks together.

"And when I am not in trade school, I can get some other education in math and reading."

Father rose to his feet. He looked down at her eyes, seeing her respect for him, feeling the sincerity of her simple request. It dawned on him. He remembered how she had always been at his side in the farm labor, all of it, working hard and being so productive. He had never needed to ask her twice for help. She was always there, willing and able, the best worker he had ever seen. He realized in that moment just how much he admired her, how much he appreciated her help.

He asked, "How old are you?" He well knew her age, but he did not know how to join her conversation.

"Sixteen."

Again, he studied her kind expression. "I suppose you *are* old enough…old enough that you can be on your own."

Elena could hardly believe what she was hearing. She threw her arms out and flung them around his waist. She held him tight.

He bent and wrapped his arms around her. "You are right. You might be safer in the city. And your God…he can watch over you now."

Elena held onto him, not wanting to let go. They stood together in the midst of the golden grain, bathed in the sunlight, lost in the moment.

Then together, they picked up their tools and resumed their labor, as always, working hard out in the field.

* * *

Soon after, Elena found Mother alone in the kitchen. She told her of her intent to go to the School of Sewing and Design in Irkutsk. Mother had been forewarned by Father that he had already consented to her request. Nevertheless, she gave a brief disagreement with the idea, like it was mandatory. Then she consented.

In her businesslike way, Mother focused on the details that remained undecided. "You should not go to Irkutsk. I have heard there are political conflicts in the Far East. If war was to break out, you may not be able to get back home safely. I suggest you go to the school in Kansk."

Elena had been to Kansk several times. It was nearer. But she was unimpressed with that city. It seemed to be second class, a cheap escape. A number of her friends had gone there, but she felt she had nothing in common with them anymore. She would rather be where no one knew her. "Mama, I want a fresh start and a top-notch school. In Irkutsk, I can start a new life."

Mother conceded. "I know a woman there."

"Who?"

"Her name is Maria Arteyevna. Her husband has been in exile here, and we met her when she came to visit him."

"Yes. I remember her. She had dinner with us several times."

"I am sure she will take you in." Mother resolved. "I will write to her."

* * *

Elena was able to return to her far and secret place one last time: the tree amidst the rose hips. There she felt God's presence. She gave him thanks for all the new things in her life and the coming changes. She would be separating again from Mitia. He would go to Kansk, and she would go to Irkutsk. But she was confident they would somehow reunite and would be married. Yet there would be troubles before then, for she knew that Mitia's family was a target of the Communists. She prayed about all this, asking God for his protection, confident that he would give it.

Before she left, she said goodbye to the birds and butterflies, her companions. She was leaving a place where her faith had grown, where she had come to trust God for everything. Yet she had a sense she would never be able to come again to this place of peace.

Part Two

12

Elena left Bunbuy on horseback, riding with her father at her side, making the three-day trek to reach the train station at Tayshet, a main stop on the Trans-Siberian Railway. There she used the only money he gave her, enough to buy a one-way ticket to Irkutsk, some 670 kilometers to the east. She would be on her own there to earn what she could to pay for her education and to buy food and clothing, or to otherwise pay for a return ticket.

Before she boarded, she made him a promise. "I will try and find a place for you and Mama so that you can move close to me…that is when the Communists come and take away the farm."

Father leaned back. "We will have to see about that."

Elena could read his doubt, doubt that a young girl could possibly understand the ways of the world. But she did not want to argue with him. They embraced and said their goodbyes.

The train ride east took nearly twenty-four hours. The powerful engine puffed out a tall line of steam and thick black smoke as it chugged along, dragging its cars behind, winding through the pristine taiga, twisting and turning through the foothills that line the Mongolian border, climbing steadily uphill and onward into Irkutsk. Irkutsk was a large city near the southern edge of Siberia, situated at the discharge of Lake Baikal, the massive body of fresh water that irrigated the heart of Russia by means of its sinuous outflow that wound its way north and east some 3,500 kilometers to its point of discharge into the Arctic Ocean.

It was midmorning on a brisk sunny day when the train pulled into the station. Elena followed the directions her mother received in the mail from Maria Arteyevna. She walked from Irkutsk station to the Glaskovsky Bridge, with its five great arches that spanned the Angara River, leading her eastward to the main part of the city. In about thirty minutes, she worked her way near to her destination, resting often while enjoying the sights, bearing her bag of clothing slung over her shoulder.

Elena rounded the corner and onto Maria Arteyevna's street. She noted the stately appearance of the buildings lining both sides, some gated, an area of obvious wealth. But Elena saw straightway the evidence of emerging disrepair. The trees and shrubs had overgrown and overtaken the structures. Weeds were coming up through the pavement and along the curbs. The buildings were in need of touch-up paint on the trim and a good wash for the windows.

Despite this, the architecture of the houses was an immediate fascination to Elena: closely spaced structures, large, urban, carefully planned, each unique, yet complimenting each other with craftsmanship, competing over style and ornament. But sadly, each reflected a sense of only former glory. The times had changed. Wealth was fast becoming a memory.

Elena arrived at the house number on her card. It was a tall two-story structure, dominated across the front by six symmetrically spaced, oversized floor-to-ceiling windows on each floor, projecting from the wall, supported on ornate brackets, each capped with arched headers and carved trim and flanked left and right by three-panel wood shutters. The walls faded as a backdrop to the frilly detail, walls made of horizontal hewn logs, heavy trunks that had weathered to a dark brown and together rested on the brick foundation. The four corners of the structure were formal, with white fluted trim that covered the ends of the logs and stretched up as a visual support for the metal roof, a roof edged with an elaborate frieze all around, intricately molded in wood, conjuring a whimsical image like gingerbread. All the trim and shutters had been artistically painted in two tones: white and tan, the latter having faded to a dusty pink.

As Elena stood drinking in the detail, the large front door swung open. A very attractive woman stepped outside and onto the porch. Elena recognized her right away.

Maria called to her, "Elena! So glad you made it." She ran down to the curb and welcomed her into her arms. "Did you have any trouble finding us?"

"None at all." Elena smiled. "Your directions were quite clear. And I *so* enjoyed seeing the river along the way. And this city, Irkutsk, is so much grander than I ever imagined."

"Come, let me show you inside."

Elena followed Maria up the walk and they stepped into the foyer. It was an opulent space. Overhead was a chandelier with electric lights that lent a golden glow to the space. Elena marveled at so much hand-carved woodwork: the paneling, the trim, and the sweeping banister of the curved staircase that led to the second floor.

Maria noted Elena's fascination and proudly explained, "This is my house. Ilya, my husband, he gave it to me." She pointed to the top of the stairs. "Upstairs is an apartment. We have tenants there, and their maid. You will meet them at dinner." She looked at Elena's bag. "Here, let's put that in your room. Come with me."

They stepped into the parlor.

Maria pointed. "Through there is the living room. We also have tenants there." She leaned forward and spoke quietly, which seemed odd since no one else appeared to be home. "The Communists, they are making everyone rent their empty rooms. There is simply no place to put anyone anymore; there are so many refugees nowadays. But I…I did not want to have total strangers living in my house. You never know who you can trust. There are so many spies.

"Well," she continued, "I knew they were doing this, so I chose the people who would come and live with me. I reached out and invited them in." She looked proudly at Elena. "I know these people. And they can be trusted. They are dependable. And I think that you will like them. They really are quite nice. And they, my dear, I am sure they will like you too. They will like you as much as I do."

Maria seemed to have gotten herself wound tight like a music box, and Elena was all too happy to let her play out. She fixed her gaze on the woman and listened carefully to everything.

"You do know that I was so delighted to hear from your mother. She is so nice. I cannot believe how good she was to me when I was there in Bunbuy to visit Ilya. Well, when she said that you wanted to live in Irkutsk and go to school here, I was so excited. I was excited because I have one more empty room that I was going to have to fill. And I thought, *How perfect!* I need to fill this room, and you, you want to be here. And I am so much in need of another set of hands to help me here. My coachman, you see, you will meet him later, he is just too old now to do the work any longer. And your hands are young and strong. Now you can do that work instead. And I, I will provide you with the food you need." She sighed to catch her breath. "I mean, isn't that just perfect?"

Maria entered a hall that led out of the back of the parlor. Elena followed close behind. She came to the first door and opened it. "And here it is. This will be your room."

The two of them stepped inside. Elena examined her quarters. It was a comfortable size and well furnished. There was a twin bed, a dresser, a make-up stand with mirror, and a wardrobe. They were all handcrafted pieces of furniture, like heirlooms: dark wood, polished, exquisite. She sighed and looked up at the plaster ceiling and noticed the light, noticed it just as Maria was flipping on the switch. Elena was speechless. She had never lived in such luxury.

"You can leave your bag here and we can finish the tour."

They continued their walk through the back part of the first floor and looked into the other bedrooms.

"Now I have three children. They are at school and will be home after lunch. So you will meet them soon. Their names are Galya, she is twelve, Mariama, she is ten, and little Ilya, he is seven. I will need your help with them." She turned and retraced her steps back toward the parlor. "Let's go and have some tea, and I will tell you more."

They came into the kitchen. It was a large space, with a long table surrounded by twelve chairs. There was a stove there for cooking and a hand pump at the sink. Elena could not believe the modern conveniences. It was a multi-purpose space with laundry equipment and ironing board in one corner.

Maria put a kettle on the stove and brewed the tea. They sat at the table as Maria continued.

"Now I have some chores for you." She pulled a piece of paper out of her pocket and looked at her notes.

"You will wash the clothes for my family, fold them, and do the ironing.

"You will clean the house.

"You will keep the garden in the back.

"You will clean the dishes after every meal.

"In the winter, you will shovel the snow each day. The coachman will do some of the sidewalks, but he is getting too old, and you will be his helper.

"You will buy all the groceries and, in the wintertime, use a sled to pull them home.

"Now you will also have responsibilities for my children." She got up, poured two cups of tea, brought them over, sat down, and picked up her teacup. She took a sip, carefully eyeing Elena. She made her decision. She put the cup down.

"I trust your mother."

Elena's eyes shot across at Maria's.

"She is an honest woman. And I have observed you as well. I know that you can be trusted too."

Elena leaned forward.

"You will bring up my children like you are their mother. Bring them up in such a way that they will have your standards. Teach them to be clean and honest, simple but with developed minds, decent and fair, and teach them morality as well. You will put the children to bed for me, as I do not have the patience with them. And you will care for them whenever I get together with the Intelligent Circle of Friends, it is a club, or when I go to a party. Oh, and you will need to take the children to the bathhouse too. That is out in the back."

Maria sat back like she had just finished her speech. She picked up her teacup. But Elena was soon to find out how much more Maria had to unload.

Maria took a sip of tea and lamented, "If I did not have this house in my name, I do not know where I would be living now. Ilya had three other houses in his name and the business. He was a merchant. He ran a trading company that served all of Irkutsk, with a sales area that extended down even into Mongolia. Well, when the Communists came into town two years ago and again last year, they put a stop to his business. They seized everything. They took Ilya's houses, and they sent Ilya off to Bunbuy for some sort of 'rehabilitation'...the *rascals!*"

Maria caught herself as her face turned beet red. She looked at Elena. "I am so sorry. I should not speak that way. Will you please accept my apology?"

Elena nodded. Though she had said nothing yet, Elena still remained fully engaged with all she was hearing.

"You know, Ilya and I never married. The children, they have his last name, Sergeyevich. Ilya is Mohammedan, a Tatar. Me? I am Russian Orthodox. Neither of our churches would marry us. And our parents, hah! They forbid it too. But we loved each other...I mean love each other. If I will ever see him again.

"Do you know all the family wealth was in Ilya's name? And when the Communists came, he gave them half our gold. And do you know," she wagged her finger, "that...*that* was not enough for them?"

Maria got up suddenly from the table and held up one finger. "I will be right back." She hurried out of the room.

Minutes later, she returned carrying two heavy leather bags. She placed them on the table in front of Elena. Their contents made a clinking sound, a clear ringing of metal. Maria sat back down, stared at Elena, and continued, "I am depending on you for everything and am telling you all my secrets. I trust you completely."

Elena felt at last the urge to prove she was engaged in the discussion. "Yes," she said.

"I am trusting you with my finances...all the rest of the gold. You will hide it and only *you* will know where it is. My children, they are too young and are not able to make wise decisions. But I am trusting you with everything."

Maria leaned forward across the table and placed her hand on Elena's. "The Communists are watching me continuously, but you...*you* they will not suspect." Maria looked at the bags. "Because of this gold, I almost wound up in prison. Please keep this a secret."

Maria sat back in her chair and picked up her cup. "Whenever we need money, I will ask you, and you will take the gold things to the Trakcin. It is a government store where you can exchange it for cash to make our purchases." Maria tilted her cup all the way back and drained it, then set it down on the table. "Now, do you have any questions?"

Elena sat up straight. "I might have some later. But I think I understand it all." She smiled at her host, grateful to be there, but in wonder of all that lay before her.

13

Elena made fast connections with new sewing customers. The first was Maria, for her family. Next were the tenants. They were attracted to her own clothes, which she was quick to explain to them she had designed and made herself. The money she received was at first small, as she kept her prices low to secure the commissions. And she did not need that much money to get started in school. Classes were only eight rubles each, though every ruble she earned was precious to her purpose for being there.

Elena enrolled in the School of Sewing and Design in Irkutsk, located a twenty-minute walk from Maria's house. Her training was Monday through Friday from 8:00 a.m. till noon. Her first class was in sewing theory and learning how to draw designs: an eight-month course that she completed in two. The different stitches came easy to Elena, as she already knew most of them. She quickly moved on to the advanced courses.

In the afternoons, Elena performed her enormous household responsibilities for Maria. She found the children to be surprisingly immature, a product of being pampered and apparently ignored by their mother. Elena saw straightway the need to fix that. She did not shy away from setting them on a new path—hers. She was very strict with them.

Pretty soon, she had them washing themselves in the bathhouse. All she had to do was inspect to see if they were clean. And though she had become their hard master, they learned to yield to her discipline because they could see that she did love them. And they soon loved her in return.

In the evenings from 6:00 to 8:00 p.m., Elena went to school, intent on earning her high school diploma. She began by enrolling in the first grade. The weekends Elena spent alone, restocking her energy. She had no extra money for recreation or social events.

Elena made many fast acquaintances at school. She kept her eyes and ears open, hoping she might meet another Christian. She found none among the other girls and could not relate to their interests. But she did become friends with some of the older ladies.

Elena longed for a chance to discuss her faith with someone, anyone. She had ample opportunity to meet people her age and older. Many gentlemen showed an interest in her.

Maria Arteyevna wanted to fix her up with an engineer who was thirteen years older than she was. But Elena was not thinking about marriage, even though she really liked him. Since she had become a Christian, she had no interest in seeing any man who was not also a believer. She obeyed the words of Jesus, who taught it was best to not be "unequally yoked," not tied to someone who would pull her away from her faith. Still, Elena determined it best to be kind to these people, and so she prayed that God would also draw them to himself. And ever present in her conscience was her commitment to remain faithful to Mitia.

Elena could see that many of Maria's friends were highly educated. But Elena had no fear of engaging in conversation with them, even speaking at their level. They enjoyed listening to her and were surprised to learn she was just a village girl. She made many good contacts and thus expanded her income opportunities as a seamstress.

But despite this failure to find a truly satisfying friendship with any other believer, Elena was not to be deterred from her diligent execution of the many responsibilities at Maria's house. Hard work was something she had never been lax to perform. And she always did a good job, doing so with joy. The longer she worked there and cared for the children, the more Maria appreciated her, which further warmed their relationship.

After several months, when the two of them were alone in the home, Maria made them both a treat: blintzes. She set the warm thin cakes on a plate, dabbed on a dollop of cheese sauce, then rolled them up and sprinkled on some sugar. She carried the plates to the table and they sat down together to eat.

Maria proudly watched as Elena cut off a piece with her fork and raised the morsel to her mouth.

Elena closed her eyes. "Mmm." She delighted as the sauce and sugar melted in her mouth. She lifted the back of her hand to shield her mouth as she spoke, still chewing, "You have really outdone yourself this time."

Maria straightened proudly. "It is my mother's recipe. She always made the best blini. And her charlotte cake…I'll have to make you one of those as soon as strawberries are in season."

"Mmm, yes." Elena had to pause her eating to get the words out. "Something else to look forward to…aside from the end of winter."

Maria took several bites, finding great pleasure in her own dessert. She had something she had wanted to say. The time was right. "You know, the children really do love you, Elena."

"They are very good children. You should be proud of them."

Maria nodded. "I think Galya needs to get out and visit, meet some nice friends. I was thinking you could help her."

"Yes, she is certainly old enough." Elena knew that by the age of twelve, any girl in Bunbuy would have been far more independent than Galya. But she had no intention of saying anything negative about her to Maria.

"I was thinking she should go to the theater or a movie or a concert or dance or something."

"Yes. That would be good."

"You should go with her, of course."

"Of course." Elena knew all too well that Galya would need a chaperone. She took another bite and chewed it slowly. "Your mother, she must be a great cook."

"Yes, she *was* the best. She passed on..." Maria lifted her eyes toward the ceiling. "It was ten years ago."

"Oh, I am sorry."

"You don't have to apologize. But I do miss her. Whenever I bake, that is my time to remember her."

"Your mother, was she Orthodox, like you?"

Maria startled. "Huh?"

"Orthodox?"

"Oh, yes. Yes, she was. She was the one in the family that was so serious about church. I think if she hadn't been, then she might have approved my marriage. My father, he didn't care at all about church."

"He didn't believe in God?"

Maria set her fork down and looked at Elena. "No. I don't think he did. When he died, they just put him in a box and stuck him in the ground. No funeral. No visit from the priest. None of that. That was the way he wanted it."

"Did that bother your mother?"

"Oh, Mama, she was terrible after father died. She was a wreck. Dad did everything around the house. No. She was in no shape to protest, to arrange for a funeral. And she respected his wishes." Maria's eyes grew wet as her face reddened. "Mama didn't last more than a year without him before she died."

"Your mother, did she believe in God?"

Maria stiffened. "Well, she was at the church a lot. And we did give her a funeral. The priest spoke. It was a nice ceremony. My sisters were there with their families. It was kind of a family reunion."

Elena realized her question hadn't been answered. She wiped her fork around the edge of the plate, scraped up the last of the cheese sauce and put it in her mouth. She thought a moment before saying, "I believe in God."

Maria had finished her desert. She reached across the table and grabbed Elena's plate, then took it to the sink, knowing it was Elena's job to do the dishes.

Elena continued, "I have been studying the Bible, reading it myself. And I am so excited to find out all that there is in there, so much about God that was kept from me."

Maria stayed silent at the sink as she washed their plates. Elena came to her side and took a towel to dry. She had many thoughts that had been pent up for so long. With excitement, she began to explain her discoveries, everything that was on her heart. They finished cleaning up and returned to the table. The whole time, Elena never stopped explaining what she believed. Maria said nothing, just listened.

At last, Elena caught her breath. She sensed she had revealed too much too fast. Uncomfortably, she asked, "Do *you* believe in God?"

Maria looked down. "Elena. There is so much I admire about you...your honesty, your goals, your ambitions, and your standards. You have high standards, and I do not hesitate to trust you with raising my children, even with my gold."

"But what about God?" Elena fixed her eyes on Maria.

Maria looked up. "That is all well and good for you, my dear. But what a person believes is…is *very personal*. I mean, if you want to believe in nonsense, then who am I to be your judge?"

Elena felt a chill.

Maria got up from the table. She looked at the clock. "The children will be home soon. I am going to read for a bit and then rest." She left the room.

* * *

Soon after, Elena was reading the newspaper. In the corner of the back page, she found an article that piqued her interest.

QUESTIONABLE CONCERTS: Irkutsk. Warning. A group of young people have been traveling in the area, singing, playing instruments, and preaching. This group has proved to be a trap for our youth, poisoning the minds of the simple, anyone easily misled by their foolish message. The government is looking for your help, as these opportunities for wrongful indoctrination need to be stopped!

Elena imagined excitedly, *They must be Christian.* She wanted to find them, to go to a concert to see who they were. *Couldn't this be the opportunity to take Galya to hear a good concert?*

She found Maria in the next room and showed her the article.

Maria read the words, then looked up at Elena with curiosity. "What are you asking?"

"I was wondering if you had ever heard of this group, if you know where they meet."

"Yes. I heard about them. Why do you ask?"

"I am interested in going to one of their concerts, to find out about them. Maybe they are evangelicals."

Maria's face turned red. "*Elena!* What is *wrong* with you? Have you lost your mind? As long as you live with me, you will *never* go to such a place. These people are into witchcraft. They poison people's minds."

Elena leaned back. "Do you really believe that?"

"Of course. A friend of ours visited them and remained with them." She wagged her finger at Elena. "You will *never* go to see these people as long as you are in my house."

Elena hated the sudden tension between them. She nodded politely and left the room. And not wanting any further discord in their relationship, she made a decision right then that she could no longer speak with Maria on anything about religion or her efforts to find other believers.

Elena reached out to others instead. She got to know the tenants. One was an aeronautical engineer; he lived upstairs with his wife and maid. The other was an industrial worker; he lived in the downstairs living room with his wife and son. The aeronautical engineer was a Communist; his wife (an older woman) was Russian Orthodox. The wife of the industrial worker was a young woman, a schoolteacher.

Elena had to be careful in what she said, not sure she could trust them. But soon, both women became friends and responded kindly to Elena's interests, her desire to talk about God. They became engaged in talking about religion and were surprised to hear how much Elena knew about the Bible, taken by her seriousness about God. The older woman asked Elena a lot of questions. But in all the many interchanges that followed, neither woman seemed to be truly sympathetic to her faith. And neither knew of any place to gather to worship.

Six months passed and she was not able to find a church or any believers. One day, a winter day, Elena was rushing to get to school. She was running on Karl Marx Street and passed by an old Orthodox church. There she saw an elderly woman standing in front of the church, looking up at the cupola, crossing herself.

Gripped with curiosity, Elena crossed the street and ran toward her, waving. "Hello, I see that you are a religious person."

"Yes, I am," the woman replied, startled. She caught herself, then fearlessly continued, "And I never walk past a church without stopping and crossing myself."

Elena animated. "I, too, believe in God. I am looking for an evangelical church. Would you happen to know of one?"

"Of course, I do. There is a large one on Blinovskaya Street. I do not know the exact number of the building. But it is on the corner of Pistierovska Street and Blinovskaya. You will see a red house with a plaque describing the time and day the services are held."

Elena placed her hand on the woman's shoulder. "Thank you *so* much." She turned and ran the rest of the way to school.

After classes, instead of going home, Elena ran to Blinovskaya Street. There she spotted the red house, which was surrounded by a wrought iron fence. A small plaque was mounted on the fence beside the gate. She approached with excitement and read it.

Evangelical Christian Church
Services are on Sundays at 10:00 a.m.
& evenings at 6:00–8:00 p.m.
Bible Study on Tuesday evenings at 6:00 p.m.
Prayer meetings on Thursday evenings at 6:00 p.m.
WELCOME ALL, FREE OF CHARGE!

Elena could hardly believe she had finally found a place to worship.

She ran home, started her chores, and rushed to get everything done as soon as she could. But she worried. *How do I tell Maria I am going to church? She will not allow me to go.*

While she worked, she labored over what she would say or do. *How do I do this? Can I just leave without telling her? She will be asking me where I am going. I cannot tell a lie.* She prayed, "Dear God, please guide me."

They ate dinner. Elena cleaned the dishes, put them away, and approached her landlady. "Maria, I need to be at a meeting at 6:00 tonight. I should be home by 8:30."

Maria glanced at her. "Okay, my dear, if you need to go, then go."

Elena was so relieved. She said in her heart, *Maria must have thought this was a school meeting. Thank you, Jesus!*

Elena donned her hat and coat and hurried off to the meeting, anxious over what she might find there.

14

Elena was walking to the church meeting, rushing to get there and worrying at the same time. *All the bad things I have heard about evangelicals, are they true? What if they really are witches? Are they poisoning people's minds? Trapping them?*

She prayed, "Jesus, please protect me. Guide me. You are my strength. You know I am looking for you in this place. Please help me. Will I find you there?"

She arrived at the church and found the doors open. She walked in nervously. She saw a young man in the front, well dressed. No one else was there. She sat down on the last bench close by the door. She made a plan. *In a few minutes, others will arrive. If I notice anything suspicious, I can quickly run out the door.*

A group of young ladies came in next. She studied them...*normal looking.* Then a husband and wife entered and went straight to the front and sat down. Elena looked around the room. She noticed there were verses of the Bible posted on the walls:

"Go and sin no more"

"We preach Christ Crucified"

"For God so loved the world - John 3:16"

She remembered reading those verses in her Bible. She took a deep breath and relaxed.

Another woman came in and went to the very front. Elena recognized her. *Lyudmila Ivanovna Rayevskaya!* She was one of Elena's sewing teachers in school. *Oh my goodness! I have been in school the last six months and have been searching for believers. I had no idea she was evangelical. Had I known, I could have been worshipping here with her all that time.* She caught herself. *But she could have lost her job if I had said something.* Lyudmila could not have known Elena had been searching for a church or that she was a believer.

In a few minutes, the rest of the room filled with people. The young man who had been there when Elena first entered rose to his feet. He approached the rostrum to commence the service. She reasoned, *He must be the leader.* Hymns were sung. Time was spent in prayer. And then the leader, the pastor, delivered a message. This was the very first time in Elena's whole life that she had heard preaching, heard anyone explain the scriptures. She hung onto every word he spoke.

At the end of the service, everyone knelt down to pray. Several came to the front and prayed out loud. Elena ran forward. She fell on her knees and prayed aloud, "Thank you, Jesus!" Her words flew out freely, for she had no fear of the others there listening. "Thank you, Lord. Thank you for helping me to find this church." She was certain that God's spirit had guided her there.

As the prayer time ended, members of the church, young and old, came up to meet Elena. They crowded around her, shook her hand and hugged her, welcoming her to their service. They asked many questions about her background and how she had found the church. Elena examined their faces, their smiles, their genuine interest, their warm concern and touch. She had never experienced such love.

Lyudmila pressed through the crowd that had formed around Elena. She extended both hands to her. Elena wrapped her arms around her. The two hugged a long time as tears formed in Elena's eyes. "I am so happy, so happy to know you are a Christian."

Lyudmila said, "And the pastor that was preaching, he is my son."

Elena left the meeting glowing, exuding a warmth that stayed with her all the way home.

A few days later at the school, Lyudmila did not show up for work. Elena soon heard the whispers.

"Lyudmila has been fired."

"I heard why."

"Me too. It is because her son is a preacher."

Elena's face turned white. She spun away from them and stared at her sewing machine, vainly trying to hide her emotions. She agonized. *How did the Communists find out? How did they learn that Lyudmila's son was a preacher? I've been here just six months in this school and had no clue she was even a Christian. She has been a teacher here for many years…my favorite teacher…and now this?*

The students gathered for a job meeting. As they waited for the meeting to begin, several whispered.

"Someone spied on her."

"Yes. That is how they found out she was going to that church."

"Someone turned her in."

Elena could not stop thinking about what had happened. Everywhere she went, everything she did, while buried in her many responsibilities, she worried about Lyudmila.

After Lyudmila's dismissal, Elena felt awkward when she went to church. She felt a change there, something different about the people. She could read it in their faces. The people who had been so friendly to her on that first night were different now. They were cooler, distant, disinterested in having a conversation with her. They turned their head away when she approached. Elena knew something was wrong.

Elena sought out Lyudmila after a service. The two of them stepped to the side and spoke privately. Lyudmila's eyes were heavy. She wiped them, as she spoke, "I can't get a job anywhere." She explained the details of her visits to another school to find employment, even her attempts to work in stores or for vendors, anywhere. All her options were closed. "With my experience, my qualifications, with so many friends, I should be able to find *something*. I just don't know how this happened. My reputation is ruined."

Elena hugged her. They cried together.

After the next service, an elderly man approached Elena and introduced himself. "I am Yevgeni Kropanin, one of the elders." He could see she did not know what an elder was, so he explained his role as one of the elected leaders in the organized governance of the church.

Elena recognized him as a man of good temperance, of some importance. She was polite and shook his hand.

"I would like to get to know you, young lady, seeing as you are new here...find out about your family." His lips stiffened. He caught himself and forced a smile. "So we can better understand how we can help you and...and pray for you, of course."

They spoke for a few minutes, niceties and such, then everyone else was filtering out. Elena felt that the discussion should conclude. She wanted to get going. They said their goodbyes, but not before Yevgeni shook her hand and said, "We need to speak some more."

At the next several meetings, each time after the service ended, Yevgeni made his way over to Elena to speak with her. Elena held nothing back. She revealed to him many details of her life, her conversion, about Karpenko, her beliefs, her knowledge of the Bible, facts about her family, her reliance on God to guide her there to the church.

Then she moved on to where she lived, stating that Maria Arteyevna did not know she was coming to the church and Elena's efforts to keep that secret. "Maria was a friend of my mother. She took me in so that I could go to school. I am a maid at Maria's in exchange for room and board. Those were the arrangements my mother made with her.

"But Maria is an atheist and would not allow me to come to church, if she knew. That is why I rarely come.

"I am praying to God to find a different place to live so that I can come to church freely and without worry...a place where I can live with someone else, where I can do things around the house instead of pay rent...since I am a student." Elena reflected on her landlady. "Maria is good to me, but she gives me no freedom to worship."

Yevgeni listened carefully.

At the next meeting, he introduced Elena to a railroad engineer who was a member of the church. He and his wife had three children and were looking for a nanny, as both had to work. Here was a welcome new opportunity for Elena.

It was during this introduction that Elena detected a change in Yevgeni's attitude toward her. His expression was different, no longer aloof; he seemed genuinely friendly. As she watched him speak, she recalled the first night she had visited the church, remembering how friendly everyone had been. She saw that same kindness return in him. And then she figured it out, figured out what she had been sensing all along. *He has been checking me out all this time; the church sent him. They picked an elder to see if I was for real. Everyone thought I was a spy for the Communists...that I had been the one that told on Lyudmila. They surely thought I would turn them in next! No wonder they kept their distance.*

Elena studied Yevgeni's face as he completed introducing Elena to this couple. He retold her story to them while she stood at his side and listened; retold it with confidence, like he believed it himself. She knew then he was satisfied, satisfied Elena was not a threat.

Yet she could see that others in the church clung to their suspicions. They remained unwilling to believe that Elena was not really an informer.

15

Each time Elena had wanted to go to church, Maria asked her where she was going. This had become to her an insufferable burden. *To not tell her is to lie, and to lie is a sin. But if I tell her the truth, she will not let me go.* Elena had to think of ways to go without telling a lie, which constantly weighed on her conscience. And now the railroad engineer and his wife agreed to take Elena into their home, doing so on the same conditions posed by Maria Arteyevna. She could attend school and then do whatever was needed around the house in exchange for food and a place to live; and she would no longer have to hide her church attendance from her landlady. At last, Elena's problem would be solved.

But there was the dilemma. *How do I tell Maria I will be leaving?* She fretted. *Maria has treated me like her own daughter, shared many secrets with me. She has trusted me completely. I have done everything for her. Who will she find to replace me, to do all I do and without pay? She has provided for me and been good to me. Can I leave her now?*

Elena had one more worry. Her mother had made all the arrangements for Elena to live there with Maria. Mother had approved her move to Irkutsk, her going to school, her being away from home—all this with an understanding, the knowledge that Elena was living under the protection of someone Mother trusted. *How do I let Mama know of my new situation, who they are, where they live, all the details?* Elena knew that letters were not getting through to people; the Communists opened the mail. *I cannot write such personal matters, especially because of the reason for my move... 'I want to go to a Christian church.' They will arrest me. They will close the church.*

She prayed, "God, you are first in my heart. I know you want me to have fellowship and gain spiritual growth among believers." It was clearly more important that Elena go to church. It was the right thing to do, to move. She made her decision. She would have to tell Mother later. Mother would approve.

Then came the matter of timing, when to tell. Maria was a wonderful person to Elena, but she had a bad temper and was extremely controlling. This would be a terrible discussion. She dreaded the thought of it. So she prayed about what to say and when. In the meantime, her new family kept asking when she could start. Elena delayed.

She was not able to go to church for a while, unable any longer to bring herself to explain to Maria about where she wanted to go, and unwilling to lie.

The first day of May was Spring and Labor Day, a Russian holiday. Maria was alone in the kitchen, sitting at the table, reading the newspaper.

Elena approached and stood at attention in front of her. She swallowed hard and began, "Maria, I have something to say."

Maria looked up over the corner of the newspaper, eyes trained on Elena's face.

"I have found another place to live." Elena took a breath. "I am leaving."

Maria's face turned white. She lowered her gaze. She stared unseeing at the newspaper, blinked, and refocused on Elena. "O-okay." She hesitated then asked, "And when will you be leaving?"

"This afternoon." Elena could not believe how well this discussion was going. She stood awkwardly a moment,

130

wondering what had just happened. Then it occurred to her. *Maria must think someone at the school told me to leave because Maria was a politically suspicious person, on account of the way the government treated her and her husband. Or maybe she is guilty that I am so overworked?* Either thought directed the cause at Maria for Elena's decision to leave, producing Maria's apparent guilt, guilt over what others might think of her, nothing to do with the real reason. *How amazing!*

Elena formed her lips into a smile. "And I want to thank you for taking me in." She curtsied.

Maria folded the newspaper and stood stiffly. "You're welcome, my dear." She was much taller than the petite Elena. She looked down at her and extended a gentle hand. "And I hope you will come by and visit often, whenever you have a chance."

Elena could read Maria's worry in her whole body. But the decision was made. Incredibly, there was nothing that Elena had needed to explain. This discussion was over. They shook hands.

Maria never fully understood Elena's reason for leaving, but respected her. The two remained friends, and Elena continued to take care of her gold, to take it to the place of exchange, faithfully guarding Maria's secrets.

* * *

Elena's work for her new family was very hard but not as hard as it had been with Maria. The family was not rich. They did not have all the wealth to worry about as had Maria. And they loved Elena. They trusted her completely with the care of their children. They allowed her to make decisions without asking their permission. But in this household, there was another sort of a problem. The husband, Sergey, he was a good man. But the wife, also called Maria (Maria Petrovna), she was secretly seeing another man.

As Elena lived with them, Maria's affair became obvious to her, though Sergey remained oblivious to it. Elena was deeply troubled by what she saw, knowing it was wrong according to the teachings of the Bible. Finally, she decided she had better speak with Maria.

Elena waited until they were alone together to confront her. "Sergey is trusting you, and you…you are cheating on him."

Maria's jaw dropped. Her face turned red. She leaned forward, placed her hand on the table, and slumped into her seat. Elena pulled out a chair and joined her.

Maria sat still, looking away. She wiped her face. "I remember that look in his eye, the first time I saw him. And that smile. He was…*is* so handsome."

Then Maria opened her heart. She poured out her story, uninterrupted, rattling on and on. She filled in all the details of how she and her lover met, then how one thing led to another, and now the relationship has been established. She turned to Elena, unflinching in her sadness. "What can I do? I love him. I cannot live without him." She looked down. "I do not love Sergey."

Elena leaned forward. "You have three children. You need to think about *them*."

Maria nodded as tears ran down her cheeks.

Elena put her hand on Maria's. "We should pray about this."

The two held hands, bowed their heads, and quietly prayed together. Maria asked the Lord for forgiveness, crying with all sincerity in her voice. They finished. They stood and hugged. Elena hoped now that this would be the end, that the affair was over.

They talked several more times in private and prayed together. Yet Maria kept on seeing her lover, no longer in fear of Elena's notice. Elena saw him. He was a younger man, a student.

Elena again confronted Maria. "He is taking advantage of you. When he finishes his studies, he will move, and you will not see him again."

"No." Maria shook her head. "He...he said he loves me. He said that as soon as he finishes school, I can move with him, marry him, and divorce my husband."

As the affair continued, Sergey started noticing his wife's odd behavior. Elena felt the awkward tension between them. Participating in keeping the secret made her feel awful.

One Sunday, Sergey had some work to do and intended to stay home with the children. He addressed Maria, "You can go to church with Elena."

Soon after they left the house, Maria stopped walking and turned to Elena. "You go on without me."

Elena's eyes widened.

"If you are done with church before I get back, wait for me on that bench by the theater." She pointed. "If I get back before you, I will wait for you there."

Elena dropped her hands in disgust. "I cannot do this." She took a deep breath. "I will tell Sergey what you are doing. I have to."

Maria measured Elena, seeing her resolve. She sighed. "You...you are right." She turned and resumed walking toward the church.

Elena followed.

From then on, Elena hated being at Maria's house. Her environment had again become horrible. She could see that immorality was destroying the family, and she had become an unwilling partner in keeping it a secret. She labored with her thoughts. *What do I do? I do not want to go back to*

Maria Arteyevna. And I cannot live like this either. Meanwhile, Maria started to treat Elena better, fearful that her secret would be revealed to Sergey.

Elena lived with them three months, continually looking for another place. In church, she met an elderly gentleman, Gospodin Kalmikov. She got to know and trust him. On one occasion, she revealed, "I am living with Sergey and Maria, and it is just too awful."

Gospodin Kalmikov turned his kind eyes toward her. "You can tell me, my dear. I will keep your secret."

Elena told him just enough of the details so that he could understand. "I simply cannot live there anymore. I cannot."

He leaned forward and whispered, "Your secret is safe with me, and I will pray for you." He smiled at her. "Let me ask around. Maybe I can help."

A week later, Gospodin Kalmikov approached Elena after the service. He clasped her hand in both of his, as he spoke softly, "I discussed your situation with my wife, and we have decided. We want you to come and live with us." He turned around and spotted his wife, standing to the side. He waved her over and introduced her. "And here is my wife, my dear, sweet Nina."

Gospozha Kalmikova happily extended her hand. "Yes, dear. We would love to have you come and live with us."

Elena was overcome with surprise. She had not asked him for a place to live. She had only explained her situation. "Thank you," she said, feeling otherwise speechless.

Maria Petrovna did not take the word from Elena very well. She cried. Then she and Sergey both tried to talk Elena out of leaving. "The children are so used to you, and we all love you." Their appeals convinced Elena to remain a while longer.

Gospodin Kalmikov and his wife kept approaching Elena at church. They asked many times, "Why do you stay? This is not good for you."

Finally, Gospodin and Gospozha Kalmikov both came to Maria Petrovna's house to find Elena. They pleaded with her, "You must come. You will become like our daughter. You will not have to do so much work, not like here. Please. Come with us."

The thought of less work had an immediate appeal to Elena. With all her chores, all her responsibilities, all her schooling, she was exhausted. Elena was at last wooed by them.

She gathered her things and followed them to their home, filled with relief.

16

Elena mastered the entire sewing curriculum offered at the School of Sewing and Design, finishing the three-year program in one. Meanwhile, she also attended her evening education classes and completed the third grade. When the summer break came, she returned home to visit her family.

It was early evening when she arrived in Bunbuy. The family was expecting her. They poured out of the house to greet her, forming a receiving line: first Anna, then her stepbrothers Semion and Mitia, then Father. Mother stood at the end, at the top of the steps in the open doorway.

One at a time, Elena embraced them and gave them a kiss. At last, she worked her way up the stairs and there melted into Mother's arms. She stood there for the longest time, fighting back her tears of joy.

The familiar smell of Mother's cooking wafted out through the opening.

Mother said, "You are just in time for dinner."

As they sat, everyone wanted to know what had happened in Irkutsk. Elena told them all that she had learned in school, proud of her accomplishments. Then, finally, she told them she no longer was living with Maria Arteyevna.

Mother's eyes narrowed. But before she could even speak, Father stood.

He rested both hands on the table and leaned forward. "Elena, you were right. We were *fools* not to believe you. Already a number of families are put into prison and everything confiscated from them." He listed the families. "Collectivization has already begun in our own village. *Nothing* is owned by farmers. *Everything* belongs to the government." He trained his heavy eyes at her. "I was a *fool*, Elena. I should have listened to you. I should have sold the equipment. Now I am giving it away to the Communists."

Elena just listened. There was nothing she could say.

Father sat. "The Communists have dispossessed the rich and separated families; males they send to different parts of Siberia, sent without anything. The Communists keep everything, including now the houses. The smaller farms, like ours, we are forced to pay big taxes. We give the government more than half our goods, our milk, meat, eggs, yarn, and grain; so that there is not enough left for us to survive."

Elena looked at their plates, heaped with food, just like in the old days. She wondered.

Father smiled as he picked up his fork. "But tonight...*tonight* is special. Tonight, we have a feast because you, Elena, *you* are home." He filled his fork and lifted it to his mouth.

Mother had been waiting anxiously to pose her question. She saw her opportunity and asked, "And where do you live now?"

"Gospodin and Gospozha Kalmikov have invited me into their home. I am so thankful to them. They have two young boys. These children were born late in their marriage, so they are an older couple. And they are so nice." She picked up her meat with her fork. "They are not wealthy, not at all like Maria Arteyevna, so they do not have to worry about the Communists. Gospodin Kalmikov, he does not make a lot of money, but Gospozha Kalmikova, she has a garden. She grows all their own food—they have a big garden—and sells her produce in the market. They also have two goats, so there is plenty of milk and cheese. She is the most amazing woman. She works so hard. I cannot describe all the things she does." Elena took a bite, chewed, and swallowed. She finished her thought. "And they both are Christians."

Everyone stopped eating. They looked at her but said nothing.

Semion broke the silence. "The Pavlovichs...they are gone. After the Communists took their store and farm, they sent Gospodin Pavlovich and Erik off somewhere."

"Where?"

He paused, as he chewed. "No one knows. And Mitia Pavlovich..."

Elena's eyes shot across at Semion.

"I heard he finished school. But he did not come home...I guess he heard what was happening; that they were looking for him. He must have decided he had better hide before they grabbed him too."

"Where is he?"

"His neighbor thinks he is hiding on an island in the East Siberian Sea."

Elena stopped eating. That place was very far away, far to the north. There would be no means to communicate with him.

Semion shook his head. "We could not write to you to let you know."

Elena stared at her plate and sighed. "I understand." She wondered how she could ever get in touch with Mitia. And where was he really? Their relationship seemed now to be hopeless. *Will we ever marry?*

The table again turned quiet and stayed that way for the rest of the meal.

* * *

Early the next morning, the entire house was awakened by a stern knock on the door. Elena opened the door to see who it was.

A woman stood on the porch with her hands held out, her face red with anguish. "Please...*please* let me in!"

Elena opened the door to her and the woman stumbled into the kitchen, breathing heavy, in a fit of sweat, frantic. She grabbed her face and screamed, "Oh! Oh, it is terrible. *He keeps doing it!*"

By now, the whole family had entered the room to see the commotion.

Mother gently took the woman by the arms, soothing her. "It will be okay. Everything is all right." Mother pulled out a chair and helped the woman to sit. Then she poured a glass of water and brought it to the table. "Here you go."

The woman lifted the glass and drained it. "Thank you...I...I can't thank you enough." She lifted her hands to her face and dug her fingers into her cheeks. "I can't believe this is happening!" She started to cry.

Elena noticed that the woman had welts on her arms.

Mother sat down close and placed her hand on the woman's shoulder. She spoke to her softly, "What is wrong? Why are you crying, dear?"

Mother glanced up at the boys and Anna and motioned with her eyes—that she wanted privacy for an adult talk. They immediately understood, opened the door to the outside and left. Elena and Father sat down and joined them.

Mother handed the woman a damp cloth and she wiped her face. Her breathing eased and she sniffed back her tears. At last, she spoke. "It is my husband. He has locked my mother in the basement and is beating her with a stick. I tried to stop him, and he hit me too; hit me a few good times."

Mother took the cloth from her, then used it to gently wipe the woman's hands as if she were tending a small child. The woman let her do it.

"And why was he beating her?" Mother asked.

"Oh, he is *drunk* again!" She was instantly agitated, worked up afresh.

Mother took hold of her hand. "It is okay. You can tell me."

"He...he started beating my mother because he wanted her to wait on him, to feed him." She took a deep breath and let it out slowly. The sound of her exhaling rattled like a washboard. "He gets drunk all the time anymore. And Mama...Mama can't stand it when he gets that way, so she just ignores him. And he...he is so high and mighty, he doesn't take that from her."

Father turned to Elena. "Her husband is the new secretary of the communist party." He fixed his eyes on the woman's face as he continued, "He gets drunk all the time. And everyone in town is petrified of him. Whatever he demands, he gets. If he wants sour cream, he gets sour cream. If he demands bread, he gets bread. If it is eggs, he gets eggs. If it is milk or clothing he wants, then milk or clothing he gets. People bring him what he wants, or he puts a gun to their heads. So he gets whatever he wants."

Elena instantly worried. *Shouldn't Father keep his thoughts to himself?*

The woman looked up at Father. She was calm now. She held her chin high as she spoke, "You are a very brave man, Comrade Briuchanov. You know I can turn you in."

Father did not flinch. "Turn me in for *what?* For speaking the truth?"

The woman curled her brow and sneered. "The truth...*Hah!*"

Mother interrupted. "Is there anything we can do to help you?"

The woman stared at Mother and sighed. "I don't think there is anything you *can* do. I...I just didn't know where to go. I...I've seen you around town a lot. You don't seem like 'Party' people, so...so I thought this would be a good safe place to come. I didn't know where else to go."

Mother held her hand. "You can come here anytime you want. My house is your house."

The woman rolled her eyes and smirked. "Well, *that* is true!"

Mother's face turned bright red, suddenly getting the joke that the government actually did own her home. "No. That is not what I meant."

The woman reached across and took hold of Mother's hand. "I know. *I know.* You are very sweet. And I thank you for letting me into *your* home."

Mother smiled. Then feeling the need to change the subject, she asked, "Can I fix you a cup of tea?"

The woman relaxed. "Surely. I would like that a lot."

Mother fixed the tea, and the four of them talked for a long time.

* * *

Elena visited with her old friends. She found out that Andrei, the secretary of the Young Komsomols, had left Bunbuy to study in a technical school. There was now much discord over the new secretary and several of his cohorts. Their reputation for cruelty and being drunk all the time had spread throughout the village. The feeling among Elena's friends was one of hopelessness, as there was nothing to be done to put a stop to the nonsense. Those who had been bold enough to speak out, to complain, they had been hauled off to work camps. The town no longer seemed the same. It had become a terrible place to live. There was great fear of the Komsomols' power.

Elena began to worry about her younger sister, Anna, who had just finished the fifth grade, the highest grade available in the villages. She recognized the need to protect her, to somehow get her out of town, away from those drunken men. A young, attractive girl would be an easy target. Elena came up with a plan and approached Mother. "How are we going to send Anna somewhere so that she can get a higher education?"

Mother shook her head. "Everything is taken away. We have nothing left to sell."

"If I am eighteen, I can be allowed to work in Irkutsk, and I can legally have some of your assets. The farm animals are still yours; you can sell them. If I just had some money, I could buy a new sewing machine to make clothing for sale. Then I could save for her education. And I can pay you back."

"But you are not eighteen, Lena."

"I know someone. He is a young adult who was part of the communist party. We have been friends a long time. He is the chairman of the village now. I am sure he can get me the papers I need."

Mother studied Elena. "How can you do this? To do this is to lie."

Elena felt suddenly trapped in her own standards. She closed her eyes and pondered the problem. She sighed. "If I do nothing, then Anna will be stuck here in this terrible place. And…and I just can't imagine what will happen to her. These leaders, these drunkards, they have no sense of right or wrong. There no longer is any law. Yes, it would be a lie, but it would be a lie that hurts no one. It would be the right thing to do."

"Let me speak with Papa. If he says it is okay with him, then it will be okay with me."

Mother and Father later gave Elena their blessing. Soon after, the village chairman looked into Elena's records. He revealed to those in charge that "the village had the wrong date listed on her birth certificate." Thus, he gave Elena a revised one, one that said she was eighteen. The new papers were legitimate.

With her papers now in order and her legal share of her parent's property in hand, her modest assets, Elena said goodbye again to her family. She boarded the train bound for Irkutsk. The lawlessness she left behind in Bunbuy was simply mind-boggling to her. She had to leave, and she had no intention ever to return.

17

With her new birth certificate in hand, showing Elena was eighteen, the government allowed her to work. She got her first job at a clothing factory, Igla, which means "needle." She was hired there into the division of seamstresses, as master seamstress. Thrilled with the position and excited to work, she did her best to please her manager and dressmaking cutter, as the three worked together to satisfy each and every order, striving to delight every customer. Elena was pleased by how well they all got along. Her manager and cutter loved Elena's work, and they loved her too. But it was the customers who were the most pleased. They kept coming back for more of Elena's work.

In the evenings, Elena advanced to the next term of classes for the uneducated. She intended to complete the fourth and fifth grades within the year.

Elena continued to live with the Kalmikov family. With the income from her new job, she could afford to pay them rent. They, on the other hand, would not accept her money and, surprisingly, did not expect her to do anything to help around the house. While Elena was at work or in school, Gospozha Kalmikova already had the house clean, dishes done, gardening done. There was nothing left for Elena to do. Gospozha Kalmikova would wash the family's clothing and wash Elena's too. And when Elena had to work nightshifts, Gospozha Kalmikova would send her husband to come and meet her, to walk her home, to keep her safe.

Elena was truly treated like a member of the family. She felt she had never had it so good.

There were other boarders who lived there with the Kalmikovs. Gospozha Kalmikova's brother and another member from church each had rooms; thus, when Elena arrived, all the rooms had previously been filled. So instead of a private room, Elena was given space in the corner of the kitchen, the main reason Gospozha Kalmikova voiced when she refused to accept her rent money. The other reason was, "We love you like a daughter." It truly showed.

To thank her guardians, Elena made them clothing. She sewed something for each of their children and for gospodin and gospozha, something they could use. She saw they needed dress shirts or a suit, coats and dresses; so she sewed these. After a while, to return the favor, they bought the fabric for Elena to sew into garments. They realized she could not afford all that fabric for their new wardrobe, and they were getting a tremendous discount, beautifully designed and made outfits at a mere fraction of the cost. As a gift, they also bought fabric for Elena's own use. This they did for her many times.

Gospodin and Gospozha Kalmikov showed their good character, the character of mature Christians. They were active in the church and openly discussed their faith. They believed the teachings of Jesus and showed it in their lives, not only in how they treated each other, but in the hospitality and generosity that they extended toward Elena, not hesitating to share the little that they had. Their practical Christian living became an encouragement to Elena, who was only beginning her newfound faith. And as she learned from them, she knew she was growing spiritually by just being there.

The Kalmikovs often invited a lot of young people into their home. Elena met many great folks as a result. She soon became active in the church youth group and participated in all their events. In time, Elena even became one of the young leaders. In October, she joined the church.

* * *

When winter came, Akulina arrived unannounced in Irkutsk. Elena was overjoyed to see her. But Mother wore anguish in her eyes.

"What is wrong, Mama?"

Akulina winced and grabbed her side. "These awful pains." Her body tightened and quaked as she squinted her eyes shut. After a moment, the tension in her cheeks eased. "I came to see the doctor in the big hospital here. They could do nothing for me in Bunbuy."

Elena stiffened with worry. Mother was her best friend, someone she could always trust. She gently placed her hand on Mother's shoulder. "I will go with you."

Elena looked her over, still absorbing the reality that Mother was actually there with her in Irkutsk. She noted Mother's outfit, remembering how she always wore her best clothes out in public or when traveling. A modest linen cap sat atop her head, delicately embroidered by Mother's own skillful hands. Some of Mother's long blond hair fell out around the edges, hair now streaked with silver. Elena peered up into Mother's eyes, detecting a sense of burden there, burden that could not be hidden. She probed, "What else?"

Mother leaned forward confidentially. "It is the Communists. Someone told on us. They said we had gold."

"Gold?" Elena leaned away. Her eyes flashed.

"They came with their shovels. They dug holes all over our yard looking for treasure. All they found was rocks and clay." She winced and held her side again.

Elena wrapped her arm around her tenderly. "You will stay with me, Mama. Here, of course."

The Kalmikovs welcomed yet another guest into their home. Mother stayed with Elena in her corner of the kitchen. They both slept on the same put-away bed, a twin-size bed. Elena had been planning to move to an apartment of her own. This now heightened the need.

That need was soon met. Elena had become friends with a couple in her church. The wife's name was Pasha. Their house was near to Igla and not far from the church. Pasha's husband was away frequently because of his job, which left the woman alone in her home. They had an extra room that they wanted to rent to someone from the church so that she could have the security of company and extra income. Pasha offered the room to Elena.

Gospodin and Gospozha Kalmikov were very understanding, happy that Elena could be independent, pleased with the location of her new quarters, and respecting of her new landlord; and now very glad for Elena.

For Elena's part, being able to afford to live on her own brought with it a sense of accomplishment. And even though the Kalmikovs had loved her and treated her like their own daughter, she had constantly felt indebted to them, since they did so much for her. That burden now was lifted.

As she left the Kalmikov's house, she embraced and thanked them. She walked away, praying, *Thank you, Lord. Thank you for guiding me here. I thank you for them, how they protected me and helped me in my time of need. As long as I live, I will never forget them.*

* * *

Elena went with Mother to the hospital to see the doctor to determine the cause of her pains. The doctor diagnosed gallstones, the source of her frequent and severe pain attacks. He told her that she should have them removed, a very serious surgery with possible complications. A lesser alternative, but one that might not work, was to go on a strict diet. Mother decided to give the diet a chance, fearful of the surgery.

Akulina stayed in Irkutsk under the care of the doctor and continued to live with Elena, always happy to go with her wherever she went. Elena saw this as an opportunity to talk to her about matters of faith, doing so as often as she could. They went together to Elena's church, Christian Alliance, for services. They also attended another nearby Baptist church for Elena's fellowship with other young people. Elena felt blessed, convinced that God had prepared her room at Pasha's house just for her, that she could be able to accommodate Mother, that they could be together, that they could read the Bible together, and that they could speak freely about God.

In the meantime, Elena completed the fifth grade. She applied to and was accepted into the high school where she soon completed the seventh grade. Now she would be allowed to go to technical college, the Workers Faculty, where she would be trained to teach others how to design and sew. She signed up, passed the test, and was admitted. She was thrilled. Now she could quit her job, live on campus, and study. The cost of school was forty rubles per year, but readily afforded with the money she earned on the side from her expanding list of sewing customers, each of whom loved the quality of her work and her unusual designs.

* * *

As the winter of 1930 waned, Elena received more unexpected guests: her sister, Anna, and her two stepbrothers, Semion and Mitia. They had fled Bunbuy and left everything to come to Irkutsk, having only the clothing they wore on their backs.

Semion explained, "It is Father. He has been arrested."

Elena and Mother braced themselves and listened.

Semion explained, "They took him somewhere. Where, we do not know. He could not keep the 'quota.'"

"Quota?"

"The Communists! They have all these quotas now. There is a 'meat quota,' a 'grain quota,' a 'milk quota,' a 'yarn quota.' All these quotas." He hung his head in disgust. "If you can't supply your quota, they haul you off to jail."

Elena's eyes narrowed.

Semion continued, "So Father had to keep all these quotas. We had enough grain, and there was enough milk. But if we kill the cows or sheep to fill the meat quota, then we cannot supply the milk quota or the yarn quota." His face turned redder as he spoke. The veins in his neck were popping out. "There was nothing we could do!"

Anna interjected, "This was happening to everyone. The farms were shut down. There is no food in Bunbuy. We were starving."

Elena turned to her mother. They both looked at the three.

Anna was flush, shaking, weak with hunger. "We could not stay any longer in Bunbuy. We were terrified." She was at the point of tears. "So we came here...here to be with you."

18

What do I do now? The whole family had come to live with Elena in the one room she was renting from Pasha. *There are five of us now. I cannot afford to feed them all.* But she could not allow her family to be homeless.

Elena quit the Worker's Faculty, the one thing in her whole life for which she had been striving. There was no choice. Either she quit school or her family would starve. She cried over having to leave, but it was the right decision.

Elena went back to Igla and worked both days and evenings, taking customer's orders and sewing. She had more work than she could handle. Her coworkers wondered where she was getting so many customer orders. The answer was in her initiative, her drive. She felt that if someone gave her an order once, she should do her best, do all she could to make them not want anyone else to make their clothes. She would labor to remain their seamstress and designer of choice. And they kept coming back for more.

Though having enough money to support her family was soon resolved, five people living in a single room was simply too much to bear. They needed a whole new apartment to rent for themselves.

Not far from Pasha's house, another person who went to her church had an empty unit. He was an engineer. His apartment had three bedrooms and a large kitchen with a pantry. It was brand new. He offered it to Elena and she took it. While Elena worked, Anna and Mitia were able to continue their schooling in Irkutsk. Semion, who was two years older, took a vocational class in driver's education, hoping to qualify for a job making deliveries. Elena's income made it all possible.

Then, as the weather warmed, Elena's church announced that there would be a baptism for the new members. They had acquired a special permit from the government to do this, since church activities were strictly regulated. She expressed her desire to be baptized. Yevgeni Kropanin instructed her to meet with the elders to discuss what was involved with baptism. She was to tell them her testimony, the story of how she came to believe in Christ. They would listen to ascertain if she understood the basic tenets of the faith and to determine if she was ready to be baptized.

After the meeting, Yevgeni called her aside. He extended his hand to her, expressing their acceptance of her. "Thank you, young lady. Thank you for sharing."

Elena took his hand and smiled. "I am so glad to be here."

"And we are glad you came."

She brightened. "I do hope that Pastor Rayevski will be well enough to baptize me." He was Lyudmila's son, presently sick with typhus.

"Yes, we all hope he is doing better."

"I am so sorry what happened to her...to Lyudmila."

Yevgeni studied her, discerning the reason behind her probing. He stepped close. "We know it was not you, not you that turned her in."

Elena eased.

He continued, "We know what happened."

"You do?"

"One of our deacons had a picture of everyone in the church at her house. Her neighbor had a daughter who went to the same sewing school that you were attending; she was a

Young Komsomol. Sometime before the confiscations started, she came to this deacon's house and saw this portrait. She questioned the identity of everyone in the photo. The deacon thought nothing of it and started to witness to this Young Komsomol, then said the people in the photo belonged to her church and that Lyudmila, an educated person, believed in God, and that her son was the minister.

"This young lady then told the director of the school that Lyudmila believed in God and that she should be removed. That is what happened right at the time you arrived in our church. You know that Lyudmila has not been able to find a job again. But, praise God, because she is such a great seamstress, people from the church hire her to make their clothing. Now she is able to get all the money she needs to survive."

Elena listened carefully to all he said, storing up the message in her heart. She was grateful at last to be exonerated, to be fully accepted by them. At the same time, she understood that in Siberia, suspicion was ever present in the church. Members took risks each day in the course of casual conversation.

That afternoon, Elena told her mother that she had been offered the chance to be baptized. Out of respect, she asked for Mother's permission. Mother did not hesitate to give it.

Two weeks later, Elena and her family, all five of them, boarded a southbound train, bound for the southern tip of Lake Baikal. They travelled with a contingent from the church to the tiny railway village of Kultuk, which was perched on the shores of the lake. It was late morning when they arrived, disembarking under a brilliant cloudless sky. The group walked together from the tracks down to the beach, then along the water's edge a short distance around a bend and into to a private cove.

Elena had to stop and stare to drink it all in. The lake dominated the scene. In the still air, the water was clear, clear like crystal, permitting a view to the deep bottom as it fell away from the shore. The lake was immense, so large that it might have been an ocean. Surrounding the lake were steep mountains. From the far and distant side of this inland sea, the purple hills drew closer, merging to deep green, revealing their covering of pine trees. The azure of the hills and crisp blue of the sky blended and filled the water with teal. The color was stunning.

As the group of them filtered into the cove, the elders of the church arranged everyone on the narrow curve of sand, several dozen parishioners, young and old. They stood with their backs to the trees. One of the elders stepped forward to the water's edge (Pastor Rayevski was still too ill to come). He turned his back to the lake and began to speak. First, he led them in prayer and then delivered his message.

"Today, we are here to baptize six new members of our church, six people who have come to follow in obedience to Christ, to follow him into the waters of baptism.

"Baptism is one of the two sacraments that God has given us to follow, the other is the Lord's Supper. Neither sacrament does anything to save the believer, for we know from scripture that it is by the grace of God that we are saved. It is not through our good works, so that none of us has anything to boast about when we say we have become acceptable to God. Jesus is the one that has made us acceptable. He alone has done this.

"So why do we baptize? We do this sacrament to show our obedience to God and to demonstrate our commitment to others, even those that do not believe. We do this to show them that we have faith and that we are not ashamed or afraid to follow Jesus."

He opened his Bible. "I have some scripture to share with you from 1st Peter, chapter 3. Here is God's Word:

"Who is there to harm you if you are eager to do good? But even if you should suffer for what is right, you are blessed."

He looked up from the book. "For do we not all suffer here a little?" He paused to let the silence of the scene sweep over them. He returned his eyes to the page:

"And do not fear their intimidation, and do not be troubled, but honor Christ as Lord in your hearts, always being ready to make a defense to everyone who asks you to give a reason for the hope that is in you, yet with gentleness and respect; and keep a clear conscience so that those who speak maliciously against your good behavior in Christ may be ashamed of their slander. For it is better, if God should will it so, better that you suffer for doing what is right rather than for doing what is wrong. For Christ also died for sins, once for all, the just for the unjust, so that He might bring us to God, having been put to death in the flesh, but made alive in the spirit; Corresponding to that, baptism now saves you—not the removal of dirt from the flesh, but an appeal to God for a good conscience—through the resurrection of Jesus Christ, who is at the right hand of God, having gone into heaven, after angels and authorities and powers had been subjected to Him."

He closed the book and looked up at them as he preached. "Christ himself was baptized. He came to John at the River Jordan, and there he was baptized. And though John protested, saying that he was unfit, rather that *he* should be baptized by Jesus, he conceded to the instruction of the Lord who said 'it was fitting to fulfill all righteousness.' And so Jesus went down into the water and was baptized by John.

"And then there is the command of the Lord, who, before he ascended into heaven, told His disciples to 'go into all the world to make disciples and to baptize them in the name of the Father, and the Son, and the Holy Spirit.'

"That is what brings us here today. That we might obey both the *pattern* and the *words* of our Lord, that those who first believe may follow their faith into the waters of baptism." He handed his Bible to a woman standing there, removed his shoes, and stepped to the water's edge. "Now those of you to be baptized, please follow after me."

Three men and two women stepped forward.

Elena turned to Mother. She removed her shoes and handed them to her, then followed after the other converts, standing in a line at the water's edge. The elder waded out into the lake. The bottom was steep, so it was just a short ways until the water was over his waist. He turned and motioned to the first person to enter the water.

As they came out one at a time and stood by him, he asked them questions so that everyone standing on the shore could hear their answers. Then he laid them backward into the water and lifted them out. They emerged soaked and shivering as they returned to the shore.

Elena was the last to come. She stepped into the lake and felt the shocking chill of the water—the lake had only recently lost its winter coating of ice. In less than a minute, she felt her feet going numb. But she was determined to do this. She stepped farther out, in over her waist, and stood before the Elder.

He addressed her, as he had the others, "Do you, Elena, confess that you are a sinner in the eyes of God?"

She focused on the moment. "I do."

"Do you acknowledge that there is nothing you can do, not by good works, nothing you can do to earn the favor of God?"

"I do."

"Do you acknowledge that Jesus, himself, having committed no sin, gave his life for the payment of the penalty of your sins on the cross, and that he died, was buried, and rose again on the third day?"

She trembled in the frigid water. "I do."

"And do you acknowledge that he has ascended into heaven and sits at the right hand of the Father as Lord of all the earth and that he is coming back again?"

"I do."

"Do you confess him now, here before all these witnesses, do you confess him as your Lord and Savior?"

Elena turned and looked up at the crowd. She focused on her mother, as she spoke the final, "I do."

"Then, Elena Ivanovna Nosova, based on the testimony of your mouth, I baptize you in the name of the Father, the Son, and the Holy Spirit."

He turned Elena to the side, laid her back into the water, speaking these words, "You are buried together with Christ." And lifting her up, out of the water, he continued, "And raised with him into newness of life!"

Elena came up drenched and shaking from the icy water.

And as they had with the others, the people on the beach sang in praise.

"All those who are baptized into Christ,
They have clothed themselves in Christ.
Hallelujah!"

Elena dredged herself up to the shore and stepped into the arms of Mother, who wrapped her in a towel.

The elder remained yet standing in the lake. He addressed them, "And now I extend this offer to any of you. Seeing that there is plenty of water here, what is there to prevent you now from being baptized? There is nothing to prevent you, except if you do not believe. Do you believe? Will you come?"

Elena was half frozen from her baptism, feeling Mother's hands as they rubbed her back and arms with the warmth of the towel. But on hearing these words, Mother's hands had stopped moving. Elena looked at her. Mother returned the glance.

Once more, the Elder asked, "Will you come?"

Mother turned away from Elena. She bent and removed her shoes, dropped them on the sand, and ran out into the lake.

There she confessed Christ as her Lord. There Mother was baptized.

19

It was late in the spring when Akulina found out where her husband had been imprisoned, taken off to a work camp in Kansk. She had heard the story from her network of trusted friends, an accidental conversation with an acquaintance of an acquaintance who had heard the rumor. Akulina immediately wrote to a friend that lived in Kansk. A few weeks later she received a note that confirmed Sidor was there, and that the conditions in the camp were deplorable. The prisoners there were underfed and forced to rely on their family to bring them food. Prisoners with no family to help were effectively condemned to starvation.

Akulina was anxious. She knew she must go to Kansk to help him. She again wrote to her friend and arranged to watch this woman's children in exchange for room and board. She packed a bag and made ready to depart. Elena bought her a ticket and gave her money for the journey.

Elena went with Mother to the station. They stood together on the platform, holding hands as Elena prayed for Mother's safe journey. Elena looked up at her, worried for her traveling alone, but realizing this was a trip that had to happen and knowing she could not afford time off from work to accompany her. "Write to me when you have found Papa."

At the same time, Akulina hated to leave her daughter. But Sidor needed help, so the decision was already made. "Of course. I will let you know he is well." Akulina understood the limits of what she could safely put in any letter.

The two embraced and Akulina climbed on board the train.

The train ride west from Irkutsk to Kansk took the better part of two days. After a short stop in Ilanski, the train followed alongside the bends in the river, worming its way through the narrow hills, then around the big bend and southward into the outskirts of Kansk. Akulina sat fixed at the window, absorbing the scene. They passed the lumberyards that lined the tracks on one side, with the shabby worker shanties on the other. The engine slowed as it rattled across the steel-truss bridge that spanned the Kan River. From there, she observed a row of smokestacks downriver (Kansk was an industrial center that supplied building materials by rail to the west). A few minutes later, the train came to a stop at the station in the center of the city.

As soon as Akulina got settled at her friend's, she went to look for Sidor. He was supposedly working at the brick plant. She took a small bag of food and stepped outside, having been given directions.

She turned to the north and spotted a row of gigantic smokestacks in the distance, spewing a thick plume of smoke that ascended straight up, high into the air, each pumping an endless supply of grey that dissolved and became indistinguishable from the dismal overhead expanse. These stacks marked her way to the plant, the brick kilns, with fires that never cooled, firing clay billets into bricks twenty-four hours a day, every day of the year. She walked in that direction.

Akulina approached a fence that surrounded the plant, tall pine trunks driven into the ground with rusting steel mesh stretched from pole to pole, a barrier to keep the public out and the forced laborers in. Along the top of the fence were three strands of barbed wire. The road turned to the right and ran beside the fence, then angled a hundred meters down toward the river. To her left, through the fence, was the brickyard, with great mounds of red-brown dirt that obstructed her view in, making it impossible to see any workers. There was nothing green inside the yard, just dirt and soot everywhere, some of it falling out onto the road.

Eventually, she came to a set of railroad tracks, a spur off the main line that ran through an open gate to her left and into the plant. To the side of the gate was a sign that read, "Kansk Kirpichnyy Zavod" ("Kansk Brick Works").

Two guards flanked the gate, seated in their drab green uniforms, each with a rifle at their side. They watched Akulina approach before they stood and slowly picked up their weapons. One asked in a disinterested tone, "Papers?"

She pulled them out of her pocket and silently handed them to him.

The guard studied the documents. "Why are you here?"

Akulina lifted her bag. "I have food for my husband. He is working here."

"His name?"

"Sidor Davidovich Briuchanov."

The guard raised his eyes up at her. He glanced down one more time and studied the papers, in no hurry at all. After what seemed like an eternity of seconds, he lifted his gaze and examined her up and down. He stared into her eyes without saying a word. A rise in his brow made her realize he was enjoying making her wait.

Akulina's stomach tightened. She swallowed, fearful he would not let her in.

The guard turned and looked across at the other. Neither spoke. He turned back to her, stood tall, stiff and stern, shoulders back, stomach pulled in. He took a deep breath and held it.

He made his decision. He handed the papers back to Akulina and pointed into the yard. "The family area is over there. That is where you wait. The workers will come there when they have a break."

Akulina tucked her papers away and walked along the tracks and into the yard. She followed the gravel path on the right that led straight to an area where there were tables and benches. Every surface was covered in soot. She dusted a bench off and sat down.

The family area was walled off from a view into the center of the plant, walled by two-meter-high stacks of red bricks on shipping pallets, stacks that extended continuously to the right for a hundred meters alongside the tracks. At the end of the stacks were the kilns, a row of six immense brick chimneys that rose more than thirty meters high, each spewing soot from the wood fires within. Over her right shoulder, the fence continued, separating the yard from the riverbank, a bit of welcome beauty visible from the edge of this industrial wasteland, where the only green things were the trampled-on weeds that came up through the gravel, dirt, and soot.

Akulina sat alone for hours as the day wore on. When the afternoon grew late, other visitors arrived at the plant. Each entered at the gate and walked back to join her in the family area.

A half hour later, a line of guards marched out from the edge of the kilns, walking beside the stacks of bricks. They spaced themselves to the right, along the fence. Each guard stood with his back to the river. Several came into the family area, gripping their rifles in both hands.

The first of the workers emerged out of a gap between the stacks of bricks. Akulina was suddenly anxious. Like the other family members there, she rose to her feet and studied the man as he approached.

The worker's shoulders were slumped, there was a noticeable limp in his walk, and his tattered clothing was the color of red dirt. As he grew nearer, she studied his face. He might have been a young man; his beard and hair were black. His forehead, nose, and ears were utterly filthy. As he drew close, she studied his eyes, blue eyes staring out from a snuff-colored face.

He was not Sidor.

The prisoner walked past and approached a young woman. The two embraced. The woman showed no reticence in touching him. She handed him a small bag. The two sat. He pulled out a piece of bread and chewed off a bite. His hands were shaking.

One at a time, more of the men came. Each was the image of grime and frailty, men defeated by their labor. After they greeted their loved one and ate their meal, a guard came over and ushered them away. They shuffled alongside the brick stacks toward the opening back into the brickyard. When they came to the opening, they stopped and looked back at their family member. They lingered a moment, hoping it could last longer, waved, hung their heads, stepped through the opening, and disappeared from view. Then the family member turned and walked to the main gate and left.

Akulina had been waiting an hour after the last person came and went. There were no other family members with her now. The sky was getting dark. Her worry reached its zenith.

In the distance, one more man appeared. He came through the opening and stopped. He looked toward the river, studied the fence, and then eyed the guards. At last, he turned toward Akulina. He stood a moment, his posture tilting.

Akulina's heart raced.

The prisoner took a step forward. In a few more steps, he began to jog, then to run.

Akulina stood firm. She threw her arms open, and he ran into them.

Sidor held her.

They wept together.

* * *

In the months while Mother was away, Semion finished his driver education, got a job as a mechanic, and moved out on his own. Mitia graduated from trade school, turned eighteen, and took a job as an electrician, able now to support himself. But he remained living with Elena, who was supporting Anna as she continued her education.

Elena had not heard from her mother in all that time. Concerned, she wrote to Mother's friend in Kansk. But there was no response. Elena continued to pray for her parents every day as a new challenge swept across the Soviet Union and arrived in Irkutsk: starvation.

Throughout the Soviet Union, farmers were losing their lands to government seizure. Many farmers gave up their livelihood and fled to the cities, where they had heard the government would give them food and housing for a day's work. But this mass flight was not without consequences. With so few hands remaining on the farms to grow the food, production collapsed. Food of any kind, especially bread, fell into short supply.

To manage the shortage and to control the distribution of food, the government developed a card system. A card entitled a person to receive one kilogram of bread, that is, if they were working; if they did not have a job, they received a half portion. Anyone without a card could not buy bread at all. People stood in lines for days to get their one-kilogram. Families with more than one person required a card for each member of the family, and they could not send just one representative to buy bread with it. Each individual had to stand in line with their own card for their own ration.

In the marketplace, food prices skyrocketed. Frozen milk and frozen potatoes were available, but the cost was out of reach for most. Except for special occasions, the boredom of bread dominated the diet. Malnutrition took hold on the population.

The scene in the streets became unimaginable. The only places to buy food were the government stores, and there were not many of these. As a result, long food lines formed, stretching for blocks, some longer than a kilometer. People stood waiting in these lines for days to get their one loaf of bread.

As Elena waited in line for her portion, she wondered about Mother and Father. She prayed for them both.

* * *

Akulina returned each day to the plant and brought Sidor the little extra food she was able to acquire. They visited together in these brief interludes, while she brought wet towels to clean him up and scissors to trim his hair and beard. She was trying to keep him looking respectable, to encourage him, to restore his sense of dignity. This was now a psychological war, and Akulina was doing all she could to help Sidor win. She could tell with each visit that he was getting stronger, that life was returning to his eyes.

During one of these visits, while she was waiting for Sidor, a woman approached her. The woman studied her face then asked, "Akulina? Akulina Nosova?"

Akulina thought the woman looked familiar. Still, she acted aloof. "No. My name is Akulina Briuchanova."

The woman wagged her finger in Akulina's face; her voice was loud enough that everyone there could hear what she was saying. "I remember you. Your husband was Ivan. He and his two brothers ran that store in Kondratyevo. I saw you many times in the store. My mother bought her fabric there. You were *rich*."

Akulina felt suddenly insecure, seeing the others watch and listen. One of the guards trained his eyes on her.

"I'm...I'm from Bunbuy. We have a farm."

The woman stepped close. Akulina was taller. She looked up at her and studied Akulina's eyes. Akulina looked away. The woman thought a moment, and then backed up a few steps. She glanced at the guard who was staring at her, tightening his grip on his gun. She relented. "Yeah, I suppose so. My mistake. But it is funny how much you look like her."

By now, Sidor had arrived.

The woman sized them up together and sat down on the bench. Soon her relative came, and she became engaged in her own visit.

Akulina finished her time with Sidor and decided she should stay away for a couple days. When she finally did return, the guard stopped her at the gate. He took Akulina's papers and did not give them back. "Wait here," he said.

He looked into the yard and motioned to another guard, a guard who was standing beside a woman. Both came toward the gate. As the woman approached, Akulina recognized her right away as the one who had confronted her earlier in the week. When she got close, the woman pointed. "That is her. She is the one. Her name is Nosova. Her family had a large store in Kondratyevo. They were rich."

The guard looked at Akulina's papers. He asked, "It says here your name is Briuchanova. You know it is a crime to make false papers?" He clenched his jaw and glared at her. "We can put you in prison for that."

A chill shot up Akulina's spine. *What should I do? This woman has properly identified me. If I am caught in a lie, they will torture me. My life will be over.* She settled herself. She would tell the truth. *That is what Elena would do. The truth is always the best.*

Akulina stared at the guard. "My name is Briuchanova. I remarried after my first husband died. I have not lived in Kondratyevo in many years." She turned and looked at the woman. "And my family is no longer rich. My husband and one brother are dead, the other one in a work camp…*if* he is alive." She straightened her posture and glared at her accuser. "And the government already took all our gold and everything else we ever had."

Akulina stood waiting in front of the guard, waiting for some sort of backlash. It never came. He handed her back her papers and let her go into the yard to see her husband.

But the next afternoon, there was a truck waiting at the gate when she came for her visit. Akulina was taken into custody. They took her papers from her, put her in the back, locked the door, and drove away.

Akulina's jail cell was a small room with walls made of hewn logs. The floor was dirt, covered in bits of straw. She imagined she was in some sort of barn, as there yet lingered the smell of manure. There was no way to confirm where she was. There were no windows.

As the seasons turned from summer into fall, then into winter, the temperature dropped. The building had no heat. Her room was so cold she could see her breath. The living conditions were deplorable. Each day, she was given a piece of bread, a cup of water, and an empty bucket to relieve herself.

Once a day, two guards came and took her out from her cell into the space directly in front of her door. There was a table there with a lamp, the only light in the building. There were two chairs at the table where the guards sat.

They began their routine. They ordered Akulina to stand in front of them while they asked her questions. The questions and answers were always the same.

"Where is the gold that belonged to your family?"

"There is no more gold."

"Your family were merchants, they supplied all the businesses for many miles around. They had several stores, teams of animals, and the biggest house in Kondratyevo. And you are telling me that they did not have any gold?"

"I never said we didn't have any gold."

"Oh, so you *did* have gold?"

"What I said before, I will tell you again. We gave all the gold—I mean the government *took* all the gold we had. And now...*now* we do not have any more."

This questioning took place several times a day. For the whole of the day, Akulina was made to stand on one spot. She was not allowed to sit. Afterward, she was returned to her cell to collapse, to fall asleep on the filthy floor, to become ready to resume the cycle again the next day.

* * *

As starvation took hold in Irkutsk, tensions in the food line ran high. If a person had to leave the line for any reason at all and wanted to come back to the same place, no one would let them in. They forced that person to go to the end of the line to start over again. It could be two to three days before they received their bread. Desperation set in. Anyone that tried to cut into line would get pulled out and severely beaten. In many cases, riots broke out.

Since Elena was working, she could not afford to stand in line all day for bread. Work was her means to support herself. If she did not show up at the factory, even if she was late, whatever the reason, she would be dismissed. She tried waiting in line after working hours and stood all night. When morning came, it was time to go to work, but she was still nowhere near the store. This happened several times. Each time, she walked away without any food.

Undernourished, she prayed that God would sustain her and Anna. And she prayed for Mother's quest to find and feed Father, trying to imagine their circumstances.

Elena continued to work each day and stand in the bread line at night, with hopes of obtaining a single loaf. Weak with malnutrition, Elena found she was getting dizzy, unable to concentrate on her work. She prayed that God would help her to buy bread.

And then the idea came to her. She decided to go to the store during her lunch break. She had one hour, and there was a store just a kilometer from Igla. She prayed as she walked there.

Rounding the last corner, she saw the line. It stretched to the right, down the street for many blocks, as far as she could see. To the left was the store, two blocks away. She sighed, but crossed the street to join the line anyway.

Just then a thought flashed in her mind. She did not go to the right toward the end of the line. Instead, she turned and went to the left, toward the store. She passed by the many people who had been standing there for more than a day. She prayed as she went.

She came up to the front of the line and stopped, turned, and looked over her shoulder, back down the line, seeing all the hungry people, their shoulders slumped, their eyes dull;

the line of them extended beyond her sight. And right there, beside her, was the door, the destination of them all.

Before she had a chance to turn around, to walk toward her spot at the far end of the line, she noticed the man standing there first in line. Quietly, he motioned to her with his hand, motioning that she should get in line, in front of him. If she stepped there, she would be the next person served.

She studied his face, wondering if she had understood his hand motion. He was an elderly man. He nodded, affirming his intent.

She stepped in front of him, looked at no one, and kept her eyes fixed ahead at the door.

Just then the door opened. Elena stepped inside. Her heart was racing. She looked at the attendant. She fumbled in her purse to find her card. Finding it, she caught her breath. She showed her card to him. She waited, shaking with hunger. Her stomach tightened. She tasted the acid of her nervousness rise into her throat. She swallowed to hold it down.

He reached down behind the counter and gave her one-kilogram of bread. She paid him.

Elena stepped back outside and looked at the man that had let her in. No one else seemed to notice she had cut in line. No one else even looked at her. There was no riot. *Did they see me?* she wondered.

She flashed a thankful eye at him, clutched her loaf tight to her chest, and ran back to work. Elena cried as she ran. "Thank you, Lord! Thank you for helping me! Thank you for that kind man that allowed me into the line! Thank you!"

She arrived back at work in time before her hour ended.

That night, she shared the bread with her sister. It was just enough for them for the day.

The next day, when lunchtime came, Elena again felt drawn to go stand in line for her bread. Like she had the day before, she prayed as she walked. She asked, "Lord, please open another heart today."

She came upon the line and again walked up toward the door. She looked at the people standing there. No one looked up. They each stared, fixated at the back of the person immediately in front of them. They looked sad and hopeless, like prisoners of a defeated army.

When Elena was just a few people from the front of the line, a woman looked up at her; she pulled the edge of her scarf back from her face. "Here is your spot." The woman smiled. "Don't you recognize me?" She was elderly. Elena had never seen the woman before.

Elena stepped in front of her into the line. In a few minutes, it was Elena's turn. The door opened. She entered, bought her bread, and came out.

Elena stopped. She extended her hand to the woman. "Thank you."

The woman nodded.

Elena ran back to work, tears flowing down her cheeks. *Dear God, it is a miracle!*

That night Elena said a special prayer of thanks as she also prayed for Mother, oblivious as to what was befalling her.

* * *

When the simple questioning of Akulina failed to produce the answers that her captors were looking for, they resorted to torture.

She was taken from her cell into a special room. There they had a board the size of a person in width and length. The surface of the board was impaled with metal protrusions, sharp nails and fishing hooks, each connected to an electric current. They stripped their victims and lay them naked on their back on the board, then turned on the electricity. The shock of current caused the victim's body to twitch and move up and down, falling on the nails and becoming engaged with the hooks, then lifting and tearing open the flesh.

They lay Akulina there and questioned her as they turned on the power. They questioned and tortured her, but she had nothing to tell them. Eventually, she fell unconscious.

She awoke in a clinic. The doctor dressed her wounds. Her entire back, all the way down to her legs, was ripped open. In a few weeks, she recovered enough to be put to work, but not for long. New interrogation and tortures began.

This time, she was put into a freezer, a room where the ceiling, floor, and walls were encased in ice. There was a small window, through which guards could observe while the prisoner suffered in the extreme cold. To avoid becoming frozen, Akulina kept herself moving rapidly. She could not stop or she would freeze to death.

Over time, the cold took its toll. Her teeth began to gnash. She tried to keep her mouth closed to stop it, holding her jaw with her hand, but to no avail. Then her body began to shake, thrashing without control. She ran as fast as she could, moving every part of her body, yet she could not avoid the feeling of getting colder and colder.

During this freeze, her interrogators kept shouting through the small window, "Where is the gold?"

Akulina prayed, "God, take my soul. Free me from this torture. Forgive my interrogators."

She could speak no longer; her mouth was frozen. Her body ached. Her battle to stay awake was failing. She leaned against a wall of ice and slid down onto the floor, unconscious.

Akulina awoke in a bed in the clinic. How she was brought back to life, she did not know. Twice now she had been brought near to death, but they had not let her die. She knew the twisted truth behind their "mercy." If she were to die, they would never find the gold—the gold she did not have.

Again, she recovered completely. They returned her to her original cell and closed the door.

The next day, she was taken out for more questioning. This time, she noticed there was another prisoner standing to her right, a very old man. She gasped, "Grandpa!" He was Sidor's grandfather. He was 105 years old.

A guard stepped out from behind the table and scolded her, "We did not say that you could speak!" He raised his fist. She braced herself. The guard mysteriously withheld his wrath. He stepped back behind the table and sat.

The questions came just as before. This time, they asked the old man.

The answers were the same.

The guards turned toward Akulina and continued the questioning. Akulina was exhausted. To make matters worse, her gallstones were acting up. She stood firm before them and gave them the same answers she had always given. As the day wore on, she felt faint and sat on the floor.

The guard came around to the front of the table and glared down at her. "You are not allowed to sit. You must stand."

Her head sagged. "I cannot stand any longer." She gritted her teeth and looked up at him. "I am sitting...sitting no matter what you say."

The second guard came over close. "Do you know what we do to people that do not stand?"

She looked up at him, unflinching.

"We *kill* them." He puffed out his chest. "And do not think that because you are a woman, that we will hesitate to kill you too."

"*Good.*" She scoffed. "Then I will not have to go through this torture. I will be in the presence of God, where there is no pain, where there are no tears."

The guard raised his fist to strike her.

The other grabbed his arm and stopped him. "I think we are done for the day." He helped Akulina to her feet. "Back to your cell. We will see what you have to say tomorrow."

They locked Akulina in her cell and continued to question the old man.

* * *

The whole of the rest of the year, Elena went to the food store at lunchtime to buy bread. Each day, the same thing happened. Someone let her into line in front of them. She never knew any of these people; and never saw any of them a second time. They were young. They were old. She did not know if they were believers or if they were atheists. But she knew something special was happening, that God had laid kindness on all their hearts.

There was never a problem when she cut in line. No one else standing behind her caused a commotion. It was as if the others never saw her. Each and every time Elena went, she prayed to find the right person. And each and every time, she gave thanks to God for their kindness.

And as she gave thanks to God for her and Anna's provision, she continued her vigil of prayer for Mother, asking for some word of her situation.

At long last a letter arrived from Mother's friend in Kansk, breaking the silence. The message was short, but clear. Mother was now in prison, but where she did not know.

Anna now joined with Elena as they prayed together for Mother.

* * *

The daily inquisition of Akulina continued for five months. Then finding always the same answer, that "there was no more gold," the guards grew weary. They kept Sidor's grandfather a while longer, hoping he might yet tell them the answer they wanted to hear, but Akulina they set free.

Akulina stepped forward out into the daylight. Her eyes were unaccustomed to it, blinded by the sun. She followed the road that led away from her place of imprisonment, a one-lane track, heavily rutted. She labored with each step, weak from torture and malnutrition. At a rise in the road, she could see ahead a good distance. The smokestacks of Kansk were nowhere to be seen. She had no idea where she was.

Farther down the road, she came to an urban neighborhood. She knocked on the first door she came to. The door opened a crack. A woman looked out.

Akulina asked, "Can you tell me which is the way to Kansk?"

"Oh, it is that way to the east." The woman pointed. "You are not walking there, are you?" She sized up Akulina, who was filthy. "It is too far to walk." Having caught a whiff of her, she placed her hand over her nose and mouth and began to close the door.

Akulina felt embarrassed. She backed away and appealed, "Do you have some bread?"

The woman peeked out. "I am sorry, truly sorry. We do not have enough food even for ourselves. I wish I could help you. I do, but I cannot." The door closed tight.

Akulina set off in the direction of Kansk. She stopped and knocked on dozens of doors along the way, begging for food. Once in a while, someone gave her a little of what they had, but never more than a few bites. At the end of her first day, she came to a farm. The proprietor was kind enough to let her sleep the night in his barn. She was glad it was no longer winter, unable to imagine another night of shivering.

For days and days, Akulina continued her march. With the little help she received, she grew ever weaker and depressed. At a rise in the road, she came to a pile of boulders on the shoulder; she found a flat spot and sat there to rest. Looking out on the scene, seeing the beauty in it, she felt refreshed. She remembered her family and wondered if she would ever see them again. She thought about Elena, wondering what she would have done in this situation. It came to her.

Akulina closed her eyes and prayed.

Later that afternoon, she came upon a group of men walking along the road. One of them, a young man, recognized her from years ago, when he was a boy in Kondratyevo. He took pity on her and invited her to follow him home. There he fed her and gave her clean clothes and a bed to sleep. From there, Akulina wrote to her daughters, Elena in Irkutsk and Pana in Vydrino. She asked for money to buy a ticket to return home.

Three weeks later, a letter came to Akulina from Pana. In it was a ticket to Vydrino.

Akulina rode the train east and stopped at Tayshet. There she got off and made her way to Bunbuy. She found her house empty, ransacked. The windows had been broken, and there was no food. She knew she could not stay there.

She resumed her travel east, all the way to Vydrino. There Pana cared for her. Pana's husband, a veterinarian doctor, tended to her wounds. There they fed Akulina and nursed her back to health.

And as summer arrived, Mother made her plans to return to Irkutsk. She was coming back to Elena.

* * *

In 1931, throughout the Soviet Union, many, many people died.

20

The food shortage in Irkutsk remained an impossible situation. Even though Mother had returned and now was the one that could stand in line for food, there was never enough of it. Elena and her family were always hungry.

An opportunity presented itself to Elena, one she could not turn down. There was a need for a seamstress instructor in the Far East, a high paying job, a means for her to better support her family. With her director's permission, she took time off from her job at Igla and departed. She boarded a train bound for the Far East, skirting along the southern bank of Lake Baikal, through Vydrino, then turning north and east, climbing up and over the top of China, crossing the border out of Siberia and into Amur in the Far East.

Four days and two thousand kilometers later, the train pulled to a stop at Station Ol'doy, a gold mining town perched on the banks of the Tipara stream, which flowed south into the Amur River. Gold was discovered there in the 1850's, and mining persisted there ever since. Intelligent and educated people from all over the Soviet Union came there, many from Moscow. They came there as a duty to their government for providing them with a free education. Upon graduation, they were not yet allowed to pursue work of their choice; they were sent to different places, places where there were needs for their profession, places like Station Ol'doy. They must serve there three to four years to complete their duty, performing their labor during normal hours, just like anyone else, but without pay. Evenings they had free, and many joined in theater work; some were movie stars.

Elena was able to teach courses in Ol'doy, courses in cutting different fabrics and sewing. Her students were of various ages, most much older than Elena. She taught three classes per day, three hours each: morning, afternoon, and evening, nine-hour days. She was paid five rubles an hour, a very good wage. She was happy with the workload, particularly happy because she was being compensated more even than most highly-educated engineers and other professionals.

After her working hours, Elena did volunteer work. With the permission of the government, she opened a sewing shop, where she managed her students who served as her staff. Her students were then able to make money selling the work of their hands, but Elena received nothing, that is, no payment in the form of cash. Instead she received something far more valuable: she established contacts with government officials and merchants who dealt with fabrics and those in charge of the area stores. Thus her circle of working friends grew. Everyone in that area got to know Elena and came to appreciate her design and sewing abilities, seeing she was highly recommended. They recognized her skill and energy. Her authority grew.

These were good times for Elena. Through her government contacts, she was able to go to any store and factory to select all the fabric she needed or wanted; and with cash in hand, she could buy it. Elena was also able to enter food warehouses to buy goods and produce in quantity: canned vegetables, jars of vegetable oil, flour. Few Russians had such opportunity; the public never had access to these luxuries. Once a week, Elena would gather a package of these items and send them to her mother and sister: food, clothing, and money for Anna's education. These were their survival packages. Elena always put in a note suggesting that whatever they could not use themselves, they could sell for extra money. For herself, Elena bought the best fabrics and sewed outfits that otherwise she could never have had—suits, coats, jackets, blouses, and skirts, anything her heart desired.

Elena completed her year in Ol'doy and the officials there asked her to stay one more. But she wanted to get home. Her family was no longer in crisis, her impetus to coming there, and she had done her service to the government. She missed her family and her church. It was time to go home.

When she returned to Irkutsk, Elena had money saved, a new wardrobe, and a family whose needs had been met. She was thankful for the year.

21

The first Sunday that Elena was back, she was excited to go again to church with her sister and mother.

After the service, Anna spotted a young man across the room. She waved him over as she whispered to Elena, "There is someone new that I would like you to meet."

A tall, nicely dressed young man worked his way through the people. He came up to them and flashed his bright eyes. "Hi, Anna..." He turned to Mother. "...and Gospozha Briuchanova."

Elena studied his face. He was very handsome.

Anna said, "This is Arkadiy, and this is my sister, Elena."

He extended his hand to her. "I've heard so much about you."

Elena took his hand. "I hope it was good." She looked at Anna.

"It was," he said.

They chatted a few minutes. It quickly seemed like time to leave.

Arkadiy asked, "I would like to hear about your time in Ol'doy. Can I walk you home?"

Elena was taken aback by his forwardness. But she could not say no or be inhospitable. She nodded. They left together.

The entire walk home, Elena was open, telling Arkadiy many of the details of her year away. She did all the talking, hardly imagining her story would be that interesting to him. He just listened.

She explained what had driven her there, her care for her family. She had been providing for them all of her adult life and even before. Without voicing it, she showed her hard outer shell, a protective shell that would not permit her the time or luxury to have a relationship with a man. There was no room in her life for that. Her time for a relationship would come, surely, someday. Someday, she could love one man above her family. But not now. Not just yet.

When they arrived at the front of Elena's apartment building, she turned and looked up at him.

"I really would like to hear more," he said.

She could tell he wanted to come in, hoping she would invite him to have lunch. Considering herself a good judge of character, she studied his eyes. She saw something there: honesty and integrity. But she wasn't ready.

"Yes," she said. "We should talk some more." She tilted her head. "Thank you for walking me home."

Arkadiy got the message. He nodded politely, backed up a few steps, turned and walked away.

A month later, Arkadiy's job took him to Slavgorod, which was several hours west of Kansk. He frequently returned to visit the church and to see Elena. After church each Sunday, he came to Elena's house. He was falling in love with her. He did not hesitate. He proposed.

Elena turned him down. She was indeed attracted to him. He was good looking. But she was looking for more than just looks. That is, if she was even looking.

Other young men in the church also showed their interest in Elena. She had many boyfriends and had little interest in falling in love with any of them. She was very comfortable with all the fellows with whom she socialized. She relished talking and discussing passages of scripture with them. It was her faith that excited her. If they loved her, it was not on account of any moves she made to curry their favor, it was because they loved her for just being herself.

Several more proposed. One at a time, she turned them down.

Rather than pursue romance, Elena had a different focus. She wanted to dedicate her life to Christian service. But persecution of Christians increased with each year. As it did, she realized that service for the Lord could not happen without personal sacrifice and challenges. The Communists controlled where people were allowed to meet, Bible studies were not allowed in homes, and the mention of God in conversations was strictly forbidden. The only place where one could legally talk about God was in a sanctioned church building. But none of this difficulty caused Elena to shrink away, to depart from the direction she saw for her life. She would not fall away from her faith, and she developed an expectation that her future husband must be just as committed. But before that unknown day, she was content in fully absorbing herself in church and family. There she found satisfaction.

* * *

During Elena's work holiday, her cousin Klava came for a visit. They decided they should travel to see some friends. They went to the train station.

While they were standing in line at the ticket window, a gentleman approached them. He asked, "Is this by chance Elena Nosova?"

Elena turned and studied his face for a split second. "Oh my goodness...*Mitia?*" She had not seen him in five years. She threw her arms open, and they embraced.

He pulled away from her and glanced over his shoulder. "My train...it is leaving."

He took several steps in that direction, looked back at Elena, then ran toward the train. She followed. The train was already pulling away slowly. He ran up the stairs, into the car, and stuck his head out the last window. Elena ran alongside the train, looking up at him.

"Please give me your address!"

But Elena could not keep up. The train pulled away and left her standing beside the empty tracks. She wondered, *Will I ever see him again?* So many thoughts raced through her mind. His proposal had been all those years ago. So much had changed since then. Their lives had gone on, apart from one another. She had become a Christian, and Mitia was not a believer. That fact was central. It loomed as a barrier too important for Elena to ignore.

And yet there he was again, glancing off the edge of her life, like a skipping stone.

Why? she wondered. *It is probably over. It surely is.*

22

Ivan Rukasuyev, the husband of Elena's older sister Pana, was arrested and sentenced to five years in the Far East for his crime, the "crime" of being educated, a veterinarian, a wealthy man.

Ivan was exiled to Bukachacha, which was at the easternmost edge of Siberia, high in the mountains. It was a coal-mining town, and there was no train service there. The nearest train stop was Chernyshevsk, some ninety kilometers to the south, a station stop on the Trans-Siberian railway. From there, horses were used to transport people to and from the mines and to pull wagonloads of coal down the narrow mountain roads. His sentence, his duty, was to tend the horses. And because the animals might need care anywhere along the route, he was not confined; he was free to travel up and down the one road. But for his labor he received no pay.

Pana wrote to Elena to explain the situation and to note that he could receive visitors. She also had been evicted from her apartment with three small children and a fourth due any day. Elena shared the letter with her mother and sister.

"Someone turned him in." Mother shook her head in disgust.

It didn't have to be said. Ivan was guilty of nothing, of course. Anyone could go into a government office and report someone, to accuse them of being rich, educated, or religious, merely acting out of envy or hatred. There was no trial. The accused was questioned, dispossessed, then sent into exile.

The women knew they had to do something to help Ivan. Anna had a friend that was an official in the communist party. She and Elena thought it would be a good idea to go and see him, intending to plead their case.

They stepped into the government building and went down a long corridor of closed doors. They came to the door marked "Passports," opened it, and stepped inside. A secretary greeted them, took their names, then ushered them into the director's office.

A man in uniform was seated behind the desk as they entered. He abruptly rose to his feet and stepped around to greet them. "Anna, so nice to see you again." He turned to Elena. "Is this your sister?"

"Yes, this is Elena."

"I am Leonid." He extended his hand, palm down, a purposeful means of demonstrating his superiority of office.

"Very nice to meet you," Elena said, as she twisted her hand and yielded to his handshake. She sized him up quickly: clean-shaven, thick dark hair, slicked back and glistening, his uniform neatly pressed, coal black eyes. He was young and handsome. He had high energy.

He pointed to the empty chairs in front of his desk. "Have a seat."

Elena watched the official's eyes as Anna lowered herself into the chair. He was studying her, obviously attracted. Anna had a nice figure and she was beautifully dressed. At seventeen, she could turn a few heads.

Leonid stepped behind his desk and sat down. Elena sat in the other chair beside her sister as he leaned back in his, smiling at Anna.

Anna sat up straight and explained the situation. "My older sister, Pana, she needs help. She has three children and a fourth one on the way, and her husband is in prison." She leaned forward. "He really didn't do anything wrong."

He sat up, listening carefully.

"He is a veterinarian, he—"

The official stood, waved his hand, motioning for quiet. "Just a minute." He stepped out from behind his desk, went and closed the door to his office, and returned to his chair.

He wagged his finger. "I do not need to have an explanation." He turned toward Elena. "And I do not want one. Understand?"

The girls glanced at each other, turned, and stared at him.

The corner of his mouth curled. "I can help."

Anna's eyes brightened.

"I can get you a clean passport." He spoke softly. "It will only cost you a small fee."

Leonid pushed his chair back, got up and stepped over to his credenza, opened a drawer, took out some papers. He began to process them, flipping through the pages and pounding each one with an ink stamp. Elena and Anna silently looked at each other.

He finished the document, studied it a second, nodded to himself, came back to his desk, and sat down. He leaned forward and showed it to them, turning the pages. "With this passport, you can go anywhere you want to. Just write in the place *here*, and the stamp is already *there*. I put a stamp on every page." He smiled. "Just pay me one hundred rubles."

The sisters raised their brows.

"If you want to see your brother-in-law, now you can."

Anna leaned forward. "This is not for me, is it? Or for Elena?"

Leonid took a breath and blinked. "No."

Elena and Anna looked at each other with blank expressions.

"No…This is for your brother-in-law." He grinned.

Elena's mouth dropped opened.

"And what is his name?" He sat back and dipped his pen in the inkwell.

Anna told him.

They watched as he wrote it in.

Elena reached into her purse, paid him, took the passport, and tucked it out of sight. They both left.

As they walked away, Elena whispered to Anna, "Now we just have to figure out how to get this to Ivan." The passport could not be sent in the mail. Mail to prisoners was opened by the government. After some discussion, Elena decided she should take the passport herself.

To do this, she would have to take time off from work. She approached her director. "I have to travel to the Far East for personal reasons and would appreciate time off…without pay, of course."

He laughed and said, "What? You have a boyfriend there?"

Elena smiled, as if to agree.

He studied her expression for a moment, mindful that she had been in the Far East last year. "All right. You can have a week off."

Before she could make ready to depart, Elena was faced with a real dilemma: how to get a train ticket. In the past year, the government had imposed tight restrictions on travel. There was only one rail line going east, and the trains were always filled with postmen, passengers, soldiers on business trips, and prisoners. Deportation of exiles was a constant thing, and prisoners were transferred from one prison to another along the train line. It was impossible for the average person to get a ticket.

Arkadiy happened to be visiting at the house when they were discussing the travel plans. Though he had no idea of the purpose of the trip, its secret nature, he offered to help. He promised to get her a ticket.

Two months later, Arkadiy showed up with a ticket, a special class ticket for party members, soldiers, and business travelers. He did not explain how he got it, and Elena didn't ask.

The scheduled day of departure arrived. It was evening, and Arkadiy took Elena to the train station. He carried her suitcase, following her into the sleeping coach. When she came to the bunks, she pointed. "I would like to sleep up top."

The train lurched forward. It was already leaving. In a hurry, he tossed the suitcase up top, then spotted a uniform coat was already up there, but no bag. The coat appeared like those worn by soldiers and government officials. He turned to get off the train. "You will have to get that soldier to put it down onto the bottom bunk." He ran to the end of the car, shouted, "Have a safe trip!" and jumped off.

Just then the government official returned to the car. He looked up at the suitcase on his bunk. Elena apologized. "My boyfriend had to leave quickly and did not have time to move it. He didn't see your jacket. I am happy to sleep on the bottom bunk."

"No. You can have it." He retrieved his coat. The two of them were alone in the compartment. He studied her. "Your boyfriend must be in love with you, to treat you so well, to pick the best spot for you."

She ignored the comment, took off her hat and coat, and sat down at the small table beside the window. She looked outside and watched the lights of the train yard fade as they pulled away from the station. He sat with her at the table.

They chatted for a while. It was already late, so each of them got situated, retired to their bunks, and went to sleep.

In the morning, Elena tried to sleep in, being uncomfortable in the same compartment with a government official, afraid of having a conversation with him. *What if he asks me who I am and why am I traveling? What can I answer? 'I am not going for any business at all. I am going to visit a prisoner to take him false papers. I do not have a legal ticket. I should not even be on this train!'* She felt the sudden peril and pretended she was sleeping.

The trip was very long, and she knew she would eventually have to get up. She listened carefully to what was going on, hearing his movements. Finally, and to her great relief, he stepped out of the compartment and left her alone. At last she got up washed and made herself presentable. A short while later, breakfast was delivered and she enjoyed her meal while looking out the window. The travel accommodation, the comfort, the food, the service, and the privacy were like nothing she had ever experienced.

The government official returned to the car. He brought several of his friends with him, all of them men. Elena felt odd, perhaps the only woman on the train, imagining what they would think of her: young, well dressed, a spectacle. She tried to relax.

As they talked among themselves, she stayed quiet, resolutely staring out the window, trying to reach down into herself for some sort of confidence.

It dawned on her. They must be thinking, *Look at her. She is well dressed. She must surely be a government official, obviously traveling on government business. Maybe she is here to see what I am up to?* The whole rest of the day she never spoke a word. And they never asked her a thing.

The first day came to an end.

Early the following morning, Elena made ready to get off the train, to change to another one that would take her to the Far East. At 5:00 a.m., they arrived at the destination, Station Pashina. It was November and already very cold. Snow was on the ground. Everyone was still sleeping when Elena exited her car and walked to the station to board her next train.

The inside of the station was shocking. It was packed with people lying on the floor, on benches, some standing. There was absolutely no room for another person. Elena had to step over them to get to the information desk.

As she approached, she studied the bodies, straining in the dim light of a few bare bulbs to make out the details. They were sleeping restlessly, exhausted, filthy, crawling with lice the size of cockroaches. She pulled the hem of her fur coat up, fearing lice would jump onto it.

When she got to the information desk, the office door was locked. She looked in through the window, saw someone inside and knocked. They opened it a crack.

"What time is the next train going east?" Elena asked.

"9:00 p.m. Come back later. You can buy your ticket when we open."

Elena turned over her shoulder, looking back over the disaster. The room smelled like a stable. She thought, *I cannot stay here all day. But it is freezing outside.* She dreaded the options.

At that moment, the door to the outside swung open and a gentleman stepped in. He was very well dressed and held two leather suitcases. *A government official,* she concluded.

He looked at the human swarm on the floor and then toward the information desk where Elena was standing. She stood out from everyone, well dressed, a fur coat, polished black leather boots, a black beret on top of her neatly coiffed hair.

Their eyes met.

He stood in the entryway, not moving. Elena approached him, carefully retracing her steps back over the people. "What time is your train?" she asked.

"Tonight at 9:00 p.m."

She stepped close to him. "Mine too."

"Where are you spending the day?" he asked.

Elena looked around the room, then back up at him. She shrugged her shoulders. "Here? I suppose?"

"Listen. I travel through here a lot. There is a real good restaurant right down the street." He looked around the room at the huddled, crawling filth on the floor. "I am not waiting here. Why don't you join me?"

Elena glanced past him, over his shoulder, out through the glass to the outside. It was pitch black; the government always turned off the lights overnight to save money. She was uneasy. "I...I think I will just stand here near the door." She had sized him up. "Thank you for offering. There is usually a long line at restaurants, and I do not want to wait in the dark. Maybe I will wait until daylight." She hoped now he would just leave her alone.

In the dim light, he strained to read her eyes. "The restaurant is very close, nearby, and this is a restaurant for specially educated workers of high class only. The only thing we need to have..." he had assessed her attire and assumed she was a fellow government official, "...is a certificate of registration, a reason for travel, and where you are going."

Elena had no such certificate. And she was not about to disclose to anyone her reason for travel. "Thank you again. But I think I will wait here until later...maybe."

He left.

Elena stood holding the doorknob with one hand and her suitcase with the other, afraid to move, afraid to set it down, afraid to get near any one of the dirty people. She knew that lice loved to get into fur. She longed for the daylight so she could just get out of there and step outside. She stood, petrified.

A short while later, the gentleman returned. "Good news. There is lots of room in the restaurant, there is no line, and you can go with me as my guest. Let me treat you."

She glanced out the window. It was starting to get light. She looked up at his eyes. Seeing only kind intentions, and now dreading to remain there a second longer. She relented. "Okay."

He extended his hand and took her suitcase. On the way to the restaurant, she finally confessed, "I do not have a certificate."

He turned to her.

"I am traveling on personal business through Chernyshevsk to Bukachacha. I will not be allowed to get into the restaurant."

"You do not have to worry, I will help you. I...I am a doctor you see. I was in Moscow for three months for various seminars. I am on my way home. I work in Chernyshevsk. I pass through this village, here, many times, and everyone in this restaurant knows me well."

"They know *you*. But they do not know me."

"Well, do not worry," he said. "I will tell them you are traveling with me and that you have just finished the school of dentistry and are a dentist."

Elena stopped walking. "How can I lie? I am not a dentist."

He laughed. "This is not a cardinal sin. Do not worry. This is a very small town, and there are no other places for us government officials to eat." He grinned. "And if we do not go there, you will freeze out here. I cannot let that happen. I am concerned for you."

Reluctantly, she followed him. They arrived at the restaurant. Before they entered, he asked, "Tell me your last name."

"Nosova."

He entered. Elena followed, trembling.

He went straight to register. "Hello, so good to see you again. I would like you to register my guest here, Doctor Nosova. She is a dentist."

The registrar looked at Elena. She tilted her head toward him.

The registrar made some notes, picked up two menus, and said, "Follow me."

They entered the dining room, sat, and ordered their meal. A short time later, breakfast was served: warm blintzes with jam and tea with lemon. The food was wonderful and delicious. Afterward, there was no bill. The meal was free for all the government officials. Elena was included.

After the table had been cleared, the doctor showed Elena around. In the back, there were rooms for the officials to rest while waiting for the trains. Elena entered one and lay down, hoping to take a nap. She tossed and turned, bothered by the thought that these officials could have so much luxury while her family suffered. She got no rest at all.

At dinnertime, she came out into the dining room and saw her new friend already seated at a table along with a group of others. There was an empty chair, and he waved her over with insistence. The people there introduced themselves. Some were doctors, some lawyers.

"And this is Doctor Nosova. She just finished the school of dentistry."

Elena said nothing.

At that moment, a waiter rushed out from the kitchen to the table, greatly disturbed. "One of our waitresses is ill in the kitchen!"

Four men promptly got up from the table and went to see. By now a crowd of people had formed, wondering what was going on. A woman moaned loudly in the next room. The door to the kitchen burst open, and the four officials returned. One of them looked at Elena. "The waitress has one heckuva toothache. It is a good thing you are here, Doctor Nosova."

Everyone looked at Elena.

Her heart was racing. The consequences of doing nothing or getting exposed as a "fake" overwhelmed her.

She stood. "I...uh, I am traveling without any of my medicine or equipment." She studied their anxious faces and thought a moment, realizing her quandary. She set her napkin down on the table and stepped forward. "But I think I can help her."

She followed them into the kitchen. The waitress was sitting on the floor, holding her head, bent over in agony.

Elena got down on her knees. "Here, let me look into your mouth. Open wide."

The woman's gums were scarlet, swollen and bleeding.

"It is an infection," observed Elena.

The waitress groaned.

Elena looked up at the officials standing there. She barked at them, "Someone get me some clean gauze, rubbing alcohol, and a bandage. And I'll need warm water."

They remained standing, gawking.

"*Quick!*"

They sprang into action and brought her the items. Elena mixed the rubbing alcohol into the warm water. She neatly folded the gauze into little squares and dipped them into the liquid, making warm compresses. Gingerly, she positioned them in the woman's mouth and then wrapped a bandage around her head and jaw to hold it all in place. Elena was grateful she had taken a class in first aid. Elena stood and helped the waitress to her feet. She guided her into one of the private rooms and helped her lie down to rest.

In the evening, after dinner had been served, while they were still eating, the waitress came out from the back.

She bent and hugged Elena. "Oh, thank goodness you were here. I am feeling *so* much better. You would not *believe* how painful that was, but then you were here, and the pain is gone. Thank you. Thank you. *Thank you!*" The waitress was crying.

The officials at the table, doctors, lawyers, and other professionals beamed in amazement, marveling at the coincidence, that Elena just happened to be there at the right time to help this poor young woman. They praised her skills. They started discussing plans for the future when they all reached the Far East. "We need to get together with you, Doctor Nosova, and get to know each other better."

The day ended. Elena and the others in the restaurant were well fed and warm, enjoying their clean surroundings. But Elena's mind was on the poor people waiting at the train station, the way they had to live, the rear militias, the prisoners, the destitute, the homeless. They had no money to buy a ticket to get to their destinations. They just stayed at the station to keep warm, struggling to remain alive. She silently prayed, *God, you know all the details of each of those lives.*

Elena and the doctor boarded the nine-o'clock train. They sat together in the same compartment, no one else with them. This was a high official train. Prisoners were not allowed there; prisoners rode with the cargo. The doctor was proving himself to be a very nice gentleman. He was about thirty-five years old, tall, and handsome.

Elena asked, "How did you come up with such ideas so quickly to rescue me?"

"It is a talent I acquired." His expression grew serious. "Knowing you had no passport certificate and are not traveling on business, then just what *are* you doing? You must be going to see a relative who lives there..." He studied her eyes. "...or visiting a prisoner."

Elena found herself believing and trusting him. *He probably can get me where I need to go, to see Ivan.*

In the long hours of their trip that followed, they had many conversations on different topics. Elena told him about Irkutsk. He had never been there, except passing by train. Eventually, she let her guard down and confessed, "I am going to see my brother-in-law. He has just been sentenced to prison."

He leaned forward.

"He is a veterinarian doctor. I hope that my sister and their children could move to be near him and possibly get a job to support themselves."

"I know the town. There are not many jobs there, except that they are always looking for seamstresses."

Elena's eyes brightened. Pana was a master seamstress.

"If your sister can sew, she could get a job there. If she is a good seamstress, she will be able to get work from many of the workers and make more than enough money to survive."

Elena felt comforted. Still, she made no mention of Ivan's passport.

He looked at his watch. "We will be coming to the station soon. There will be a taxi waiting. I would like to offer you a place to stay tonight."

She felt suddenly uneasy.

He leaned and smiled. "My mother lives with me. We have an extra bedroom."

She measured him.

"Listen, Chernyshevsk is not the safest place for a young woman. The soldiers and security guards simply cannot be trusted. They are here only to move the prisoners. They are not trustworthy. And...I have to leave early in the morning on business. When I come back, I will take you to the government headquarters so you can find your brother-in-law."

When they got off the train, there was a taxi waiting, just as he said. The taxi driver put them in the backseat and gave them blankets. The weather was freezing; it was a blizzard.

As they drove, Elena strained to look out the windows. She saw the many shabby buildings and all the men standing around, huddled together in the howling wind and swirling snow. It did not seem at all like a safe place to be. She glanced at the doctor beside her and prayed silently, *God, you are protecting me.*

The doctor's apartment was very small and crowded with furniture, but everything was clean. It seemed indeed like the home of a professional, a doctor. He introduced Elena to his mother, a woman about sixty years old. The doctor's mother prepared a very nice meal for them. Her hospitality was a blessing to Elena. Afterward, she was able to have a good night's rest in a private room.

The doctor returned from his errand the next morning and took Elena to the government building in the village, the central point of connection for the travelers. There were stables there to shelter the many horses.

At the information desk, Elena asked for the whereabouts of Ivan Rukasuyev.

"Yes. He is here. You can see him at noon."

Elena's heart was bursting. She turned to the doctor. "I can't thank you enough." She hugged him and thought, *God led me to you, and you kept me safe.*

He pushed back from her, suddenly bashful. "I…I am glad I was able to help." He changed the subject. "I hope you will stop by my apartment and see me before you go back to Irkutsk."

"If I can. I just don't know how long I am going to be here."

They shook hands, and he bid her goodbye.

As he walked away, she realized she had never gotten his name.

23

While Elena waited at the government building, she noticed a roster posted of prisoners and citizens. To her surprise, she found Pana's name and address. She got directions.

Elena bundled up and stepped out into the blizzard. A few blocks away, she came to the apartment. Pana's mother-in-law greeted her warmly and let her in. She explained to Elena, bringing her up to date in all the family matters. Pana was at work, a seamstress; daughters Zoya and Anna were in school; little Ilya was there running around; and Eugene, the newborn, was a few weeks old. Then she asked, "How on earth did you get here?"

Elena gave a brief recount. She was bursting with questions of her own. "And how did *you* get here?" The last she knew, they were still in Vydrino.

"When Ivan was deported, we had to get out of the apartment within twenty-four hours. We had nowhere to go, so we boarded the same train as Ivan. I could not believe they allowed us to do that. But here we are. We found this apartment right away, and Pana has not stopped working while we've been here. She is making good money. Now, let me show you around."

Elena got a tour. There was a kitchen, the entry and living area, and two bedrooms. She was amazed. No one even in Irkutsk had such a nice apartment.

At noon, Pana arrived, followed by Ivan. The government did not feed the prisoners and left them to fend for themselves; he came home for lunch. As they got reacquainted, Elena listened to the details of Ivan's imprisonment, the hundreds of men that slaved there for the government without pay, sentenced merely on unproven accusations and lies. Ivan confirmed he had done nothing wrong. Neither had the other prisoners.

Elena retrieved her purse and pulled out the passport. She handed it to Ivan. "This is for you."

He took it. "What is this?" He opened it and read his name on the first page.

Elena explained, "Anna knew someone in the Party. He gave it to us. It is a clean passport. Maybe you could use it someday."

He handed it back, scowling. "No. I would rather not use it. It is illegal. If they confiscate it and find out I have an illegal passport, it will be worse."

Elena handed it toward Pana, hoping she might change his mind.

Ivan got up from the table and grabbed it. He went over to the stove, opened the door, and tossed it in. It burst into flames.

He came back and sat down. "I would rather live out the five years and do everything right. After that, maybe they will allow me to live in peace."

Elena glanced at the stove, watching her one-hundred-rubles go up in smoke.

Ivan placed his hand on Elena's. "I appreciate, rather, Pana and I appreciate your heart's concern to help us. We know that you really care about our family. Your coming here is enough. We are so glad to see you."

Elena stared at the stove. She turned and studied Ivan's confidence. She wondered out loud, "I don't get why."

"Why did I burn it?" He stood. "We have to do what is right. We are to submit to the authority of our government."

Elena blinked. "*W-what* did you say?"

"I said, 'We have to submit to the authority—'"

Elena finished his sentence. "—of the government."

"Yes." He looked down at her with surprise.

Elena hesitated then decided she had to speak her mind. "Th-that is from the Bible."

He swallowed hard. "Yes. Yes, it is." He looked at Pana then back at his sister-in-law. He held his head high. "We have become Christians."

Elena's body tingled. A smile filled her face; she burst out, "So am I!"

Pana and Elena both leaped from their chairs and grabbed each other. All three embraced, speaking out many words of praise, hardly believing what they were hearing, wondering and then sharing each of their stories, the circumstances of their belief.

* * *

Elena stayed with Pana and Ivan for several days, as they shared their stories with each other and the fullness of their joy.

Elena was able to get a return train to Pashina Station without incident. However, there were no seats or sleeping rooms available on any train going west from there. No one could get a ticket. The trains that came into the yard did not open the doors for people to be able to board. She waited one whole day at the train station trying to make some sort of arrangements to get onto a train, any train. *What do I do? How do I get home?*

Evening came and it grew dark. She despaired.

A train pulled into the yard. She stepped outside to get a look. Through the windows, she could see the lights on inside and all the passengers seated. It was a very long train, car after car filled with soldiers. The train finally came to a stop. But the doors did not open.

It was very dark; all the lights in the yard were out. Elena took a walk toward the last car, hoping, now feeling desperate for any opportunity to board the train. She couldn't imagine waiting another day there in Pashina, and she knew if she did not get back to Irkutsk, she would be dismissed from her job. She was already a day late.

The train lurched forward. It was pulling away, out of the station.

Her heart in her throat, Elena ran a few steps and grabbed with one hand onto the handrail of the last car, her suitcase in the other. The wind was howling, and she could hardly keep up. She ran with all her speed and swung one leg up onto the first step, then climbed up onto the platform, gasping out clouds of steam. She straightened and reached for the door handle to go inside.

It was locked.

The train was now at full speed, and Pashina was well behind them. It was freezing out on the platform.

Elena turned and huddled against the car wall, pulling her fur collar up around her face. The folly of what she had just done, jumping on the train, sank in. *I am going to freeze to death out here all night. And this is a military train. I do not have a ticket. If I get caught...when I am caught...they will think I am a spy.*

The wind continued to blow like a blizzard. The rear door to the car burst open. Elena was on the hinge side, shielded behind the open door. She huddled against the wall, anxious to stay out of sight. The thought of jumping off the speeding train flashed through her mind. But that would only lead to death.

The light from the open door illumined the back of a soldier. He closed the door, turned on a flashlight, and stepped to the back rail to urinate.

He finished and turned to go in. That was when he saw her. He shined the light in her face, then spoke, "You will freeze to death standing here."

Elena was still too shocked at being discovered. She said nothing.

He sized her up. "This is a military train, and you are a civilian and not allowed on it. You had better get off at the first stop." He looked at her more closely and softened. He extended his hand to her.

She kindly took it. "My dear soldier, I know what you said is true. I know this is a military train. I know I am not allowed to stand on this platform. I know this is very dangerous. But I am in a predicament that I cannot get out of."

He bent near.

"I must be home tomorrow to go to work. I was not able to buy a ticket and decided to just jump on this train, even if they find me. That is why I am here."

He scratched his head as he studied her pretty face. "What can I do with you?" Then very quietly, he said, "Follow me." He reached for the handle and opened the door. "And do not say a word."

He took her by the hand and led her to his bunk. It was already very late; so all the other soldiers were sleeping. He lifted her up onto the top bunk and then her bag. He looked up at her, placed his finger to his lip, motioning to be quiet and to lie down.

Elena lay down in her fur coat atop the covers. After a while, he came back to her and motioned that she should take the fur coat off. He reached up and covered her with a blanket. Elena followed his instructions perfectly, barely breathing, petrified. *But what can I do? At least I am on the train.* She looked around. All the soldiers were sound asleep. She prayed, *Dear God, protect me. Guide the rest of my trip. Give me peace.*

She fell asleep.

Early in the morning, she awoke to laughter.

Someone asked, "Hey, Yurka! Who is that on your top bunk?"

Yurka answered, "That is my sister."

Another soldier laughed. "Your sister? How did she arrive here all of a sudden?"

"Well, let me tell you, such miracles do not happen often. I go out in the middle of the night to urinate. The train stops, and I see my sister outside, stepping onto the platform. I grabbed her and pulled her inside. You all know how it is in getting tickets these days. She and I were both so excited at this happening. Well, I thought, we all know each other here, so I put her on my bunk."

Everyone laughed.

"Yeah, tell me another one."

"Well, tell us. Is she a good-looking girl, this sister of yours?"

Yurka said, "What can I tell you? You will see for yourself when she wakes up."

"This is fantastic. We haven't seen a girl in our midst in a long time. This is great!"

Yurka warned, "You all better stay away from her. She is a very clean girl."

Elena lay in bed, completely still, afraid to get up, fearing what would be next. She kept the blanket pulled tight over her head.

"Hey, Yurka. Why don't you wake her up so we all can go to get kasha for breakfast. Or we can start singing very loud to make sure she wakes up."

They burst into song, singing very loudly, continuing their laughter.

Elena decided she could fake it no longer. She pulled the covers back, sat up on her bunk, and rubbed her eyes. She dangled her feet over the edge.

The soldiers got quiet.

Yurka stepped over and extended his hands up to help her down. "Well, sister, how was your sleep?"

"Very well," she said with a smile.

She got down and sat there with the men, who were very quiet now. They ate their kasha, a hot cereal similar to oatmeal. After breakfast, some started to play cards, some dominos. Several picked up their guitars and played. Each group wanted Elena to sit with them.

Elena replied, "I do not know how to play dominos or cards." Instead, she sat with the guitar players and singers. They gave Elena a guitar, and she joined them, playing. She knew the Russian folk songs and joined in, happy to be the center of attention.

Yurka came close and whispered, "I finished my time served and am on my way home. I live in Kansk and would love to get your address and see you again sometime." Others overheard and also asked for her address.

"I live in Irkutsk. I will probably never come this way again."

Half the day passed. The conductor walked into the car, holding onto some journals to give to the men. He spotted Elena. "And what is this?" He pointed at her.

The soldiers, as if planned, replied in unison, "This is a relative of Yurka, and we all know her."

"And how did she get here?"

They gave a variety of answers, interrupting each other. Elena remained seated in silence.

He stared down at her. "This is not a place for a woman. Where will you sleep? There is no room." He did not ask her anything, not where she was going or how much longer she would be on the train. "Follow me," he said sternly.

The soldiers pleaded, "Leave her here with us. She does not have to go until tonight, when it is time to sleep."

He ignored their pleas. He took Elena by the hand, and she followed him to the observation car. This car was clean, nonsmoking. There was an empty bed there, already made. "This is yours," he said.

Elena was suddenly afraid, afraid that the conductor would ask her all kinds of questions. She would rather have stayed with the simple soldiers. But here she was with the conductor.

"My coat, my suitcase...they are in the car."

"I will get them." In a moment, he returned with her things. "Can I get you something to eat?"

"That would be very nice. Thank you."

A short time later, he returned with a tray full of desserts, things Elena could never afford. She smiled and took them.

At night, she slept in the bed prepared for her. During the night, people came through the car periodically, so she felt safe. In the middle of the night, the conductor woke Elena to check her ticket.

She looked up at him. "I do not have a ticket."

He looked befuddled, worried. *"You have to have a ticket.* I am going off duty, and the next conductor is coming on. If you do not have a ticket, I am going to be in real trouble." He lifted the edge of his hat and scratched his head. "Just a minute." He walked quickly out of the car.

Elena began to worry. She expected he was going to grab one of the intelligentsia to come back and arrest her. She agonized.

A few moments later, he returned, looking flush. "Here," he said, as he handed her the ticket. "Now you are all set...and so am I."

Elena looked up at the conductor. Her heart was racing. She studied his face, which had a lopsided grin. She blinked and steadied herself. "Where are we?"

"We are coming into Irkutsk. That is our next stop."

"Oh, good. That is my destination." She stood and picked up her coat.

He looked at her nervously. "Excuse me. Can I get your address?"

"I...I, uh," she yawned and held her hand over her mouth for a moment. She shook her head. "For the life of me, I can't remember it."

When the train arrived and Elena stepped off, there was Arkadiy. He had been waiting for two days, not knowing which train she might arrive on. She was a day late. He took her bag and walked with her back home.

At work, Elena's boss allowed her back without a problem, understanding the delay. "I know how hard it can be to get a ticket."

She nodded and thought, *You have no idea how hard.*

24

This was the time of certification. Throughout the Soviet Union, people who had a personal license or other identity paperwork were required to submit these to the police to receive a passport. The passport registered a person to their village or city district. It entitled them to receive a ticket book by which they could purchase food. Without a passport, they could not purchase food, so their survival became virtually impossible.

Mother could not get a passport. She had no identity papers. Her paperwork had been taken from her when she was imprisoned and had not been returned. Without her passport, she could no longer live in Irkutsk. It was only a matter of time until she would be discovered and deported.

Mother thought that she should return to Bunbuy to obtain a replacement copy of her papers. But there was always the risk when she arrived that they would look past her new married name, Briuchanova, and discover her first marriage to Ivan Nosov. If they did that, they would know she was from a family of wealthy merchants. Then they would throw her in prison, and she would again have to endure the torture: the government seeking after hidden wealth, wealth that was no more.

Elena refused to let Mother return to Bunbuy and resolved to go there herself to get Mother's new papers. Even though Elena had the name Nosova, her own paperwork from the Bunbuy Village Council listed her social position as "peasant," a safe classification. Still, there were risks. The Communists had imposed new laws and placed added staff in charge of everyone's personal records. The new staff came with a fresh set of eyes and a fervent desire to look deeper into everyone's past. If there were enemies of the state anywhere, they would surely find them out, catch them, and send them to hard labor camps or to slave away on collective farms. But despite the fearful consequences, something had to be done for Mother. Elena would wait until her vacation time, then go.

Elena shared nothing of her problem with anyone at church. The risks were too high that the wrong person might discover her family's past. As far as they knew, she was just a peasant girl from Irkutsk, an accomplished seamstress.

The time of Elena's vacation came. After church, Arkadiy came to their house for lunch, just as he had been doing for quite some time (though Elena had turned down his proposal, he was not deterred from being a good friend). As the only man around, he was quick to offer help to the family, doing chores, making repairs, and helping out in any way he could. He had become a fixture of sorts.

After lunch, he talked to her privately. "What is this...you are going to Bunbuy?"

Elena tried to brush him off. "I have some time off from work, so...so I just wanted to go back to my old home, see the old village." She took a step toward the door, hoping to go outside. She intended he would follow her and then leave.

He stood directly in front of her and studied her face. "You told me you never wanted to go back to Bunbuy."

She looked away and stepped around him. "Well, a have some good memories there."

He followed her. "You told me how frightened you were of the place...the lawlessness." He knew how delighted she had been that her family had left Bunbuy and followed her to Irkutsk.

She reached for the doorknob. He put his hand on the door and stopped it from opening. He looked down at her. "And you told me how the men went after the young women, and your fear for Anna if she stayed there."

Elena refused to look up at him.

"You are not telling me everything, are you, Elena?"

She stood still, staring at his hand. Finally, she looked up. "I have to go there to get Mother's papers. She never got them back when they let her out of prison. And the men are coming through the neighborhoods looking for anyone who is not registered. If they find Mother..." Elena furled her brow and stared into his eyes. "...they could take her away again."

He put his hand on her shoulder. "You cannot go to Bunbuy. You could be in danger there. You know that."

She nodded. "But something needs to be done."

"No buts." He placed both hands on her shoulders. "I can help. Let me see first what I can do. Okay?"

"Okay."

Arkadiy got the particulars he needed: Mother's date and place of birth. Elena insisted on giving him some money. He took it and left.

A week later, Arkadiy returned with Mother's birth papers and a legal passport. How he got it, Elena wasn't told.

And she didn't ask.

25

With Arkadiy's help, Mother had her new passport in hand, her problem solved. Now she admired and had special respect for him, invited him always to come over for meals, and treated him like a part of the family. She loved him. He was at their apartment nearly every day.

No longer focused entirely on survival, it seemed things were getting better for Elena's family. Anna finished her education and got a good paying job in an office as a bookkeeper. She was ever grateful to her big sister for the support she had long given. "It was because of you, Lena, because of you that I have my education and am able to get this good job." Now Anna was able to supplement the family income.

Stepbrother Mitia had become established as an electrician. Though he made enough to support himself, he preferred to live with his stepsisters and stepmother to remain a part of the family. Mitia had good character; he was unflappable like his father Sidor. Anna and Elena loved him as if he was their brother by birth. He was handsome, medium height, and Elena always made sure he looked good by sewing him clothing that was in style. He was a little lazy as far as helping around the house, but Mother always said, "Men do not enjoy women's work." So Anna and Elena agreed to leave him alone.

Mother became the joy of her family. She took charge of cleaning and cooking. Meals were always ready for her children when they returned home from work. Each of the three gave their full paycheck to her, and she took charge of managing the finances. Their combined income had become significant, lifting them out of their trouble. When any one of them had a need, it was met. They were always well dressed and well cared for. Mother did not have to work, and with her new passport, she could get the food; Elena no longer had to stand in line. Life was good.

Anna and Elena were involved in church activities and often had young people visiting in their home. Elena sang in choir, played in the orchestra, and served as a youth leader. She also became church treasurer and a deacon. Both young women had lots of suitors. They were experiencing and relishing the ways of urban life. They were able to have fun.

One Sunday afternoon, after lunch, while the house was filled with family, there came a loud knock on the door.

"I'll get it," said Elena, thinking it was one of her friends from church. She ran to the door and pulled it open.

Standing there was an old man, his clothing well worn but clean. He had a thick beard laced with gray. He doffed his hat and looked at her. She studied his face a second. His skin was weathered, red from the sun. She looked into his deep brown eyes. The unmistakable memory of them pierced her heart.

"*Papa!*" she yelled. She leaped forward and flung her arms around him.

He held her, crying, "Lena, my dear, sweet Lena."

Elena turned, wiped the tears off her cheeks, and yelled into the apartment, "*Mama, Anna, Mitia…it is Papa!*" She dragged him in through the door.

Everyone jumped from their chairs and surrounded him.

"I am free," he said, as he kissed them all. "I am free."

Mother fixed him a meal as they crowded around the table. Semion came over, so they all were reunited. They were a family again.

Sidor filled in the details of his imprisonment. He also told them, "Grandfather was tortured until he lost his mind. But he has been released. He is living now with my aunt Sofia." He was 107 years old.

As he ate, he looked at Elena. "I should have listened to you, Lena. I should have listened to you."

"That is okay, Papa. You are here, and that is all that matters."

He looked at his sons. "You have become men."

One at a time, they told him the details of their lives since coming to Irkutsk. He leaned back in his chair, studied their faces, and smiled broadly as they spoke.

Mother fixed a dessert and brought it to him. "You should come and live with us now."

He picked up a forkful of blintz and raised it to his mouth. "I have a new job now." He closed his eyes and savored the taste. "I am a tour guide. The Communists pay me to take people on expeditions into the Taiga. I am through being a farmer."

Mother interjected, "So I should come home then."

He glanced around the apartment, their new furniture, their fine clothing. He waved his hand. "I am always in the woods, not at home. You cannot come with me. You would be all alone. You have your place here with everyone."

Akulina pleaded, "But I want to be with you."

"I will come here whenever I have a vacation. I promise."

Anna chimed in, "And we love having Mama here."

Sidor looked at Anna then at Elena. "But you soon will both be married."

Elena said, "My future husband may not want to have his mother-in-law living with us."

Anna got up and hugged her mother. "Then I will never get married. My future husband will have to go on my terms, or we do not get married."

They sat and talked for several hours. When evening came, Sidor went for a walk with Elena. She took him to go see her church. Along the way, he said, "I can't tell you how proud I am of my sons." He held her hand. "They have finished their school and have good jobs."

She squeezed his hand.

He stopped walking and turned to face her. "It is you, Elena. You have provided for them. You have supported and provided for everyone." He began to cry.

She looked up at him and gently corrected him. "No, Papa. It was not me that provided for them. It was God."

He cupped her cheek with his palm and pulled her to him. "I suppose so. I suppose so."

26

The list was never written down, but Elena knew it by heart: all the things she wanted in a man that would make him qualified to be her husband. At the top of the list were these things: good character, exceptional abilities, strong in faith, and able to take care of her. Certainly, there were other things on the list, including good looks, but those were down the list a ways. These would be seen as fringe benefits if the most important qualities were fulfilled.

From the beginning of Arkadiy's interest in Elena, she was not taken by him. Without realizing it, she was constantly comparing him with her list and finding him lacking. At the start, he had one big strike against him. She had decided he would never be able to take good care of her.

First, he was a year younger than Elena.

Second, he made less money than she did. He was a bookkeeper with a median range salary.

Third and last, he did not have a higher education.

Knowing these things, she had refused his first proposal. But Arkadiy was patient and very much in love with Elena from the first moment he saw her. Slowly, over time, she was able to see his many good qualities. He was faithful, honest, trustworthy, and hardworking and could do anything with his hands. He was a good Christian, helping in church, making himself available to anyone in need. He had integrity. Around the apartment, he did many chores for all the family. By doing these, he was slowly and steadily winning their hearts.

And he was good-looking too.

His one-sided relationship with Elena had continued for nearly two years. To Elena, Arkadiy was just a good friend.

As Elena spent more time with him, certain facts about his past emerged, facts that had a very familiar ring. His family in the Ukraine had at one time been wealthy, and he had been held back from getting a higher education. Arkadiy's father had died shortly after the Revolution in one of the typhus epidemics, and his mother had later remarried. She felt a strong connection there, a sudden sympathy. Her heart began to warm to him. Some of her prior judgments were being revisited. She had been wrong.

Arkadiy was now around all the time, like a part of the family. If they needed food, he would be the one to stand in line, glad to give Mother a break. Everything he brought back was for all the family to use. He had become an excellent provider and caregiver.

Elena soon made up her mind about him and discussed it with Mother. But she told Arkadiy nothing. Quietly, she admired his patience, his faithfulness, and his persistence. She was in no rush to tell him.

One day, they left to go to the market together. The road there took them down a steep hill. Snow was still on the ground, and the street was slick with ice. Coming down the slope, they started to slide.

"Be careful." He reached out for her. "Here, take my hand." He kept them both from falling, as they slid all the way to the bottom, squealing and laughing.

At the bottom, he expressed his relief. "How good it is to be together and we both are safe and you still want to wait."

She tilted her head coyly. "Who said I wanted to wait?"

He spun around and stared at her, speechless. He studied her face. She grinned and walked off briskly toward the market. He followed, running to catch up.

She stared ahead. "I do love you. And I have decided I will marry you. And since you will be drafted this year, we might as well get married so that when you leave, you will already be my husband."

Arkadiy was wide-eyed and pale. He said nothing.

They were quiet the rest of the way to the market. They purchased what they needed and walked home silently.

The next day, Arkadiy came over to see Elena. "I need to talk to you."

They went out for a walk.

After they had walked a good long ways, he asked, "Did you mean what you said yesterday?"

She took hold of his arm and leaned on him. "I do love you. Yes, I want to get married."

He stopped. She looked up at his face. He was beaming.

He lifted her high in the air. She fell into his arms and they embraced.

They started to make wedding plans, intending to get married as soon as possible. They looked for a large apartment, since Elena wanted her mother to live with them. Her current apartment was not big enough. In particular, they needed an extra bedroom.

That kind of an apartment proved impossible to find. After weeks of looking, they found nothing. Arkadiy succumbed. "With the housing conditions in Irkutsk, we are lucky to have what we do. How about we start our marriage with just the two of us?"

Elena placed her hand on him. "Mother will live with us until she dies." She put her other hand on her hip. "Promise me."

He took her hands in his and held them. "Yes. I promise."

"You will never complain?"

"Never."

Elena took a breath. "And Anna?" Her sister also needed a place to live until she found a husband.

He found himself in a sudden and unavoidable pattern of accommodation. "Yes, Anna too."

Still, after more searching, they could not find a larger apartment. They knew they would have to stay in the same place. At least Mitia had gotten married and moved out to live with his wife's family. This made some room for Arkadiy and Elena to have a room of their own.

And so they registered and got their marriage license in May. Then on June 17, 1935, they were married at the Evangelical Christian Church in Irkutsk, Siberia, Russia.

Their new life together was just beginning.

27

In October of the year they were married, Arkadiy was drafted into the army and sent to the Manchurian border. There he worked at the headquarters as a clerk to the general. Every day, he wrote a letter to Elena, and each day, she wrote one to him.

Soon Elena found out she was pregnant. At the age of twenty-three, she was thrilled to have a baby on the way. She wrote to him with the exciting news. But in the Russian Army, soldiers were not allowed to come home, so he knew he would not see his child until he or she was two years old. They continued to correspond and share their joy from a distance.

Now the wife of a Red Army soldier, Elena was afforded certain privileges. The law said that "If the wife is working and makes more than three hundred rubles a month, then she is able to support herself; but if she makes less, then the government would make up the difference." At work, Elena was awarded as a "Stakhanovite," that is a Soviet worker that regularly surpasses production quotas, a special honor that was highly compensated. Her monthly salary was seven hundred rubles, so she had no government assistance, no paycheck for her husband's army service. But she had no need.

She continued to see if she could find a bigger apartment and something closer to work so that she would be able to come home during lunch hour to feed the baby. She registered at the housing authority for a bigger apartment. It took quite a while, but she finally found something she liked in the right location. With everyone's help, she was able to move and get settled before the baby arrived.

On June 10, 1936, her first child was born, a daughter named Lubow Arkadiyevna Bondar. Lubow means love. She called her Luba for short.

While she was in the hospital, Elena got very sick with kidney inflammation, an illness that lasted three months. Filled with concern for her family and unable to work, she sent telegrams to Arkadiy, but the army would not let him come home. Yet she survived her illness and returned to her apartment, able again to work.

Arkadiy continued his assignment at the army headquarters, and the months apart flew past. Then by some chance, he was sent to Irkutsk for one day, there to purchase supplies for the Army, as he had done only once before. He seized the opportunity to come home. He told no one he was coming. It was a surprise.

When he arrived at the apartment, Elena was at work, but Luba was there with her grandmother, Akulina, whom she always called "Babusia." The name stuck.

Luba was now eighteen months old and well-spoken for her age. She played with Arkadiy all day long, very open, glad to be with this man.

Elena entered the apartment to a shocking surprise. "Arkadiy! How come? How can this be? You are home!"

"But not for long." Arkadiy explained he had to return the next day.

Later that night, at bedtime, little Luba confronted Arkadiy, pointing at the bed. "You cannot stay here and sleep with Mommy."

"I cannot? And why is that?" he gently asked.

"Only my daddy can sleep with my mommy."

"But I am your daddy."

"No, you are not. My daddy is in the army."

No matter how many times they tried to explain who Arkadiy was, Luba refused to believe it. She kept on crying. "No. My daddy is in the army."

Elena and Arkadiy enjoyed all too brief a night together. The next morning, he had to return to duty.

During Arkadiy's absence, Elena's family lived very well. In addition to her salary from Igla, she made another three to four hundred rubles per month sewing in the evenings. Anna also made a good salary. With their combined income, they were able to purchase new furniture that was made to order, very expensive and beautiful luxuries. By the time Arkadiy finished his term and returned, the apartment was fully furnished.

They welcomed him home.

28

In the spring, Anna met someone and fell in love. His name was Stephan Pavlovich Kiselov. He was a medical doctor and engaged in research at Irkutsk University. Arkadiy helped them with their wedding. But Anna could not find a place for her and her husband. Instead, they moved out and lived with Stephan's mother.

Another period of "cleansing" by the Communists began, seeking after anyone that could be considered an enemy of the state. The arrests followed endlessly. This time, they reached deeper into all organizations.

In September, Elena was summoned to the NKVD offices.

On her way there, she fretted. *They have found out that my identity papers are false, my birth certificate. An informer, someone must have turned me in. But who?*

Arriving at the government building, she was directed down the hall to an office. A soldier stood there at attention, armed with two pistols. He looked down at her, sized her up. She showed him the summons. He studied it a moment, handed it back, and opened the door.

Elena stepped inside the office as the door shut behind her. She looked ahead. An official sat behind the desk in full uniform, a man in his early thirties. On the wall behind him was a large portrait of Stalin, flanked either side by brass poles draped with brilliant red Soviet flags.

The official put his hand up and motioned for her to step closer. "Let me see your summons."

She handed it to him.

"You are Elena Ivanovna Nosova Bondar?"

"Yes."

She turned to her left and glanced at the empty chair. She placed her hand on the high curve of her stomach. Elena was seven months pregnant. "May I sit down?"

"No." He didn't look at her as he turned open his notebook on top of his desk. He flipped through many of the pages and slowed, found the one he wanted, and ran his finger down the text to the entry he was looking for. He studied it a moment, grunted, and then looked up.

She braced herself for the question.

"I see that you are a Christian."

Elena blanched. "Yes," she said. "Yes, I am."

"Hmmm." He nodded, picked up his pencil, and made a note. He looked up at her. "And tell me, how did you become a Christian?"

Elena blinked. She hadn't been prepared for this line of questioning. She looked down at his desk and noticed the newspaper *Bezbozhnik* ("Godless"). She glanced at the pin on his lapel, a gear with a star in the center and the letters *"Сб"* (SVB)—he was a member of the League of the Militant Godless (LMG). She fumbled for her words. "Well, uh, I read the Bible. I, uh, thought about what it said. And I, uh, I believed it. I mean, it said that…the Bible said…that I should believe in God, to place my trust in Jesus, and that I should follow after him. So that makes me one of his disciples. That is what makes me a Christian."

He had been twirling his pencil around as she was talking. He set the tip down on the paper. "When did this happen?"

"When did I become a Christian?"

"Yes."

"It was April in 19…1928. Yes, 1928."

He made his note. Keeping his pencil there, again, he looked up at her. "And who helped you to become a Christian?"

"Who helped me?"

He remained ready to write. "Yes. Who helped you?"

Elena squirmed. She understood that her right to believe was protected under the constitution, but she well understood that the communists used militant groups like the LMG to carry out their true intent to destroy Christianity through propaganda, striving to convert everyone to atheism, while imprisoning and killing those that worked against them. Spreading Christianity was definitely working against them. She carefully chose her words. "There wasn't anybody that helped me." She caught her breath and continued in a deliberately-sweet voice. "I told you. I read the Bible by myself. I believed it by myself. I became a Christian by myself."

He twirled his pencil again. He looked down at his notes. "And you say this happened in April 1929?"

Elena shook her head. "No. I said, '1928.'"

"I thought you said, '1929.' Yes, that is what I wrote down. That is what you said."

"No. I specifically said, '1928. April 1928.'"

"And now you are changing the month?" He pushed his chair back and stood up.

Elena took a deep breath. "I said April. It was April."

He drummed his fingers on the desk and sat back down. "Now tell me more about how you became a Christian."

Elena repeated her story. She gave a bit more detail this time but was careful not to mention Karpenko or how she got her Bible. He never did ask how she got it. She wondered how she could have answered that question without implicating him, while saying the truth. But she did not have to.

The questioning went on for four hours. The same questions were repeated over and over, changing the order. Elena could see through his efforts, his efforts to confuse her. Nevertheless, in her condition, standing the entire time, she was getting exhausted. But she did not falter, and she mentioned no other names, no one from her church.

He was getting tired too, and visibly frustrated. He took a breath to regroup. "You *must* have been told how to become a Christian. Someone helped you. Someone told you what to do."

"No. No one told me what to do. No one told me how to become a Christian."

He slammed his pencil down on the desk. "You lie!" He shoved his chair back and shot to his feet.

"I am not lying."

He hammered his fist on the desk. "You lie!" He shook his head and screamed, "You are protecting someone!"

Elena bit her lip and lowered her voice. "I am not lying."

He rounded his desk and stepped up close to her. He bent over her, glaring, inches from her face, clenching his jaw. His eyes narrowed. He seethed. "You are a *sly* woman."

Elena responded gently, "It may be difficult to say whether I am sly or maybe I am very smart."

He held his breath as his face became red. He turned his head to the side and let it out slowly. He settled down.

While he stood there close, she added, "You have been questioning me for the past four hours, not even noticing that I am seven months pregnant. Do you realize that this could affect my baby? And if the baby is born with complications, *you* will be responsible?"

He looked down at her hands, now resting on her stomach. He grunted. He turned and stepped over to his credenza, poured her a glass of water, then handed it to her.

She took it from him, staring at his face as she drank it. She handed him the empty glass. "Thank you," she said.

He measured her another moment and then shook his head. "Okay. You are free to go."

Elena did not hesitate. "I need a note from you. It must say that you questioned me for four hours and that no one should interrogate me anymore." She was afraid someone would grab her on the way out of the headquarters and begin the questioning all over again.

The corner of his mouth curled in a grin.

She leaned forward confidently, waiting for his compliance.

He turned and stepped behind his desk, pulled out a piece of paper, wrote the note, and handed it to her silently. Elena took it from him with her head held high. She spun around and walked out of the building.

Having escaped, she was thankful that God had given her courage to survive the interrogation. But she feared that Arkadiy would be questioned as well because his background was so similar.

* * *

On November 14, 1938, a son was born to Elena, Vitaliy Arkadiyevich Bondar. She had wanted to name him Vsyevolod, and Arkadiy did not protest, but somehow, his birth certificate carried the name of Vitaliy. They would grow accustomed to the new name. Now they had five people living in their modest apartment: Elena's family and Akulina, one big happy family.

But it was a family that was not yet big enough.

Elena's sister Pana showed up at her doorstep. She had with her, her mother-in-law and her (now) five children: two daughters, two sons, and an infant boy.

"Ivan has been arrested again!" she cried. "They sent him away to somewhere; where we do not know."

Elena asked, "But his term, his five years were up?"

Pana held her hands up. "This is new. I do not understand." She grew red in the face. "They gave us twenty-four hours to get out of our apartment. We had a little bit of money, enough to buy a ticket to come here. We had to leave everything. We had nowhere else to go."

So Elena welcomed seven new family members into their apartment, which had an open living area of just nineteen square meters. But there was no other choice. As the wife of an exile, Pana had no rights. The government did not care where she had to go to survive. She had no passport and was not allowed to live in Irkutsk and had no legal right to work. She would have to live off whatever the other members of her family could earn.

But Elena loved her sister dearly.

How can I afford to feed seven more people? She knew better. *With God's help, we will survive.*

29

For a year, Pana's family stayed with them. Arkadiy and Elena constantly looked for ways to get her a passport so that she could get some kind of a room of her own and be able to buy food. At last they had success, found her a room and made a few connections so that she could get some sewing jobs. After Pana's family moved out, Elena felt the pressure released; more room in the apartment and fewer mouths to feed.

When the weather warmed and April turned into May, Elena became very sick. Barely able to breath, she labored just to climb the stairs to their second floor apartment. The feeling persisted, even grew worse with each passing day. Worried it could be pneumonia, she went to the doctor. She had x-rays taken. These showed her lungs were clear but revealed an unexpected surprise: her heart was severely enlarged. *Why?* she wondered. The doctors could give her no answer.

The strange illness continued. Her energy drained. She lost her appetite.

Elena decided to check in with a gynecologist, suspecting she was pregnant. They confirmed she was. But now what? Why was she experiencing a heart problem? It made no sense.

Four doctors looked at her test results. All four concluded the same thing, that the baby was causing the problem. They each told her, "You will not be able to carry this baby to full term. Your heart will not be able to take it. You need to have an abortion."

The horror of the prognosis sank in. Elena placed her hand on her heart and felt it laboring. She asked, "When?"

"Immediately. This cannot wait. Your health is at risk. If you wait, you will die."

"But I thought abortions were not allowed?"

"In a situation such as yours, where your life it at risk, there is no prohibition. This is a necessary procedure. We have no choice."

The last doctor that she saw gave her a medical leave of absence, which was almost unheard of in Russia. He scheduled the abortion in a few weeks, giving her the longest time possible for her heart problem to go away on its own, if it might. But he set a limit. "It has to be before the first movement of the baby is felt, before the end of your fourth month. You could not survive after that."

Elena left the hospital deeply disturbed. She went straight to see her pastor. She sat with him and explained her problem, the recommendation of the doctors, and how she felt about it.

He consoled her. "I understand this is not your desire, not your choice to have an abortion. But the doctors see no other way to save your life. You should obey the doctors. They are experienced in these things."

Elena sat in disbelief. "I must *kill* my child? I cannot do that!"

"But you are not doing it because you do not want this child. The operation is necessary, according to the doctor." He shook his head. "If you do not follow his advice, you will die."

She left the church feeling wholly dissatisfied with his advice.

Elena and Arkadiy labored together over the subject. He did not want to lose her. He loved her. He sided with the doctors.

Elena talked with her friends. They all said the same thing: "The doctors are right."

She talked to Mother, the one person who usually agreed with her on everything. Mother gently held her hand and reasoned. "God knows that you are not just trying to get rid of this child. You already have two children, a girl and a boy. They are so little. You are needed by both of them. If you die, who will take care of them?"

Elena and Arkadiy's Christian friends came and visited her at her apartment, as she rested. They told her, "There is no sin in this instance because it is not by your choice that this needs to be done. This is only to save your life."

"Maybe it is not a sin to *you*. But to *me*, it is!"

Elena considered all she was hearing. No one agreed with her. She felt all alone.

Pana came over for a visit; they had not seen each other in nearly a month. Elena was delighted she would finally have someone to talk to, someone to whom she could explain her predicament, someone who might understand and give her the support she so desired.

But Pana was crying when she arrived. Elena promptly forgot about herself as she gave her sister a handkerchief. "What is wrong?" she asked. They sat together in the kitchen.

Pana collected herself. "Two weeks ago, I came home from work and found Babushka (Ivan's Mama) sitting at the kitchen table, distraught. She was absolutely beside herself, b-because two government social workers had come and taken Leonid away..."

Elena raised her hands to her mouth.

"...and now he is in the pediatric hospital."

"What! What is wrong?"

"I don't know. I...I haven't been able to get in and see him. I go to the hospital every day after work, but they won't let me in...they don't let the public in. There is a daily notice that they post at the gate that gives his condition. It says always the same thing, that he has dysentery, but his temperature is normal."

"How? How did this happen?"

"When I came home and found Babushka, she kept saying she 'never should have let them in the apartment.' She told me that Leonid had a runny bowel when they examined him that morning, so they just scowled at her, said he had dysentery, grabbed him up and took him. They left a card saying where they were taking him."

"I don't know how they can do this..."

"I asked the guard at the hospital gate the same thing. He told me there is a new city ordinance...that the medical staff is going around, checking every household that has young children." Pana face was red with anger. She gripped the arms of her chair so hard that her knuckles went white.

"Do they have any visiting hours?"

"On Thursdays from 3:00 to 4:00 pm." Pana took a deep breath and sighed. "I have to work then. If I went to see him, I would lose my job."

Elena knew all too well that there was little to be done. Regular citizens had been seeing their rights systematically taken away by the government, and Pana's situation was even worse because she was an exile. Elena leaned forward and gently placed her hand on Pana's. "Let's pray about this."

Pana nodded. They held hands and prayed together. Then Pana got up, hugged Elena, and whispered, "Thank you." She smiled at her and left.

Elena had not even had a chance to share with her sister the challenge she was facing in her own life.

* * *

Pana left Elena's apartment determined to find a way, any way to get in to see her baby. She ran all the way to the hospital. The hospital compound was surrounded on all sides by a fence. The only way in was through the front gate, where a guard was posted twenty-four hours a day. So she went around to the rear. Seeing no one about, she climbed over the fence, and stared at the hospital building, wondering what to do next. Just then the rear door swung open and two nurses stepped out into the yard.

Pana anxiously approached them. "My son is here in the hospital. I haven't seen him in weeks. I really need to see how he is doing."

The nurses looked at each other.

One asked, "How old is he?"

"One."

"What is his name?"

"Leonid Rukasuyev."

"Inside this door, down the hall, your first right." The nurse pointed. "That is the infant ward. You can see him through the glass."

"Thank you!" exclaimed Pana. She opened the door and rushed inside.

When she arrived at the window, she anxiously looked into the room at all the cribs. She spotted him and cried, "Leonid!" He was sitting up and playing with a balloon. She raised her hands to her face and sighed, *He looks so good.*

A nurse turned the corner and came down the hall. She paused, glanced at her watch, looked up and glared at Pana. "Gospozha! You cannot stand here. Come on. You have to go."

"But that is my baby in there." Pana pointed.

The nurse put her hands on her hips. "I don't care who is in there. *You* don't belong here."

Pana left.

Several days later, Pana again climbed over the fence and entered into the hospital, carefully looking around, hoping not to see that surly nurse again. She went to the same window and looked into the infant room. Leonid was not in his crib. Another child was there.

Frantic, she looked at the next crib. Leonid was not there. One at a time, she looked at every crib. No Leonid anywhere.

She looked to her left, down the hall. There was another window to another ward. She ran there, anxiously scanning every bed and crib. No sign of Leonid.

She searched farther down the hall and found another ward. Again, she scanned the beds. *There he is.* He was lying on his back. His chest, arms, legs, and face were covered in red dots.

A nurse in the room saw her looking in through the window. She stepped out into the hall and confronted Pana. "You can't stand here."

"That is my son. Can I come in and see him?"

"I am sorry, gospozha. This is a measles ward. No one is allowed in."

Pana stood, holding her hands to her heart, pleading.

"I am sorry, gospozha. You are going to have to leave before I call someone."

Pana took one more look through the glass, turned, and left. She went to the gatehouse and spoke with the guard. She begged for permission to be able to get in. But none was given.

Several days later, Pana again climbed the fence and went in. She found Leonid in yet another ward. This time, she could see him lying in his bed, his little chest pumping up and down. He was obviously struggling to breathe.

Again, one of the nurses stepped out into the hall. "May I help you?"

Pana was distraught. "That is my son there. What is wrong with him?"

The nurse looked at her kindly. "He...he has pneumonia."

Pana's face reddened. "May I come in and sit with him?"

The nurse put her hand on her shoulder. "I am sorry, this is a contagious area. No one is allowed in." She made eye contact. "I am sorry."

"Please?" she pleaded.

"No, gospozha. You will just have to wait until he gets better."

Pana's breath was stolen. She walked away holding her chest.

* * *

As the days passed, the time for Elena's abortion grew nearer. All the while, a battle raged within. Her conscience told her one thing, her mind another. She felt no peace. And her illness only intensified. She felt sick now all the time. *Maybe the doctors are right. How can I leave my husband and children?*

Yet the thought of willfully killing her child was too horrid. *Lord, you give and take life, you alone.* She worried, if she were to choose to take the life, that she would no longer be able to pray to him. The thought of violating God's will seemed worse to her than dying. She waited. She prayed.

And she stopped talking to and getting advice from anyone. She didn't even talk to Arkadiy or her mother, and

Pana was not around. She withdrew her thoughts into isolation.

Then Pana arrived again for a visit, deeply distraught over something.

"It is Leonid. I have been able to get in and see him." She clasped her arms to her chest and sighed. "*He is my last child...a special child. I do not know if I will ever see Ivan again...I cannot have another baby.*" Pana's body was shaking as she sobbed.

Elena got up and wrapped her arms around her sister. "You will see Ivan again."

"How I love that little boy! His eyes...that curl of his smile is just like his daddy. I remember how I laid him on my chest and looked into his eyes and told him, 'How very much I love you.' He used to be so happy, so strong, so full of life, and so quick! He would rest on my shoulders, and I would hold him tight."

"We don't know yet what will happen..."

"I would never want him to grow up...so that I can keep on carrying him close to me. Oh, how I love him! Oh, how I miss him!"

Elena comforted her sister as she cried and cried. Somehow her own problem seemed like nothing compared to what Pana was facing. She said nothing of her concerns. After a while Pana left.

The day before the scheduled abortion arrived. When evening came, Elena found herself alone. Luba and Vitaliy were in bed. She fell on her bed pillow, sobbing. Her tears were not prayers, neither were they flowing out of fear. The tears were her realization that she had no choice. *Why aren't my very closest family, Mama and Arkadiy, why are they not standing with me in my decision? Why are they not upholding me and helping me spiritually? Why is everyone on the doctor's side?*

She lay agonizing for an hour, sobbing. But then it came to her. *I am not alone. Oh, Lord, you…you are with me! You are greater than Mama, greater than my husband, greater than my brothers and sisters in Christ, and you are greater than the doctors!* She decided. *I will not have the abortion. I would rather die.*

Peace at last entered her heart. She fell asleep.

In the morning, she told Arkadiy and her mother her decision. She did not go to the hospital that day, and they did not force her to go.

* * *

When Pana returned to work, all she could think about each day, all day, was her little Leonid.

Several days later, she received a notice while she was at work, summoning her to the hospital. Feeling a knot in her stomach, she ran the whole way to the gate. She showed the note and the guard let her in. A nurse guided her to the ward. When she stepped into the room, she saw Leonid lying in a crib. She went to him. He looked up at her and silently stretched his little hands up. He was too weak to sit.

"Oh, sweetie," she cried. She bent and picked him up.

As she held him, she seethed inside. *Why? You doctors and nurses…why? Why did you not let me tend to my child myself?* She clenched her fist and scowled at them standing there, watching.

She felt his labored breathing and refocused her eyes on his. He looked into her eyes. He took one more weak breath and died.

She held him, screaming inside herself, *How can you do this to me! I…I will sue you all! He is gone! My baby, my love is gone! You doctors, you nurses…you let this happen!*

Sobbing, she bent forward and lay his little body down into the crib. She stood over him, staring at his lifeless form.

And then it came to her. In her silent rage, she felt an unexpected change.

Isn't it said in scripture that not a single sparrow will fall, apart from the will of God? A soul is so much more important to God than a sparrow. It must be God's will that he died. Who can argue with God? She knew the difficult truth, that his death was not an accident. *His death was not the doctors' fault.*

She looked longingly at Leonid's dear, sweet face. His lips were formed into a smile. He was at rest.

Pana's fists loosened. Her fingers relaxed. Her breathing eased. Her rage gave way to peace. But it made no sense to her. How had her anger waned?

She wiped the tears from her face and thanked the attendants for calling her and allowing her in. She left the hospital.

On her long walk home, she found release. *My son is with you now, Lord, in your presence. Someday, I will come and be with you too. I will see him then. Oh, how marvelous you are Lord!*

Pana went to Elena's home, bringing with her the terrible news of Leonid's death. The sisters cried together. Again, Elena kept her own burden to herself as Pana talked about her plans for the funeral, how she had ordered a casket and chosen a burial plot.

Then Pana opened up. "While my child was in the hospital, I was very angry...*furious*...indignant that they would not allow me to see him and take care of him. But now...now I no longer blame them. I am very grateful to the Lord God, grateful for how he showed me his grace. He has always comforted me in my trials." Pana recounted her frantic flight to Irkutsk from the east last year, bringing her five children to move in with Elena; it was a fifteen-day journey.

She took hold of Elena's hand, "And you, my little sister, you took us in. And now we have our own apartment, and we have fresh food every day that Babushka prepares for the children." She looked at Elena as tears rolled down her cheeks. "Death claimed my baby without asking. I have seen many of my loved ones die…four of my eight children."

Pana wiped back her tears and fixed her eyes on Elena's. "I've learned that the Lord has always given me courage to go on. I must trust him no matter how hard my circumstance."

Elena embraced her sister. She had just been told all that she needed to hear.

*　*　*

It was the end of June, the end of Elena's fourth month. She went again to see the doctor to check on the condition of her heart, bearing the ever-present pain.

The doctor chastened her. "You are out of your mind! You surely have only a few days to live. Let me admit you today, and we can get this procedure over with."

She remained steadfast in her decision. "I cannot have this abortion." She did not tell the doctor why she thought it was wrong. *He will never understand.* She stood, turned, and dragged herself out of his office.

Back at the apartment, Elena made no mention of her prognosis, that she was only given a few days to live.

The few days passed, yet death did not come.

Two more weeks passed.

In early July, Elena felt it: the first movement of her baby. This should have been the end. Yet in that very moment, the pain in her chest subsided. It faded to nothing, like steam leaving a cooling kettle. She could breathe again. She felt normal. And she was very hungry.

She returned to the doctors. All four came into the room, together with several of the nurses that had been involved with her prognosis. They examined her and found nothing wrong with her heart. They threw their hands up in disbelief. They pronounced her "completely healed." Nevertheless, they warned her not to get pregnant again, stating that her heart had been weakened by her ordeal. "You will continue to have problems if you have more children."

Elena's appetite was back to routine. She gained back some weight and looked much better. With renewed energy, she was even able to return to work and to carry her baby to full term.

Then on December 3, 1940, Elena gave birth to her second daughter.

Arkadiy asked, "What shall she be called?"

Elena smiled. "Vera," which means faith, "because it was only by faith that she was born."

Not only were the doctors and nurses amazed, but so were all the people in her church, including the pastor. Several dared to call it a "miracle" of God.

There was a woman from Elena's church who was the head of nursing at the maternity hospital where Vera was born. This nurse had made sure she was there when Elena delivered, there to help in case there had been complications. She placed Vera into her own ward, then stayed with her past the end of her shift. When Elena was completely taken care of, only then did she leave. She told Elena, "I learned a very big lesson by watching you suffer and then by watching you triumph over temptation."

Elena smiled at her, proudly holding Vera. Elena looked down at her newborn, seeing with her own eyes that she had learned a lesson too.

30

When Elena and Arkadiy came home from the hospital with Vera, she found her mother sitting with Pana and Anna in the living room. It looked like a family meeting had been purposefully arranged. She could tell from their faces that they were holding something back.

"What is it?" Elena asked.

The three women looked at each other, then at Elena. Pana's face grew red. She erupted. "Ivan, he...*he has been shot!*"

Elena handed the baby to Arkadiy and ran to her sister. She embraced her, saying, "Oh my!" over and over again. She held Pana in her arms as they all four sobbed together.

Mother interrupted, "And Pana is on a blacklist." She handed Elena a piece of paper.

Elena took it and read it. "When did you get this?"

"When you were giving birth," said Mother. She placed her hand on Elena's shoulder. "We have to move. We should go to Kiev." Kiev was where Arkadiy was from; his parents still lived there.

"Kiev?"

"Yes. Arkadiy, Pana, and you should all be able to find work there and get resettled. It is six time zones to the west, far away from where the Party will be looking for Pana."

Elena listened to them explain the advantages. She realized they had already been discussing what to do and were well prepared, having kept the matter from her while she had been in the hospital, apparently not wishing to make her upset.

She silently bemoaned, *But we are all settled here.* She looked around the room at all the nice furniture. She glanced through the doorway of the room that had been set up for Vera. The thought of moving and the difficulty of starting all over again swept over her like a wave. And she loved Irkutsk; she did not want to move. *But this isn't about me.*

Elena looked at Pana, red in the face, wiping back tears. She closed her eyes and sighed. "When do we move?"

Arkadiy stepped forward. "We must go right away."

The four women formulated a plan. Pana would travel with Arkadiy to Kiev to find a place to resettle and to find work. Her four children would be divided between Elena and Anna to care for them while she was away. The key was to get Pana to safety first, to find a place to hide her from those seeking her life.

A few days later, Arkadiy and Pana boarded a train, westbound toward Kiev.

* * *

Right after they left, Vera got very sick with bronchitis. The doctor prescribed a mustard treatment with hot bottles, a procedure that was common to the time. But the bottles he gave Elena were entirely too large to fit on the chest of a tiny two-week-old. Elena improvised. She cut patches of fabric that fit Vera's little body and drenched them in the hot mustard mix, then laid these directly on her chest. The heated mustard could easily burn the tender skin, so she had to watch carefully to see when the skin started to turn red, then remove the patch immediately. Once the skin had been allowed to cool, then she would start over with a new patch. This went on for two weeks, until little Vera finally started getting better. With this care, she was able to make a full recovery.

* * *

In May 1941, Arkadiy returned to Irkutsk.

He and Pana had stayed with his parents while he looked for two apartments and jobs for them both. It was difficult to find housing in the Soviet Union; there was a constant shortage. In order to find an apartment in Kiev, he needed to register, the same procedure required for finding a job. It could take many months, sometimes years, for the applicant's number to come up. The apartments available were intended for the people of Kiev, which gave Arkadiy an advantage, since that was his hometown. Pana, on the other hand, was an outsider, which would make finding something for her nearly impossible. It had taken Arkadiy four months, but he had been able to find a place to live and a job. Then, using his network of trusted friends, he had also found Pana an apartment and a place to work.

Now the task was for the rest of the family to prepare to leave Irkutsk. In just a few days, their clothing was packed and they were ready to go. They would leave everything else behind.

Elena and her sister Anna finalized their plans concerning Pana's children. Anna would continue to care for Anna (fourteen) and Ilya (eight), while Elena would take the other two with her, Zoya (sixteen) and Eugene (six). Anna hoped to be able to relocate her job in the near future to Moscow, then to Ukraine where they could all reunite.

At the end of May and after saying many tearful goodbyes, Elena and seven others (Arkadiy, Luba, Vitaliy, Vera, Mother, Zoya, and Eugene) all boarded a train bound west toward Kiev. They rode together into an uncertain future, wondering if they would ever see Elena's sister Anna and Pana's other two children again.

Part Three

31

Elena and her extended family, all eight, boarded the westbound Trans-Siberian train in Irkutsk. It was a fast train, carrying them more than five thousand kilometers through the heart of Russia, crossing the Ural Mountains, out of Asia and into Eastern Europe. They had purchased first class tickets, which placed them in a luxury coach, occupying two separate sleeping compartments. Mother, Luba, and Vitaliy were in one. Elena, Arkadiy, Vera, Zoya, and Eugene shared the other. As they rode along, they sat together by the windows and watched the scenery fly by, day after day, admiring its beauty. Even Luba, almost age five, was transfixed by it. As she sat there, she relished the food that was served to them, enamored with the taste of condensed milk, something entirely new.

After a week, the train arrived in Moscow. There they would change trains to continue to Kiev, but not before taking time to see the sights. That night, they celebrated Luba's birthday at a restaurant in their hotel. The children were delighted by food they had never seen before, including a dessert of fresh fruits served in long-stem crystal bowls. Luba was especially taken by the sight of green grapes. She put one in her mouth and savored the sweetness. She looked up wide-eyed at Elena. "I have never had fruit before, Mama."

Elena gently corrected. "When you were a baby, your Aunt Anna would bring you an apple or an orange every day." The food shortages had since put an end to that luxury.

After dinner, they spent the night at the hotel.

The next day, they went to see the tomb of Lenin in Red Square. They stood in line several hours before they could get in, admiring the vast and powerful expanse of the paved space and the stunning turrets and architectural details of the towers of Saint Basil's Cathedral, the brilliant colors, red and orange, green and blue, the patterns, the dots, the swirls, standing as a fantasy, like a cluster of uniquely and ornately decorated ice cream cones, each with golden balls instead of cherries on their tops.

The next morning, they left Moscow on a train bound for Kiev, traveling south and west some 870 kilometers. It was another all day and overnight trip.

Arriving in Kiev, Pana met them at the station. Zoya and Eugene flew down the platform and into her arms. Many tears were shed, great tears of joy. Behind Pana stood an older couple, Arkadiy's parents, Olga and Georgiy Bondar. Georgiy was Arkadiy's stepfather and uncle; he was the younger brother of his father, Faddey.

Arkadiy embraced them both, then turned and introduced his family. Elena had never met them. Olga studied Elena a moment. She glanced at Arkadiy then gushed, "Where did you ever find this adorable, little gypsy? She is like a living doll!"

They embraced.

Elena was immediately impressed with Arkadiy's parents. Olga was a very beautiful woman, and Georgiy was quite handsome. They both were well dressed, something she never failed to notice. Her quick study of them detected some of Arkadiy's features, seeing the family resemblance in both of them: the color of his eyes, the shape of his forehead and ears. Then as they became engaged in conversation, she could tell they were well-educated and intelligent, people of high class, thoughtful and gentle...a surprise of sorts, a welcome surprise. She hadn't known quite what to expect in them.

There at the station, they transferred to another train that took them to Irpin, a suburb of Kiev, a short ride to the west. That was where Arkadiy's parents lived. They had a small apartment there within walking distance of the station. When they arrived at the unit, there were more reunions and introductions to the rest of the family. They met Arkadiy's stepsister Taisa, nineteen, a recent graduate from the Railway College, and stepbrother Feon, sixteen, still in school. The large family, all united, then enjoyed the rest of day together, and Elena was grateful to be able to relax after the long trek, while someone else entertained her children.

After dinner, Arkadiy took Elena and their children to see their new home. It was located in Bucha, a short train ride, the next station stop to the north—a long walk indeed, but technically within walking distance of his parents. Arkadiy and Elena's new apartment was just a few blocks from the Bucha station. It was in a house that was owned by a doctor and his wife. The doctor had been exiled, caught in the recent wave of cleansing. The wife, therefore, had been forced to rent part of her home to make ends meet. She kept just two rooms for herself and shared the kitchen with her tenant. The part she rented had its own entrance through a porch. The structure was large and lovely, a tribute to the doctor's former wealth and standing in the community.

The landlady greeted them, unlocked the door, and gave them a tour. Arkadiy and Elena spent the next week acquiring furniture. With Arkadiy's new job and his good income, they were able to buy all that they needed. By week's end, they had moved in.

The first morning there, before anyone else was up, Elena arose and went to the kitchen. She swung the back door open and stepped outside onto the rear porch, gazing into the yard. The swifts were singing in the trees: large tulip trees in full bloom with pretty pink and white petals. The fragrance, the color, the life, all of it was magnificent. She stood there, drinking it all in, listening to the birds.

A breeze rose up off the warmth of the lawn and rustled through the trees. It tugged on the branches, pulled off some of the petals, and these fell lazily around her feet. She closed her eyes and felt the warmth glancing off her cheeks and sweeping through her hair, savoring it, hardly believing all this beauty was there for her, giving God thanks and wondering, wondering just how long it would last.

32

Elena and Arkadiy began to settle into their new apartment. After having taken all that time off to relocate his family, he needed to get back to work. His job was in Kiev, about a half hour train ride away, which was very convenient. In the meantime, Elena was busy with Mother making improvements to their quarters. They were able to purchase drapery fabrics and began to finish off the trimmings, making it feel more like it was their home. It was a labor of love.

The children enjoyed the new place, exploring the gardens, playing in the yard. But they remained obedient, playing only where Elena would allow them, careful to respect the property of their landlady. In the evenings, Elena sat and wrote letters to her sister Anna to keep her apprised of all the wonderful things they were enjoying.

The very next Sunday, June 22, everything changed.

Early in the morning, word filtered through the town that war had begun. Germany had invaded the Soviet Union. Everyone sheltered indoors, fearful, anxious to know what was going on. Elena and her family sat beside the radio, listening for news.

Before noon, Soviet foreign minister Vyacheslav Molotov came on to address the people:

> *"Without a declaration of war, German forces fell on our country, attacked our frontiers in many places. The Red Army and the whole nation will wage a victorious Patriotic War for our beloved country, for honor, for*

liberty. Our cause is just. The enemy will be beaten. Victory will be ours!"

The hours that followed were only anxious.

The next morning, Arkadiy purchased several newspapers and brought them home to study. He learned that the enemy invasion force had attacked along an immense front, a front that extended all the way from Romania, from the shores of the Black Sea in the south, dividing Europe, through Hungary and Poland to the Baltic in the north, an incredible distance of 2,900 kilometers. One newspaper reporter said, "This attack is the largest war effort in human history."

Two days later, Arkadiy was drafted to return to duty. He was given the rank of captain and placed in command of an artillery battalion. He was told to report immediately to duty.

Elena assembled the family together as Arkadiy donned his uniform and gathered his things. He stepped into the entry hall, his bag slung over his shoulder, ready to depart.

Elena said, "We will come with you to the station."

"No. I would rather say goodbye here." He looked past her, through the open doors to the living room, seeing half a new set of drapes hanging on one of windows and Elena's sewing machine set up there. The apartment had not yet begun to feel like home.

He turned and studied his family, standing in a line, all their eyes fixed on him. First was Akulina, who was holding Vera. He kissed her, then the baby. Next he bent and picked up Vitaliy, who was fascinated by his hat. He gave him a hug and set him back down, then handed him the hat. He bent and kissed Luba. "Now you will have to be a big help to Mama while I am away." She nodded, red-faced, wiping back a tear.

Finally, he came to Elena. The two embraced.

"God will watch you. I know it," she said as she clung to him.

"I know. I know he will."

At last, he turned toward the door and started to leave.

Vitaliy said, "Daddy! You are going to need your hat!" He hurriedly handed it to him. Arkadiy took it, smiled at him, and put it on. He turned and stepped outside.

Elena felt a tightening of her stomach. She knew it was fear, the fear that she might not ever see him again. She fought against it.

* * *

Within days, the bombing of Kiev commenced. There were frequent air raids. Constant booms could be heard in the distance. Many stayed indoors, leaving the streets mostly empty. On occasion, people were seen running to do their business. Between the booms, it was eerily quiet. At night, all the lights were out.

To Elena, the conditions had become too scary, too chaotic to bear any longer. She confronted Mother. "I think we should go somewhere safe, back to Irkutsk."

Mother had tried to busy herself with the sewing machine. She just listened.

"We have no idea when Arkadiy will return. We are here alone, two women and three children. I am not familiar with the area. I have no job. I really do not know anyone. How are we going to survive?"

At that moment there was a distant boom.

"How are we going to survive like this?"

Mother turned off the sewing machine and looked up.

Elena continued, "At least if we went back to Irkutsk...at least then I would have all my contacts. I...I could easily get a job." Elena looked all around the room. "Staying here we will only be killed."

Mother stood and came over to Elena. She wrapped her arms around her. "You should do whatever you think is best."

Elena left the apartment and made the short walk to the train station. There was a long line of people waiting at the ticket window. She got in line.

After nearly an hour, she made it to the window and addressed the man behind the counter, "I would like to get tickets to Irkutsk."

The ticket man looked at her in surprise. "Gospozha, you cannot get tickets to go there."

"Why not?"

"There are no passenger trains to the east. Only troop trains are allowed on the line."

"Since when?"

"Listen. That is all I know. That is all they told me. There are no passenger trains." He looked past Elena's shoulder. "Next customer."

Elena did not budge. She looked at the man. "Well, since *you* don't know, who does?"

He stared at her, obviously miffed. She stared back. He drummed his fingers on the counter. "Just a minute." He stepped to the side of the window and opened the door. From there he said, "Come inside."

Elena stepped in as he closed the door.

He whispered to her, "Step over to that office over there." He pointed. "That man is the head of the railway department, uh, my boss. If there is anyone that knows any more, it would be him." He straightened his hat and returned to the customer window.

Elena walked over to the office. She looked inside and saw an official seated behind a desk. She tapped on the door to get his attention.

He looked up at her. "Oh, uh, yes. May I help you, gospozha?"

"I am trying to get to Irkutsk, and I understand there are no passenger trains traveling that way any longer."

"Yes. That is right."

"Listen, with all this bombing going on, I am concerned about the safety of my children. Uh, my husband is in the army."

He placed his hand on the table.

"Well, I am from Irkutsk, and I really need to get back there so that I can work and be able to support my family."

He rolled his tongue around his cheek, then looked down at his log. He flipped a couple pages. "I could get you and your family on a mail train." He looked up. "Of course, you would have to travel with the cargo."

Elena sighed. "That would work."

"The train leaves this afternoon, 3:00 p.m., from track one." He looked again at his log. "It goes through Kharkov."

"Oh, no. No. The Germans are bombing Kharkov. I would much rather travel through Moscow." She stepped closer and tried to read his log herself.

He placed his hand over the page. "There are only troop trains going through Moscow. No. The only way you could possible get to Irkutsk would be through Kharkov." He started looking at the fare sheet. "So how many tickets would you like?"

Elena stood transfixed. She stared away into the corner before turning back to him. "I am going to need to think about this. Can I get back to you later?"

"Sure. But if I do not hear from you by noon, it will be too late."

Elena thanked him, walked out of his office, and returned to the apartment. Back at home, she explained the details to Mother.

Mother answered, "Maybe it is God's will to stay put?"

Elena looked out the windows. Most of the petals had fallen off the tulip tree. "Yes. Yes, I suppose it is."

Elena knew there were many families faced with the same situation. Yet she would be able to get a small salary as the wife of a soldier. *We should be able to survive, with God's help. He will surely protect us.*

From that day onward, Elena lost all contact with her relatives. A short time later, the evacuations of Kiev began. She had no idea where they would wind up.

33

By August 25, the Germans were less than twenty kilometers from Kiev. Ukrainians were being evacuated to makeshift refugee camps. Survival in the urban areas was about to become impossible.

One of Elena's neighbors, Stanislav, came to her in a panic, understanding Elena's plight: two women with three small children alone with no husband. He wanted to help them. "We are leaving tonight at midnight to escape the evacuation. Would you like to join us?" There was great fear of being taken with the masses to the refugee camps, fear the conditions would be overcrowded, lacking food, shelter, and proper care. "We have a friend with a horse and buggy that will take us east. There is a bit of a walk to reach him."

The thought of evacuating with the general population was too horrible for Elena, and remaining behind to be overrun by Nazis was even worse. His offer made sense. She consented.

As the evening grew late, she paced back and forth, trying to figure out what to take. It couldn't be much. When the time came, Mother took Vitaliy and Luba by the hands, while Elena carried Vera (eight months old) and a small suitcase with some dry bread, a few candy bars, and a jar of water.

At midnight, they left and met up with Stanislav and his wife, then set right off as he directed. They walked together all night, escaping beyond the evacuation zone. From there, they entered the woods, walking hour after hour in the dark.

As the sky began to brighten, they came to the appointed rendezvous point, stepping out from the trees and onto a narrow road. A man and his wife stood there beside a buggy. The horses were harnessed and ready to leave.

Stanislav introduced Elena's family to his friends.

The man looked at the small children, then at Akulina, the grandmother. He shook his head. "I cannot take you. This...this is too much responsibility for us." He looked at Elena and then at Stanislav. He was insistent. "I am sorry."

Stanislav pleaded with his friend. But it became clear that this was not going to work. He stepped close to Elena. "I don't know what to say." He placed his hand on his forehead. "I...I mean, it is not my horse and buggy."

Elena was stunned. *What do we do now?* she wondered. *I am not even sure which way we came and how to get back. And if we get back, the evacuations will be over. There will be no one to take us to safety.* The thought of being occupied by the German enemy fell on her with force.

Stanislav's friend was seated in the buggy and ready to depart. He called out, "Come on, Stan. We need to get going."

Stanislav took hold of Elena's hand. "I am so sorry." He and his wife turned, stepped over to the carriage, and climbed in.

Elena watched as the driver whipped the horses and drove away in a hurry. In a moment, they were left alone, standing beside the road, in the middle of nowhere. She looked down at Luba.

"Where will we go now, Mama?" Luba asked.

Elena gently cupped her cheek in her hand. "We will go to the Lord."

They faced back into the woods and set off in the direction from which they had come, or so they thought. Mother and Elena prayed as they went. They walked all day without rest, unsure of direction and with no idea where they were. But they did not stop. Elena picked up Vitaliy in one arm and held Vera in the other. Mother picked up Luba. The older ones fell asleep.

As the day grew late and the sun set, they heard voices ahead in the distance, where they saw smoke curling into the darkening sky. They walked toward the smoke. As they got closer, they could hear people talking. It was already dark and difficult to make out what was being said. They saw the light of a bonfire and the shadows of figures moving around it.

Elena and Mother approached the edge of the fire and strained to make out faces. They recognized no one. They said "Hello," introduced themselves. "May we join you?"

"If you can find a spot."

A short distance from the fire was a large building. Elena and Mother went closer to examine it, hoping to find a place there to rest. They opened the door and looked inside, finding it packed with refugees, wall-to-wall with people. Elena pressed between them, stepped over others, and squeezed her way through, looking for an open area. There was nothing, no place to stand, no space even to set her children down. She silently prayed.

She looked at them. "My dear people, would you possibly be able to squeeze in a little so that I can put my children down?"

"Can't you see there is no room?"

"Can you squeeze in a little more? I have three children, and we have walked all night and all day and need just a little bit of room, just enough room to put the children down? Mother and I will stand."

The people started to shift around. A space opened up in one corner, just enough to put down Luba and Vitaliy. There was straw on the floor. As she positioned them, the people around her watched her little ones, measuring Elena as she held her infant. They squeezed in further and made more space, enough so that even she and Mother were able to lie down beside their children.

Elena nodded in gratitude to them. She closed her eyes and sighed. *God, you heard my prayer!*

Elena looked around the room, studying the many faces. There were all different kinds of people there: elderly, middle aged, and young adults. Everyone was talking, some were scared, some complained. All were in the same predicament. The room was filled with noise.

As Elena rested, her heart was full of thanks to God, thanks that they had a roof over their heads, grateful to be among the living. As the evening grew late, everyone around her lay on the straw, close to one another: men, women, and children all in one room packed together as tight as could be. Little by little, the room grew quiet.

Early in the morning, Elena and the people around her introduced themselves. Each had his or her own story to tell. Elena found out that they had been sleeping in an animal shelter with many rooms; the windows had been closed up with bales of straw.

With time, everyone filtered outside and found the bonfire still blazing. Some people were cooking whatever they had brought with them on the fire. Elena asked around, and it became clear that no one knew how long they were going to be there or whether there would be enough food to survive. There was nothing nearby: no stores, no farms, and no houses. This shelter was truly isolated, set apart in the woods.

Elena opened her suitcase and dispensed what she had to Luba and Vitaliy: the dry bread, the candy bars, and the water. Elena had been nursing Vera, but when she tried to feed her, she realized that she had no milk. She was completely dried up.

After their snack, Elena, Mother, and the children went into the woods to look for mushrooms. They found a few and thought it would be enough for one day. But when they returned and cleaned them, they realized that they had nothing to cook them in. Fortunately, someone offered them a pail.

Thankful for the use of the pail, Elena offered some of their pickings, but they were refused. Mother and Elena ate the mushrooms without spices, butter, or bread, just boiled.

Evening came. Elena could not fall asleep. She was trying to imagine how she could feed her children, especially Vera, who had not had anything in more than a day, only water. She was very hungry. Elena silently prayed, *Lord, will you provide something for my children?*

The room was noisy. Some people were just talking, some played cards, some argued. Starving, shaking with hunger, Elena closed her eyes and tried to relax. She continued to pray as the room grew quiet. After a while, she drifted into fitful exhaustion.

A voice came to Elena, a gentle whisper in her ear. "Why are you worried? You have an empty bottle. Take it. Go out into the hallway, and you will see one window that is not closed up. Put your empty bottle on that windowsill."

Elena opened her eyes and looked around. She looked at Mother sound asleep. Her children were all sleeping too, so were the others nearby. The room had become quiet. *Who was that?* she wondered. She glanced at her suitcase at her side, picked it up, and laid it on her lap. Careful not to make a sound, she opened it.

There was the empty bottle.

Elena stood, holding the bottle, seeing all those around her sound asleep. She stepped carefully and quietly over them and made her way into the hallway. She looked all the way down to its end. Sure enough, there was one window there that had not been closed up. She walked to the end of the hall and set her bottle on the sill. She looked at it, prayed, and returned to her place. She lay down and fell asleep.

Elena snapped awake early in the morning, while it was yet dark, before any others were stirring. She quietly got up and tiptoed out of her room and down the hall to the window, staring at the sill. To her amazement, the bottle was full of milk.

She whispered, "Who on earth put this milk into my bottle?" She gazed out the window at the stars shining and prayed, "Oh, Lord! Praise your holy name. I have milk for my family. God almighty, you have heard my prayer!"

She quietly returned to her place, with both arms wrapped around the bottle. There was enough fresh milk for that day, not only for Vera, but also enough for Luba and Vitaliy. She told no one else about the milk.

Discreetly, Elena asked around, trying to find the person that had the cow. She wanted to thank that person for being so thoughtful and to make arrangements to pay them once she returned home. But no one said they had a cow.

That evening, Elena put the empty bottle again on the windowsill before she went to sleep. In the morning, she again found it filled with milk. Again, she was able to feed her children. Again, she asked around quietly. Again, no one admitted to having a cow.

For eighteen straight days, Elena placed the bottle there. For eighteen straight days, she had milk for her children. But she never found the person with the cow to thank them. Yet she knew that however that bottle was getting filled, it was surely God that was behind it. She said many prayers of thanks to him.

There was an older couple that was sleeping near them. On the morning of the eighteenth day, the wife noticed Elena had the bottle of milk.

She whispered, "Hey! Where did you get that?"

Elena came close. "I am not really sure myself. I put the bottle on the windowsill each night, and someone fills it."

The woman's eyes narrowed. "There is no one here with a cow."

"I know. I asked around." Elena looked at the bottle filled with fresh milk and smiled. She spoke confidently, "God keeps filling my bottle."

The woman leaned back and scoffed. "God? There is no God!" She threw her hands up and turned away. "You are a crazy woman!"

The woman's husband had been listening intently. He looked at Elena and shrugged.

By now, others had overheard her exclamation. They stared at Elena holding the bottle. She bravely addressed them, "God is the one providing for my children. He is my hope. He is my protector."

The scoffer looked at the faces of all the others as they listened to Elena. She laughed at them. "There is no such thing as God. Look at yourselves. Look where we are. There is no God!" She pointed at Elena. "Do not believe this woman."

Later that morning, word came throughout their shelter that it was safe for them to return to their homes. Elena and Mother received directions back to Bucha. They took the children and began the long walk home. They passed through and out of the woods, onto the road. The area there now looked familiar. Ahead was a steeple. They were not far from home.

Elena turned and looked over her shoulder, seeing others coming after them, stepping out from the trees onto the road, then separating off in various directions. Following a ways behind her was the scoffing woman with her husband.

They were walking through a residential district just a few kilometers from home when an explosion behind them shattered the air. Elena and Mother ducked instinctively and held their ears, ringing from the blast. They cautiously turned around to see what had happened.

Two houses down the street, a cloud of smoke ascended into the air. There the husband of the scoffer was kneeling, bent over in his front yard. He was sobbing, holding his wife's torso in his arms. She had stepped on a land mine. Her legs lay behind him in the street.

34

By September 19, the Germans had taken control of Kiev.

The days had been filled with the constant sound of bombs exploding. The stores quickly ran out of food, and most of Kiev had no running water. Bucha fortunately had water. But Elena had nothing left to feed her family.

Mother looked at the empty cupboard. "Well, let us just pray and sing praises to our God. We can do nothing else, for we will die here without food."

Elena frowned. "Since when have you become so pessimistic? My neighbor knows of farms in the villages where we can work. And we *can* still work. We are not dead yet." She smiled. "Don't you think God will give us our daily bread?"

Mother stayed at home to watch the children while Elena went next door to meet up with her neighbor Maya. They were going to see if they could find work.

Maya stepped out of her house dressed like a peasant. She stared wide-eyed at Elena. "You are going like that?"

Elena looked down at her black suit, standing tall in a pair of heels. "What's wrong with this?"

Maya shook her head and started walking down the block.

"Listen. I don't have any old clothes." Elena clopped along on the cobbles to catch up.

They walked for many kilometers until they were out in the country. They passed from one village to the next, looking for someone to hire them. They were willing to do any kind of work, especially if it paid in food. The collective farms had been taken over by the Germans. The private farms were worked by their owners—these seemed to them to be the best opportunity.

As the day grew late, they came to a private farm where the owner, a woman, was standing at the edge of her field, watching the refugees walk by, interested in hiring someone to dig her potatoes. She agreed to hire Maya and then turned to Elena. "Are you looking to be hired as well?" The woman stared at Elena's clean, pressed suit, then at her heels. "Do you even know how to work?"

Elena straightened. "Try me out for one day."

The farmer declined, then entered into negotiations with Maya, to establish the amount of pay.

By this time, the farmer's neighbor from across the road had walked up to the women and was listening to the negotiations. She looked at Elena. "I will hire you."

Elena turned to her.

"But I will only pay half the price she is paying."

Elena took a deep breath and sighed, "Okay." She reasoned that half of something was better than going home empty handed. Elena promised to return the next morning to get started.

Early the next day, Elena knocked on Maya's door.

Maya opened the door and peeked out, sleepy eyed. "I am not going. I can't." She held up her clean and delicate hands. "I don't think I can do that type of work."

Elena was disappointed; disappointed, but not surprised. She stayed positive. "I will bring you back a couple potatoes then." Elena left, having surmised what Maya was really thinking, that digging potatoes was beneath her, since her husband was an engineer. She recalled how Maya had her own garden filled with raspberries, and had shared them with Elena as inducement to get her to pick them for her, so she wouldn't have to get her own fingers dirty. Maya was obviously opposed to real work, no matter the circumstance.

Elena arrived to dig the potatoes for the farmer, just as she had promised. The woman showed Elena the field and where she should put the harvested potatoes, then left.

Elena worked all day without eating. When the sun was getting low, the farmer came to take an account of the harvest. Elena stood barefoot beside her pile of potatoes, a pile she estimated was more than ten-bushels-worth.

The farmer stared at the enormity of the pile. Her jaw dropped. She looked at Elena. Her hands and clothes were filthy. There was a big smudge of mud on one cheek. The woman smiled. "I bet you are hungry."

The farmer invited Elena into her house and got her cleaned up. Then she sat her at the kitchen table and fed her a large bowl of borsch. As they were eating together, Elena shared her concern, "I am so grateful for a chance to earn some food." She told the woman about her children and her need to work to provide for them. Elena drained her bowl. The woman refilled it.

Elena explained, "My husband...he is in the army. He was drafted and I do not know...with all this war going on...I do not know if I will ever see him again." Elena's body shook with repressed sobs.

After Elena had eaten her fill, the woman filled a sack with the potatoes as she had promised. She also gave Elena a liter of milk and told her, "If you come back again tomorrow, I will pay you full price."

Elena walked away, praising God for his provision.

The next day, Elena earned so many potatoes she could not carry them all. A few days later, she had harvested the entire crop. As Elena left, the farmer from across the road stopped her. That woman's potatoes were still in the ground, since Maya had never come. "Can I hire you?" she asked.

Elena stood proudly in her heels, feeling the weight of the sack slung over her shoulder. "Thank you for the offer, truly. But I think I have enough now." She walked away, grateful for God's blessing.

35

With the German occupation, it was impossible for Elena to earn her stipend as the wife of a soldier in the Red Army. So she sought out and was able to find sewing work, intent to earn enough to purchase staples like bread and butter. In the afternoon, she was in the living room, busy at her sewing machine.

Luba screamed and ran into the living room. Elena stood and stared at her daughter.

"Papa is in the kitchen!"

Elena dropped her sewing and ran into the next room. A man stood there, filthy, in rags, his face scratched with dried blood.

She flung her arms around him, pressing her head into his chest, squeezing him. She pushed back and looked up into his blue eyes, crying, "Is it you?"

"It is me." He cupped her cheeks with both hands and kissed her.

By now, the entire family had streamed in to see what was going on. They crowded and kissed him. Vitaliy was jumping up and down, squealing with glee. Elena stood by, clasping her hands to her heart, watching them reunite, still trying to believe it was real. *Yes. This is Arkadiy. My husband has returned!*

As he stood there, holding Vera, he began to explain what had happened. "I was told to go to Kharkov to join up with the others. On the way there, I decided to stop in and see if you and the children were still alive."

Elena took hold of Vera and corrected him. "You are *not* going to Kharkov." She handed the baby to Mother. "Germans are everywhere. They will take you prisoner. We need to let things quiet down a little, see what happens, then decide. But right now, I am *not* letting you leave."

She turned and looked more closely at his face. He hadn't shaved in days. There were scratches on his forehead then down his right cheek to his neck. She lifted the collar to get a better look at his cuts. They were black and oozing. He winced.

She looked into his eyes. She could read it. He was hurt bad.

Elena's instincts took over. "Let us get you cleaned up." She turned to Mother. "We need to be alone."

Mother took the kids, left the room and closed the door, leaving them alone.

Elena took hold of his lapel and gently peeled open the front of his jacket, watching his face, seeing him twinge with pain. Next was the shirt. This was more difficult. His back had been ripped by shrapnel. His untreated wounds were oozing. Some of the blood had dried. The filthy fabric was stuck to the scabs. She took a basin, filled it with water, dipped a towel, and used it to soften the fabric to be able to pull it off. She changed the water and dabbed his wounds over and over, as gently as she could, cleaning out the cuts, the gashes.

As she washed him, she silently agonized. *You suffered so much. But you are alive. Thank God! Though your flesh is torn, it will heal.* Elena's heart was aching. Her hands began to shake uncontrollably.

He turned to face her. She reached up and wiped the scratches on his neck then on his face. He studied her pretty face. Her brow was wrinkled with pain. Tears were streaming down her cheeks.

He stared into her eyes, wiped her tears with his fingers, and spoke softly. "You are right. I will not go to Kharkov. My place is here with you. I will *never* leave you again."

She silently nodded and took a deep breath to regain control of herself. Then confidently and tenderly, she finished dressing his wounds.

36

Elena kept Arkadiy inside the apartment, away from the curiosity of the neighbors. Outside, the German occupation had taken a firm hold. With time, his physical wounds healed, but he still had not spoken a word about what had happened or how he had been injured. Elena gave him the space to recover. She did not ask.

Late in the evening, he was sitting in the kitchen, staring out the window into the darkness. Elena came into the room. Everyone else was already in bed. "Would you like some tea?" she asked.

"Sure."

She put the water on the stove and sat down.

He turned from the window and stared at her. "Did I ever tell you how *beautiful* you are?"

She reached across the table and took his hand.

"I...I couldn't imagine not coming home."

She squeezed his hand.

He looked down, then lifted his face; it grew red. He looked up at the ceiling. Tears welled in his eyes. "I...I was given command of an artillery battalion." He kept looking away. "And they...the Germans...they had been bombing our position for days and days, a-and...and we sat there waiting and waiting for our chance...for our chance to fight, to shoot back, but the bombs kept *exploding* all around us." He caught his breath. "Fortunately, no one was hit or killed by the bombs, but many of them fell close. Four of them landed right in front of us and two more behind, *massive* explosions. M-my ears were ringing. I...I couldn't hear a thing, and there were clouds of smoke all around us and showers of dirt and sand raining down on us. And the looks on the faces of the men...well, I had never seen such *terror* in their eyes. W-we were expecting one of those bombs would land on our ordinance, and then we would all be goners.

"But then...then it got real quiet. The dust settled, and the smoke and haze began to lift, e-except for some of the trees and scrub that were on fire from the bombardment. The smoke curled up into where we were, burning our lungs. We huddled in our holes, coughing and choking until the fires burned themselves out.

"When the last of the smoke cleared, that was when we heard them...the panzers. I looked out over the field. There were so many tanks rolling toward us, I could not count, maybe a hundred, flanked by so many troops marching, holding their guns. A-and they were headed straight to where we were. So I ordered my men up out of their holes, to their guns, to fire at them."

Just then the kettle on the stove began to shriek.

Elena got up to fetch it. "Go ahead. I am listening."

He waited as she poured the tea, brought it to the table, and sat down. "So...so I gave the command to 'fire!' but none of the howitzers would shoot. I...I ran from gun to gun, yelling 'fire!' at my men, a-and they kept trying, b-but one of them said, 'Captain. My gun is full of sand.' I ran up and down the line, and everyone said the same thing...all the guns were full of sand.

"By this time, the Luftwaffe was screaming in over us, strafing us...hundreds, thousands of bullets raining down on us. The young soldier next to me was hit, then others all around me. One at a time, they fell, and the bullets never stopped...they never stopped. I fell over next to two of the bodies. Something exploded near me; I felt it hit me in the back. I lay there very still." He paused. "A half hour later, it was all over."

Arkadiy looked down at his teacup. He put both hands on it. "When I could not hear the tanks any longer, I finally looked up.

"There were bodies everywhere, bloody; none of them moving. I stood up and looked around. First, I looked off to the right, all along our position. Nothing was moving. I just saw bodies lying there. Then I turned to my left and saw the same thing, except there was one soldier standing there very still. He saw me and came to me. He...he was a private. It was his first week in the army. So we decided that we had better find our troops and join up with them. Unfortunately, we did not encounter any. So that meant we had to make our way to Kharkov.

"After that, we decided to hide in the day and crawl along at night. There were Germans near us. I could hear them talking. I understood what they were saying, so I could figure out what direction they were headed so that we could avoid them. Some nights, we slept in open fields, hidden among the grain. Other nights, we slept in barns and begged for food. One elderly man gave me an outfit and an empty grain sack to hide my uniform.

"And so by the grace of God, I made it home."

He looked at her straight-faced and picked up his tea. He drained it and set his cup down.

"Would you like more?" she asked.

"No, thanks." He stared into the empty cup. "I am done now."

She put her hand on his.

37

Another month into the German occupation, the reality that the invaders were going to stay sank in with the Ukrainians. Tensions eased on both sides. The occupiers had largely eliminated the resistance, and the occupied only wanted to be able to live. To live, they had to eat.

The scarcity of food continued to be a problem for Elena's family. Their best hope, it seemed, was to try and find another place where they could dig potatoes. Elena and Arkadiy both went out to see what opportunity they could find. By then, however, all the private farms had been picked clean.

Late in the day they were discouraged, having found nothing. Before they turned home, they decided to pray for guidance and for provision. On their way back, they passed by several collective farms. At one, there was a German troop truck parked by the side of the road. Two armed soldiers were standing by it, chatting with each other.

Arkadiy whispered to Elena, "I have an idea." She looked at him, wide-eyed. He jogged ahead and went straight up to the men. The soldiers saw him coming and raised their rifles, wary of trouble.

Arkadiy slowed. He addressed them in a friendly tone, "*Wie gehts?*"

The soldiers looked at him, startled.

Arkadiy glanced up at the blue sky. It was a warm day for December. "*Schöner tag, ja?*"

One soldier turned his gun to the side. He nodded tentatively. *"Ja."*

The other shifted his weight and nodded.

"Sie brauchen jemanden, kartoffeln zu holen?" Arkadiy's German accent was flawless.

The two looked at each other. One answered, *"Die kartoffeln sind noch im boden."*

"Uh..." He turned and pointed at Elena before he continued. She had been watching him from afar, worried what sort of trouble he might get them both into. Yet she knew he spoke German perfectly. His mother was born in Germany, full-blooded German; she had raised him to speak both languages. Elena studied her husband and the soldiers from the distance, oblivious to what they were talking about.

Arkadiy continued to speak with the soldiers, animated, leaning forward, using his hands. They responded in a friendly fashion, smiling, looking at each other, nodding. One of them even set the butt end of his rifle down on the ground and leaned back against the truck.

At last, they seemed to have completed their negotiations.

"Gut. Zehrgut!" said Arkadiy as he turned toward Elena, then back to them. *"Wir werden morgen wieder...in ordnung?"*

The two looked at each other. *"Ja. In ordnung."*

"Gut...gut. Danke." He bowed and turned to walk away. *"Guten abend,"* he said as he waved.

They both smiled and waved. *"Guten abend."*

Arkadiy walked back confidently to Elena and whispered, "Let's go."

When they were a confidential distance away from the men, Elena's curiosity erupted. "What was that?"

Arkadiy put his arm around her and grinned. "I got us a job tomorrow: picking potatoes for the Germans."

* * *

Elena and Arkadiy were able to harvest potatoes at that collective farm for the entire week. Each day, Arkadiy spent time chatting with the soldiers, treating them like they were old friends. In return, they acted very kindly.

On the last day, the commanding German officer, a lieutenant, showed up to receive the crop. He stood by and watched as the soldiers loaded the bushel baskets onto the truck. Arkadiy and Elena were standing at a distance, putting their portion into sacks, making ready to carry them home.

The lieutenant saw them and yelled in their direction, "*Bitte. Komen sie hier!*" He waved at Arkadiy, beckoning him to come.

Elena remained while he ran over to speak with him.

In a few minutes he jogged back over, smiling. "They are going to give us a ride."

They picked up their sacks and carried them over to the truck. One of the soldiers helped Elena climb up and into the back. Arkadiy was invited to ride up in the front with the lieutenant.

When they arrived at the apartment, they got out and unloaded the potatoes. Arkadiy was beaming as they carried their haul into the apartment.

"What?" she asked, trying to understand him.

"I got a new job in Kiev."

"Kiev?"

"Yes. They need carpentry help, renovating a building that had been bombed. They want to turn it into a grocery store."

"Really?"

"And that is not all. They have a new apartment for us right across the street."

"No!" She beamed.

"Other Ukrainians are to be put to work on the project. They need me to be their translator and supervisor."

* * *

Arkadiy and Elena's new apartment was just a block from the main market in the heart of Kiev. It was in a grand-looking multifamily building, previously occupied by the well-to-do. Their unit was on the second floor. The German officers in charge of the occupation of Kiev also lived there. In the basement was a kitchen where all their meals were cooked by master chefs.

Arkadiy took Elena upstairs and opened the door to the apartment to let her see it for the first time. Filled with anticipation, Elena stepped into the vestibule, greeted there by the smell of fresh paint. The unit had been recently renovated, and the sound of construction told her that more work was underway in the buildings all around. She stood a moment drinking it all in, the high ceilings, ample light. Large double doors greeted her ahead, to the left and to the right, leading to the other rooms. To the right was a bedroom, ahead was the living room, and to the left was the dining room.

She stepped ahead into the living room. Beyond it, to the outside, was a balcony that overlooked the front courtyard. Turning to her left was the entrance to a second, larger bedroom. She worked her way back through the vestibule and into the dining room. She continued from there into the immense kitchen. Off the kitchen to her left was a second balcony that faced into the backyard. On the other side of the kitchen was a corridor that led to more rooms. The spaces were filled with tools, ladders, and paint buckets.

Arkadiy explained, "This passage and extra rooms used to be part of another apartment, but now this is also ours." He pointed into one of the rooms. "They are making this into a full bath." He walked down the hall. "Here are two more bedrooms."

Elena needed to understand it more. She turned and walked back through all the rooms again, trying to absorb it, coming to the realization that this entire unit was exclusively for her family. She had never lived in such a large space, and the appointments were simply beautiful. The colors throughout were pleasant cream-colored walls. Tall windows ran nearly floor to ceiling, bringing in plenty of light. The large living room had pastel patterns painted on the walls up high, above the chandelier and below the decorative crown molding. The carved wood doors, the wide moldings, the ceilings, all this gave a sense of quality, even grandeur.

She asked Arkadiy, "And what about this furniture?"

"Left by the former tenant. It is ours if you want it."

Elena's eyes widened. She walked a third time through the rooms to study the furnishings more carefully. The pieces were like new, many exquisite, much nicer than the handmade pieces they had in Irkutsk. She could hardly believe it.

In one bedroom, there was a large double bed, a nightstand, a desk and chair, and a medicine cabinet made of ebony with mother-of-pearl and brass inlays. The living room had a round ebony table with six chairs, a brown leather sofa, and a shelf on the back of it with a row of various sized marble elephants marching along it, arranged from the largest at one end to the smallest at the other. Against one wall stood a chaise lounge, beside it a baroque floor-to-ceiling mirror with wide gilded frame. There were several small occasional tables with vases of flowers and art objects in the room. Against another wall was an armoire with a mirror in the middle. Next to this stood an upright piano and stool.

"Now Luba can have lessons!"

The dining room had a long ebony table with twelve chairs. Above its center hung a splendid crystal chandelier. There were two china cabinets yet filled with pretty dishes. In one corner stood a beautiful green ceramic-tiled stove that stretched from floor to ceiling, which, due to its central location, heated the whole of the apartment.

She could hardly believe this was her new home.

Arkadiy and Elena spent the next week arranging the furniture and acquiring the rest of what they would need, including some lovely hand-embroidered rugs to soften the hardwood floors. With Arkadiy's new job and his connections with the Germans, they were able to obtain the rest of what they needed. By week's end, they had moved in.

38

When the renovations to the grocery store were complete, the Germans needed someone to run it. They knew that Arkadiy was fully fluent in the German language, but they also saw he was trustworthy, that he was very effective in motivating the Ukrainian workforce, and that he solved problems. Placing Arkadiy in charge of the store became for them an easy decision.

The new position required that he first hire all the staff he would need to perform the many tasks at the store. By this time, he and Elena had been attending a local church, which happened to have many capable workers, each in desperate need of a job. So he employed a good number of these to fill out his staff of cashiers, stock boys, guards, and buyers. Arkadiy also now had access to trucks for shipping produce, which he was generously permitted to use to deliver construction materials to help restore the church building. With the opening of the store and others like it throughout the region, food became widely available. The starvation period came to an end.

Because Arkadiy was the only one who could speak both Russian and German, he had to be at the store all the time—there to keep things running smoothly, to solve communication problems that could pop up at a moment's notice. He necessarily wound up working many hours. Yet this immense responsibility also came with the privilege that he could take home anything he needed for his family. He and Elena began to enjoy a true sense of luxury.

As an employee of the Third Reich, Arkadiy was able to obtain new papers, taking advantage of his interaction with the high-ranking German officials. He exchanged his Soviet passport, which had listed him as German with Russian citizenship, for a new German passport. This gave him and his family full rights and privileges under the laws of Deutschland.

When the bedrooms and new bath were completed, the family was able to spread out more. Akulina (grandmother Babusia) and Vera, then a toddler, moved into one of the bedrooms. Nadia, a live-in maid, occupied the other bedroom. She was hired to clean, do laundry, and help in the kitchen.

Once Vera started to walk, she became the family's center of attention. She was naturally adorable: tiny, yet full of life. Her hair was blond, like gold and full of tight curls; and her face had rosy cheeks. She was such a happy child. As she became more mobile, she ran along a path through the apartment, starting at one balcony then across through the living room and vestibule, into the kitchen to the other balcony, giggling as she went. Then she would reverse course and do it all over again, burning off an endless amount of energy.

To add to the family's entertainment, Vera would grab things as she ran, only to drop them off the balcony. Each yell of "No!" from her onlookers made her giggle louder and run ever faster. It was a great game, a game she gleefully made everyone else join in with her. She found a pair of shoes. Those would go over the rail. Toys, she dropped them too. Towels and dishes, those were gone. When finally she grabbed and dropped an iron. Everyone watched, aghast.

"Someone could get killed!" Luba screamed.

Elena put an end to the game after that. All loose items were placed high and out of Vera's reach. And Vera was put on full-time watch.

* * *

During the renovation and restoration of their apartment complex, building materials were left in the backyard court, an area where Luba and Vitaliy played with the neighboring children. There was a pile of lime there, and the children pretended it was flour, using it for imaginary cooking projects.

One day, Luba was carrying a cup with lime, and another child pushed her. She fell over and the lime splashed in her eyes. Immediately, it started to burn. They found some water and splashed it on her face, trying to wash it out. But when the lime got wet, it did even more harm.

Luba stood, screaming, "Mama! Mama!"

Elena came running.

"My eyes! My eyes!"

Elena acted fast. She doused Luba's face with water, rinsing it over and over again. She cradled Luba in her arms and ran to the doctor as fast as she could, an old famous doctor, an eye specialist who had his office nearby.

The doctor examined Luba. He cleaned her eyes out as best he could. By this time, Luba's eyes were swollen shut and red. She couldn't see a thing.

He pried her lids open and shined in his light. "These are badly burned. I don't know if you will ever see again, young lady." Seeing her fear, her sobbing, he placed his hand on her little shoulder. "But I will take care of you the best I can." He put in some drops to soothe her pain.

He handed a bottle of eye drops to Elena. "Put these in three times a day. And I want to see her every week."

Elena continued the regimen faithfully each day, offering up her prayers. Little by little, Luba's sight returned. When at last she made a full recovery, the doctor declared it a miracle. Elena knew Luba's recovery was only made possible by the grace of God.

After this, Elena and Arkadiy realized they needed help to watch the children. Elena hired a governess, Fräulein Schmidt, a friend from church and a former German teacher. Elena and Arkadiy wanted Luba and Vitaliy to learn German, learn words, how to count, how to read and write.

The fräulein came early each morning and left late at night, after the children were in bed. During the day, she took them for walks in the park nearby. She brought along her own three children and watched them all as they played together outside and in the fresh air. During their time together, she spoke to them only in German. She taught them good manners and etiquette and showed them how to behave in the German culture.

Every time the local evangelical church was open for services, Arkadiy and Elena went there with their young family. Luba and Vitaliy were able to walk the distance, while Arkadiy would carry Vera. When they got near the church, some young people would be happily waiting to take Vera to care for her during the service. As the family became more engaged with the church, they made many good friends, inviting them to their apartment for social visits. Elena joined the choir and sang during the worship services. Even two-year-old Vera became involved, learning certain short Bible verses and able to recite them from memory.

When Christmas came, Arkadiy secretly decorated the living room while the children slept. When he finished, he left the door to their bedroom open so that when they awoke, they could see a tree beautifully decorated and a table full of presents. They ran out into the room in the early morning, shouting with excitement, while he sat by smiling, drinking in their joy.

In the meantime, their young family was growing. On March 9, 1943, Elena gave birth to a boy, Valeriy Arkadiyevich Bondar. Now with a family of four children and seeing the older ones mature, Elena hired a friend, Tatyana Pavlovna, to come and teach Luba how to play the piano. They paid her in the same way that they compensated all their help: with food from the grocery store. Paper money was worthless.

A few weeks later, Arkadiy repeated his decoration of the apartment for Easter, putting presents out for the children. Then at Pentecost, he placed fresh cut birch trees in the corners of the living room and lined the floor with reeds. Arkadiy loved the holidays and took great joy in giving gifts to his children.

He and Elena were busy throughout these times making good memories and establishing traditions that their children would long remember. They took full advantage of this peace and prosperity, not knowing how long it would last or how quickly things could change.

39

In late August, the Russian military launched an offensive to wrest back the Soviet territory from the Germans. Only a month before, the Germans, in their last attempt to push farther east, had suffered a devastating defeat at the battle of Kursk, two years now into their war to conquer the Soviets. The tide of war had turned.

In September, the planning, equipping, and resolve of the Russians became apparent to the occupiers: they were coming back to Kiev, and they were not to be stopped. By the fifteenth, the bombing had been going on for a week. The Germans made their decision then to retreat.

The Russian Air Force dropped pamphlets in the neighborhoods, making it known that anyone found to have aided the Germans would be shot. The Soviets had a name for these traitors: they called them the "Volksdeutsch." Arkadiy was a Volksdeutsch.

He and Elena were faced with the hard question. *What to do?* Should they stay and remain loyal to their Russian heritage, with the possibility of being turned in and shot? Or should they retreat with the enemy, the occupiers, the Germans? The decision to leave was their only real choice. Arkadiy would surely have been considered a deserter, a traitor, with no shortage of local Russian citizens to testify against him.

Arkadiy had much support among the German leadership, which made them feel better about leaving their native country. But he and Elena wondered how much of their family would be able to go with them. All the decisions had to be made quickly. The Russian army was less than twenty kilometers away, nearing the east bank of the Dnieper River, making preparations to cross.

The Germans made fast arrangements to remove their troops by train, allowing the refugee families to accompany them. Each family was permitted to bring along just one suitcase. The intent was to pack eighty refugees into each railway carriage. These were not passenger cars; these were boxcars.

Herr Krakow, Arkadiy's boss and the German civilian official, was very kind to him. He allowed Arkadiy to have an entire railcar to himself for his family, relatives, and friends. He also permitted him to take food provisions from the warehouses, including barrels with flour, sugar, melted butter (which doesn't spoil), sauerkraut, pickles, salted herring, salted bacon, dry sausages and salami, cheeses, cookies, macaroni, rice preserves, jars with fruit compote, dry fruit, and many other items. The length of the journey was uncertain, and food would surely be a necessity.

There was little time to pack. On the evening of September 23, the Germans gave the order that the train would be leaving the next morning at 7:00 a.m. Arkadiy and a carpenter friend hastily assembled wooden crates for Elena to pack some of their things. They worked all night, nonstop. As they labored, they listened to the unceasing echoes of bombs exploding in the city. The electricity was out, so they used candles and worked by the light of the moon. Before the sun came up, they loaded the crates, two suitcases, an old chest, and all the warehouse goods into their boxcar. They also brought along pillows, blankets, sheets, and Elena's sewing machine. She could not imagine life without it.

By sunrise, the cars all up and down the tracks had been loaded with people, most of them in a panic; many children were crying. Arkadiy loaded his car with his family and friends. These included Elena, Luba, Vitaliy, Vera, Valeriy, and Babusia (Akulina); Elena's sister Pana Rukasuyeva and her two children, Zoya and Eugene; Arkadiy's mother, Olga (whom the children called "Omama") and stepfather, Georgiy ("Opa"); Arkadiy's aunts: Lidia and Olga, with their families; Arkadiy's cousin, Galina Fedorenko; some friends from church, Dr. Maria Ivanovna Oliver with her husband, Valentin with his wife Marta and their children; and Potapov and Bogdanov, two brothers in Christ, men who had preached on Sundays. There were thirty people in their car. Most were believers, and they took time together to thank God for giving them the night, one last night, to prepare, to pack food, and to get everyone safely on board.

At 7:00 a.m., the train sat in its place. The bombing had damaged part of the station. Nothing could move. The smell of smoke was everywhere. Arkadiy's car was hitched to a military car to its front, a car that was stockpiled with barrels of fuel. He and everyone with him sat in their car and huddled together, listening to the sounds of planes flying overhead and bombs exploding all around them, afraid to step outside, and expecting the train would leave at a moment's notice. While they waited, they knew that if a bomb landed on that fuel, they would all be dead, either from fire or explosion. All day they sat there.

When evening came, they closed the car doors. Potapov and Bogdanov opened their Bibles to read to them by flashlight. They all prayed together and sang songs, encouraged one another, and turned their hearts away from fear, away from the thoughts of death that surrounded them. They were grateful for how God was protecting them.

Throughout the night, they continued to wait as the bombs kept on falling. Still, the train did not move.

By morning, the gray of the sky turned from smoke into clouds. It started to rain and the sound of the planes faded into the distance. The train gave a sudden tug and began to move, though very slowly. They pulled west out of Kiev and into a dense forest. There the train stopped.

Arkadiy and several of the men in their car jumped out and went ahead to find out what was causing the delay. They came back and reported that guerrillas had been hiding in the trees and had attacked the train ahead of theirs. They had thrown mines at the passing cars, which had caused one to derail. Some of the passengers had been killed.

A while later, their train began to move again, now advancing at the speed of a turtle. Many times, it came to a stop. Many times, there were delays before it would get going again. Each time, they found out that some act of sabotage, mines and bombs, had destroyed the tracks, or that there had been grenades thrown or gunfire from the woods. The people in Arkadiy's car never ceased giving prayers for protection and thanksgiving to God for keeping them safe.

Under normal circumstances, the five-hundred-kilometer trip west into Poland would have taken less than a day, but the delays and downtimes were endless. Hours turned into days. Days extended into a week, and the train had made little forward progress. As they stayed cooped up in their car, they were grateful for their planning, grateful they had food and water.

But then there were the necessary issues of human life. There were no bathroom stops along the way. Elena hung some sheets in a corner of the car and a pail became their toilet. Whenever the train came to a stop to make repairs to the railroad, they opened the doors to get fresh air and to empty the pail.

There was also the issue of hygiene. Though they had plenty of water for drinking, they conserved it exclusively for that purpose, not knowing how long their trip would take. They dare not waste it to wash their bodies. So as they rode along with the doors closed, their combined smell became insufferable. They all stank, and there was nothing they could do about it. The one bright spot was that little Valeriy, at the remarkable age of seven months, became potty trained.

The stops and delays continued. Observers were posted on the engine, there to look ahead. They studied the tracks for booby traps and kept their eyes open for saboteurs. A number of times, the engineer stopped just before striking a mine.

After a month, the train finally crossed the border into Poland. Though they had suffered through their stench, they realized that they had luxury in their boxcar of thirty, compared with the cars behind them packed with nearly three times that many people. They were grateful for the food and grateful no one had lice.

When they pulled into the train yard, their boxcar was detached from the train and attached to another. No one explained why this had happened or how their course may have changed. When they finally started to move again, they immediately came to another stop and waited while the tracks ahead were repaired from yet another act of sabotage.

When they resumed, they passed by their first train that was now lying beside the tracks, cars overturned and crushed one into another. It had hit a mine and derailed. Everyone onboard had been killed.

As they passed by the remnants of the cars, seeing the bodies strewn beside the tracks, Marta, who was not a Christian, sat by the door looking out. She stared at the carnage, holding her hand to her mouth. She spun away and cried, "God is the only one that has protected us thus far. I have seen his work." She placed her hands on her heart. "If we are still alive when we get to Germany, I want to be baptized and be a believer too."

Elena embraced her, remembering how the Israelites had been rescued from their slavery in Egypt, taken through the Red Sea, and then only a few weeks later, turned to worship the golden calf. "I hope you will never forget this day and what you are saying. When times are good, you may forget. You must trust in God in good times and in bad. In him, you will never be disappointed."

Their first planned stop was in Lodz, Poland, at a transit camp. Everyone continuing on to Germany had to be processed there, their paperwork prepared for entry. Next was the disinfecting, in order to not bring disease or bugs into Germany. Each of them was sprayed with a white, stinky powder and sent to the showers for cleansing. Then they were dispatched to the bunkrooms.

That night, some of them learned what bedbugs were. They awoke with red itchy bumps all over their bodies. In the morning, Omama and Luba exchanged horror stories about their restless nights. One of the locals said, "You obviously have sweet blood." The rest of their group escaped the bedbugs.

On Sunday, Babusia stayed home with the children, while all the adults went to a Baptist church in the city to worship and give thanks. After their escape, there was no doubt in the mind of anyone that had been in Arkadiy's car that it had been God that had protected them.

40

Before the end of October, they were sent north to a refugee camp in Gilgenburg, Prussia (Dąbrówno, Poland). The camp was set up with row upon row of wooden barracks, hastily improvised quarters that had been erected on the shores of a stunning, pristine lake, a lake that was more than a kilometer wide and seven kilometers long. The land all around them was farmed, open fields as far as the eye could see.

The barracks were a straightforward design, long gabled structures with a center hall that was flanked by twenty-six small bedrooms on each side. The refugees were packed into these, each according to family size. Arkadiy's family was given two rooms. One was for him and Elena, Vera, Valeriy, and Babusia. Directly across the hall was one for Omama, Opa, Luba, and Vitaliy. Pana and her family received their own separate room.

The rooms were small, meant mainly for sleeping, so the refugees spent most of their time outdoors, enjoying the fresh air and taking in the views. The lake was yet warm from the end of summer, so for a short time, they were able to swim and bathe.

Shortly after the refugees filled the camp at Gilgenburg, a string of illnesses assaulted the children. Luba and Vitaliy ate something and got very ill with jaundice. They were put into the camp hospital where they stayed for a couple weeks. They enjoyed good care there from a nurse, Schwester (Sister) Elsa, who was very kind to them. When she was off duty, she played the accordion and sang to entertain the children, even played games with them.

One windy day, Elena went to visit. She took Vera with her, sheltering her in her jacket, holding her close, and believing this was sufficient protection for the short run to the hospital. But the next day, Vera had a very high temperature. The doctors said she had pneumonia. Elena took her to see her good friend, Dr. Maria Ivanovna Oliver, who had escaped with them from Kiev and was now at work in the hospital. Dr. Oliver was a specialist, a skilled paramedic. Knowing pneumonia was highly contagious, she suggested that Elena watch her in the barracks and indicated she would take her under her personal care, check in on her from time to time. Dr. Oliver showed Elena how to make warm compresses, which would help her little lungs to recover, and told her to take Vera down to the beach during the day so that she could get fresh air. Elena observed that whenever she took her there, that she did not cough as much, benefitting from the moist air. Elena was glad to be taking care of her daughter by herself, as there were terrible reports coming from the hospital that many of the children were dying there due to a shortage of help. There was also a common belief that the German nurses cared first and foremost for the German children, all at the expense of the refugees. Vera was sick for weeks, but she finally did get better.

While she was recovering, Valeriy contracted small pox and had to be taken to the hospital. Since he was a very little boy, Elena was allowed to stay with him in an isolation room. Dr. Oliver came to watch him at night to relieve Elena so she could catch a few hours sleep. This personal care was strictly forbidden, but Dr. Oliver was fast becoming a wonderful friend. Valeriy got well and returned to the barracks.

Next came the measles. Every child in the camp came down with it. Those that were sent to the hospital did not get well. All of them died. Elena worked with Dr. Oliver in confidence to keep her children's illness a secret from those in the barracks, caring for them in their beds. Each of Elena's children recovered.

Then came the whooping cough, which raged through the camp. Babusia, Omama, and Aunt Pana all took turns to stay with each sick child and to take them to the lake for fresh air. Hiding the sound of their coughs away from the other refugees kept them from the death sentence of being sent to the hospital. Elena's children survived this ordeal too.

Then came endless diarrheas in the camp, which affected both young and old. Many died. Elena had a remedy for diarrhea and other stomach ailments: polyn (wormwood). It had a powerful effect for anyone that took it. Within a couple days, the discomfort and stomach pain subsided. The hard part was getting it down; it was a bitter herb with a terrible taste. A cube of sugar taken right after made it less awful. After it was proven to work in her family, Elena passed on her knowledge to others in the barracks, and many recovered because of this remedy. This is how Elena became known around the camp as "Dr. Bondar."

When the onslaught of sicknesses at last subsided, Luba, who was now seven, began to attend a school that had been set up in the camp. She was enrolled in the second grade. This was her first encounter with school.

As 1943 drew to its conclusion, the family took time to celebrate Christmas. Everyone stood beside the lake as they sang hymns together and prayed. They all were there: Arkadiy, Elena, Luba, Vitaliy, Vera, Valeriy, Babusia, Omama, Opa, Pana, Zoya, Eugene, Lidia, Olga, Galina, and with Potapov, Bogdanov, Dr. Oliver, and their new friends Octaviy and Roswita. They raised their voices in song, remembering the birth of their Savior, ever grateful they could all be there together.

41

When winter came, the sicknesses continued, this time the chicken pox. It started with Luba, then Vitaliy, and then Vera. But Vera's chicken pox did not show up on her skin. It went into her body, and her lungs became very weak. Vera's chicken pox lasted more than a month. But Elena saw that God protected her once again and she survived. When the weather began to warm, Vera at last became strong. The attacks of illnesses subsided.

By March, the Russians had retaken Leningrad from the Germans and pushed the battle lines back through much of Belarus and the Ukraine. Meanwhile, the German war machine had suffered defeat on other fronts, with the loss of North Africa and the Allied invasion of Italy. In response, the Germans began to pull some of their people out of Prussia and Poland, taking them back to the Fatherland, where they could help the war effort by laboring in the factories.

With the coming of spring, the decision was made to move the refugees at Gilgenburg to the west and into Germany. The Bondar family, the Rukasuyev family, Potapov, and Bogdanov were transferred west by train one thousand kilometers, passing through the heart of the Third Reich to Dahlerbrück, Westfalia, Germany.

There, Arkadiy was put in charge of the work camp, the Ost Arbeiter ("East Workers"). That responsibility did not last very long. His honesty flew straight into the unforeseen teeth of corruption. Arkadiy was aware of the laws written for the protection of foreign workers, the "Orders for Auslander." So he demanded good living conditions and decent meals for all the workers, insisting that the rations belonging to the workers be delivered directly to the kitchen. Unfortunately, the officials higher than Arkadiy had previously been sidetracking the goods and selling them on the black market, lining their own pockets while the workers starved. When they saw that Arkadiy had been intervening and properly directing the flow of food, they called him in for a meeting. They ordered him to stop causing trouble, or he would "find himself in an unpleasant situation." Arkadiy resigned from that position.

He found replacement work right away at a nearby factory, Carl Falkenroth Söhne. They manufactured all sorts of hand tools at their plant in the neighboring village of Schalksmühle. He brought with him a number of good workers from Ost Arbeiter.

On Sundays, Arkadiy and his family sought out a place to worship. When they first arrived in Dahlerbrück, they attended Evangelische Kirche, where services were held in the German language. But a short time later, many more refugees arrived in Schalksmühle. These were laborers from the east: Polish, Ukrainian, and Russian laborers. Most were Evangelical Baptists. Feeling more comfortable with the Russian language, the Bondars started worshipping with these newcomers. They made many good friends with these families and individuals, including the Lewczuks, Gordieyevs, Berkutas, Paul Bajko, Kolesnichenko, and others.

At the end of March 1945, the Allied forces stood on the western border of Germany and prepared to cross the Rhine, intending to overrun the heart of the country and bring an end to the war. The Americans, under Generals Patton and Bradley, crossed the river south of Cologne, while the British, under General Montgomery, crossed north of Düsseldorf, leaving a stronghold of resistance between them known as the "Ruhr Pocket." The two Allied armies met up with each other to the west of the pocket on April 1, having surrounded an area of some seven thousand square kilometers, an area still occupied by the German Army. In the center of the pocket was Dahlerbrück.

By April 4, when the American Ninth Army to the north of the pocket fell back under the control of General Omar Bradley, the German will to fight had collapsed. The Allies' plan to surround the German stronghold, rather than assault it directly, had proved to be a strategy that saved many lives on both sides. The next move by the Ninth Army, southward into the villages and towns, was largely unopposed.

For weeks, the people in Dahlerbrück had been watching the Allied planes circle overhead as they returned north and bombed the major German industrial center in Hagen, a scant fifteen kilometers to their north. Several bombs also fell in Dahlerbrück and Schalksmühle. But in early April, the word filtered into the camp that all Westfalia had been surrounded.

Seeing that the war was lost, all industry in the German villages stopped, the German military scattered, and the entire region descended into anarchy. Refugees from the camps, desperate for food, pillaged the stores. The scene was utter chaos.

But the local senior citizen leaders of the towns soon wrested back control. The Germans were a proud people, a citizenry that would not tolerate the looting and rioting. Some sense of order was thus restored as they waited to be occupied by the unstoppable enemy, the victorious Allies.

On April 14, a battalion of American soldiers rode into Dahlerbrück without firing a shot. On seeing them coming, the German officials waved the white flag of surrender. Those in charge of the labor camps and factories and any of the German soldiers remaining (those that had not yet deserted) were rounded up and put into makeshift prisoner of war camps, huge open fields that were hastily enclosed by barbed wire. Meanwhile, the Americans seized control of the factory where Arkadiy had been working. He and all those with him were now officially unemployed. Arkadiy, Elena and their family were under the control of the American Army.

Two weeks later, on the banks of the Mulde River north of Leipzig, the American ground troops made first contact with the Russians, who had been advancing from the east. Finally, on May 8, the Germans surrendered. The war was over.

Shortly after, Russian officers started visiting the refugee camps, looking for former Soviet citizens and prisoners of the war, intending to return them to Russia, a right they had been granted at Yalta. They spread messages to their former comrades, propaganda, about how wonderful their life could be if they were to return to the USSR and how glad their fellow citizens would be to see them come home. Many refugees were truly lonely for their homeland and their families left behind, so they agreed to return. Thus began a period of repatriation.

A great number of those that did not volunteer to return were taken away by force. Russian military arrived and grabbed individuals, forced them into trucks, and sent them back to Russia. Some resisted being taken and were shot trying to escape. They knew they would be mistreated by the Russians, sentenced to years in the labor camps in Siberia, even executed. Some refugees committed suicide rather than be taken back. Word of forced repatriation filtered through the refugee camps and eventually to Dahlerbrück.

In late July, a caravan of the Russian military arrived at Dahlerbrück. They met with the American command and reviewed the rosters of refugees, looking for Soviet citizens on their blacklist and any other Russian surnames. They sent officers through the barracks to gather and lead them away. Arkadiy, Opa, and others of the Russian men saw they had come and stayed away from the camp.

In the afternoon, the Russians came to Elena's building. She heard a knock on her door and opened it to look out.

A Russian officer stood there. He removed his hat and smiled. "Good afternoon, I am Lieutenant Filippov." He glanced down at a clipboard and continued, "I am looking for the Bondar family."

"I am a Bondar."

He craned his neck and looked into the room. "Is your husband here?"

She glanced over her shoulder. "No."

He pressed his way past her, through the doorway. He looked at everyone there: Babusia, Omama, Pana, and all their children. He clenched his jaw. "Where is he?"

"He is at work."

"And where does he work?"

Elena thought quickly. "He does all sort of odd jobs. It is never the same thing. I am not really sure where he is today." She raised her hands. "We are refugees."

He dropped his clipboard to his side and stared at her, biting his lips. "All right then." He swept his hand in a big circle toward the door. "Then get everyone up, and we will go."

Elena's mouth dropped open. "You know we are German citizens." She picked up her papers and handed them to him.

He glanced at them only briefly and handed them back. "Once a Russian, always a Russian."

She took them back, thought a second. "Well, we certainly cannot go *now*."

He stiffened and glared at her.

"Can't you see I am in no condition to travel?" Elena was eight months pregnant. She looked down at her enormous stomach and placed both hands there for emphasis.

He glanced down, then looked up, blushing. He looked in her eyes and swallowed hard.

"Only after I deliver my baby, only after I am well, then the entire family will be able to return to our beloved Russia." She fixed her eyes on his and waited.

He raised his clipboard and drummed his fingers on the names. While he studied them, his eyes moved back and forth. He looked back at her and sighed. "All right. I understand." He put his hat on and left the room.

Elena realized she had just been given a chance.

That evening, Elena and Arkadiy met with Peter Gordieyev, a dear refugee friend who was in charge of the paperwork at the camp office. They shared their concern with him, concern they could be abducted.

Peter nodded. "The Polish refugees are being moved to a new camp in Lüdenscheid tomorrow morning. I can put you on that truck if you would like?"

They agreed. Early the next morning, the entire Bondar and Rukasuyev families were loaded on a truck with other Polish refugees and driven east to the German town of Lüdenscheid.

That evening, a group of Russian soldiers stormed the barracks of the camp at Dahlerbrück. They worked their way brusquely from room to room, dragging refugees from their beds, shuffling them outside. There were screams heard up and down the halls.

Lieutenant Filippov came to the door of Elena's room. Two soldiers stood beside him, anxiously gripping their rifles. He placed his hand on the knob, threw it open, and burst into the room.

The beds were empty. No baggage. No clothing. No people.

He clenched his fists. He turned to his soldiers and seethed.

He'd been had!

42

A month after their escape to their new camp, on August 26, Elena gave birth to her fifth child, a daughter. They named her Nadiezda (Nadia for short), which means "hope." Their three daughters now were named "Faith" (Vera), "Hope" (Nadia), and "Love" (Luba).

In Lüdenscheid, Arkadiy and Elena found many other believers among the Polish refugees. They conducted Bible studies with them in their quarters during the week and gathered each Sunday for worship in a large room on the first floor of their barracks. In mid-September, American missionaries visited the camp to minister to the refugees and organized a conference for all to attend.

Arkadiy and Elena had always invited visitors up to their room for fellowship and refreshments. In this camp, they had two rooms. One was a bedroom for all eight; the other they used for living and dining. There was a small stove there where they cooked their meals. Opa and Omama now had their own room on a different floor.

As the conference was planned, it was decided that Elena and Arkadiy would host the missionaries for a meal. Arkadiy went shopping to find something special for the guests and came home with a bushel of cranberries. Babusia agreed to make them into kisiel, a cranberry cobbler, for the desert.

When Sunday morning came, Akulina put all the ingredients in a large pot, a twenty-five-liter bucket: the water, sugar, potato starch, and cranberries. She brought this mix to a boil on top of the stove, then removed it from the heat and set it down on the floor to cool. She placed it beside the water bucket, the same size and type of pot. She left it there and went downstairs with Arkadiy and the older children to go to church.

Meanwhile, Elena was still in the bedroom, needing to nurse Nadia and finish dressing Vera before the three of them could go downstairs and join the others. As the weather was getting cooler, Elena put an extra layer of clothing on Vera, who was quite small for her age and never a good eater (she had been "living" on cucumbers): first tights, then a pretty dress. She combed Vera's hair, so she was all ready to go. Then Elena sat down on the bed to nurse the baby.

Vera asked, "Mommy. Can I get a drink of water?"

There was no sink in the room, just a bucket of water and a cup that they kept in the living area. The bucket was tall, but she could get water for herself by using a little step-stool that they kept there. Elena said, "Of course." This was routine. Vera left the room.

Seconds later, Elena heard Vera screaming. She ran from the room and saw Vera on the floor, coated head to foot in kisiel; the pot sat sideways beside her. She had tumbled off her stool, arms first into the wrong bucket. Then while trying to escape, she had dumped it all over herself.

Elena put Nadia down on the floor and grabbed Vera. The hot gooey kisiel was all over her body, burning her head to foot. Elena tried to rip the clothing off her, but every piece was stuck to her skin, continuing to burn. She grabbed a pair of scissors and cut off as much as she could. But by the time she had gotten it off, the damage had been done.

Elena ran downstairs and grabbed Arkadiy. They came back, gathered Vera, and ran her to the hospital.

There the doctor assessed Vera's condition. "She has first-, second-, and third-degree burns all over her body." He took Elena and Arkadiy aside. "I don't know if she will survive, and if she does, she may never be able to use her arms." They had been burned to the bones. "We don't have much staff here and really no medicines for burn victims, especially small children." Vera was not yet five. "You would be better off to care for her yourselves." He saw the concern weighing heavy on their faces. "I will show you what to do, and I will stop in to see her."

The doctor dressed Vera's wounds, and then gave them ointment and a few bandages. They would need more.

He showed them how to prepare sterile dressings and then explained the protocol for changing them. "These first- and second-degree burns, though painful, will eventually heal, as there yet remains underlying skin. But the third-degree burns have no underlying skin. The skin must regrow from the edges of each wound, which requires time." He pointed to her arms. "During that time, these will be open and oozing sores, sores that must be kept clean or they will become infected." He focused on their faces. "Infection can kill."

They stood silent, trying to absorb what all they had heard. Arkadiy took hold of Elena's hand. He turned to the doctor and said, "I understand."

They set about to make the necessary preparations. Elena ripped up several sheets and boiled them in pails of water to sterilize them, making as many bandages as she could. A member of their church advised that they could also lay cabbage leaves on the first- and second-degree burns, since that can help remove the heat. Arkadiy was able to find plenty of cabbage at the store.

The doctor did as he promised and visited them to see how things were going. He observed how Vera's dressings were being done and assured him, "I couldn't have done it any better myself. She really is much better being here with you...better than being in the hospital." He looked at the cabbage leaves on her skin, fascinated by it. "Even at room temperature, they do remove the heat."

Someone had to be with Vera all the time, as she was in constant pain. The whole of their church was praying for Vera, and many came and took turns to watch her. Elena made a special place for Vera to sleep. She strung a hammock in the bunk bed and lined it with soft pillows. It was too painful for her to lie on a mattress.

Arkadiy was always the one who changed the bandages. Elena was there to watch.

Vera cried and squirmed as he pulled the old dressings off; yet she remained compliant, understanding it was necessary. She looked up at Elena. "Can we sing, Mommy?"

Elena stood still, tingling, devastated by what she was witnessing. "Yes, sweetie. What would you like to sing?"

"Joyful, Joyful."

Vera led out in the singing while Elena tried to join in. She could hardly sing. Her voice cracked as tears ran down her cheeks. They sang together, over and over again, while Arkadiy finished changing the bandages.

Joyful, joyful, never ceasing.
Let's be joyful all the time.
The light of God was freely given.
It will never cease to shine.

Let us follow in God's footsteps.
Let us cling to his dear feet
so that when the trials do come,
we will not be in defeat.

Elena watched Vera lead out, seeing the strength in her, and seeing a little heart that could not imagine defeat. She prayed silently, *Please, Lord. Just save her life!*

When the old cloth bandages were removed, Elena washed them out by hand and boiled them each day to have them ready for the next change. There were no washing machines in the camp.

After the accident, Babusia was not herself. She withdrew. She stayed out of the bedroom where Vera was being tended, sitting by herself at the table.

Elena confronted her. "Mama, it was not your fault."

Akulina held her face with both hands. "It was my fault. I was the one that put the boiling pot there, right next to the water."

Elena sat down beside her. "It was a freak accident. Vera was just trying to get some water. It is not your fault." She put her arm around her mother.

Akulina shook her head and sobbed.

"Why don't we pray, Mama?" Elena composed herself and took hold of Mother's hand. "Dear Lord. Nothing is too hard for you, nothing too hard for you to do for your child. Lord, you have given us a good doctor and helped us to be able to take care for her. We are grateful for that. Please, Lord, please just save her life."

They sat quietly together for a long time, holding hands.

*　*　*

The routine of changing the bandages continued for four long months. And the prayers never ceased.

Vera survived and made a full recovery, except for the scars on her arms, scars that became reminders of how God had kept her from defeat. And she was not sick after that.

43

According to the Yalta Partition Plan, the Allies divided Germany into four occupied zones after the war. The Russians occupied the eastern half of Germany, the French took the far west near their border, the Americans the south, and the British the north. Within the three western partitions, the Allies maintained camps and temporary homes for refugees until they could be permanently resettled.

The problem of the refugees became a huge humanitarian concern. The United Nations Relief and Rehabilitation Administration (UNRRA) was organized specifically to deal with a subset of the refugees, the "Displaced Persons" (DP), those that refused to return to the Soviet Union and other Eastern European countries under communist rule. The UNRRA set up special Russian, Ukrainian, and Polish DP camps throghout western Germany. Lüdenscheid was one of these camps. It was situated within the British zone.

The Bondar family had chosen to go to the Polish DP camp in Lüdenscheid in order to escape forced repatriation to the Soviet Union. The camp was situated on a former German military base, occupied mostly by Poles, but also home to some two hundred Belorussians, Russians, and Ukrainians; most of these refugees were Baptists. These Baptists lived together in one of the many massive three-story military barracks on the base, Barrack #3. Arkadiy's family and Pana had rooms there on the second floor. Opa and Omama had their own room on the third floor.

The men of Lüdenscheid took various odd jobs to earn whatever money they could for food and other goods, working either in the town or in the camp. Those that knew English were readily employed as translators.

Sixteen-year-old Alexander Boltniew knew English. He was hired by UNRRA to work in their office in the camp. Part of his responsibility was to keep track of all who lived in Lüdenscheid. More than 1,600 individuals were on his list.

When a line of Russian trucks drove into the camp in December, Alexander was on duty in the office. He looked out the window, saw them coming, and bolted out the door. He ran to Barrack #3 and spread the word. Arkadiy, Opa, and the other Russian men promptly escaped to safety.

But the Russians would not be deterred.

In late January, the Russians returned to the camp, accompanied by a British escort. They pulled up to the office and went inside. A young British soldier sat behind the desk as they came in. The Russian officer removed his hat and saluted. "*Menya zovut Leytenant Filippov.*"

The British soldier stood and returned the salute. "I am sorry, sir. I do not speak Russian. My translator is out of the office. I am Corporal Coy."

Filippov looked at him, puzzled.

"Do you speak English?" Coy asked.

Filippov understood that much. He shook his head, held up his hand, turned, and walked out of the office. In a minute, he returned with a Russian private. He handed a paper to the private and instructed him what to say.

The private said, "We look for these people." He handed it to Coy.

"You want to find these people? Here in the camp?"

The private nodded.

Coy glanced down at the paper. "I don't usually do this. This is not my regular job."

The private translated for Filippov. The lieutenant frowned and blurted out something to the private.

"He...he want you look."

"Uh, right...right. I will try." Coy turned toward the row of binders behind him in a bookcase. He glanced down at the paper in his hand and turned back to them. "These are Russian names, eh?"

The private nodded.

Coy ran his fingers along the notebooks. The binders were labeled in Cyrillic, so he could not clearly understand what he was looking at. "Uh, maybe you can read this? I can't. Sorry."

The private stepped behind the desk. He scanned the names on the binders then pointed at one. Coy took it to the desk and sat down. He opened the binder and laid the paper list beside it. The private stepped to the side of the desk to peer over his shoulder.

Coy glanced up at him and cleared his throat deliberately. "Uh, I need to look at this." He placed his hand as a shield over the page and stared at the private.

The private stepped back and stood beside his officer.

The Brit turned the pages slowly, looking down the names, page after page, reading each name, one at a time. He was in no hurry, finding pleasure in making them wait.

In the meantime, Filippov's face was turning redder by the second. He turned his hat over and over in his hand, purposely breathing heavy.

Coy came to the last page and closed the notebook. "No, sir. Can't find any of those names. Sorry." He looked at the cover of the binder and read the small print in the corner. "Hey, this is Belorussian names." He shook his head and looked up at them. "I am bloody sorry. I had the wrong notebook."

He stood and turned to the bookcase. One at a time, he pulled the binders out and looked for the English translation on the cover. "Ah. Here it is. 'Russians.'"

He turned back to his desk and sat down. He glanced at the names on the list and then looked up at the private. "Hey. I really can't make out the writing, also in Cyrillic. Uh, can you read me the name?" He handed the paper back.

The private read the first name on the list. "Bondar, Arkadiy."

"Bondar?"

The private nodded.

Coy opened the binder and started reading from the first page. It was a slow process, as the handwriting was a challenge to read.

Filippov shifted his weight and nervously tapped one foot. He put his hand in his pocket and clenched his jaw. His eyes bugged out as he fixed them on Coy.

"Ah! Here it is—'Bondar.' B-o-n-d-a-r. Right. That is the one."

Filippov said something to the private. The private asked, "Where is he?"

"Uh, let me see." He ran his finger to the right. "It says here Barrack #3 room 306."

The private translated. Filippov put his hat on, grabbed the paper from the private's hands, and stormed out of the room.

Coy yelled after them as they left, "That is on the third floor!"

They were already out the door.

Coy looked back at the notebook. "Hey, wait a minute! I made a mistake." They were already gone out of earshot. He continued, speaking to himself, "That is Georgiy Bondar, not Arkadiy."

Filippov had already hustled out of the office with a purpose, the private in tow. He ran down the stairs, across the pavement to his truck and climbed in, then sped off farther into the camp, toward the row of barracks.

There were big numbers on the front of each of the barrack buildings. He screeched to a stop at "3" and jumped out of the truck. He ran to the back and barked orders at his soldiers. They all jumped out, toting their rifles. The lieutenant straightened his hat, pulled his pistol from its holster, and signaled two soldiers to follow him. The rest dispersed around the building as they had been directed.

Meanwhile, up in the barracks, the sound of the truck's brakes alerted one of the refugees on the third floor. He ran out into the hall in a frenzy. "*The Russians are here!*"

Georgiy had been sitting with Olga in their living area, which faced the front of the building. He jumped to the window and spied the truck. In a panic, he ran to the bedroom, which faced the back of the building. "I have to hide."

Olga ran with him. They looked around the room. There was no place to hide there.

"Quick," he said. "Help me tie sheets."

They ripped them off the bed and hastily tied them together. He took one end and hitched it to the bedpost. He threw the window open and tossed the other end out. The bitter cold air swept into the room.

By now, there was a sound of feet running down the hallway growing closer.

Georgiy looked at Olga and kissed her. He turned, grabbed the sheet, sat on the sill, and shoved his feet out the window. He spun around and lowered himself, hanging onto the sill for a moment, staring back into the unit.

Olga held her hands to her heart, anguished, staring at him. She stepped closer.

He looked up at her. "I love you."

"God will keep you safe." She touched his hand.

The door to their unit burst open. Filippov and two soldiers pressed in, brandishing their weapons. Georgiy let go of the window and put his full weight on the makeshift rope. It snapped. He plummeted to the ground and landed hard on the frozen concrete. His legs crushed beneath him. He lay in a heap.

Filippov ran to the window and looked out. Georgiy was already surrounded by soldiers. They picked him up, his legs broken, and carried him rudely to the truck.

Filippov stared at Olga.

She said something to him in German.

He had no idea what she said. He glanced at the other two soldiers, motioned toward the door, and left her alone. When he got to the bottom of the stairs, he tugged on his uniform jacket, straightened his hat and slowed his walk out of the building to the truck. He smiled at his men, stepped up into the cab and drove away. He had his man. Or so he thought.

Later that day, Alexander Boltniew returned to the camp. He found everyone in the Barracks #3 huddled together in a state of shock over the abduction. When they told him what had happened, he was devastated that he had not been there to prevent it. But they crowded around him and embraced him. Then they all together fought back their tears and lifted up their voices in prayer for Georgiy, for Opa, wherever he was.

44

In July 1946, a number of Polish refugees, among them the Bondar and Rukasuyev families, were relocated 190 kilometers north from Lüdenscheid to the German village of Frille. Some of the refugees, including close friends, were moved to the neighboring village of Wietersheim, about a thirty-minute walk to the west. Both towns had small centers for commerce that were surrounded by farms with vast open fields and orchards. The mode of transportation there was by bicycle or on foot; there were no cars or trucks. The farmers hitched their cows to wagons to pull their goods and loads. Life there was quiet, slow-paced, and pastoral.

The refugees were moved into houses of the German town-folk. School was provided for elementary education of the children of the refugees. Part of the school building in Wietersheim was set aside for the refugees to conduct their Sunday morning worship services in Polish. Many of the refugees walked to Wietersheim for this morning service and then in the evening to the German Lutheran church in Frille, where they were also allowed to hold their own Baptist services.

Elena and Arkadiy's family were moved into a farmhouse on the east side of the village that overlooked a soccer field. On the opposite side of the field, Pana moved her family into a house that they shared with two Polish families.

Pana's apartment was in the middle of the house, with a door through the entry that opened directly to the outside.

Her new neighbor's rooms were to either side, sharing the same entry hall. There were other doors between Pana's rooms and those of her neighbors that were kept closed all the time with furniture placed in front of them for some semblance of security. There was little privacy between the neighbors; each was able to hear every word spoken on the other side of the walls.

Pana formed an immediate low opinion of her neighbors, hearing their frequent drunken, raucous arguments and boastings, and seeing that they stole farm animals (pigs and rabbits) to cook for their meals. They kept this livestock in the basement, a part of the house that was accessible only through Pana's inner hallway. They often fed the animals by tossing food in through the cellar windows when Pana was not at home.

Meanwhile, on Pana's side of the thin walls, she was conducting Bible studies for young people in her church. They read the Bible and sang hymns together in Polish, aware and unashamed their neighbors could hear them. She invited her neighbors to join in. One of the men in Pana's Bible group, hoping to encourage them, gave both neighbors a Polish New Testament so that they could read scripture on their own.

As Pana's family adjusted to their new life in Frille, she found ways to make it more enjoyable. The refugees were allowed to gather fruit that had fallen to the ground beside the village roads. Pana would gather apples and pears into large sacks and carry them home. There she would painstakingly peel and cut away the good parts, discarding anything rotten or filled with worms. Her labor of love produced sweet jams and preserves that she kept in jars she stored in the basement.

One Sunday, after Pana returned from the morning church service, she found the outer door to her apartment ajar, the lock broken. She looked at the inner door to her private room. It was locked, unharmed. She went downstairs to the basement. There she saw her jams and preserves on the shelf; every jar was half empty. The other shelves were filled with food items that were not hers, goods obtained dishonestly by her neighbor. She turned and stared at the stolen rabbits that were sniffing around on the floor. Half-nibbled vegetables lay on the slab beneath the cellar window. She drew her conclusion.

Pana went upstairs to confront her neighbor, Beatrice. She knocked on the door.

Beatrice peeked out. "Yes?"

Pana pointed to the broken lock on her front door. "Perhaps you have seen who broke my lock and opened the door?"

Beatrice opened the door fully. "I did." She put her hand on her hip. "You Baptists go to your services, while I must wait to go down to feed my rabbits. Why should I wait for you?"

Pana silently studied Beatrice's face, unable to bring herself to accuse her of stealing her jams. She walked away.

Pana told one of her friends what had happened. They advised her to go to the police. "If those people don't get punished for opening your door and breaking your lock, next time, they will do something worse."

Pana thought long and hard about the advice, feeling it right that thieves *should* be punished. But before she went to the authorities, or said anything to her sister, she quietly sought the counsel of one of the leaders in her church, Peter Gordieyev. She explained her problem to him.

Peter listened carefully as she laid out the evidence and revealed the attitudes and the actions of her neighbors. Then he listened to her tell the advice she had received from her friend. He asked a few questions and sat back to hear her answers. When he was sure she was finished, he observed, "Of course, for breaking the door and lock, they will be punished and disqualified for immigration."

He leaned forward. "At the moment, we have an opportunity to share Christ with the Polish people and other nationalities. Should the villains be jailed, their friends and other Polish people will be angry and will stop listening to our witness. Thus the open door we have with them will be closed. An opportunity for the gospel will be lost."

Pana sat fixated, listening. Her face reddened. In her silence, she wept at the injustice, the thought that the thieves would get away with what they had done.

"The scripture says, 'Whoever takes your coat, do not withhold from him your shirt. Give to everyone who asks of you, and do not demand back what is yours. Be merciful, just as your Father is merciful. Pardon and you will be pardoned.'"

As Pana heard his final words, she knew Peter was telling her the truth, the hard truth. She calmly stood, thanked him, and walked away. Pana made no attempt to repair the lock. And the jams and preserves continued to be consumed down to the end.

One day, her neighbors on the right got drunk and fought, screaming at one another on the other side of the wall. Pana heard every word, like they were right in her own room. Beatrice yelled at her husband, "It would be better if you went to those cursed Baptists! They don't drink. They do no evil. They only sing hymns to their God. But you and I always fight like a cat and dog." Beatrice could be heard weeping bitterly.

Not long after, Pana had guests stay with her; guests that had come to attend a church conference. Her two Polish neighbors brought food, saying, "You have guests, and we know that you have nothing to give them."

The neighbors started a friendship with Pana. They came to her room for Bible studies and sang hymns with everyone there.

After many months, packages began to arrive from America addressed to the church, items to be divided among the needy. Pana had never considered herself "needy." To her, a needy person had nothing to wear. She had managed to sew outfits for her family, so she usually declined the help. But on one occasion, she was offered two coats, one for Zoya and another for a girl who lived with them. The coats fit perfectly, and the girls were thrilled to have them. That was the first help Pana accepted.

A short while later, a package from the United States came bearing Pana's name on it. It contained clothing for small children and three pairs of ladies shoes. Pana gave the clothing away to families that needed them. The shoes fit Zoya, but she took two pairs next door to Beatrice, who was glad to receive them. There bloomed a sense that the neighbors were becoming good friends.

In the summer of 1947, registration began for emigration to South America. Both of Pana's neighbors registered and were accepted.

Beatrice came to Pana to say goodbye, red in the face. She threw her arms around Pana, and cried on her shoulder. "I have done many hurtful things to you, and you always repaid me with goodness." Beatrice wiped back her tears. "Now I see that you are holy people, and I want an address of a church like yours where I am going. I desire to go to your church." She composed herself. "All Polish people here that I know are from my background, and they...they know me. The whole time I was here, I was afraid of them and what they would think of me if...if I became like you. When I immigrate, that will be a new place, and no one will know me there. I will be able to go to a church like yours."

Pana took her again in her arms. "I will be glad to help you." They cried together.

Later that day, Pana consulted with the church leaders and was given an address for a church near to where Beatrice was moving. She shared it with Beatrice, and they said their goodbyes.

A few weeks later, the second Polish family prepared to leave. They would be moving near to Beatrice, and came to say goodbye to Pana. "You have become like family to us. We are asking God to send us good neighbors in South America, just as you have been good neighbors to us here. We have lived with you in the same house for a year and have not heard one mean word from you." The woman proudly held up the Bible she had been given. "And I promise I will keep reading this every day."

They said their farewells.

* * *

In the springtime, Luba began suffering constant pain in her legs. Her doctor ordered bed rest. Arkadiy took her to the hospital each day for treatment, and Elena wrapped hot bags of sand around her legs to ease the discomfort. During this time, Luba's friends brought her schoolwork home so that she could keep up with her class. With the coming of summer and the return of the warm weather, her health returned.

To shorten Luba's walk to school, Elena and Arkadiy's family moved to the western edge of the village with a German family that had a large two-story farmhouse. Elena and Arkadiy were given a bedroom on the second floor where they also kept little Nadiezda. On the ground floor, they were given three more rooms: a bedroom for the older children, one for the two grandmothers, and the third room that they used as a dining and family area.

Akulina had been very ill for a while. Her strength was waning, and she stayed in bed most of the time, in need of care. Yet she convinced Elena not to put her in the hospital, preferring to be near her grandchildren to enjoy watching them play from her bed in the next room. She loved them very much. Elena and Pana took turns caring for her.

That summer, refugees were able to register to immigrate to Canada, advertising opportunities for tailors and dressmakers. Pana's friends tried to convince her to register, since she was more than qualified. But she was not yet ready to leave her mother and sister.

Pana explained the opportunity to Mother, who was always aware of everything going on. Pana remembered all that Mother had been through, her arrest, her torture, their flight from the Communists, and then the horrors of war. As she spoke, she studied Mother lying in bed, her skin turning sallow; she was a shadow of her former self. Pana knew that if they were to separate at this time, that she would not see her again alive. Mother was too sick. Immigration would surely be denied her.

Pana hugged and kissed her. "I do not want to add any more grief and sorrow to you, Mama. I want to stay here with you."

Mother took her hand and soothed it. "You should go, my daughter. I do not want you to miss this opportunity. Perhaps this is your only chance to settle down in Canada and work in the trade using your skills. Certainly, I would like to have my daughters by my side as long as I live, but I am old and sickly, and you must think about your well-being and the opportunity you have to provide for your children. Other women have spouses to look after them. You are alone. Think things through well, and pray that God may show you his will, that there will be no regrets later."

Pana looked at the love in Mother's eyes. She saw a Christian woman of good character, meek and gentle, regarding others above herself, not judging anyone, and preferring to give in rather than cause an argument. She had always been a hard worker and just. Even now Mother was worried first about Pana, that she might not lose the opportunity.

They prayed together. "As to what might befall us, Lord, we will trust in you."

Pana decided not to go to Canada.

Mother said to her, "May the Lord bless you one hundredfold, my child, for not wanting to impart the pain of separation to your old mother in her last days on this earth. He will send you a better opportunity. Just be faithful to him." Mother's face lit up with happiness.

Pana's friends and acquaintances judged her unwise for turning down the chance to immigrate. Yet once the decision had been made, Pana felt relieved.

Those that qualified for immigration to Canada soon left. Pana listened to stories from those that had relatives there who said, "It is the best country to live in."

As autumn came, Mother's condition grew worse. Her liver was failing. She needed assistance around the clock. Pana spent each night at Mother's side, while Elena, who had small children to tend and was expecting again, watched her during the day.

Late in October, Pana sensed the end was near. At night, she sat by her bed and asked, "Mama, what advice or admonition would you like to leave with me?"

Akulina smiled. "You know the Lord. He is the best teacher. You have his Word. Study it and live accordingly. It is written, 'Do not judge, and you will not be judged.' Always remember this, my child."

Pana nodded and fixed her pillows. "Go to sleep, Mama." Pana lay down on the bed beside her, with her head on the pillow close by. Mother dozed off.

Akulina suddenly opened her eyes and said, "I see Jesus." Then she closed her eyes and fell asleep forever. Her soul was now at rest with the Lord.

* * *

The family made all the arrangements for the funeral. Pana prepared her mother's body for burial, dressing her in an outfit that Elena selected. Arkadiy purchased a casket and ordered several wreaths. Mother was laid out in the casket in the dining room where those that wanted to pay their respects could come and see her for the last time.

There was a funeral service held in the dining room. It was very simple. Extra chairs were brought in for guests. Many people came, filling the dining room and two bedrooms to capacity. Everyone could hear the preacher as he told of her life, then they sang hymns together. After the service, eight pallbearers carried the casket to the cemetery, a thirty-minute walk. Some of the women carried the wreaths. There was a long line of people and many children trailing after the coffin. They sang hymns together the whole way there.

On October 29, 1947, eleven days after Mother died, Elena gave birth to her sixth child, a boy. They named him Iosif (Joseph).

Several months after Mother was laid to rest, Arkadiy had a memorial made, a concrete cross that said in the Polish language.

Bruchanowa, Akulina
25.7.1872
18.10.1947
Spoczywa w Panu
("Resting in the Lord")

Mother was buried in the Frille cemetery, in the area designated for the displaced persons.

It was especially hard for Elena to lose her mother, her best friend. Mother had lived with Elena all her life, always helping with house chores and taking care of her children. It had never mattered how tired or sick Mother was, she had never refused to look after the grandchildren. Mother had adored Arkadiy, and he had always been very good to her. But now all of them, Elena's family and Pana's family, they all had to bid Mother goodbye till they meet her again in eternity.

45

Luba completed the sixth grade in June 1948. In August, Arkadiy took her south and west to the town of Lippstadt to enroll her in a high school (gymnasium) for Polish and Slavic refugees. She was housed there in a dormitory, sharing a room with three other girls, all with a Baptist background. The other girls in the dormitory were Catholic. Several of the boys that attended were also from Baptist families, including George Boltniew. The curriculum included secular course studies and classes in religion.

During their time in Frille, Arkadiy worked as a cook and a provisional director in the school. But as the immigrations began and many of the refugees left, the camp started to be liquidated, and there was a lack of work. By the fall of 1948, Arkadiy continued his responsibilities, but as a volunteer (without pay).

When the first group of young people immigrated to England, the Baptists in the camp conducted a farewell service. Each individual came to the front of the room to leave a few words with those that were to remain behind. Pana was moved by what each expressed and cried through the whole service. She remembered the many other times when she had to say goodbye to relatives and friends, believing her separation would be only for a short time. War had separated her from loved ones for decades, *or is it for forever?* A picture of the past and present farewells overwhelmed her. She could not get a hold of herself. This was only the beginning of immigration. She wondered,

What will become of me if I cry every time someone leaves? Like many others, Pana stepped forward and gave Bible verses as a remembrance to those leaving.

A short time later, immigration to South America began. Again, the church had farewell services and more tears flowed. Families and individuals that had been with the Bondars and Rukasuyevs ever since their time in Kiev were leaving to new homes. They had been especially close, having experienced the frightful escape on the train, and then they had lived those years together in the camps. Those experiences had bonded them into one great family. It was harder to see them go. Change was all around those that were left behind, ever present in the now quiet halls, the empty classrooms, empty quarters, and empty beds.

In June 1949, the last of the refugees were moved out of Frille and Wietersheim. Both Pana's and Elena's families were relocated south one hundred kilometers to Paderborn, to a former German military camp. There they were placed in large buildings, where they had rooms beside each other. Many of the other members of their church had already immigrated to other countries, so there were just a few refugee families left. A month later, Elena gave birth to her seventh child, a son. Leonid Arkadiyevich Bondar was born on July 23, 1949.

In August, Pastor Lewczuk came to Pana's apartment with immigration applications to the United States. He filled them out for her and came to the question of marital status. There were four possible answers: married, single, divorced, and widow. He asked Pana what to put there.

Pana felt the dilemma. *I am married, but I do not have a husband. I am not divorced. How could I be a widow when I have not buried my spouse? Am I a widow?* The thought of this made her shudder. She had hoped against hope that perhaps Ivan had escaped death and was yet alive, and that one day, he would return. *Thirteen years have gone by since the NKVD arrested Ivan and threw me out from my job and home, stating that I was a wife of the "enemy of the state."*

Pana told the pastor her story. She sighed. "Write whatever you consider correct."

He marked "widow."

After completing the information and also filling out applications for Elena's family, he sent the forms to the United States. Pana and Elena both wondered what would be the result. They prayed for an open door.

Meanwhile in America, Baptist brethren, those who had previously immigrated from Russia, Poland, and Slavic countries, received the applications and passed them out among their network of Baptist churches up and down the East Coast. The hope was to find someone willing to sponsor a refugee individual or family. Sponsors had to promise to provide jobs and living quarters for the immigrants.

Pana soon received a letter that a family in North Carolina had agreed to be her sponsor. Her nerves were suddenly burdened with worry over the move to a new country. She showed the letter to Elena. "I think I should wait, wait until we can both go and be together."

"We do not know how things will work out, if we will ever get sponsored at the same time and location. You have an opportunity, a wonderful opportunity. You should not turn this down." Elena smiled. "Our chance will come somehow. We are all in God's hands. And he has never let us down."

Pana embraced her sister. She made her decision to leave.

It began again, filling out more papers.

In September, Pana received word she would be leaving for America. She hurriedly packed. On the day of her departure, the two families lined up in their rooms. Pana, Zoya, and Eugene passed along to each of them, giving them hugs and kisses.

At last, Pana came to Elena, standing at the end of the line, holding her new baby. They silently studied each other's faces. Pana thought, *My life has been harsh and painful, my husband's arrests and demise, the loss of children and constantly being chased by the Communists, then the war.* With tears in her eyes, she hugged Elena and whispered in her ear, "Our only hope remains that the Lord will not forsake us."

Elena leaned back and nodded. "We depend on him completely."

After promising to write and wiping back many tears, Pana walked away with her family, wondering, *Will I ever see my sister again?*

Yet she held out hope that Elena would also find a sponsor.

46

In transit camp, Pana's family was reunited with many of her Christian friends from various other camps. They prayed together in anxious anticipation of their departure. There they were subjected to all sorts of medical examinations. First, they had to pass the German doctors, physical and mental tests and x-rays. Then American doctors reviewed the findings of the German doctors and gave their stamp of approval. Pana failed one test and had to repeat it. She worried she would be denied immigration. Zoya and Eugene had no difficulty passing all the tests. On the second try, Pana was approved.

Next they were investigated and interrogated about their past life and ideologies. After this, there was a meeting with the American Consul. He had to place the final stamp of approval on each immigrant's application. Pana was told her ship would depart on October 1. She prepared for their voyage to the United States.

On the morning of their leaving, their hearts were filled with excitement. They were to board trucks that would take them to a train destined to their port of departure. Each refugee stood in line holding their baggage, waiting to enter the trucks. An American official checked their papers and spoke to each immigrant in their native tongue before they climbed in.

When it was Pana's turn, she handed the documents to the American, with Zoya and Eugene standing behind her.

He examined the papers and looked up at her with a worried expression. "Is this your daughter, Zoya?"

Pana nodded.

"She cannot go with you." He showed Pana the paperwork, which was written in English.

Pana could not read it.

He realized and explained, "Zoya is an adult, twenty-five. She requires her own sponsor."

Pana panicked. Her face turned white. She stared wide-eyed at the man, having clearly heard and understood. She agonized, *What can I do? I cannot sail and leave my daughter behind.* The terrible vision returned, the nightmare of leaving her other two children behind in Siberia. *It will be worse to leave Zoya alone in a foreign country with no family right here to be with her.* She turned and took hold of Zoya's hands. "I will not go to America." Pana wept.

Pana's friends stepped forward and gathered around her. "No. You should go to America. Later, you will be able to receive her. It will make it easier when her mother is already there."

The official interrupted. "Excuse me, gospozha." He pulled a sheet off the bottom of Pana's papers. "It says here that Zoya has her own sponsor. Everything is clear for her."

Pana's eyes narrowed.

"She is just not leaving today. Not with you."

She breathed easier. Still, the idea of their immediate separation was horrible.

The official looked at the line of people waiting to get onto the trucks. He glanced at his watch and refocused on Pana. "Come on, gospozha. You need to get going."

Pana took hold of her daughter and the two of them wept.

"You go on, Mama. I will be fine."

Pana anguished, wiping back her tears. *There is no better choice. It will work out.* She and Eugene said goodbye to Zoya, picked up their baggage, and climbed up into the back of the truck.

Zoya gathered her things and stepped back, watching as the other women climbed into the truck. As they drove away, Zoya stood alone on the pavement waving goodbye.

Pana held onto Eugene's hand, her tears flowing. She took a deep breath and looked at her son. "God will give us strength."

He nodded and squeezed her hand.

After they boarded the train, they got situated in their seats. Pana pulled out a notebook and began to record all that was happening on her trip. As she thought about their present travel comfort, recalling the many other times she had traveled in Russia: standing on a train for several days while holding a child, or on a horse with a baby in her arms, and walking through mud, or in a boat, alone with the children. She marveled at the comfort of her current accommodations.

When they arrived at the port, they entered the ship, the *General Mayor*. It was massive, seven stories high. Each person was given a small traveling kit and told where to go. The men and women were separated. Pana was ushered to the third deck, and Eugene was taken to the second with the men. As soon as the last passenger was aboard and in place, the ship cast off.

In the evening, Pana sat out on the deck to enjoy the scenery. Immense blue-green waves constantly moved about them, and land was no longer visible. The image of the water brought back her childhood memories of Siberia, the river where she lived, when she crossed the water in little boats, daringly cutting through the waves during storms. There were memories of her mother and aunt, how the three of them sailed while she was at the helm. As she remembered, there came an announcement that all passengers must return to their cabins.

As she descended the decks, everyone received a bedding package. In her cabin, there were three levels of sleeping berths stacked one above the other. She made her bed in one. The first night aboard was restful. She slept through a storm.

On the second day, the ocean was very calm. Everyone appeared on the deck to look around. There were small and large ships everywhere, and she could see land, a tall white wall, the English shore. They sailed close to the wall; there were white buildings on the top of it. They continued along beside the wall until they arrived at a channel between two massive rocks that jutted up from the waves. On each rock stood a lighthouse. Pana thought of the hymn, "Direct Your Lighthouse, My Brother." The ship turned between the two rocks without stopping. England remained on the right side. The second night was restful.

On the third day, passengers again came on deck. The ocean was peaceful, without one tiny wave. To their side, it was smooth like a mirror. To the front, there was a ship ahead. In one moment, the ship was higher than theirs; next it sank lower; then again it rose higher. Even though the ocean appeared calm, she understood there were large rolling waves, carrying her ship up and down all the time. With this incessant motion, the passengers lost their appetites. The night became stormy.

On the fourth day, people stopped eating entirely. The smell of food made everyone feel sick. The ocean was storming. Waves were high and angry, like they were fighting among themselves. Sprays fell on the deck; no one could be there. The sun could not be seen. The ship tossed back and forth and rocked up and down, tilting to and fro.

The people stopped wearing makeup and styling their hair. They lay still in their berths and on the floors, seasick. Somehow, Pana and Eugene managed to eat one meal. The night passed with little rest.

On the fifth day, the storm raged. Waves covered the deck. Over the loudspeakers, a pleasant voice of invitation in Russian was heard. "Please come, beautiful ladies and lovely children, to the dining hall." Very few could go. Most lay in their berths in nightdress, their hair uncombed. Their cabins were hot and stuffy, the air heavy, despite the electric fans. One woman screamed, "I do not want to go to America. Please let me die!" Men came at all hours to check on their spouses and family members, even though men were banned from the female levels. Eugene came to check on Pana, himself weak and barely able to stand.

On the sixth day, no one moved much. All were seasick and unable to get out of their berths. Thoughts of food or drink abandoned them. The passengers had each been given coupons at their time of entry to the ship. Now they heard an announcement to go redeem them. But who cared about anything? There was no will to live. But Eugene was not to be deterred. He went and redeemed their coupons for two pairs of nylons for Pana and some chocolates for himself.

On the seventh day, Pana managed to get to the deck. The sky was azure, and the ocean was lightly tossing. Slowly, others began to crawl out to the deck. Some felt better, and their appetites returned. But they were not yet interested in cosmetics. This day was Eugene's fifteenth birthday. Pana stepped with him to a corner and prayed for him, thanking God that so far they were alive and well; then she congratulated him. An announcement was heard that the captain received a telegram that his wife delivered twins. He would have liked to speed up the ship, but again, the storm would not let him. Another restless night followed.

The eighth day was Pana's birthday. But she could not even lift her head. All the women in her cabin, one hundred women, could not get out of bed. Eugene brought Pana oranges, but she could not eat. Their vessel rocked and rolled in the storm.

On the ninth day, the sun came out. People appeared on the deck. No one wanted to stay in their cabins. Their appetites returned. In the evening, there were church services for various denominations, and there were movies, dances, and entertainment. Everyone found something of interest. People at last were able to take advantage of the conveniences: showers, baths, and laundry machines. The night was peaceful and very restful. The ship sped ahead.

On the tenth day, the morning passed briskly. The weather was good. Pana still had no appetite, and Eugene did not feel well. He had a raised temperature and did not go to eat. That evening, they turned in their hand baggage. The night went by peacefully.

On the eleventh day, everyone was awakened at 4:00 a.m. They gathered the rest of their things and turned them in. Then they went to the deck where they could see boats and various vessels coming toward them. They were steaming into New York Harbor.

Instantly, everyone's mood changed. People were laughing and briskly moving and talking. Single women were parting with their belongings, throwing away old clothing they had worn on the journey. "We do not need old rags now that we are in America. We shall have new things."

In the eleven days of their journey, Pana and the other women had made many new friends. They busily exchanged addresses in their new country, promising to keep in touch with each other. There was a medical doctor, he was going to be with his mother. There were four families that Pana had grown close with during the trip. Pana had read to them from her Bible, which was always with her. She let them all know she would be moving to North Carolina where her sponsor lived.

The ship slowed. By 10:00 a.m., they could see lighthouses off the edges of the land. When they saw the Statue of Liberty, they shouted, "Hurrah!" Everyone was ecstatic. Young people hugged each other and sang songs in their native languages: German, Estonian, Lithuanian, Latvian, Hungarian, Polish, Ukrainian, and Russian.

By 11:00 a.m., they could see tall buildings. Their vessel continued at a slow speed. Two tugboats arrived, one at each side of the ship. They tied on and towed their ship into the port. Everything happening was a fascination to Pana and Eugene as they looked around.

Passengers joyfully were discussing who would be meeting them.

But Pana felt different. *There will be no one to meet me. My sponsors are in North Carolina. We do not know each other. How will we communicate?*

At 4:00 p.m., they disembarked. Pana and Eugene stood for the first time on American soil. Everyone's luggage was already there in separate piles, each labeled with an individual number. Pana found her number and sat on a box with Eugene at her side. She looked around. There were signs posted, where to go and what to do next. From there, the immigrants would be sent to their destinations as stated in their documents. Pana's luggage was addressed to North Carolina.

Pana watched from afar as her newfound friends each were met by their sponsors. She studied them. They seemed so joyful, smiling, ready to be taken to their destination without further worries. Each turned and spotted Pana. They brightened and waved enthusiastically. Pana and

Eugene waved back. One at a time, the other immigrants turned and left the pier.

Pana's worries smothered her. She felt no elation being there on American soil. She had no relatives or friends in this country, and she did not know the language. She imagined herself as deaf and mute, unable to understand what was being said and unable to speak. She felt a sudden impossibility of survival there, burdened with worry, consumed with inadequacy. She felt no comfort in knowing her sponsors were a Christian family, because all they really wanted was a housekeeper. She imagined herself scrubbing floors on her knees and cleaning laundry, all the while unable to converse or be understood. She felt completely alone.

As she sulked on her luggage, a well-dressed, intelligent looking gentleman approached. He addressed her in Russian, "Are you Gospozha Rukasuyeva?"

She stirred and looked at him. "Uh...Yes."

He held up his hand. "Just wait here. A man that speaks Russian will come and explain to you all that you need to do." He left.

Another man came and greeted them. "Hello. I am Pastor Radivoniuk from Newark Russian Ukrainian Baptist Church."

He asked Pana a few questions. They spoke briefly. "Wait here. I have to go take care of some things and will be right back."

Pana nodded with a sudden sense of relief, glad to be able to speak with someone.

The pastor returned in a few moments with a man, Mr. Klaupix. Pana knew him from her time in the German camps. He asked, "Would you like to stay in New Jersey rather than go to North Carolina?"

Pana's eyebrows raised. "Is it permissible to stay here? I have been sponsored by someone in North Carolina? Don't I owe it to my sponsors to work for them in order to repay them?"

Mr. Klaupix smiled to ease her. "All our Baptist brethren have asked members of American churches to sponsor people. But when they arrive in the United States, some of our local Russian-Ukrainian churches offer help with living arrangements and help find jobs for immigrants."

"That is legal?"

"Yes, and there are no Russian-Ukrainian speaking churches in North Carolina. But here, in New York and New Jersey, there are churches in every city that speak your language."

Pana looked at Eugene then back at the men. She beamed and enthusiastically shook their hands. "Yes. Yes, I will stay here." She could barely contain herself. She looked toward heaven and sighed. *Who am I, Lord? Such an insignificant person and you have taken such good care of me through your servants, my brothers in Christ.*

The men advised her, "When you go through registration, tell them you prefer to stay here and you will not go to North Carolina. Then just sign the papers."

From then on, Pastor Radivoniuk took care of Pana and Eugene. He took them for a glass of grapefruit juice. Pana took a tiny sip and could not swallow it. It was so bitter. She had never had grapefruit. But she was too embarrassed to not drink it. Slowly, she swallowed the entire drink, bit by bit. It was a hardship, her first taste on American soil.

After this, Pastor Radivoniuk took them to a hotel in New York City. They talked and got acquainted. He promised to find her a job and an apartment. As soon as that was taken care of, he would return to get them. They prayed together, thanked the Lord for his goodness and mercies, and said farewell to the pastor.

Pana and Eugene prayed together and retired to bed. Eugene fell asleep immediately. The night in the New York hotel was an exceptional experience, she delighted in the conveniences. Yet she could not fall asleep. Too many impressions floated through her mind. She quietly read the Bible a while and finally drifted into pleasant rest.

The next morning, Pastor Radivoniuk arrived and paid for their hotel stay. They visited briefly in the lobby, and then he left to attend to other business. While he was gone, Pana went out and looked at the store windows.

When he returned, they boarded a bus to Newark, New Jersey, then on to the city of Elizabeth. There they met their hosts, Mr. and Mrs. Green, who had a delicious dinner waiting for them. They became acquainted as they ate. After the meal, their hosts declared, "You shall join us. We shall live together as one family." Pana and Eugene stayed there that night and enjoyed a peaceful rest.

The next morning, they made ready for a trip to Manville, New Jersey, to attend a church conference. Pana was penniless, but Mrs. Green paid for a ticket so she could come. When they arrived at the church, they entered and sat in a middle pew. Quickly, all the seats were filled. Looking around, Pana had yet to see anyone she recognized.

The service began. Pastor Kovalchuk of the Manville Church stood and called several pastors to the front to take part in the service. Pana watched as Pastors Sylvesiuk, Barchuk, Lewczuk, and Gordieyev all came forward; these men had been with her in the last three camps in Germany. She wanted to stand and shout but silently thanked the Lord. The entire service that followed was conducted in the Russian language, so Pana felt right at home. After the service, Pana met with the pastors and their wives. They hugged and kissed each other and laughed together.

That evening, old friends visited and spent the night at their house. Hours were filled with conversations. It was hard to find the time to sleep.

The next day began the job search. Several uneventful days went by, and then Pana was promised a job in a factory that made clothing. A neighbor who spoke English took her to get her a social security card.

Later that week, the Greens, Pana, and Eugene went to a prayer meeting at the Newark Russian Ukrainian Baptist Church. This was Pana's first time in that congregation. Pastor Radivoniuk called her to the front to give a testimony. She spoke for a few minutes and promised to tell more later. At the end of the service and feeling right at home, she asked to be accepted in the congregation. She had with her a letter of membership from her former church in Germany and was immediately accepted by them.

On their way home, after the service, their bus was full. Mr. and Mrs. Green found seats, but Eugene and Pana had to stand. Next to Pana stood a man who had been at the same service.

He asked her, "How large is your family, and where is your husband?"

Pana's eyes tilted at the floor. "Not alive." Her body shook as she uttered the words. She realized that was the first time she had ever declared Ivan dead.

As their journey continued, they had to change buses a few times. Each time, this same man came and stood by Pana. They talked together along the way.

The following week, Mrs. Green invited neighbors and several people from the church to have a group Bible study at her house. Pastor Radivoniuk called on Pana to continue her testimony. She again saw the man that had stood with her on the bus.

He introduced himself. "I am Andrew Bogdaniuk." Andrew invited the group to come to a service at his house. He lived nearby, in Linden.

Pana went to Andrew's house the next week. A large group gathered there. After the service, Pastor Radivoniuk asked the ladies to help set the table "since brother Bogdaniuk has no wife." He prepared many delicious dishes for them. In seven years of being a widower, he had learned to take care of himself and cook. During their time there, Pana was asked to continue telling her life story. Afterward, the women helped to clean up and wash the dishes.

On only her third Sunday, Andrew Bogdaniuk approached Pana after the service. He held a letter in his hand. He smiled. "I have listened to your testimony. And I heard about you even before you came. I've written my thoughts about you in this letter." He extended it to her and asked, "Will you be my wife?"

She stood stunned.

He studied her. "I would like to hear your response right away."

Pana glanced down at the letter. She took it from his hand but did not open it. She looked up at him, trying her best to be polite. "This is strange. I do not know you at all, and you don't know me. It is too soon for me to even think about such things."

His eyes lit up. "So many other immigrants have told me about you." He clasped his hands together and unloaded his speech. "I have been praying that God would send me a truly good Christian wife. Seven years I have been praying. I have asked that God would show me the right woman, one that would be in accord with my heart. Many people have introduced me to other women in that time. I have visited with them, but not one of them seemed right. Years have gone by now, my children have grown up. Now my son and daughter are both in college. It is so hard to be alone. I have waited and waited for when the Lord would send her to me, and now you are here. I can see that God has sent me just what I asked of him. God has answered my prayer. Why should I linger? There is no reason for us to wait. When God gives his blessing, we should be happy." He dropped his hands to his side. "I shall wait for your decision."

She measured his face. *He is sweet.* But she could not escape the utter strangeness of the proposal. She tucked the letter in her purse and walked away.

People in the church heard about Pana and Andrew's conversation. Mrs. Green and Pana continued to go to all the services, and Andrew was always there. Sometimes he came to the Green's house and they sat around the table and talked.

In the second week after her arrival in Elizabeth, Pana commenced her job at the clothing factory, sewing. The factory was close enough to walk to from the Green's residence. She came home often for lunch. The pay was meager, but enough to buy food and pay the rent. She thanked God for every day of employment and asked for his blessing and guidance to continue on the next.

Pana became acquainted with the women at her work. There were Polish, Slovak, and Ukrainian women with whom she could carry on conversations. She found herself thanking God for so much: for the freedom in America and for the peaceful conditions at work. Everything seemed too good to be true. While she had been in Europe, she had never expected that such a life could exist where one did not worry that the NKVD might come at night and take them away, never to be seen again; or for being permitted to arrive a few minutes late for work and not fearing the loss of your job; or freedom from being thrown into prison without explanation; or for not having to worry who you talked to or what you said. She realized that now she could pray wherever and whenever she desired and sing to the glory of God as much as she liked.

While Pana lived with the Greens, she wrote regularly to Elena, telling her all she was experiencing. She also corresponded with many refugees that were left in Europe, sick and old people, also some friends waiting to leave. She wrote faithfully to those that she met on the ship and friends who had immigrated to other countries. When she heard back from them, she found it fascinating to learn how different their lives had become. She often stayed up past midnight corresponding. Mrs. Green would sometimes see the light was still on and come into Pana's room, gently scolding her. "You can't correspond with the whole world. You write all night and work hard all day. You will wear yourself out and die. Go to sleep."

Pana wrote to her daughter in Germany and gave her new address, telling about her new life. Zoya wrote back and included a poem that recounted her sadness over their separation.

As the weeks passed, Pana was offered help from her friends who were willing to post the necessary bond funds for Zoya to immigrate. But then a note arrived explaining that Zoya had already received her entry permit and was free at last to come; there was a date for her to arrive in America. Pana was ecstatic and thanked the Lord for his mercy.

The day came when Zoya was supposed to arrive. Pastor Radivoniuk and another church member were delegated to meet the Slavic Christian immigrants. Pastor Radivoniuk called from the port of entry and informed Pana that Zoya had arrived safely, but she had refused to stay in New Jersey, believing she had to go to North Carolina to work for the people who had sponsored her. Pana got on the phone and tried to convince her otherwise. But Zoya focused on the needs of her sponsor and the commitment she had made to serve them; her mind could not be changed. Zoya left for North Carolina without even seeing Pana. But they kept in touch with each other, writing frequent letters.

One evening after work, Pana prepared their dinner as usual. Somehow, her heart was not at ease; she was disturbed but did not know why. She set the table and was ready to call Eugene. When she looked up, the door swung open and Zoya walked in.

Pana jumped and screamed, "Oy! Oy!" They embraced.

At dinner, Zoya explained all the details of how she had gotten there, the people who had watched out for her.

When the glow of seeing Zoya again had finally waned, Pana's curiosity took over. "So why did you come?"

Zoya spoke about how much she enjoyed her new life in North Carolina, then finally got to the point. "My sponsor, a widower, wants you to come south to be his bride. He said I should bring you back with me."

Pana had no intention of moving there.

Zoya stayed a few days. They went to the Russian church in Newark, and Pastor Radivoniuk asked her to read her poems. Many people liked her and surrounded her like old friends. Some advised her to move to New Jersey to be with her mother and brother. But Zoya would not give in. Pastor Radivoniuk counseled her, "Working just for room and board is not wise. You have repaid your debt. Now it is time to start establishing your own life. Here in New Jersey you can earn a good living, if you work hard. There are many Russians here, and there is plenty of spiritual work to be done here."

But Zoya was not to be swayed. When her time there was up, she returned to North Carolina.

Pana's living situation was not without its problems. Her room was right at the entry to the apartment, so she had little privacy. In addition, her landlady would not permit her to store her trunk in the room, disliking the clutter it caused. Pana was forced to move her trunk to the church, needing to go there to get her changes of clothes. After three months, she knew it was time to move somewhere else.

She found another room for rent from an old Slovak lady in Linden. The rent would be the same, and there was enough room for her trunk and even her sewing machine. She said a friendly goodbye to the Greens and moved into her new quarters. Not long after she moved, she met neighbors from Czechoslovakia. The wife worked in a different clothing factory right there in Linden. She got Pana a job there, doubling her salary.

Since Pana now lived in Linden, her suitor came and visited more often. He reminded her again and again that he was still waiting for her response to his proposal. At times, when Pana was not yet home from work, he visited with Pana's landlady, who grew to love him and became his advocate. The Greens and several other well-wishers kept up a steady onslaught of suggesting Pana should marry Andrew, testifying that he was a "godly man." They were wearing her down. She finally began to consider the proposal.

For such an important matter, Pana would have loved to have spoken with Elena and Arkadiy to seek their advice, but they yet remained separated from her, across an ocean. She wrote to them. She wrote also to Zoya and asked her to come. Marriage was a decision she could not make on her own.

When Zoya arrived, Andrew invited Pana, Zoya, and Eugene to his house. His daughter prepared a splendid dinner, and it was a good opportunity for all of them to get acquainted. Six months had now passed from the day when Andrew had first proposed.

After they returned to their apartment, Pana discussed the proposal with Zoya and Eugene. Both were delighted with Andrew and said she should marry him. As she listened to them, something moved in her heart. She thanked them both and left the apartment to walk back over to Andrew's house.

Pana stood on Andrew's porch and knocked on the door.

He opened it and stood in the doorway, quietly studying her face.

"You wanted my answer."

He leaned forward.

Pana clasped her hands in front of her. She wet her lips as she studied his eyes. She smiled. "It is *yes*."

He stepped forward and threw his arms around her.

As soon as Pana agreed to marry him, Andrew moved quickly with the wedding plans, there was no reason to delay. Zoya stayed for the wedding and helped with the preparations. Soon everything was ready for the ceremony. Andrew covered all the expenses.

The wedding day arrived, April 23, 1950. Many guests were invited from Russian churches in other cities. This was a very happy celebration for the immigrants. The sanctuary of the church in Newark was filled. Reverend Radivoniuk officiated. Andrew's children stood next to him on the platform. Pana's daughter and son stood next to her. The pastor had a bold and inspiring message, touching the hearts of everyone. There were two church choirs that sang, one from Newark and the other from New York City.

Afterward, there was a reception in the social hall for everyone. Tables were set with many delicious dishes that the women of the congregation had prepared. There were gifts from Andrew's work. Many people from Pana's work came. Andrew's first wife's relatives came. After the celebration was over. Andrew's son George drove the bride and groom in his car. Other relatives followed in their cars and brought Pana's children to their home.

Here Pana's new life began. Everything was different. Each family member had his or her own room with all conveniences. Andrew made immediate plans to build a new house for Pana, according to her liking. She, on the other hand, thought his current home was just fine: a two-story duplex with plenty of space for everyone, two extra empty bedrooms, and a two-car garage. But he would not be stopped in showing his overflowing love for her. He would build her a gorgeous new home well beyond her needs.

From the first day after the wedding, Andrew did not allow Pana to return to work. His son, George, advised her, "There will be enough for you to do at home. You do not need to work in the factory. Papa earns enough for all of us."

Zoya did not return to North Carolina. She and Eugene remained with Pana and Andrew, while design and construction began on their new home in another part of Linden. Zoya was able to find a new job right away. She intended to save a thousand dollars to post a bond so that her fiancé, who was yet in Germany, would be able to immigrate. When Andrew learned of it, he went straight to New York and posted the bond himself.

Pana found herself living in a dream world. She loved her new husband. Her daughter and son were with her. She loved her church. She had Bible studies in her home. She loved her new life. The only thing missing were her other two children, Anna and Ilya, far away, somewhere in Russia with her baby sister.

And then there was her other sister, still waiting behind in Germany.

47

After Pana left her, Elena lost her closest friend and confidant.

One evening, after Elena had put the last of her children down to sleep, she sat in her bed and leaned back against her pillow. She looked at the nightstand. On it was a stack of letters from Pana in America. She had read each one a dozen times. Though she was happy for Pana, for Pana's new life, she missed her now, so very far away. They had been through so much together, so many troubles. But there had been many good times too. She couldn't stop thinking of her sister, wondering if she would ever see her again.

Beside the letters lay her Bible. She picked it up and held it between her palms. The leather cover felt warm to her touch. She turned it and studied the edges, all folded and worn. She had carried it with her so many years through all the camps, on the train escaping Kiev, before that on the train from Irkutsk. She remembered again the day she got it, in Bunbuy, and how she had opened it for the first time and read the note inside, "To Elena."

She opened the Bible and looked for the note, not having thought of it for a while. She thought about Karpenko, how he had appeared just long enough in her life to give her the book and then had disappeared. She turned the book over and flipped through the pages. The note was gone. It had fallen out somewhere along the way. She thought about the book itself, how its words had changed the path of her life. Pana, too, had embraced those same words, words that had guided her through her many trials. Elena just could not stop thinking of her sister.

She turned to Psalm 23, "The Lord is my shepherd, so I have everything I need," and found precious comfort in the words. She closed the book, prayed, and laid it again on the nightstand.

Elena adjusted her pillows to get more comfortable, knowing it was time for slumber. But her mind was yet stirring; she was neither tired nor ready to sleep. Beside her lay Arkadiy, resting soundly. She turned out the lamp and listened to the quiet. Nothing stirred in the other room. She was apparently the only person yet awake.

She laid her hands on her stomach, pregnant again, at the end of her ninth month. She felt the baby move a little, then settle down. She figured it wanted to sleep like the rest of them.

She thought of all her children. Her first three had been born in Irkutsk, her fourth in Kiev. That time in her life now seemed so distant. They were a young family then, building their lives together. And then came the other three, each born in a different camp, each one marking station points in her life. The earlier camps had been easier to take, with all the fellowship and support of their many Christian friends. But they all were gone now, relocated to their new countries. Wimbern, their present home, was their seventh camp. Their stays in the camps more recently had gotten shorter and shorter—and lonelier and lonelier. *Funny*, she thought, *it is sort of like birth pangs, growing closer and closer, each one more painful than the last.*

As she sat there in the quiet darkness, she felt it, her first contraction. She turned to Arkadiy, sound asleep. She would not wake him. There were hours yet to go before the baby would come. She prayed, closed her eyes, and tried to sleep.

The next day, February 15, 1951, Elena gave birth to her eighth child, a son. They named him Evgeniy Arkadiyevich Bondar. They called him Eugene.

Life in the Wimbern camp might have been the loneliest yet, with Pana gone and so many of their friends already having emigrated to other countries. But the sheer size of the Bondar family, which was now eleven individuals, left no opportunity to be lonely. Each and every day Elena and Arkadiy had the many responsibilities of looking after and caring for so many children. There was never time to be idle.

Since each family member had only two to three changes of clothes, laundry was the constant chore, the center of their daily life. Elena and Arkadiy worked together in the laundry, which was located away from the rest of the family. (Their quarters were an old barracks that had previously been occupied by nuns and monks; a building configured in the shape of the letter *E*, with the bunk areas located in the horizontal wings and shared services, including the laundry, located in the vertical spine.) At the laundry, the two parents individually scrubbed each piece of clothing by hand, using a wash board and hand plunger to agitate the load in large tubs, while recycling the limited supply of hot soapy water, which they had to boil on a stove; white clothes first, dark clothes last. Each garment was stretched smooth and hanged to dry, then stacked and carried back to their unit to fold. It took hours each day just to do the wash. Luba would often help, but her main chore was tending the newborn and keeping the floors in their unit clean and tidy from the perpetual onslaught of little running dirty feet.

The main responsibility for watching the rest of the children was entrusted to Vera. When the weather was inclement, she would entertain her siblings in the bunkroom, a space that was made private only by draping sheets. Most of the time she would take them outside into one of the courtyards located between the wings. There the children would all roll around on the grass and burn off an endless supply of energy. Vera's main job was to make sure no one got hurt. It was a job she did very well.

In the evenings the family would have their one big meal. Arkadiy would go to the commissary and carry their food to their quarters in buckets. There they would dish it out and sit down together at a long table. While they ate, the children would always ask about the old days, or about Babusia, or they would ask, "Mama, could you tell us a story?"

Elena leaned forward in her chair. "I was born in Kondratyevo, in Siberia. It was a small village near a lake. The fishermen did their fishing there, a quiet and peaceful sight. In the summer I loved to swim there very often with my family and friends.

"Across the lake, there were fields of flowers and large bushes of red currents that grew in abundance. It was a beautiful sight. We would play all day in the fields and pick the berries. With our pails full of berries, we sang together as we walked home, happy to share our pickings. The sun beamed on us all and we never had a thought this life would ever end.

"There were six children in our family: me, my sisters Pana and Anna; plus my cousins Klava, Pavlik, and Marusia (children of Uncle Don and Aunt Anfia). Of the children, I was always called 'beloved' and the others were reminded to take example of me, for my obedience and good character. Of course, I always felt embarrassed for being singled out, even though it was for good behavior. I thought it would hurt the others and make them jealous. But they all loved me nonetheless.

"Across the street there lived a family. They had a son called Kostia. During a house fire, Kostia had been badly burned and he barely survived. Later, all the neighborhood children made fun of Kostia, for his face was full of scars; so he would throw rocks at them. He also threw rocks at my sisters. But he never threw one at me. He loved playing ball with me, and had always treated me kindly. I was four and Kostia was nine.

"The adults in our family heard all about the rock throwing and so they considered Kostia to be a troublemaker. They forbade me and the others to play with him. Our yard was surrounded by a fence and he was not allowed to enter in.

"One day he stood outside the gate and saw me looking out at him through the window. He called to me, 'Elena you are the only one that forgives. If I have hurt you in any way, please forgive me. I do not know why all of a sudden I am not allowed into your yard and we cannot play ball anymore. I miss playing with you.'

"As I was looking out through the window, my heart ached for him. I said, 'The reason they don't like you Kostia, is that you throw stones at them. Restrain yourself from throwing stones, even if they laugh at you. Then you will see a difference.'

"Kostia stood there a while and thoughtfully dug a hole in the ground. He spit into the hole, took some of the soil and threw it up in the air, saying 'Elena I swear that I will never throw a stone again. You will see a difference in me from this day on.'

"Quietly he left our home. I stood by the window and watched him walk away. I felt a deep hurt for him, for he seemed so lonely."

Elena looked around at her children and smiled. "But do you know what happened after that? He never threw stones again when they made fun of him. And soon everyone else treated him nice."

Elena sat back in her chair and sighed. "There are so many good memories I have of my childhood. And though those days are gone forever, my memories are still here in my heart. I will never forget them."

After dinner, Arkadiy, Elena, Vera, and Luba were tasked with doing the dishes and then getting the little ones cleaned, washed, and ready for bed. The boys never did help with these tasks, or with any of the other household chores, creating the impression in Vera and Luba's minds that they always got off easy, or that they were lazy. But the two girls just accepted that was the way things were.

After the littler ones had been tucked in, the rest of the family returned to the living area where they sat around and repaired their clothing while singing songs together. Here even the boys learned to sew on buttons and darn their own socks. Clothing was constantly recycled, handed down, and resized. When an item was finally too old or ruined, Vera was charged with separating and carefully pulling it apart to recycle the thread for use with their needles. Elena insisted that everyone in the family always be clean and presentable, that their clothing looked nice. And though the family had nothing and could easily have said that they were poor, they never did feel that way. The Bondars always had everything they really needed, which was mostly each other.

As the evening grew late, after the chores had been completed, Arkadiy would pull out a book and read to everyone. Vera would call out "*krokodil, krokodil,*" and Arkadiy would open and read her favorite story about a crocodile; it would take three nights to make it all the way through the book. And then they would all have the pleasure of hearing it again, or another reading from a different book.

Three nights a week, Arkadiy would lead the entire family in a Bible study. He would read to them and the children would participate by memorizing the passages.

They capped every one of their nights with a time of prayer. They would pray for Opa, they would pray for Elena's sister Anna, they would pray for their many cousins and friends left behind in Russia, and they would always pray for Pana in America.

* * *

In June they moved again to Augustdorf. That was where they were in September when an American official showed up at their unit. Elena and Arkadiy invited him in.

The official had a folder in his hand and a broad grin on his face. "I think you are going to like to hear this."

They both stood with anticipation.

"You have a sponsor." He looked at the papers and struggled with the name. "Andrei Bog-dan...Bog-dan-eee...uh."

"Bogdaniuk." Elena finished the name.

He looked at the papers. "Yes, I suppose that is correct."

Elena beamed. "He is my brother-in-law."

"You are moving to New Jersey."

Elena embraced Arkadiy, then the official, bursting with gratitude and excitement.

The next day, they were transferred to their ninth camp, Wentorf. This was a special camp organized to prepare refugees for immigration. There were appointments with German doctors, the German police, and investigations to determine if all members of the family were politically safe. When the Germans decided an individual was acceptable, then there were more appointments, next with American doctors, who reviewed each individual case and put on their stamp of approval. The final appointment was with the American Consul, whose office reviewed the German paperwork. If they were not satisfied, they continued to investigate on their own. Only upon the approval of the consul could one obtain an entry visa into the United States.

Everyone in the Bondar family passed, except Omama and Luba. Both failed the medical examination. Arkadiy and Elena were told that Omama had a heart condition and the doctor said she could be re-evaluated in three months. As to Luba's failure, there was no explanation, no reason given. They were only told that she was deferred by the German doctor and that it would be up to the American doctor to examine her and make a final decision.

Elena found Luba alone in her quarters, sitting on her bed. "What is wrong, *milochka?*"

"I don't know, Mama. They didn't tell me." Luba looked down, eyes fixed on the floor.

Elena studied her daughter, recognizing her intentional distance. Elena reflected on when she herself was fifteen; having been so independent and having made many plans for her life in a world that was changing around her so fast and completely. Luba's world, too, had been changing, with all the moves from camp to camp, making new friends, boy friends, then suffering one more separation after another, dragged along by her parents, forces she could not control. Elena sympathetically placed her hand under Luba's chin, lifting her face, gazing into her eyes. "It will be okay."

"Yes, Mama."

Elena studied her face. "Do you want to tell me anything?"

Luba took a breath, then smiled. "I am okay, Mama."

Elena felt the distance; but she was unwilling to probe any further, to add more stress. She nodded, smiled at Luba, and left the room.

While the family waited for Luba's exam, they made a decision about Omama, who had pleaded for them to go ahead to America without her. Arkadiy and Elena knew they needed to do what was best for the children, to find stability and re-establish their own sense of independence. The shuffling around from camp to camp was placing a strain on their family life. They made the difficult decision to go ahead as scheduled. Omama would join them later, when she could.

When Luba heard the decision, she realized she was the one person holding the entire family back from immigration. It was a great shock to her. That night, she had a strange dream. She saw her entire family standing by a very large body of water. A ship came and took everyone, but left her behind. She was terribly frightened and upset, standing alone, watching them leave. Yet a little while later, the ship turned back and picked her up.

The next day, Luba labored over her dream. She fancied herself staying behind in Germany, being perfectly happy with that, considering all of her friends there, and the dancing—oh, how she loved the dancing! But there was a tension. *Mother and Father would never allow that to happen, for me to stay behind by myself.* They would rather everyone stay together as a family, even if it meant lingering on in the German camps. Keeping together was pre-eminent.

That night, she had another dream, just like the first. Again, she was left behind, like an outcast, separated from Mother and Father, separated from her siblings. She tossed and turned and snapped awake in a fit of sweat. She sat up in her bed, breathing heavy. She looked around. Everyone else in her room was fast asleep.

Moonlight poured in through the window. She stood and tiptoed over to the opening and glanced up at the moon. She turned and looked around the room at all the other beds, seeing her brothers and sisters lying there quietly. She stared up at the moon and whispered, "What are you telling me, Lord?"

A wisp of cloud moved across the moon, plunging her into darkness. She shivered as she thought about her life and whether she fit in with the family, overwhelmed by the sense of separation from them, like it was forever. And then it dawned on her, the reason for her separation. She knew she had been thinking only of herself in her desire to stay in Germany with her friends. *But friends are passing. They come and go. Family is forever, just like God...God, you are forever.* She realized she had never truly committed her life to Christ, just as Mother had. The cloud moved away and the light fell on her face. She knew what she had to do.

Luba knelt in the moonlight and prayed, "Lord, I have sinned. I have been in rebellion against you. Forgive me. I want to commit my life to you." She felt then a sense of relief, like a burden had been lifted. She got back up and returned to her bed in complete peace. In just a few minutes, she fell asleep.

In the morning, Luba received an order to appear before an American doctor for her examination. She prayed and went to the appointment. There were many people in the waiting room. Her body shook as she looked into each of their nervous faces. Her stomach formed into a knot; she hoped she was not getting sick. Finally, Luba's name was called, and she got up and walked down the hall to the doctor's office. She opened the door and stepped inside.

The doctor sat behind a large wooden desk. He was a young-looking man, presently examining x-rays and looking at papers. He finished reading them and lifted his eyes. He asked, "Fräulein, what should I do with you?"

Luba fidgeted, realizing this man held her destiny in his hands. She swallowed hard and answered, "I don't know."

He stood and led her to an examination room. He examined her, and they returned to his office. Luba sat in her chair and squirmed. He stepped behind his desk and sat down. He waited, contemplating something. At last, he exhaled, "I think we shall have to let you go to America."

Luba burst up from her seat and thanked him. She left the office feeling like her feet were not even touching the ground. When she got to her room, she fell on her knees, thanking God. "I know you want me to put you first in my life!"

She could hardly wait to tell her mother.

And while Elena welcomed the news and was blessed by Luba's testimony and prayers, she was thanking God for her daughter's transformed heart.

* * *

The days and weeks that followed for Elena were filled with a mixture of anxiety and hope. The thought of leaving Omama behind was very hard for everyone to take. But Omama softened the idea by reaching out to her German nephew who agreed to look out for her while she waited to get her approval. The bigger anxiety lay in moving to an entirely new and foreign culture, with the challenges of finding employment and learning English. Both were tremendous burdens. Still, these anxieties paled against the bright hope set before them, the knowledge that Pana waited to receive them, and so many of their Russian and Slavic friends would be there to welcome them to America.

By November, they were told they could board the next available transport to the United States. They left for the port of Bremen Haffen (Bremerhaven) on the North Sea to wait for their ship. There they boarded the USNS *General*

M L Hersey, a former US Navy transport ship that had been commissioned during the war.

On the ship, they were placed in separate quarters. Elena and Eugene were in a small upper cabin for mothers with babies. Arkadiy was with Vitaliy in a lower part of the ship, designated for men only. Leonid, Iosif, Nadiezda, Valeriy, and Vera remained together under Luba's supervision. Elena had constant cause to thank God for allowing her eldest to travel with her family. Every morning, Luba had to make sure they all were dressed, see to everyone's hygiene, and take them for their meals, which she did with gladness. Whenever the children were on the deck, Luba had to watch them closely so that they would not fall overboard. That was a constant challenge.

On November 22, 1951, the ship steamed into New York Harbor. Everyone stood at the railings cheering as they saw the Statue of Liberty. There was an overwhelming sense of joy for all. At the last dinner on the ship, they were introduced to grapefruit. They marveled why Americans would ever eat that fruit. Then a real Thanksgiving feast was spread out before them, exposing them to the American holiday.

Very early on Saturday morning, they were awakened, given breakfast, and told to prepare for entry to their new homeland. The ship pulled up to the pier, and the passengers filtered down onto the dock, where each stood for the first time on American soil. Elena and Arkadiy were themselves pre-occupied with keeping track of their children, who were bursting with excitement over everything new. And while many fellow immigrants bent and kissed the ground, Elena was too busy counting her children's heads and trying to figure out where they had to go to next.

The passengers formed into lines that moved toward the inspection stations and the exit, with everyone advancing at a snail's pace. Each person had to have their papers approved and stamped.

Arkadiy held Eugene, and Elena kept all their children close to them in line. Luba held Leonid at the back, keeping track of their group of eight. Elena had dressed them all in their best clothes, and made sure the boys each had their hair neatly combed. She wanted to make a good impression when she would be reunited with Pana, and would for the first time meet her sister's new husband.

Elena was stationed at the front of the family, anxious about seeing Pana again. She looked ahead of them, tipping up on her toes, stretching her four-foot-ten-inch frame as tall as she could to see over those in front of her, looking beyond the immigration officials, beyond and into the many families and friends that crowded the place, waiting to receive them. She leaned side to side, looking to find a gap to see through.

Then straining, she saw her. Elena jumped in the air and waved frantically to get her attention. "Oy! Oy!" she screamed.

Pana was standing beside Andrew. She heard the cries and looked. She saw Elena and cried back, "Oy! Oy!" Pana beamed as she wildly waved both hands.

Then Elena and Pana both dropped their hands and stood still, studying each other's faces from the distance. Though all the people around them moved about and filled the air with their conversations, the sisters focused only on each other, like they were the only two people there, in the quiet calm of just the two of them, safe, in peace, standing with their feet firmly on the shores of freedom.

Elena thought about what united them. Sure, they were sisters. But it was Christ that truly united them, the one that had guided them through all their trials. She raised one finger toward heaven and looked up.

Pana did the same.

They both closed their eyes and smiled, as they silently prayed, *Thank you, Lord. Thank you. Thank you!*

...for "Whoever will call on the name of the Lord will be saved." How then will they call on Him in whom they have not believed? How will they believe in Him whom they have not heard? And how will they hear without a preacher? How will they preach unless they are sent? Just as it is written, "How beautiful are the feet of those who bring good news of good things!"

—Rom. 10:13–15

Epilogue

The main characters, afterward:

After her second medical review, Olga Bondar (Omama) was granted a visa to come to America and be reunited with her son, Arkadiy. However, she preferred to remain in Germany, not wanting to be a financial burden to her son and his large family. By then she had resettled in Altersheim, close to her nephew, Heinrich. Omama remained there until her death on March 5, 1969.

* * *

After his capture and forced repatriation in 1946, Georgiy Nikitich Bondar (Opa) was hospitalized by the Soviets. His daughter, Taisa, who had been searching for relatives separated by the war, found him while he yet remained in intensive care, recovering from two shattered legs. He was able to make a full recovery and moved in with Taisa, who continued to care for him. He died December 27, 1950.

* * *

Since the time of Pana's immigration, her mind was constantly burdened with the thoughts of her two children left behind in Siberia. She sought every means to contact them, desperate to know if they had survived the war.

She faithfully stayed in touch with her fellow refugees from the German camps. The Russian, Polish, and Slavic refugees together formed a vast network of communication across America, corresponding with each other and often traveling great distances to attend conferences to see each other face-to-face to encourage one another. Each of them had loved ones left behind and shared a common purpose: to reunite with family. At the conferences, delegates arrived from Eastern Europe to preach the gospel to strengthen the refugees spiritually.

At one of these conferences, Pana recognized one of the delegates, a preacher from her former church in Kiev, Jerzy Sacewicz. She was unable to talk to him personally, as he did not mingle with the audience, forbidden to do so by informers from the homeland who watched their every move. Nevertheless, she was able to pass a note to him with her address, which he later took back to Poland. Pana wondered what would come of it.

Finally, in 1956, Pana received a short letter from Anna Kiselova, her sister, their first contact in fifteen years. Many tears of joy were shed by Pana and Elena as they pored over the note.

Over the next months and then years, both sisters wrote to Anna, now separated from them behind the "Iron Curtain." Letters coming and going were opened and read by the Soviets, and many were never delivered. Both sides understood that messages had to be coded and then analyzed. Despite this challenge, Elena and Pana were eventually able to piece together enough of the facts to understand what had become of Pana's children.

Pana's daughter, Anna Rukasuyeva, had married Boris Serdiuk and was then living in Norilsk, the most northerly city of Krasnoyarsk Krai, Siberia. Pana's son, Ilya Rukasuyev, was at that time a grown man, working, and on assignment to another region of the Soviet Union. He had sent his sister, Anna, a letter, intending to return home soon, but he never showed. Whatever became of Ilya remains unknown to this day.

After seven years of marriage to Pana, Andrew suffered a major heart attack. The doctors indicated he could not return to work and advised that they move to a warmer climate. They sold their home and moved to Miami, Florida. In 1962, after just twelve years of marriage, Andrew Bogdaniuk passed away. Their love for each other was cut far too short.

In 1971, after thirty-one years of correspondence and separation, Elena and Pana's baby sister, Anna Kiselova, was allowed to come to the United States for a visit. The whole Bondar clan met her at the airport. There was great joy at the reunion, and many tears were shed.

Since that first visit, Anna came back to the United States several times. Her last visit was in 1991. As she was leaving this last time, Anna told Elena and Pana, "You know, when I get back to Siberia, I will not be able to tell the relatives anything that I have seen here about all the prosperity. They will never believe me or even begin to understand." Anna remained in Russia and passed away there on May 29, 1999, at the age of eighty-three.

In 1979, Pana's daughter, Anna Rukasuyeva Serdiuk, was permitted to come to the United States for the first time, where she was reunited with her mother, brother Eugene, and sister Zoya. She was able to return several times and finally immigrated to the United States, moving in with her mother, until she was able to buy her own home in Miami. Later, Pana sold her house and came to live with Anna, where she stayed until the time of her death on January 20, 1994, at the age of eighty-five.

* * *

When Elena's family arrived in America, the ten of them lived several months with her sister Pana and her husband

Andrew Bogdaniuk in Linden, New Jersey. After the calendar turned to 1952, Elena's family moved into their own home in nearby Elizabeth. Andrew and Mr. Green (from church) helped with a loan for their closing costs.

Arkadiy took a job right away working at a factory in Elizabeth. Money was tight, but he earned enough to cover their expenses. Each week, he divided his pay in cash into four envelopes that were labeled: "church (ten percent)," "bus fare," "mortgage," and "groceries, etc." His children watched him and learned how to set their priorities. Giving to God's work was always first.

In their first years in New Jersey, Elena's children were immersed in learning English. As they became a part of their new culture, most took on new names. Luba became Linda, Vitaliy became Victor, Nadiezda became Nancy, and Valeriy became Larry. Vera's name was never a challenge for her American friends to pronounce.

On September 27, 1953, Elena gave birth to their ninth child, another son. They named him Walter Arkadiyevich Bondar. Now there were six boys and three girls in the Bondar family. Walter was later teased by his siblings as being the only member of the family eligible to become president of the United States. With the responsibility to raise their nine children, Elena did not work outside the home. Her full-time job was caring for them.

Within a few years, Arkadiy had learned enough English to confidently communicate. He left his factory job and started his own business as a building contractor. As his new business expanded, he purchased their first car, a Buick. All eleven family members could squeeze in; the smaller ones rode on the laps of their siblings. This was long before the invention of seat belts and child safety laws.

From the beginning of their time in America, Arkadiy and Elena became members of the Russian Baptist Church in Newark, New Jersey. There the whole family was active in the many programs, being at the church nearly as often as the doors were open.

In 1965, Elena was approached by Alex Leonovich from Slavic Missionary Service (SMS) to write Christian children's programs in the Russian language, programs to be transmitted via short wave by Trans World Radio into the Soviet Union. At that time, missionaries were prohibited from entering Russia; the gospel was outlawed. Elena happily agreed and began her radio ministry.

In 1967, Arkadiy and Elena moved to Maryland, into a house right next door to her daughter Linda and her husband Adam Korenczuk. Adam was the senior pastor of the Slavic Church of Christ in nearby Baltimore, where sermons were preached in Russian, Ukrainian, and Polish languages. Elena could now be near family, share and hear the gospel in her native tongue, have her whole family engaged in the culture of a familiar and dynamic Slavic church community, and enjoy better health by living in a less-industrialized part of the country. There Elena continued to write and record her daily radio programs in a soundproof studio that Arkadiy built for her in their basement. Year after year, Elena's voice was broadcast as "Tiotya Lena" (Aunt Elena), reaching the ears, hearts, and minds of untold numbers of Russian children and adults. Elena had at last become a "star"—yet one of far greater importance than she had ever dreamed or imagined back when she was fifteen.

Arkadiy and Elena lived for many years in their home in Joppatowne, Maryland. Arkadiy continued his construction business there while Elena was involved in the radio ministry. They both remained active in their church, never missing a service, and saw all their children marry and themselves become active in American churches. Then following a long illness, all the while being aided by Linda and Adam, on April 24, 1985, Arkadiy died at the age of seventy-two.

A while later, Elena sold her house and moved in with her daughter Linda. Having completed seventeen years of radio ministry, Elena yet felt the need to do more for her Lord. Between 1982 and 1999, she wrote and published three books in the Russian language. Elena passed away on December 20, 1999, at the age of eighty-seven.

* * *

Any uncertainty that Pana and Elena carried with them concerning the final circumstance of Pana's first husband, Ivan Rukasuyev, was laid to rest in America, when the bitter word of how he died came to Elena through the network of Russian refugees. The story of Ivan's demise is told in the Appendix.

* * *

Alexei Karpenko, the man who had singularly and faithfully delivered the gospel to Elena in Bunbuy in 1927, forever transforming her family, was later exiled to the Far East to the city of Vydrino. There he sought out Pana, whose address he carried with him in his pocket, written on the slip of paper he received from Akulina. Pana welcomed him into her home and ministered to him, while he shared the gospel with her and her husband Ivan. That same message pierced Pana's heart and transformed the lives of her entire family.

Pana also received from Karpenko the story of his earlier arrest, his imprisonment in Minsk, and his 1927 exile to Siberia. Her record of these events is the source of the story presented in the Appendix of this book.

After spending some time with Pana and Ivan, Karpenko was again arrested and taken away by the Communists. Before he left, apparently feeling his end was near, Karpenko parted with his most treasured earthly possession, a family photo showing his wife and children with his youngest son holding his violin. A copy is in the appendix.

After this Karpenko disappeared.

Appendix

Ivan
Rukasuyev

After Ivan Rukasuyev finished his five-year exile in Bukachacha, the government decided he was still an enemy. They had come and roused him from his house, evicted Pana (who left for Irkutsk), and sent him to another assignment farther east in Tupik.

Tupik was a small village, well north of the Trans-Siberian Railway line, in the middle of nowhere, perched on the banks of the Tungur River. It had been founded in 1911 as a result of an unsuccessful attempt to pave a road to Yakutsk. That project had ended abruptly right there in Tupik with the outbreak of World War I. That was how the village got its name: Tupik means "cul-de-sac." In 1938, Tupik had been chosen to be the administrative center of Tungiro-Olyokminsky District, and the Communists set up a headquarters there. Travel to and from Tupik was largely by horse, so Ivan's veterinarian skills were put to work there.

While Ivan was serving out his exile, he traveled on occasion to Mogocha to obtain veterinary supplies. Mogocha was located one hundred kilometers to the south of Tupik, situated on the main rail line, one of the more established villages in eastern Siberia. On one such trip to Mogocha, he was sent to obtain medical supplies for Tupik's doctor. He went to the train station to receive the shipment. While he was waiting in the station, he saw a man, poorly dressed, standing with a woman and three children. He watched as the man helped them onto a train, waved goodbye, and then walked away.

Ivan studied the man's face, his eyes. They seemed strangely familiar. Then he recalled. "Robyert? Is that you?"

The man turned to him. "How do you know my name?"

"It is me, Ivan...Ivan Rukasuyev. Don't you recognize me?" Ivan's family had befriended Robyert years before when he was growing up in Vydrino. Robyert had been neglected by his family. Ivan's father had taken him in and given him food and clothing.

"Oh yes! Ivan!" He extended his hand, and they shook.

"Was that your family?"

"Huh? Oh yes. Uh, they are going back west."

"To Vydrino?"

"Uh, yeah. Vydrino. That is right. Uh-huh."

Ivan got a whiff of vodka on Robyert's breath. He studied his face. Several of his teeth were missing, the rest were brown. He hadn't shaved in days. The gray hairs on his head were matted in filth. He was a shocking sight. "Listen, Robyert."

"Huh?" He made eye contact.

"Would you like to get some lunch?"

Robyert placed his hand inside his tattered jacket and grabbed hold of his scrawny stomach. "Sure," he said. He looked up and announced, "I am buying."

They walked out of the station, down the main street, and turned into a restaurant. The place was crowded, but they did not have to wait that long before a table opened up. When the meal arrived, Ivan watched as Robyert cleared his plate, then as he ran his filthy finger around the surface and licked off the last of the sauce. He also downed six cups of coffee. There was not much conversation, just eating.

When the bill arrived, Robyert stared at it. Ivan studied the machinations going on behind the man's eyes. He picked up the bill. "How about I pay this time?"

Robyert placed his hands on the table. "Sure. But the next one *has* to be on me."

When they walked out of the restaurant, Ivan asked, "Do you live here in Mogocha?"

Robyert pointed at himself. "Me?"

Ivan nodded.

"I uh, well, uh…"

"Do you need a place to stay?"

Robyert put his finger to his mouth. "Uh, I have kind of had a tough time lately. B-but I will be doing fine real soon."

Ivan put his hand on his shoulder. "How about you stay with me for a while? I have an extra bed."

Robyert lifted his eyes slowly and grinned. "Sure," he said.

Ivan took Robyert home with him to Tupik. He fed him, bought him new clothes, and got him cleaned up and presentable. He asked around and found Robyert a job. He even gave him some money to help the man with his family.

But Robyert did not send the money to his family; he used it to buy vodka. He became drunk and lay in the street, shouting and making a scene.

The police heard the shouts and came to question him. "Okay, fellow, you can't just lay here. Come on, let's take you home. Where do you live?"

"I live over there." He pointed. "I live with a vet…a vetri-narian."

They helped him to his feet.

"I have known this man a very long time. He used to be very *rich*, and…and he still is *rich*."

When Ivan returned to his apartment, there were police standing in the open doorway. "Are you Ivan Rukasuyev?"

"Yes." He glanced inside. The place had been ransacked. An official stood in the living area, holding a pile of Ivan's papers.

"Where were you?"

"I...I am a veterinarian. I was taking care of the horses at the stable down the street." He pointed. "I have a license." He reached into his vest pocket, pulled it out, and showed it to the officer.

The police took the papers from Ivan and placed him under arrest. They led him away to the communist headquarters and locked him up. Ivan was held two days in a prison cell without food or water, no light; it was impossible to know if it was day or night. At last, they pulled him out of his cell and took him to a room for questioning. There was a table there with one chair. He was ordered to stand in front of the table and wait. Daylight filtered in through a small window near the ceiling.

After an hour of waiting, the door to the room opened. In came an official of some rank, wearing his Soviet uniform. He closed the door, removed his hat, set it on the table, and sat down. He had a folder of papers that he laid open on the table. Ivan could see his license on top.

The official picked it up. "How did you get this?"

"I am a veterinarian. The region had no veterinarian, and so the government issued me a license to head this veterinary center here in Tupik."

He put the license down. He pointed at Ivan. "You. *You* are a '*lishonetz*.'" It means a "have not." A lishonetz had no rights, could not work, could not make money. A lishonetz was one that had been well off, that was evicted from their home, not permitted to take anything. The lishonetz were sent to slave labor camps. The lishonetz never had such privileges as Ivan had been afforded. The official stood and placed both fists on the table. "Now *how* did you get this license?"

The questioning went on for an hour. Ivan gave the same answers over and over.

Frustrated, the official stood. "Have a seat here."

He went to the door and left. In a few minutes, he returned with paper and pencil. "Here. Write down all the medicines that you have."

Ivan looked up at him with narrowed eyes.

"Write them down."

Ivan finished writing and handed him the paper.

The official looked at it and grunted. He walked over to the door and held it open. "You are free to go. You may live in your apartment. But when your replacement comes, you will have to leave."

Ivan stepped close. "Replacement?"

"I suggest you go now before I change my mind."

Ivan walked out of the room and returned to his apartment.

* * *

After three months, two police officers appeared at his door. Ivan let them into the apartment. He had all his medicines neatly arranged on the table. He showed them what he had.

"Good," one of them said.

"Do I get to meet my replacement?" Ivan asked.

"No. That is not necessary."

Ivan looked around at the apartment, all his things. He would have to leave them behind, just as he had done before. He looked at one of the officers. "Where do I go to now? What is my next assignment?"

"Come with us. You will find out."

They led him to the government building, then took him to the interrogation room. They let him sit at the table, then left the room, closing the door. Ivan waited several hours. At last, the door swung open. The official he had first spoken with stood in the doorway, in full uniform, pistol at his waist. Ivan had never learned the official's name.

The official looked at him and spoke dryly, "Come with me."

Ivan followed the man. They walked out of the headquarters and down a road that led in the direction of the stables, where Ivan had previously worked.

"Where am I going to next?" Ivan asked as they walked.

"You will see. Your ride is up ahead."

Ivan tried to be optimistic. "You know, I liked being here, being able to help with the horses."

The man grunted.

Ivan continued, "A horse is such a useful animal, powerful, *magnificent*, really. The horse is one of God's most beautiful creations."

Silence.

"I think about God every day. I think how he has taken good care of me, given me the chance to have a good job, like the one I had."

No response.

"I am so glad I met the man who told me about God."

The official stopped walking. Ivan went ahead another step, stopped, and spun around.

"What man?" the official asked.

"Oh, there was a man that came to our house when we lived in Vydrino. He told me and Pana—she is my wife—told us both about God."

"What was his name?"

Ivan hesitated a moment, then looked down at the road. "Funny. I, uh, I can't remember."

"Was he an exile? A lishonetz?"

Ivan looked up. "Yes. He was an exile. He was an electrician and a pastor of a church. He was highly educated."

"And you can't remember his name?"

Ivan studied the man's cold black eyes. He realized what was going on now, the "innocent" questioning. He would withhold the name. He lifted his hands. "No. I can't remember."

The official read the purpose in Ivan's expression, the withholding of information. He had seen that look so many times. But he was getting tired of the game, and he needed to get back to what he was doing. He stepped forward. "Come on. Let's get you going to your next assignment."

They resumed their walk in the direction of the stables. They were close now, ahead, just around the bend. The road narrowed there to the width of one man. The official slowed and let Ivan walk ahead of him.

"Where is my next assignment?" Ivan asked.

"You will see."

Ivan heard a snapping sound, the sound of the man's holster being opened. He took a few more steps and stopped. Ahead was the stable. It was empty. He stood still, waiting.

The official came up close behind him, aiming his pistol to the back of Ivan's head. "You know where your next assignment is, don't you?"

"Yes. Yes, I do." Ivan closed his eyes and prayed, grateful that he had listened to that man, that exile all those years ago, the man who had no fear, the man who held the burden of following Christ, of sharing the gospel in such high regard that he could never be silenced. He prayed to the Lord, grateful to now be a believer. And he thanked the Lord for sending him Karpenko.

The official seethed, *"Lishonetz!"* and squeezed the trigger.

Karpenko's Exile

Katya sat beside her husband, nervously holding his hand. They waited together, silently staring at the picture of Stalin on the wall behind the desk. It was a huge picture of the very handsome man, his thick black hair combed back and shining, the overlarge mustache, curling up at the edges with the faintest of a smile. The odd thing about the image was the eyes, which were not looking at the camera; they were angled up and away, as though fixated at some distant ideal.

The door to the office opened and a man in a uniform stepped in. He was tall and fit, powerful looking, his uniform neat and pressed; he was a member of the NKVD. He carried a folder in his hand. He glanced at them, then stepped around behind the desk and sat down. The name placard on the desk read, "Komandir Kalugin," matching the name embroidered on his pocket.

Kalugin opened the folder and read the name, "Alexei Makayevich Karpenko." He looked up. "Is that you?"

Karpenko leaned forward. "Yes, sir." He smiled.

Kalugin directed his eyes back into his folder. He flipped through several pages, reading the dates. He sighed, closed it, laid it on the desk, and looked up. "You are apparently unable to learn from your mistakes. I see that you have been here several times." He closed his mouth and glanced toward the window. "And when troublemakers like *you* refuse to reform, then they finally bring them to me." He stood and leaned forward, holding onto his desk. "Do you know why they bring them to me?"

Karpenko thought a second. "No."

Kalugin pounded the desk with his fist so hard that his name placard bounced. "Because I get results!"

Katya flinched. Her eyes opened wide.

Kalugin tugged on his uniform as he clenched his jaw. He put his hand to his mouth and stroked his chin. "Let me get right to the point." He leaned forward and glared at Karpenko. "All this talking about God…such *stupidity*…it is going to stop." He angled his thick forefinger straight down at his desk. "And I mean right now!"

He wagged his finger at Karpenko and furled his brow, then pointed at Katya. "And this husband of yours will be arrested and put in jail, while you and your children will be sent to exile as *lishonetz*." He puffed out his chest. "I will do this…" He pointed at her husband. "…if *he* can't learn to keep his tongue behind his teeth!"

She started shaking. Karpenko placed his hand on hers to calm her.

The official again tugged on his uniform and sat down. He pulled out a pad of paper and wrote something on it. He read it a second time, grunted, spun it around, and pushed it to the front of the desk. He handed the pencil toward Karpenko. "Sign this."

Karpenko leaned forward on the edge of his chair and read it to himself. It read, "From this day forward, I will not speak to anyone about God."

The official reached closer to hand him the pencil.

Karpenko did not take it. He sat silent.

"Sign this or we will put you behind bars!" He glared at Katya.

Karpenko did not move or change his expression.

Kalugin stepped around to the front of his desk and towered over him, clenching his fists.

Karpenko turned to his wife. She was clasping her hands together, pleading that he comply. He closed his eyes, sighed, turned up toward the official and took the pencil. He set it on the page and signed his name.

Kalugin took the paper and added it to his file.

They waited a second until it became clear the meeting was over. They looked at each other, got up, and headed toward the door. Kalugin pointed at Karpenko as they were walking out. "The first word from you about 'God' and you will be punished harshly."

They left. As they were walking home, Katya clung to his arm and spoke quietly, "They cannot stop you from believing what you have in your heart."

He placed his hand on hers. "Yes…yes."

"You just have to stop telling the factory workers about God."

He said nothing as they finished walking home.

At home, Karpenko spent some time with his three children. Then as it was getting late, he kissed them and told them to go and get in bed. The children were obedient and went straight to their rooms.

Karpenko sat with Katya in the kitchen.

She pleaded, "You must not break your promise."

He gently took hold of her hands. "Let's pray together."

He stepped away from the table and knelt. She joined him. He closed his eyes and began, "Lord, you see our situation. You know my desire, and you also know my decision today in the office of the NKVD. I believe that you gave me the thought when I didn't know what to do, even before I gave my word to keep silent. And you have reminded me that in silence, there is also witness. Help me to be your witness. With your help, I want to do your will. Amen."

Katya said, "Amen."

He got up, retrieved his Bible and some paper, and sat down at the table. Karpenko used to have many Bibles, but he had given them all way, and it was impossible now to obtain any more. He cut the paper into small pieces, took his pencil, and began to transcribe Bible verses onto them. He had a plan.

In the middle of the night, long after Katya had left for bed, Karpenko finished writing on his last piece of paper. He folded all the papers neatly and put them in the pockets of his work slacks and jacket. He went to lie down and sleep for a while.

In the early morning, Karpenko awoke to his usual routine. He opened his Bible, read a bit, and spent some time in prayer. Then he left for work. The factory was a good distance away. On the way there, he greeted many strangers with a friendly, "Hello," as he handed each of them a piece of paper with a Bible verse. He smiled at them, but did not say a word about God.

At the factory, there were many coworkers with whom he had previously spoken about God. They came to him with questions about God, just like they had done on other days. But he did not speak a word to them. Instead, he just smiled and handed each one a piece of paper with a Bible verse.

One confronted him. "Why are you not speaking today?"

Karpenko placed his hand on the man's shoulder. "You should feel free to discuss your questions among yourselves."

By the end of the day, Karpenko had passed out all his papers.

When he came home, he prayed, "Thank you, God, for the purposeful day, for the opportunity to pass on your Word. Dear God, do your work in the hearts of the people when they read the scriptures, that they would accept you as their Savior."

Katya was very happy to have her husband home. He shared with her all that had taken place that day. "I prayed for you all day," she said.

They shared a simple dinner and thanked God together for his provision. After dinner, Karpenko got more paper out and copied more verses, again staying up late into the night, making ready for the next day. For many days, Karpenko passed out his small pieces of paper at the factory. And every night, he stayed up late to prepare the next day's batch.

The people at the factory began to catch a sense of excitement when they would see him approach. They were glad to receive his small pieces of paper and to unfold them and read what he had so carefully transcribed for them. They began to meet with each other and exchange verses, excited to read what the other had received from Karpenko. Some of them were very glad to talk about the passages together. Many understood what they were reading and embraced the meaning, giving their hearts to God, seeking after his presence in their lives. Then once they recognized that they had become believers, they began to pray together and to invite others to join in their belief.

Meanwhile, the atmosphere in the factory changed. Workers were noticeably kind to one another. They did not have harsh words toward others, having become obedient to the way of life depicted in the many verses. Some went so far as to openly praise the Lord with their lips. And as their attitudes toward one another improved, so did their productivity. Their diligence and better performance became obvious to the managers. This was especially evident in the attitude of five individuals who had previously been labeled as habitual complainers. These malcontents had been "magically" transformed. They had become entirely different people. The attitude of joy was becoming visible everywhere in surprising ways.

But not everyone was happy.

Some began to laugh and harass those who had been passing around the notes. They scoffed. "They are all becoming a bunch of holy people like Karpenko. Look at those idiots. They will believe any fairy tale."

They joked among themselves and poked each other to get a laugh. Then they turned to harsher tactics and tipped over the work of the new believers. "Looks like you need another miracle. Ha, ha!"

Not all the acts of sabotage were so small or easily corrected. Management noticed the disruptions and launched an investigation. They called a meeting after work to get to the bottom of it. All the workers assembled together on the factory floor.

The plant manager descended the steps from his office and looked out over the crowd of workers. Before he could begin the questioning, one of the scoffers yelled, "It is those that pray. They did it. They are damaging our productivity."

The manager asked, "Who? Who are those that pray?"

More than half the people in the room raised their hands.

The manager flinched. He panned around the room and studied the faces of those that were holding up their hands. They were smiling.

He scowled and addressed everyone. "There is no time to find the individual that has been damaging the goods. This is a very serious matter to those that try and sabotage the government. We will call in the NKVD. You are all free to go."

One of the scoffers yelled, "It is Karpenko! He is making everyone into a holy roller."

The manager scanned the faces in the crowd. His eyes fell on Karpenko, one of his better workers, an honest man. He closed his mouth, turned, and walked swiftly back up the stairs to his office and closed the door. He was seen through the glass speaking with the rest of his crew of supervisors.

One of the new believers took hold of Karpenko's hand. "Those that understand that life without God is death for the soul will not fear to suffer for the truth."

Karpenko silently squeezed his hand.

He continued each night to prepare more Bible verses and each day to distribute them at the factory.

Karpenko was summoned to the NKVD building. He was returned to Kalugin's office.

Kalugin stormed into the room with two other soldiers, carrying his folder. He laid it on his desk and glared at Karpenko. "You were forbidden to speak about God. You promised to be silent. You have broken your word!"

"No. I have not broken my promise of silence. Since I gave you my word, you will not find anyone in the factory that says I have spoken to them about God."

Kalugin recoiled and slapped Karpenko in the face, striking so hard that he knocked him down. "Don't you lie to me!" He kicked Karpenko several times in the stomach, as he yelled, "You are telling me that *you* did not tell the worker's about God? Half of the workforce is infected with your stupidity!" He kicked him one more time then looked at his soldiers. He straightened, ran his fingers through his hair, tugged on his uniform, and went back behind his desk to sit down, breathing heavily.

Karpenko lay a moment on the floor, writhing in pain. He collected himself, rolled to his knees, and stood up slowly. He focused calmly on Kalugin.

Kalugin looked at the soldiers and waved his hand dismissively. "Take him downstairs for questioning."

The soldiers grabbed Karpenko rudely by the arms and dragged him out of the office. They took him downstairs to a closed cell. There they beat him for hours until he fell senseless on the floor. They kept him there for several days, continuing the torture. Karpenko stayed silent.

Meanwhile, the NKVD launched an in-depth investigation. They interviewed everyone at the factory that had raised their hand, admitting to having prayed. None of them said that Karpenko had ever spoken a single word to them about God.

Karpenko was released and allowed to return to work.

Everyone now was keeping an eye on Karpenko and also on anyone else who had shown sympathy for him. At lunchtime, one of the scoffers noticed several of the believers passing notes and reading them. He ran and complained to his supervisor. "Some of those praying people are exchanging secret messages."

The supervisor came into the lunchroom.

Several quickly stuffed their papers into their pocket.

"What is that?" he asked.

One handed the paper to him. "It is just a Bible verse."

He looked at it. He recognized the handwriting. The supervisor went around to all the workers, confiscating their papers. The next day, Karpenko was again dragged into Kalugin's office. He was seated there under the portrait of Stalin. A pile of folded Bible verse papers lay on his desk.

Kalugin looked up at him. "Are these papers your work?"

Karpenko looked down at the papers. One was conspicuously unfolded. It read, "You will know the truth, and the truth shall set you free."

He looked up, smiling. "Yes."

The soldiers dragged Karpenko away. After he was beaten, they threw him into prison to be tortured. Yet while he was there, he was not despondent or regretful of anything he had done or said that had brought him there. Instead, he felt the great pleasure of knowing that he had done the right thing. For all he had done, all he had said, and all he had written was done out of love. *What a worse tragedy it would have been*, he thought, *if no one had ever received the good news of Jesus Christ.*

After this, Karpenko was sentenced to labor in Siberia and sent there to the obscure village of Bunbuy.

Images

Elena age 18 (right) and her sister Paraskovia ("Pana") Rukasuyeva, age 22. Photo taken October 1930 in Irkutsk.

Elena (right) and her sister Anna. Photo taken around 1931 in Irkutsk.

Elena's childhood home in Kondratievo, Siberia. The property had several buildings including a store, run by the three Nosov brothers: Ivan (Elena's father), Don, and Vlas. After the Revolution reached Siberia in 1918, the property was seized by the Communists and turned into a party headquarters. The brothers and their parents, then living there, would all suffer their demise. The building was later converted to a school, which it is to this day.

Standing, from left to right: Anna Nosova, age 15; Semion Briuchanov (Elena's stepbrother and first cousin), age 20. Seated, from left to right: Akulina Briuchanova (age 59) and Elena (age 19). Photo taken in 1931 in Irkutsk after the family left Bunbuy and came to live with Elena.

Elena and Arkadiy's wedding day, June 17, 1935.

Photo taken in Irkutsk in 1937. First row, left to right: Sidor Davidovich Briuchanov, Nina Vlasovna (Elena's cousin from her father's side, daughter of Uncle Vlas), and Akulina. Second row, left to right: Sikleta, Mitia, Elena holding Luba, Kharissa (Larissa). Sikleta, Mitia, and Larissa are Sidor's children from his first wife, Nataliya, Akulina's sister. Sidor's four children are Elena's cousins from her mother's side as well as stepbrothers and stepsisters.

Pana and her husband, Ivan Rukasuyev, circa 1938. This was the last time they were together before Ivan's re-exile farther east and eventual execution.

Pana and her children, from left to right: Zoya, age 14; Anna, age 12; Ilya, age 8; and Eugene, age 6. Photo taken in 1940 in Irkutsk. When Pana fled to Kiev in December 1940, she left Anna and Ilya behind in Irkutsk with her sister Anna. Pana would never again see Ilya. Pana was reunited with Anna in America more than three decades later.

Left to right, front row: Zoya and Anna Rukasuyeva. Middle row: Anna Nosova, Akulina Briuchanova holding granddaughter Luba Bondar, Elena Bondar. Back row: Pana Rukasuyeva (Elena's sister) and Arkadiy Bondar. Photo taken in 1937 in Irkutsk.

Elena and Arkadiy with daughter Luba. Photo taken in 1938 in Irkutsk.

Vera ("Faith"), age one, 1942.

Nadiezda ("Hope"), age 2, 1947.

Luba ("Love"), age 2, 1938.

The Bondar and Rukasuyev families and some friends who escaped from Soviet Union in the same railroad boxcar. Photo taken in 1943 in the DP refugee camp in Gilgenburg, Prussia. First row, left to right: Dr. Maria Ivanovna Oliver and her husband, Mr. Oliver. Second row, left to right: Pana Rukasuyeva, Akulina Briuchanova, Elena Bondar, Olga Bondar ("Omama"), Georgiy Bondar ("Opa"). Third row, left to right: Arkadiy Bondar holding Valeriy, Luba, Vitaliy, Vera, Eugene Rukasuyev, Mr. Potapov, Zoya Rukasuyeva.

The funeral of Akulina Nosova Briuchanova on October 19, 1947 in Frille, Germany. From right to left: first row behind the casket: Valeriy Bondar, age 4; Vera Bondar, age 7; Vitaliy Bondar, age 9; Luba Bondar, age 11; George Boltniew (blond boy); Eugene Rukasuyev, age 13. Second row: Zoya Rukasuyeva, age 21; Elena Nosova Bondar, age 35; Pana Nosova Rukasuyeva, age 39; Olga Bondar ("Omama"); woman; Brother Peter Gordieyev. Third row: Arkadiy Bondar, age 35, holding Nadiezda Bondar, age 2. Others are church friends.

Akulina's grave in the DP burial ground in Frille, Germany. Left to right: Pana, Olga Bondar, and Elena.

Elena and her children at the DP refugee camp in Paderborn, Germany, 1949. From right to left: Luba, Vitaliy, Vera, Valeriy, Nadiezda, and Iosif. Elena is standing in the rear holding Leonid.

Pana and her second husband, Andrew Bogdaniuk, on their wedding day, April 23, 1950.

The Bondar family crossing the Atlantic to America onboard the USNA *General M. L. Hersey,* November 1951. Left to right, first row: Eugene (held by Elena, who is out of picture), Iosif, Leonid, Valeriy. Second row: Vitaliy, Vera, Nadiezda, Luba, and the ship's chaplain.

Alexei Karpenko, his wife Katya, and three children (circa 1926). The girl standing on the right may be a sibling. The woman standing in the back may be Alexei's mother. Alexei carried this picture with him through his exiles and left it with Pana.